The Last Harp of Dunluce

David A Dunlop

Cover Design by Jim Allen
featuring
'The Lost Harp' (chalk pastel on card)
By Jim Allen
and
'Artist's Impression of Dunluce 1641' (ink on paper)
By Mark Strong

2nd Edition
Copyright © 2022 David A Dunlop

Dedication

For peace-makers and music-makers everywhere

Contents

Map of North Antrim showing key places during the conflict of 1641

Dunluce Castle as it may have looked in 1641 (etched on stone)

The Last Harp of Dunluce	1- 331
Author's Notes and Acknowledgements	334
Appendix 1 Fictional and Historical Characters in 'The Last Harp of Dunluce'	335
Appendix 2 Notes on Historical Characters	337
McDonnell Family Tree	339
Additional characters	340
Appendix 3 Notes on Historical Places and Events	341
Appendix 4 Ulster-Scots Glossary	342
Appendix 5 References	345

Map of North Antrim showing key places during the conflict of 1641

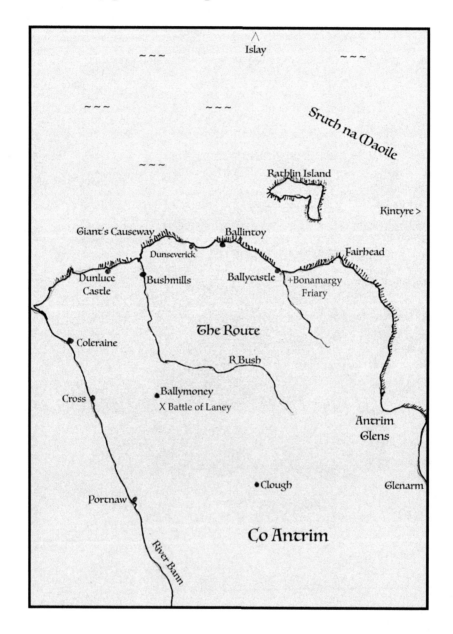

1 inch = 6 miles

Artist's Impression of Dunluce in 1641

Key A - Manor House   B - Gatehouse   C - Inner Ward
     D - Upper Ward   E - Drawbridge   F - Outer ward
     G - Gardens   H - Workshops & Stables
     I - Dunluce Village

The Last Harp of Dunluce

Chapter 1

The Handsome Young Man

Katie McKay

The first time I ever set eyes on him was on the high cliffs above the Giant's Causeway. I remember that, as he walked in my direction, a startled pheasant rose with a scriegh from the path between us and flurried itself away in a blaze of coppery-russet over the summer-green bog. I did not watch its course. I saw only the face of the young man coming towards me and I could not divert my gaze, not if someone had offered me a gold sovereign.

Did he stop to stare as I did? I suppose he must have, although I can't quite recall; everything seemed to freeze, to tell the truth, but somehow we got beyond each other, he stepping well back off the narrowness of the track so that I would not have to walk close to the cliff-edge as I passed him.

His eyes! Mesmerising, like something from another world, an animal of a different forest: the strange light in them, a vivid blue-green, the shade of the still surface of the ocean far below in that shining summer weather: the pupils black as the Causeway rock beneath. They held me, those eyes, with their intense mixture of curiosity and sincerity and…yes, a hint of amusement.

His crow-dark hair hung straight to his neck, like the well-trimmed mane of a pony. His beard was just a suggestion, as if it hadn't made up its mind yet whether or not he merited one. It certainly did not hide the strength of his face; his features were well-defined but full of gentleness, even kindness, I judged. In all my days I had never witnessed a face that so entranced me.

Not a word passed between us in those seconds. That in itself was unusual, for our rearing would have had us be mannerly and greet any person we met, stranger or not, Irish or Scot. The language would not have been a problem either. Our common Gaelic tongue in the northern fringes of Antrim, different only in dialect and grammar from the language of the Scottish islands, made basic conversation easy enough, even if both parties didn't have the English.

But, although language seemed to dry up in my mouth at that moment, in my head there were plenty of questions. They were jumping over each other like frogs in a bucket. I wanted to ask, "Who are you, mysterious stranger? Where do you live? How, why do you look so… Why have I never seen you before in this tight wee strip of coastline that we inhabit? Are you Irish, or a settler like me? Why on earth are you carrying that strangely-shaped limb of a tree that looks far too heavy for you? And why are you gaping at me? Why are you staring…the same way that I am staring at you?" But of course none of these thoughts made it out into the open, despite my half-hanging mouth.

Did I really slow up so much that the passing of him on that dangerously high path seemed to take several minutes? Did my eyes never leave his face, despite my natural shyness and the reddening blush I felt about my neck? Did I really only succeed in walking half a dozen further paces before I found myself turning to study his progress towards my giggling sisters?

I was secretly delighted that Connie and Alice had lagged so far behind on this return walk to our Ballintoy home. They had not therefore been witness to the sudden surrender of my wits. I watched the stranger's back as he approached them and then repeated his mannerly stand-aside. Even from a distance I could see the girls react as they passed him, eyes wide and dancing, hands to their mouths as if that would disguise their silly embarrassment. I had a split-second instinct to run back after him and explain that Connie was only fifteen and Alice twelve, but then I considered my own response as a seventeen year old and was ashamed of my transparent stricken-ness.

He disappeared in stages, his tall figure descending jerkily towards the strand at Runkerry.

The scent of the sea rose strongly to me and I sucked it in deeply. Some folks from places further inland might not know what I mean by 'the scent' of the sea, but we who live at the coast have no trouble discerning it. If there is an off-shore wind you can smell the homely aroma of turf reek, warm earth, the blossoms of whin and heather. An on-shore breeze brings none of these, so you might think it doesn't have any odour. You would be wrong though. The ocean entirely fills the space with the purity of its freshness and sparkle. You do sometimes get a whiff of rotting seaweed, or the stench of a heap of herring guts, discarded and decaying on the foreshore, but usually the smell of the ocean is as crystal clean as the water itself.

In the pale sky to the north-west a wedge-shaped formation of several small clouds appeared and drifted past towards Kintyre. I half-closed my eyes to squint at them; it wasn't hard to imagine that they were a group of fabled swans, *ealachan* in my Gaelic dialect, flying home to Scotland. I was loving the clear air as I waited for the girls to catch up. And for the inevitable questions, not unlike my own.

"Who under heaven is he?"

I pretended indifference. "I have no idea," I said disinterestedly. "Do you see the flock of gulls diving out there beyond Great Stookan? Look, there! See them Alice? There must be hundreds of them. It's like a blizzard of birds. There has to be a shoal of mackerel or something below."

Alice followed my gaze to the flat calm of Port Ganny, the bay immediately below us, but I could feel Connie's eyes still focussed on my face.

"You liked him, didn't you? You fell for him?"

I ignored her. "Daddy would have loved to be out there today, wouldn't he Alice? He'd have caught a barrel-full of lovely fish for us."

As soon as I said it I regretted it. Alice turned towards me and the pain in her eyes was my instant rebuke.

"Why did you have to spoil today, Katie? That wasn't fair," she murmured.

Of course it wasn't fair, but then nothing about our father's passing was fair. Our present walk would soon be taking us past the old graveyard where we had laid him to rest four years ago. He had left us in his forties, far too young an age. Although his health had never been all that sound, nobody in the parish could credit his death. Nor that he had been found stone cold dead in his own boat in Rathlin Sound. He had been alone, so we could only presume that his heart had failed him.

"I am sorry," I told my youngest sister. "I was only saying, you know, he would have….Listen, we'll soon be at Templastragh graveyard. Why don't you try to find some wild flowers for him? We can put them on his grave, that would be nice, wouldn't it?"

But Alice had turned away from me, I presumed to hide a tear. I was wrong though. She was looking out to sea, to the grey slab of an island on the skyline, the home of our ancestors. Islay lay twenty five miles away to the north.

"The saddest thing about it is," she said, "that he never got back to where he was born and reared."

She was right, but I don't ever recall our father being in too big a bother about that.

"He was so young when he married and brought mammy to Ballintoy," I told her. "He must have been happy enough to leave Islay."

"Maybe, but he must have missed it, do you not think?"

"Likely he did. I just never heard him talk about it much."

"Well I did," insisted Alice. "He would tell me stories about Port Ellen. All I had to do was ask him to tell me about when he was a wee lad. Imagine, him as a wee lad! And now he is buried here. Do you think his spirit can come up at night and look over to see Islay?"

Connie had had enough of this kind of conversation. "Would you two ever shut up with all these sad stories! I thought we were supposed to be out in the sunshine for a bit of an adventure. The only exciting thing that happened today was meeting *an duine òg eireachdail sin.*"

That handsome young man indeed! (Where did he go? Where was home for him?) I changed the subject.

"Did you not enjoy the walk today?"

"I did," she said, "but it was a wile long walk just to see a brown river and a lock o' fish trying to hide from us."

(Maybe he's a town-dweller, maybe Bushmills or Dunluce, or perhaps the village of Portballintrae that lay beyond the river?)

The idea of a visit to see the river Bush had been planted in my head by Alex, our older brother, now our only provider and protector. Last autumn he had spent a few days fishing at Bushmills for Lord Antrim. The Earl had wanted to employ some local men as there was an unusually large number of salmon running up the river. His agent, our good neighbour in Ballintoy, Archibald Stewart, had kindly recommended my brother. It would be a wonderful opportunity for Alex to be under the notice of the famous Randal McDonnell, Earl of Antrim, and of course there would be a few shillings in it for the family. The day Alex returned from Bushmills he was so excited by what he had witnessed.

"We weren't catching *na bradán* by the dozen," he told us, "we were catching them by the ton. You should have seen it, the river black with salmon. Unbelievable. The nets could hardly cope with the weight of them. Oul Randal will be making a fortune o' money from what we caught. Yet if I went poaching for a couple of trout on his river he'd deport me!"

I recall my mother telling him off for even mentioning poaching. Then she had said something about how Lord Randal needs all the money he can get. Despite the fact that he owns half the county it seems he is hugely in debt. For all his royal connections and his rich English wife he is a terrible gambler. Imagine marrying a widow who was the Duchess of some place called Buckingham. The talk was that she was the real boss…and the big spender. Dunluce Castle was said to be full of expensive treasures. None of us would ever even get to view them of course. I had never even seen the castle myself, never been beyond the Bush river, but from what I gathered the Earl's home was a completely different world to ours.

(I couldn't help it, my mind flipping back to the stranger. So gallant, wasn't he, stepping towards the cliff-edge to let me take the safer path. It came to me suddenly that I had had no sense of fear of him. The wariness of male strangers that my mother and my clergyman had instructed me to have, that and my inbuilt reticence, why had those instincts deserted me?)

We had been walking since morning. We had left on our expedition just after I'd milked our cow, fed the pigs and our various fowl. Now the sun was starting to dip behind us in the western sky and we still hadn't reached Portbradden. We had probably walked fifteen miles already and still had another couple to go. Alice was tiring, even though we had taken this fairly gently and had rested here and there. An old bent woman had stopped us near Dunseverick Castle and very kindly given us bowls of water. She was chatty too; we didn't know her but by her tongue and her expressions she was Irish.

"Yous wouldn't be Stewarts or Boyds, I don't think," she said in a wheezy voice, giving us a good once-over. Our clothes were a lot less grand than if we had been from those families, believe me! "So who are yous?" she wanted to know.

We told her we were Daniel McKay's girls. She blessed herself and wished God's rest on him, so I guessed she knew our father.

"Where were yous the day? Did yous go by the Causeway?"

"We did," Alice said, pleased to be the centre of the woman's attention.

"What about them rocks, the strange shape o' them? Did ye see them?"

"I did, and I seen them before," Alice replied.

"An' I sure ye heard the story o' *Fionn Mac Cumhaill* and how he bate the Scottish giant. That was how the causeway come aboot, ye know that?"

Alice looked at me as if for help in answering this, but I just nodded to her to speak up for herself. The woman was kindly wanting to get a conversation going with our youngest so it wouldn't have done for me to interfere. 'Go on!' I mouthed to Alice.

"Aye, I heard that story from my father when I was wee," Alice said, "but it likely wasn't true."

"Oh aye, it was true enough," the woman insisted. "Just you ask anybody aroun' here. They'll tell you the truth o' it."

Alice wasn't done yet. "Our minister told us it had nothing to do with Finn McCool. It was just that God made those rocks that shape when he was doing creation."

"Aye well, maybe you're right," the woman said with a smile. "He musta been right and good at the design, mus'n't he?"

"I'd say he was," agreed Alice. We all laughed at her conclusion.

My two sisters left and wandered on ahead, impatient to be home. I stayed longer with this woman, a neighbour I had never met before although she lived only three miles from our home. That was how things were in the Route, indeed in most parts of Ulster, I am told. If you did not meet somebody in your church, (because they hadn't yet converted to the Protestant faith and likely still sneaked away to their Mass somewhere else), you could be living in the same town-land but have little to do with each other. To the outsider we had so much in common with these neighbours. Our way of life, our Gaelic tongue, our music, our dance, our legends, all very much the same. But religion held us apart. So we missed the chance to get to know each other. Maybe that was why I had missed out on meeting the Causeway stranger before. He was most likely Irish.

I talked to the woman about mundane things, about people she knew that mostly I didn't. She complained angrily about the local magistrate, Gilladubh O'Cahan, and us standing not a stone's throw away from his Dunseverick fortress; it seems he had ruled against her in some dispute about a stray pig that had turned up in her shed. 'Of its own free will', she said. She had to return it to the rightful owner; it didn't help that the owner was a Martin, one of the recent arrivals from Gigha, and a Presbyterian.

It crossed my mind to ask this lady if she knew the young man we had met earlier, but I held myself in check. She was not someone that I knew or could trust. Maybe I should ask Alex if he has come across him, but how would I describe him, and why should I risk the brotherly teasing?
Or the disapproval! No, I should just put him out of my mind and get on with the narrow little life I had been leading.

But those eyes! That spark of hope, of recognition of something beyond the normal…there's no point in denying that a small, slow-burning flame had been ignited deep inside me and I was helpless to do anything about it.

Chapter 2

An Unwelcome Letter

Archibald Stewart sat on the bottom step of the grand stair-case in his entrance hall. His modest stronghold stood resolutely on the flat and fertile plain above Ballintoy harbour. He did not often rest on his staircase but today he did, dejectedly so, perhaps feeling the need for something as solidly reassuring as the smooth oak step beneath his broad buttocks.

Stewart was an able and serious citizen. He seldom felt any inclination to smile and, if and when he did, he would always weigh up the benefits against the possibility of misunderstanding. His whole persona spoke of wisdom and gravity; the very shape of his large, bald head, with wide-set eyes and small nose, gave the impression that he had descended from a long and honourable line of owls.

The scroll he held in his closed fist flopped between his knees, his jutting chin propped in the cup of his other hand. Stewart's thoughts were racing, both backwards to past unsettling events and forwards to what he feared might be a precarious future. He remained there, his body motionless while his mind somersaulted over the possibilities. And that is where his wife found him, some time later as she emerged from overseeing her kitchen staff in their preparations for the meals of the day.

"What ails you, husband?"

Archibald took a few seconds to raise his head from his melancholic pose. "This," he said, wafting the scroll towards her.

"And what is this that it bears so heavily on you?"

"You must read it yourself, Mary," he said. "I have perused it twice already and I doubt if I can bear to do so again."

"Oh dear, is it such serious news? Who sends it?"

Her husband paused before forming an answer.

"You recall my journey to Scotland on behalf of the Earl last year?"

"Of course I do; how could I not! You were gone for several months. I had begun to think you would never return," she said, a hint of mischief in her eyes. "I had taken to wondering if I should be starting to search for a younger replacement…"

"Mary, this is not a time to be funny," he rebuked her, too sharply. "This letter may change the course of our lives."

"My apologies, husband. Please explain."

"That was a foolish and a futile mission," recalled Stewart. "I had to do it as Randal's ambassador, but its failure has not done him any favours, either in Scotland or with his friend the King."

"How so?"

"Do you recall me describing my meeting with Alaster McColla McDonnell?"

"McColla? The one who is believed to eat raw toads?"

Stewart nodded. "The very same. He has a fearsome reputation, whether it all be true or not."

"I remember, and I remember being glad that such a frightful warrior was on our side, even if the Earl's plans came to nothing at that time. Better to have him as a friend rather than as an enemy surely?"

"That is what I thought too, at the time. But more importantly, better to have him as a distant friend, one who operates in Scotland rather than here in Antrim. Now, it seems, that is about to change."

"What do you mean, 'about to change'? Is he intending to come to Ireland?" Mrs Stewart looked worried.

"I am afraid so. Not only is he intending to come to Ireland, he is intending to take up temporary residence very close to here."

"At Dunluce, you mean?"

"Closer, much closer."

"Surely not Dunseverick, with Gilladubh?"

"Closer still!"

Mary Stewart's face changed colour and her hand went to her forehead as her husband continued.

"We are to have a guest, my dear. A very dangerous guest!"

Mary stared at the scroll as if it might be leprous. "Please," she whispered, "tell me the worst." She squeezed herself into the narrow space beside him on the steps as he read.

15th July 1641
Castle Colonsay
My Dear Cousin Archibald, It has been some twelve months or more since your auspicious visit to our Castle Colonsay. I need hardly rehearse to you the excellent impression made by your good self upon our family here.

It was with deep regret and not a little annoyance that we learned of the failure of the proposal made by my kinsman, The Earl of Antrim, to rise against Campbell the Argyll. You will recall our discussion of the injustice whereby Campbell occupies McDonnell lands in Kintyre and other places. We would have been honoured and delighted to assist in a rising against those Covenanting enemies of King Charles here in Scotland. Sadly it was not to be.

It is my present intention to cross to your Antrim shores in the very near future as matters have turned bitterly against me in a local dispute here. May I presume upon your friendship, good cousin, by entreating you to return the hospitality enjoyed by you in our accommodation last year and so inviting myself, my brother Raghnall and a small party of my Highland kinsmen to quarter in your excellent abode at Caisteal Baile an Tuaigh. If we can be of any assistance to your endeavours while in residence with you we will be delighted to oblige. Our arrival shall be within a matter of a few days.

I remain your loving cousin,
Alaster McColla McDonnell'

After a moment of sober silence Mary Stewart jumped to her feet.
"Who brought this letter?" she asked.
"Some courier from Ballycastle."
"Where is he now? Has he gone already?"
"Not yet," replied Archibald. "Kerr is looking after him. I believe he is having some vittles in the yard while his horse is being watered and rubbed down. Why do you ask?"
"Because, don't you see, Archibald, that it is vital to draft a refusal at once so that it can be taken back to Ballycastle and sent on its way to this impudent relative!"
The husband held up his hand. "Wait now Mary. You don't understand the implications of a refusal. This man is not someone you refuse. He is one of the greatest presences in the whole of Scotland's military landscape. He is close kin to our Earl, Randal's cousin of some degree, far closer than he is to us."
"How is he a cousin? I thought…"
Again Archibald raised his hand, hushing her while he considered the genealogy. "Alaster's father was the legendary Coll Kittagh, the great left-handed warrior. I'm sure you've heard of him. Born at Lough Lynch near here, fled to Colonsay as a child where he grew up, married and had three sons, including these two, Alaster and Raghnall. Great warriors, by all accounts. And you suggest I refuse a man of this pedigree?"
"Why doesn't he invite himself to stay with the Earl then?" asked Mary. "Dunluce is far bigger and far grander than Ballintoy."
Archibald reflected on this. "I think the answer to that is two-fold. Firstly, he did entertain me last year, and secondly, he is probably unsure on which side of his family's quarrel our Lord Randal may sit. He would lose face, hugely so, if Randal turned him away, you understand?"
"I see that," Mary said, "but he is brazen enough to impose himself on us? We are merely the poor relations."
"Let's face it, we are only the land stewards, the Earl's local agents. We are here simply to serve. My father was fortunate enough to have been invited over here from Bute by Randal's father forty years ago and given a tract of land."
"'Given a tract of land?'" Mary scorned. "Land that wasn't his, as I recall. I understood that this tract of land that your family received was 'given' in payment of a long-standing debt which the McDonnells couldn't pay?"

"Yes, and you are correct, but that does not affect this present situation. The McDonnells know how to get what they want. I have no way of refusing McColla, not even if I wanted to…and believe me, everything in my spirit warns me against too close a connection with this…this man of violence. He may be the greatest soldier in Scotland, but I am wary of his whims. Anyhow, any message we would send would not reach him in time. That ship has sailed, as they say. It sounds from his words that he may already be on his way. All we can do at this stage, my dear, is prepare as best we can."

"He said 'A small party of Highlanders'? Where are we going to put them? How many? And for what? Does he feel he needs protection?"

"I have no idea," answered her husband.

"And how is the Earl going to like this invasion?"

"I cannot see him welcoming it. McColla is unpredictable. A great friendly man, although every time I looked at him I was always wondering what exactly he was thinking. He has the air of an arch-schemer about him. Randal will be on his guard, I imagine, but better to have him drinking rum inside the castle than throwing rocks over the walls, as they say."

"Well, I don't know where we are going to get rum for him; he'll have to do with a sup of our best Bushmills spirit I'm afraid," said Mary.

"Look, can I ask you to take charge of that aspect of things. Talk to Kerr; he will have ideas about where to put them. Some of them will have to quarter with our tenants; the ones with larger houses."

"How many guests are we to expect?"

Stewart the letter again. "He doesn't specify how many in this…"

"We will need additional help," Mary interrupted. "Kitchen staff, yard staff, housemaids."

Her husband grimaced. "Knowing what McColla's like I wouldn't be having too many maids about the place," he said. "Not if they want to stay maids. The Highlanders can look after themselves."

"Maybe so, but can I get more help in the kitchen?"

"If you must, my dear. Do you have anyone in mind?"

"I am thinking Jean Kennedy, and maybe Isobel McKay's oldest girl, what's her name? The pretty one?"

"Ah, Katie; aye, that's a good idea. They are good people and I am sure they could use the work."

"Good. I'll send Kerr round to ask."

"I need to give some thought to having some sort of welcoming feast for these…these guests. They held one in my honour. I can do no less."

Mary Stewart winced at the suggestion. "Goodbye quietness and normality. Welcome whiskey and mad Highlanders and crazy chaos. Is that how it is going to be?"

"For the time being, my dear. For the time being."

Chapter 3

Kirk

Katie McKay

A key article of faith for our clergyman, Reverend James Blare, was that if a sermon was worth preaching it should be listened to for as long a period as possible. That Sabbath in late July was no exception. I did my best to pay attention to what was clearly a very impassioned performance, but, between the excitement in me at the turn my life had taken this past week and the fatigue I felt in my bones as a result, my level of concentration let me down several times.

I looked up through the shafts of dusty sunlight at the beams and rafters of the building. I counted the various timbers. I watched spiders fight with unfortunate flies. Some of the window openings had had their shutters taken down for the service; the curtains of woven cloth and animal hides swayed as the breeze swirled around the kirk. I examined the blemishes on the lime-cast walls and wondered when anyone would think to repair them.

I stole glances across the aisle to where the Boyd family sat, everyone of them in wrapt attention, apart from the youngest boy who seemed to be counting shells from one pocket to the other. And in the front row, Archibald Stewart and his impressive wife, nodding along as if in agreement with the clergyman, as if to encourage his every utterance. It crossed my mind to imagine the pride Mr Stewart must feel, to be sitting in this kirk that he had commissioned. It had been built as a 'Chapel of Ease' for his nearby 'Ballintoy Castle', or, as we thought of it, the Manor House. I did not recall exactly when it had been built, I being very young at the time.

The drone of his reverence's voice continued, constant as the background hum of waves breaking on the rocks below.

Rev Blare, my mother told me, had been a Presbyterian from Scotland when he was ordained by Bishop Echlin years ago so he could be the clergyman in the parishes of Billy and Ballintoy. It suited us, with our strong Presbyterian roots, that he still preached like a Presbyterian, but in recent times he had had to appear to toe the line and be a loyal Anglican. It seemed that being a non-conformist in present-day Ireland was nearly as big a problem as being Catholic. For all that, Rev Blare still tried to use both languages in his service, but I was not alone in noticing that when he got really worked up about something his English deserted him and his voice rose into noisy Gaelic, the language and dialect of his native Arran. I was able to understand both of course, but there would have been some in our congregation who struggled with the switches. It was alright for those families who were originally from the highlands and islands; in most cases Gaelic was still our first language, even those of us born here in Antrim. But for some of the congregation, the Boyds and the Kerrs, for example, it was more of a struggle. They were originally from the central part of Scotland and spoke lowland Scots. Not all of them would have had the Gaelic, especially those who had been born over here.

"And so you see, dearly beloved brethren of the covenant, you are not the first people that God has led out of bondage into a promised land."

I was wondering why it was just the men who always seemed to be so led; the women obviously just had to follow along.

"He hath brought us hither and given us a land that floweth with milk and honey," he read from the scriptures. It sounded rosy and, to be fair, our cow did give plenty of milk and there was wild honey to be had in the sand-hills beside White Park Bay.

"Therefore, when you look out towards the coasts of Islay or Kintyre, do not look back to the former things, to your Egypt. This is your Promised Land. And when you face your enemies be strong in the Lord, be of good courage. He is on our side and victory will be His."

There was a general stirring in the congregation at this and I looked around at my neighbours. Eyes were shining brightly back at the pulpit and a few men mouthed, 'Amen'. My fellow Presbyterians were being inspired by this sermon today. Victory sounded good but I couldn't help wonder who we were supposed to be fighting. There were very few enemies around Ballintoy. Things were going very smoothly for our community. We got on well enough with our Irish neighbours and, to be fair to them, the majority were welcoming and friendly. Yes, there were some families who seemed to have a bit of resentment, I don't really know what about, but the Irish are so like ourselves; we feel like cousins.

My mind began to wander to other things, as had happened far too often since the walk to Portballintrae, this day two weeks ago. I tried to recall exactly the face of the stranger on the Causeway path. I didn't find that too much of an effort. 'But here, this is kirk and I should be listening,' I thought as I caught myself on.

Mr Blare was reading a passage from the book of Ezra, he said. Ah well, I could tune in again when he got to the end of his reading.

I had so much to be thankful for that week. I had a new job in the Manor House, learning how to be an assistant to the cook, along with my friend Jean. I couldn't believe it when James Kerr had arrived in our cottage and asked me to come down to talk to Mrs Stewart about working in her kitchen. My mother was delighted and....Mr Blare's voice rose and interrupted my thankfulness.

"Are you hearing the Word of the Lord here, young people? 'Do not take a wife from among the Canaanites!' The Lord wants to protect you from the contamination of relations with a Canaanite woman, you understand? Take wives only from the Covenant people of God."

'Ah well, that's not so bad,' I thought. He was speaking to the men again; it didn't say a word about the other way around, did it? But it did. I was too quick to rejoice. He broadened the point, including us women too.

In my mind I went back to the cliff-top.

Of what tribe was the dark haired one? How would he fit into these theological categories? Would I ever see him again? Maybe I should content myself and think no more about such strangers. There were plenty of other lads around Ballintoy and I knew one or two of them had been looking at me. But then, I hadn't exactly been looking back, had I, apart from a brief and awkward flirtation with Bruce McClure?

The clergyman was continuing. He had moved on from marriage prohibitions to something more mundane but, from the tone and pitch of his voice, equally important to him.

"It is true, is it not, that some of you farmers have refrained from removing the old heathen fairy-thorns in your new fields? Some have left in their place the pagan oak trees that stand in your way." His voice rose angrily. "And the reason, I am told, is that people are afraid of offending! For fear of offending who, might I ask? The fairies? No, the native Irish who hold these pagan objects to be of sacred value."

What was this point he was making? I was not the only one to be puzzled here. A couple of farmers had shifted uneasily in their pews.

"Brethern, the Lord hath given you this land. He hath driven out your enemies before you, so do not be afraid of giving offence. Rather be afraid of offending your Lord and Saviour. In Deuteronomy we read, 'Ye shall utterly destroy all the places wherein the nations ye shall possess served their Gods, upon the high mountains and under every green tree. Ye shall overthrow their altars, break their pillars, and burn their groves with fire; and ye shall hew down the graven images of their gods.'"

Goodness, that was a tall order, I was thinking. How would it go down with our neighbours if we start destroying the trees and the sacred stone monuments that they have been cherishing for generations? I had a look around at some of the congregation close to me. One or two were nodding their heads in agreement, it seemed, but others had dropped their faces and were finding interest in either their footwear or the floor. It was all very well for his reverence to take such a hard-line approach to obeying Scripture, but he did not have to live among these native Irish as neighbours. He could ride back in his pony and trap to his big house beside his church at Billy and no harm would come to him.

The service eventually finished with the singing of our most treasured Psalm, the Twenty Third, and our unaccompanied voices uniting in simple harmony seemed to restore some vigour to us all after the slaughtering of that sermon. We emerged from the rear door of the kirk and shook hands with the clergyman, most of us avoiding his stare and hurrying past him to freedom. As I watched I was surprised to see my brother Alex have a warm conversation with Reverend Blare. This intrigued me, as Alex wouldn't have been the most devoted to his religion. My father's spinster sister, Aunt Biddy, who lived with us, was fussing around the minister as usual, but that was of no account; Biddy had always had a special place in her heart for clergymen, for any man in fine clothes or uniform, sometimes embarrassing the rest of the family with her inappropriate chat to them. My mother always excused her and told us to pay her no heed. "She's always had a wee want about her," was mother's way of forgiving Biddy's rashness.

It was our habit after the service to gather with our friends around the sea-ward side of the building. The craic was always good there, but for the previous three or four weeks I had denied myself the pleasure. My self-imposed 'exile' was all down to an unhappy rift in a friendship with one of the local lads. I had known Bruce since childhood; we had always been playmates, good friends, but Bruce had developed feelings for me which I could never return, try as I might. There was nothing wrong with him as a person; he looked fine, big and handsome of himself and civil enough…except that he had a dogged way about him that I found tiresome, annoying even. So, the more he presumed about the nature of our relationship, the more he tried to force it towards a courtship, the more I had pulled away from him. It had come to a head about a month back when he followed me on one of my quiet, lonely walks to Carrick-a-rede along the coast. I was in no mood to accept his insistence that he accompany me, that I somehow 'belonged' to him, that us being a couple was meant to be. I had been more brutal in my words to him that day than was merited and I knew I had hurt him. It couldn't be helped. I had hoped it would pass and that we could return to a more normal type of friendship, as we had enjoyed before all this intensity. But each time I saw him I became aggravated by the accusing way he looked at me, the sort of rebuking stare you would give a sheep-dog that had not understood your commands. How different his dark stare to that of the stranger at the Causeway.

So I was slightly tentative that Sabbath as I joined the group after the service. I was hoping it wouldn't be awkward, but I was nervous and determined to avoid engaging with Bruce. The mood seemed jolly, however. That was good; we all needed a lightening of the atmosphere after Rev Blare's heavy words.

As often happened, Thomas Smith, a solid young fellow who tended to be the easy target for our banter, was having to suffer some ridicule at the hands of his mates. As I approached the group someone addressed me, drawing me into the light-hearted abuse.

"Katie, didn't you notice Blare having a go at Thomas there?"

I had no idea what was being referred to but I played along.

"Indeed. He certainly hit Tommy very hard today," I agreed.

"How so?" Thomas objected. "He wasn't talking any more to me than any of the rest of you."

"Aye, he was surely," Matt Taggart joined in. "Sure he was forever staring down at you. I saw it. We all saw it Tommy, we did surely." Matt was a great man for the 'surelys'. Behind his back we called him, 'Aye surely'.

"He never was," argued Thomas. "Yous are making this up. Why would he be looking at me, for God's sake?"

"Sssh, Tommy! He might hear you," chided our Connie who had appeared at that moment, closely followed by the solid figure of our brother, Alex.

"I don't care if he does," Tommy said to her. "They're saying…I don't know what they're saying, Connie, but it wasn't me, whatever they're saying."

This was interesting, the apology to our Connie. Although she was only fifteen, Connie had a flirtatious thing about her that endeared her to some of the lads, Tommy being the most recent admirer. Connie just gave him a look of mock annoyance, but she couldn't hide the grin behind it.

Bruce, who had been conspicuously staying on the fringes of the exchange, took up the mock attack again. "You have to admit that when he was talking about courting a Canaanite woman he was looking down straight at you, Tommy. We all noticed it!"

"What has that got to do with me, will yous tell me?" Tommy shouted, reddening about his cheeks. "There's not a lot o' them Canaanite woman around Ballintoy….or if there is I must have missed them."

Jean took his arm consolingly, while addressing the rest of us in a confidential tone.

"And believe me folks, there's not many women around here that our Tommy has missed," she announced knowingly.

We roared with laughter at poor Thomas.

"You sound like you would know, Jean," said Matt. "Tell us more."

"Nothing to tell," Jean laughed. "But there's what's-her-name? Wee Bridget something? Up the glen. I hear he's been taking walks in her direction."

"I have not indeed and you know it," Tommy complained.

The chat moved on to other things as we tired of persecuting Tommy, but I noticed that he still felt the need to defend himself to my sister. I heard him quietly protest to her, "That's a load of nonsense, Connie. That stuff about me going after wee Bridget, whoever she is. You believe me, don't you?"

Connie, ever as sharp as a pin, replied, "Of course I believe you, Tommy. Sure how could she stand the smell o' the sheep off you?"

She laughed and turned back to the main conversation, leaving Tommy looking badly wounded. The poor chap was out of his depth tangling with our sharp-tongued Connie.

"What was that other nonsense Blare was ranting about?" asked Matt. "Trees and altars and high places or something?"

"No idea. I wasn't really listening," replied Bruce, with what was meant to be a meaningful sideways glance in my direction.

"Alex, what did you make of it?" Matt continued. "I heard you chatting to his reverence there, somethin' about fairy trees."

For once Alex seemed to be a bit embarrassed and didn't immediately respond. I thought I would try to rescue him.

"It was all a bit strange, to be honest," I said. "Does he seriously expect us to go searching for trees that annoy us? Or what about the Druid's Altar up on the hill near our bog? If it is some sort of pagan thing, are we supposed to try to pull it down?"

"Good luck with that," Matt said. "Sure it's massive."

Alex stepped forward into the discussion, having considered carefully what he wanted to say. "I was talking to him about the fairy thorn thing. Do yous remember when my father died? Well, a few days before that he had chopped down an old thorn bush between our high field and Reid's bit of bog. It never occurred to us that anybody would think it sacred. It didn't look like a fairy thorn. It wasn't stuck out somewhere by itself, it was growing on a march ditch. But of course the rumour started that he had died because he interfered with a fairy thorn. The Reid crowd did nothing to stop the rumour either."

"How do you stop a rumour though? It is like trying to gather straw in a storm," said Jean wisely.

"I know, but I just wanted to know Mr Blare's opinion about it."

"And what did he say?"

"As you'd expect, he said that it is all the more reason to go after these pagan trees; destroy the superstitions and be done with all that nonsense."

There was a silence as people thought about the implications of Alex's words. Was he really serious about this?

"So you'll have a go at it today then?" I asked him.

He gave me a long hard stare. "Not on the Sabbath, Kate," he glowered.

"Ah right," I said. "As long as it's not just superstition…"

"Of course it's not superstition. It's one of the Ten Commandments."

That was me put in my place. Mind you, I always felt it was my right to throw a stone into the smooth waters of our usual ways and opinions. The rebel in me I suppose, but surely things needed a bit of a challenge, even for argument's sake.

On the way home from kirk I walked by myself, well behind Alex and Connie. Mammy, Aunt Biddy and Alice had already gone and were no doubt getting our meal ready.

The conversation after the service had unsettled me. I could not quite put my finger on why. For me Sabbath worship had always been a thing of comfort, of reassurance, a sort of warm blanket of community togetherness and shared intention. Today I did not sense those kinds of feelings. Why did these conversations and ideas seem to jar with the words we had just been singing before we left the service?

I decided to sing them to myself as I wandered along the short lane towards our humble cottage. So I did. The Twenty Third Psalm in my native Scots Gaelic. I was thankful for the idea that God would *'lead me by the quiet waters'*.

Aye, but it was a different idea that was soon drawing me that Sabbath afternoon. Before we were halfway through the meal of fried mackerel I had decided that today would be a fine day for a walk, on my own this time. I would most likely go along the strand, whether the waters of the bay were quiet or not. I would walk as far as Portbradden and maybe even Dunseverick. I would sing my own psalm to myself, if that wasn't too sacrilegious for the day that was in it.

On the white strand he will lead me, beside the crashing waves.

You never know your luck.

Chapter 4

The Harp Maker

The small flock of loyal followers filed silently out of the tiny 'chapel' in Dunluce Castle at the end of Mass, faces turned to the high curtain wall, heads bent, as if against recognition. They scurried across the drawbridge, through the outer ward and the main gates, then disappeared in different directions. Some headed inland towards the hills. Others slipped into the narrow streets of humble dwellings nearby. Dunluce, the village, was sited safely on the mainland, only a matter of feet away from the fortress itself. In stark contrast to this unassuming settlement, the ancient castle seemed sedately unaware of its dramatic location, perched precariously, as it was, on a steep-sided promontory which jutted daringly out into the sea.

Father Patrick McGlaim, the priest who was visiting from Bonamargy Friary at distant Ballycastle, was hastily tidying up the eucharistic objects on the simple altar when he became aware of footsteps entering from the inner ward. He turned his bearded face around to watch a tall figure wandering shyly up the short aisle and paused in his work to observe him. In the half-light of the building recognition was not easy. The priest waited nervously, peering short-sightedly into the gloom. Was this a friend, a late parishioner perhaps, or might it be an agent of the establishment who would report back to his masters that Mass had again been served in the shelter of the McDonnell seat?

A smile of relief flitted across the priest's face.

"Ah…God bless you, my young friend. I wasn't sure who you were until you came into the beam of light. How are you?"

"I am fine, Father. Good to have you with us."

"Thank you. I thought I should recognise that face when I saw you at the altar. Very good to see you again after all these years. How long now since you were studying with us in Bonamargy?"

"It is all of seven years, unbelievably."

"Seven years? That hardly seems possible. You must excuse me, I am afraid that my recall of names is not what it used to be; I seem to think you are an O'Cahan but, forgive me, your first name is…"

"I am Darach, Darach O'Cahan."

"Of course you are. How could I forget 'Darach', the boy of 'dark oak'…And remind me. Are you a Dunseverick O'Cahan? One of

Gilladubh's boys?"

"No, no," Darach answered, perhaps too abruptly. "Gilladubh is my uncle. My father is Martin. You met him when he came to take me from the Friary, I think. He lives over in the town-land of Straid."

"Ah right. I think I did meet him indeed. So, if you live away over there how come you are at Mass here today?"

"It's a long story Father," replied Darach. "After we decided that I wasn't cut out for the religious life I was in my own home for a few months. Then my father thought I should learn carpentry instead. So I was fostered out to the McSparran family here at Dunluce. They would be kin to my mother and they had no children of their own. John McSparran was the resident carpenter here at the castle and I was to be his apprentice and follow him."

"Ah I see. So how did you take to being fostered?"

Darach looked down as he considered how to answer this question. Fostering was an age-old practice in Irish families. It was thought of as a normal custom, one that served to reinforce bonds of kinship and bind in families which, for whatever reason, may have been considered to be in danger of being distanced from the tribe.

"It was difficult at the start, but I got used to it," he said thoughtfully. "John and Eilish have been very good to me."

"Good. I'm glad. So you continued your education here with them?"

"I did, but it is a very different type of education from the reading and writing I learned in Bonamargy."

"And which do you enjoy more?" the priest asked him.

Darach smiled. This was an easy question to answer. "The carpentry. I have learned so much from John, especially about making harps. From Eilish too. She has a great way with the salley rods. She's well known for her creels and baskets."

"Is she indeed? And you are interested in the making of harps? Good for you."

"Well you see, years ago John had taught himself the basics of harp making, and he'd made a few good ones before his fingers twisted in on him, so I sort of felt it on me to learn the tradition and take over."

"It's a noble calling; even better if you can play. Do you play? Maybe you are already a *cruitireachta*?" McGlaim asked.

Darach laughed. "I'm afraid I am no master-harper, Father. I try, but I am not very accomplished."

"I'm sure that's not true. You must let me hear your tunes sometime."

The priest turned to finish his tidying. Darach waited for him.

"Isn't it just as well you are born in this century though, Master O'Cahan?"

"Why do you say that, Father?"

"Because if you had been a harper in the last century you could have been hung for it."

Darach looked puzzled and the priest continued.

"During the reign of Elizabeth, only forty, fifty years ago, harpers were *persona non grata* here in Ireland. The English didn't like the harp. Harpers were a persecuted profession. Hunted almost to extinction, you might say, and on the instructions of Queen Elizabeth herself."

"But why? What harm could come of playing harps? They are our sacred instrument, always have been."

"Exactly. That is the point. It was part of undermining our Gaelic culture. You have to bear in mind that back then England was at war with many of our chieftains. Some were loyal to the Crown, some were not. And, as you know, the traditional harp players travelled between the great houses and castles of the chieftains. Elizabeth got it into her head that the harpers were spies, that they carried tales between chieftains and helped in spreading plots against the British authorities. So she put out an edict that harpers were to be arrested and hung; their harps had to be burned. It was not a good time to be a musician, believe me. Many fine men lost their lives. Many harps were burned to cinders."

"My God," said Darach, "I didn't know that. It is unbelievable. I'm glad I am alive now, rather than then."

"Indeed you should be, my son," McGlaim said as he finished tidying his altar. "Now I think I am ready for the road."

"Would you like to come for vittles before you go home, Father? John sent me back to ask. We live in the village, close by. We would be honoured."

Father McGlaim eagerly took him up on his offer and, following the meal with the two ageing McSparrans, Darach was obliged to produce his latest instrument and play a slow air. The priest was moved by the performance and commented on the brightness of sound of Darach's harp.

"It has a beautifully vibrant tone, great resonance altogether. And do you have any songs?"

"He does indeed," Eilish said proudly. "We hear him at the songs when he doesn't know we are listening. He is as good a singer as you will hear in Antrim."

Slightly embarrassed by this, Darach looked at his feet and shook his head.

"I am no great singer, indeed I'm not. I only make up tunes, sometimes songs, just to suit myself. I seldom let anybody else hear them."

"Well, if you want to make an exception today, my young friend, I will be delighted to make my own judgement of your talent. Please sing me a song of your making."

"Ah no, I wouldn't be confident enough to sing one of my own."

"Go away on with you, Darach," Eilish rebuked him. "He is just trying to be modest, Father. We hear him every night singing his own verses. Very good, they are."

"That's great," said the priest. "You have the right mind for it. I would know that from your time studying with us. So now you are becoming a bit of a bard, are you?"

Darach smiled self-consciously. He spoke softly from behind the curtain of his hanging hair. "I suppose you might call me that," he said, "but I am only a beginner. I have learned from some of the great travelling poets and players."

"We all had to begin sometime," McGlaim said. "Please let me hear your music."

Darach's fingers fell on the wire strings and he twanged the opening arpeggio of a recent piece he had written. It began softly, slowly, pensively, but as the tune progressed a regular rhythm developed, a repeated phrase which seemed to grow in pulsing crescendoes. His nails cascaded across the strings, creating regular crashing sounds. He was playing strongly, bravely, his natural reticence being overtaken by the power of his composition…and then the tune seemed to settle again into a melodic cadence that rose and fell mesmerically until it faded away to a very quiet finale, almost as if disappearing over a horizon.

Father McGlaim put his hands together warmly at its end. "Excellent. It is a great piece of music, and very well played. Where did you get the inspiration for this, may I ask?"

"I live beside the sea," Darach said simply.

"Ah, the sea! Of course it's the sea. Wonderful," the priest said. "I heard the breaking waves there for sure. You're very good. You'll be taking to the roads before long to play in all the great houses of Ireland."

"Hardly likely. I am happy enough with what I am doing here in my native county," replied Darach. "I'll leave the wandering to better players than me. That way I will be safe from any charges of spying."

"Fair enough, but tell me, do you ever get the chance to play for her ladyship?"

"Lady Katherine? She has heard me play, yes," he answered humbly.

"I am sure she was impressed?"

Darach hesitated but Mrs McSparran filled the silence. "Very impressed, Father. We don't even know how she found out that he could play, do we John?"

John did though, and smiled at the memory. "The two of us were replacing a bit of damaged panelling in the great hall. The Earl's harp was sitting there and yer man here couldn't keep his hands to himself. He just played a couple of bars of a tune, but here wasn't her Ladyship passing the door and landed in on us. I thought Darach was going to be in hot water over it, but naw! She was all interest! 'Extraordinary', she said. First time I ever heard of anything being 'extraordinary', especially our Darach."

"And did she ask you to play?" McGlaim asked.

"She did." Darach wasn't very forth-coming.

"And you did?"

"Aye, just a wee bit of an air."

"You're very humble. And what did she think?"

Darach hesitated, glancing at Eilish. "I don't know," he mumbled.

Eilish took up his cause. "You know rightly," she rebuked him. "She liked it very much. So much so that she asked him to play for her guests. She had been entertaining visitors. After the wining and dining she brought them out to the gardens to watch the sunset over Portrush. It was a grand night. She had asked Darach to sit up on the balcony and play for these folk. They were all very impressed and had to have him down so they could see this young harper. Somebody told me that she thinks Darach is a lot better at it than her husband!"

"So the Earl plays the harp as well?" asked Father McGlaim.

"He does, and he even gave Darach his first commission," Eilish said proudly.

The priest looked puzzled. "First commission? How do you mean?"

"Well, when he heard that John was teaching him the art of harp making, he asked for Darach to make him one."

"Really? That was a great honour for you, Darach. And how did you get on?" McGlaim asked.

Darach looked again to his foster parents.

"Go on, tell him!" John said with a smile.

"It went well, I think. He seems to like it."

"Great," the priest said.

"'He seems to like it'?" Eilish said. "He was a lot more enthusiastic than that, Darach. If I remember right, he said it sounded every bit as good as the one he brought from London."

"That is wonderful, Darach," the priest grinned. "You should be delighted with that compliment. And he paid you well for it, I imagine?"

It was Darach's turn to smile. "Well, he said he would. I'm still waiting for it, but I am sure he hasn't forgotten."

"Be patient with him, son," Eilish said. "He has a lot on his mind. The Duchess won't let him forget. They are such an interesting pair, the two of them. It is such a pity that they are away in Dublin. They seem to travel so much; you never know when they are going to be here and when they are away."

"Yes indeed," Father McGlaim said. "When the messenger brought the invitation to say Mass here today I imagined they would be present."

"So you haven't met the Duchess yet?"

"I haven't had the pleasure. What is she like? As uppity as you'd expect of such a wealthy lady?"

Darach rose to the defence of the Duchess. "We think she has really tried to understand us and fit in, as far as she can anyhow. She has her English ways and her strong ideas, and she has spent a fortune in improving and furnishing the castle. But she has been generous to the people around here too."

"She even renovated St Cuthbert's Church for the Protestants of our village," added John, "and her not even one herself. It had fallen into a ruin, needed a stack of work. A new thatched roof, new doors, new ceiling all painted blue with stars on it, new benches for the folk to sit on. It looks lovely now. That was all her idea. You couldn't ask for more decency than that. I was busy at that job for months."

"I'm sure you were. But I hear that she has switched her religion more than once?" the priest remarked.

"You could be right. I wouldn't know about that," answered John.

"The McDonnells were always clever," added his wife wryly, tapping the side of her head. "They know what side their bread is buttered on."

"Maybe, but she takes an interest in matters in the village," said Darach. "The children; things like their sport and games, and their music, even though it's probably nothing like she is used to."

"I am delighted to hear that," said the priest, nodding his head. "She sounds like a much kinder person than I had been led to believe. And I am pleased she has appreciated your music too." He leaned over to look more closely at Darach's harp, tapping the decorative edging along the frame with his fingertips. "Such a lovely instrument. And what wood is this? Is it oak or what?"

"Ah no; the neck, *'an corr'*, at the top here, it is from an alder tree; so is the fore-pillar, *an lámh-chrann*."

"*An fhearnóg*," mused the priest. "The same wood that was used in making our traditional shields."

"Indeed; it was a piece John had been seasoning for a good lot of years," Darach continued. "*An com* is salley, the soundbox, do you see? A hollowed out length of salley. Easy to work with and it helps give that lasting sound you want, do you hear that?" He plucked a few strings again.

"I do hear that," McGlaim said. "Lovely. And I see you have a little oak leaf engraved on the side here? A reference to your name, I take it?"

"It is. I just thought it was a way to signify me as the maker."

"Indeed. I like this head you have carved. A hawk or an eagle I think?"

Darach smiled. "I must be doing alright; aye, this is my eagle harp. I do a different bird on each instrument, so I remember who buys each one. The one I made for the Earl has a swan on it. I think it is my prettiest, certainly my best one so far. The last one I made has a puffin's head. It went to Ballycastle, to Hugh MacNeill's wife. I'm sure you know the MacNeills?"

"Of course I do. So Dunynie Castle has one of your creations? Hugh bought one for his good lady? You will become famous now," he laughed.

Darach shook his head. "I am not sure I would welcome that."

"And tell me, do you find it easy enough to get the right kind of timber?" asked the priest.

Darach looked at the McSparrans. "We were just talking about that yesterday," he said. "No sir, I have to say it isn't easy and it is time consuming going to search the area south of here. A lot of our trees have been cut down since….they were needed for the building of these new towns, Coleraine and the like."

"I understand," the priest nodded knowingly.

"And this strip along the coast wouldn't have the same tree cover you get inland," Darach continued.

"Of course not; the salty breezes up here see to that."

"Exactly. You see, the timber has to be well seasoned and of a certain age. I have been fortunate that John never discards any wood. He has a store of timber cuts that he has saved and keeps for repairs in his shed behind the house here. Sometimes I find a suitable piece that has been discarded when they were doing renovations."

"So you have a ready supply?"

"It's not bad, but I have a duty to try to replenish his stock. Whiles I search the shoreline for driftwood that might be suitable when it dries out. Alder isn't so hard to find around here but getting sturdy lengths of sally that have been aged is difficult."

Father McGlaim sat in thought for a few moments.

"I have an idea," he said. "Would you ever come with me to a place I have experience of, an ancient wood that has been fairly untouched by local people; I am not sure that any of our more recent settlers even know of its existence. Many trees grow beside the wee burn that flows down a little valley, so there should be plenty of alder, salley too, for they like the damp ground. I could take you there and you could spend a bit of time having a look at trees that have fallen over the years. You might find something useful. It's not far away from the hearth of your own folks in Straid."

Darach was immediately excited by the prospect. "Really? That is very kind. I would be delighted to take you up on your offer, if it is not too much trouble?"

"No trouble, my pleasure indeed."

A date and a meeting point were arranged before the priest left to make his way back to his cell at Bonamargy Friary.

He took his time on the journey, loving the solitude and peacefulness of these rides between parishes. He made good use of the opportunity for prayer, and could be seen by the folks he met, apparently making conversation with himself, oblivious to the curious onlookers. McGlaim was really thankful to God that, in this northern-most part of Ireland, he could still travel openly in his priestly attire, something that would not have been advisable in those parts of Ulster which had been planted so overwhelmingly by the English. The local Scots were much more accepting of his faith, being mainly non-conformist by inclination themselves. Nevertheless, he had developed an instinct to avoid public scrutiny as far as possible. Keeping a low profile in this new dispensation of anti-Catholic constraints was the key to survival. His people needed him and he would do his best to be there for them for as long as he could.

Today he decided to leave the normal inland route and take the scenic and more isolated path along the coast. The spectacle from the top of the Causeway cliffs did nothing to distract him from his meditations, indeed it enhanced his feelings of thankfulness. Ahead Rathlin Island, or Raghery, as the locals called it, dominated the sea-scape, its magnificent cliffs of black basalt topping the gleaming white band of limestone underneath. Beyond the island he could see the hump of the Mull of Kintyre. It was only a dozen miles further to the east across *An Sruth na Maoile,* the Straights of Moyle, that separated Antrim from the Scottish islands and mainland. The azure surface of Rathlin Sound seemed so calm and placid when looking down from this altitude.

Beside him gulls and ravens hovered and swooped on the upward currents of air by the rock face, barely moving a wing. Chaffinches chittered as he approached and hopped ahead of him from bush to whin, as if to show him the way.

Nearing Dunseverick he descended from the cliff-path towards the harbour there. Sensing that his ageing mule, *Pádraig,* was in need of a rest he dismounted and led it along a narrow track between the cliff and the sea. As he rounded a particularly tight bend the priest found himself face to face with a strikingly pretty young woman in a flowing, flaxen garment. The light breeze from the west funnelling along the edge of the rock-face played with her dress and wafted her long hair back from her face. Her eyes, the colour of wet moss, held his with modest confidence. Both stopped abruptly, unable to pass.

"I'm sorry," the priest said. "Let me back up a bit."

"It's alright," she said brightly, not at all thrown by his clerical garb. "I don't think your mule would be happy having to turn here. Easier for me to go back." She turned on her heel to retreat to a wider spot where they could pass.

"Thank you," Father McGlaim muttered. "You're very kind."

"Not at all," she called back over her shoulder.

"She may not be of my flock but isn't she the perfect vision of Irish womanhood," he thought, consciously diverting his gaze from her tall, swaying figure and tugging at *Pádraig's* reins to hurry him forward. Ahead, the young woman hitched up her skirts and leapt girlishly to balance daringly on a rough outcrop of rock by the track, allowing him to pass. She said nothing, but her grin was as wide and warming as a field of ripe corn. Father McGlaim returned her smile and touched his hat as he passed.

"God bless you," he said. Minutes later he was praying again. "I am a priest of your church, oh Lord Jesus Christ, and my love and devotion and service are only to you and your Holy Mother…and so forgive me. And let me also give you eternal thanks for the wonderful creations I have witnessed on my journey today," he breathed as he blessed himself, soon reaching the sheltered harbour of Dunseverick.

Chapter 5

The Pagan Places

Alex McKay was determined to act resolutely on what he was fairly certain were his beliefs, or at least on those of his clergyman. He had taken to heart the urgings of Reverend Blare a few Sabbath Days ago and was determined to strike a blow for his God, the one of the book of Deuteronomy. So on this August morning in the year of his Lord, 1641, Alex would climb the hill, literally and figuratively, in obedience to the Scripture. He did so in spite of cautious advice from his mother, and worried looks from his sisters. It hadn't struck him either that his Aunt Biddy's vociferous enthusiasm for his planned course of action should have rung warning bells in his head. Biddy's reasoning, if it deserved to be awarded that appellation, had less to do with the merit of the argument and everything to do with her naive fixation with the person of the clergyman himself.

As with several other local tenancies, a portion of the McKay holding lay separate from the main part, high on boggy terrain, well inland from Ballintoy. While the majority of their farm prospered on the fertile coastal plain that stretched from the rim of the cliffs above the bay to the rising hills in the south, this mountainy acreage of scattered rock, prickly whins and scrawny, wind-bent bushes was anything but prosperous. You could dig reasonable turf up there, and you could run a few sheep on its poor grass, but compared to the output from the loamy fields near the Protestant kirk the hill ground was a disappointment.

But in Alex's mind that was only half of the problem. The other half was that nobody had thought to clear the area of its untidy scrubland, not even his father before him. Admittedly, poor Daniel's industriousness had been held back by his physical weaknesses and ultimately by his early passing. Now it seemed to fall on the shoulders of his son and heir to make a start on the task. The Sabbath sermon had inspired him to action, particularly the reference to destroying the pagan fairy thorn trees that were far too common up there, two of them on the McKay plot of land itself. Not alone the thorn bushes though; there were clumps of boulders that should be shifted to the ditch, and one or two standing stones that had no place on his land, no matter what their sacred significance to the Irish. They were only taking up space and getting in the way of any possibility of drainage.

His mother's caveat had nothing to do with a perceived need for more cultivatable land. It had still less to do with present spiritual instruction. Her arguments were historical.

"It's the Reids," she had said.

"What about the Reids?" Alex gerned dismissively, his mouth full of morning porridge.

"You know the background," Mrs McKay said.

"No I don't know the background. Anyway, that has nothing to do with now, has it?"

"But it does," she argued. "Everything to do with it."

"Go on then. Explain!"

"Well, you know that the Reids own the land up there that marches on ours; that bit on the other side of the boundary stones?"

"Of course I know that but I don't…"

"The Reids are a bad crowd," said Biddy, shaking her head as she joined the argument.

"Did you know that they used to own that whole mountain? Did you know that those fields out there between us and the sea, those fields that you farm every day, they used to belong to the Reids as well? Did you know that?"

Alex looked confused and a bit flustered. "But we are tenants of Archibald Stewart. This is all his land, surely?"

"And how do you think he got it?"

"He got it from Randal McDonnell, the old one, way back."

"You are right. He got it as a grant of land from the First Earl but the thing is, it wasn't Randal's to give. It belonged to the Reid clan, to old Maeldearg, the red chief as he was called."

"It's ours now," said Biddy from the fringes of the conversation.

"Alright, but I imagine McDonnell bought it off the Reids, surely?" Alex said. "He must have."

"You would imagine so, but you'd be wrong. The story was that there was a whole fight about it, up on Knocksoughey hill. It was rough. People talked about it for years after. The red chief was killed and some of his people fled. Only a few stayed and some of their land was confiscated; that's how it came into Archibald Stewart's hands."

"Really? That story doesn't sound too good, but it was maybe thirty or forty years ago. It has nothing to do with me going up to our land today and doing what needs to be done with it, surely?"

"Maybe not Alex, but I think you have to be careful up there. Old wounds don't really heal around here. If you were a Reid and you saw some young Protestant on what had been your land, and he's destroying it, you would…"

"He is not destroying it, Isobel," Aunt Biddy interrupted. "Alex is fixing it."

"We might see it that way, but the Reids will have their own way of looking at it."

"I can handle them," Alex said as he gathered up his spade and axe. "I will be up there all day so don't expect me back till late."

"I will keep you a meal," his mother promised.

Alex worked all day in the heat of the late summer sun. He paid little attention to the birds that scattered and gave him a wide berth, the darting snipe, the curlews and grouse who liked their moorland privacy, but he was always amused by the jarring voices of many bogland fowl. Occasionally he heard the rasping cry of a pheasant. More soothing was the happy piping of skylarks in the still air above him.

'If only I could play pipes half as well as they sound,' he thought.

He shifted boulders using his spade as a lever. He fought with the stubborn roots of whin bushes, digging them out from deep crevices in the rock and piling them up for burning once they had dried out a bit. He chopped down straggly hawthorn bushes and lonely rowans until he blunted his axe. In the wettest bit of the plot he dug out a couple of drains to soak the brown water away from where he could imagine sowing oats next year.

'If I could get a few cart-loads of wrack drawn up here I could make a decent bit of a field,' he thought to himself. 'Nothing to beat well-rotted seaweed for fertilising poor soil.'

He drank often from an oilskin of spring water he had brought from home. The sweat coursed down his back; beads of it stood on his sun-burnt forehead but he was loving this. A bit of godly order was being restored to this degenerated Garden of Eden. The high altars were going to be a thing of the past. These tall stones he would need help with but there was just the one more tree to chop down, a lonely thorn bush, twisted and bent over by the westerly winds so that it resembled a very old man leaning on a stick. The local Irish may regard it as a sacred fairy tree, but he had no time for such superstition, especially after that sermon. It was in the way; it was an affront to his narrow, Presbyterian view of things; it had to be hagged down, heathen imposter that it was.

"A few good thumps with this hatchet and your troubles will be over," he said aloud as he looked at it. "Fairy thorn, my arse."

He felt the axe-blade with his forefinger; it needed sharpening so he propped his rear end against a standing stone, relaxing for a second to appreciate the view towards Rathlin.

"Have a whiff o' that," he said as his fart ripped loudly against the stone's cold surface. From his pouch he took his father's whetstone, felt its roughness in his hand and began the rhythmic scraping on the blade.

He did not see what hit him.

The half-pound rock collided squarely and forcefully with the back of his head and he fell face-forward from the ancient monument to the mossy ground. The sparks of light faded quickly from his eyes as he lost consciousness.

"*Maeldearg abú!*" yelled Michaél Reid at the top of his voice.

"Great shot," said his brother, Sean. "You got him first time."

"I did," replied Michaél, rising from beyond the stone wall. "Sure I couldn't miss when you see the size of the head on him. Wasn't I right to say not to rush him? He coulda felled us with that hatchet."

"You were right, no question. And him about to take down one of our trees, the madman. Has he never heard the stories?"

"You would wonder that, wouldn't you," Michaél said, his mind wandering back to a tale he'd been told in childhood by his father. A Murphy girl had apparently collected up some branches that had broken off a fairy tree. When she went home and was about to burn them her mother told her that their cow had fallen over, foaming at the mouth. So she took the sticks back and threw them on the ground. When she got home again there wasn't a thing wrong with her cow; it was standing chewing its cud. The moral of the story? Don't mess around with any part of a fairy tree!

"Anyways, we were right to protect it!" Sean said. "And we have the bastard now."

"But what'll we do with him?" asked Michaél.

"Cut his throat for one thing and get to hell out of here," said Sean.

"Are you sure? Maybe just leave him to the fairies?"

Sean gave him a look.

"Or maybe just give him a hiding that he'll never forget."

"No point in that," Sean said. "We would always be looking over our shoulders for him. Look brother, they didn't show any mercy to *Maeldearg*, did they? We take our vengeance, we take it here and now. One less of the bastards."

"It doesn't drive them off our land though, does it?"

"No but it's the first step. He is an only son, this one. The father is dead, we made sure of that out in the Sound, remember? The mother will up and leave with her lanky looking daughters and we'll have a chance of getting the land back."

Sean had it all worked out. He clambered across the old wall and walked towards Alex McKay, drawing his *scian* from his belt.

Chapter 6

A Letter to the Earl

27th July 1641
Ballintoy House
My Lord Earl,
I have learned of your safe arrival back in Dunluce, following your sojourn in Dublin. I trust that your business there prospered and that Lady Katherine found the place more to her liking this time.
I am obliged to inform you that your instruction regarding the raising of tenancy rent has been fulfilled as of three weeks ago.
It is only fair to inform Your Grace that not everyone was content with the new stipend. Our good provost, Gilladubh O'Cahan, raised some concern that the timing of this increase is most inopportune. He pointed to the fact that, as you are aware, the weather this year has been extremely cold, with snow lying unusually long on the land during the period when crops would normally have been sown. As a result harvest yields will likely be poorer than normal. There is fear that food shortages are bound to be a problem in the Spring of next year. I feel it my duty to report these opinions to you without prejudice.
I welcome your return at this propitious moment for the following reason. Some days ago I received a communication from your cousin, the honourable Alaster McColla McDonnell. (You will recall my alliance with him in the matter of the your proposed campaign against Campbell of Argyll.) My present communication is to inform you that Alaster, his brother Raghnall and a party of Highlanders will be arriving here at Ballintoy one week from today. I hasten to assure you that this has not been the result of any entreaty from me; our mutual friend invited himself. I am sorry if his presence here in Antrim causes any embarrassment or difficulty to your good self.
I intend to host a small feast of welcome for McColla upon his arrival. To that end I proffer to you and Lady Antrim our warmest invitation to be present with us at Ballintoy House on Tuesday 6th August.
I intend to provide some local music and dance in honour of McColla's illustrious military career. We have pipers and dancers aplenty in the Ballintoy area, though most are proficient in Scottish rather than Irish traditional arts. You may be able to help to balance matters up in the following manner. I have heard good reports concerning the young harper, an O'Cahan I believe, who is in your employ at Dunluce. Could I entreat your kindness to allow this musician to be present to play for us that evening? Thank you in anticipation.
In Your Service,
Archibald Stewart

Chapter 7

Questions in O'Cahan's Kitchen

Darach O'Cahan

My father's house. I am back home. The place of my cradling. My parent's simple dwelling, a hovel in clay and wattle. Their names are Martin and Bríd; O'Cahan of course. *Sráid* is their town-land, Straid in the English. It is really just a long straight rodden through soft bogland, sheltered behind low hills, a morning's walk southward of the Causeway cliffs. Ours is a town-land of salleys and reeds, but also a place that is now slowly taking more of a shape to itself, with small fields laid out. Some new Presbyterian settlers have put their order on the squelching land, digging sheughs through swamps, lifting stones from where we had ignored them to pile up march ditches. Squaring off their tenancies to shame their Irish neighbours. Our native landscape is becoming prayer-book neat.

Our uncle, Gilladubh, lives in a castle. An old decaying castle at Dunseverick, but a castle nonetheless. Father's abode is well down the scale from Dunseverick. This, it seems, befits the younger members of a large family. Our walls could not be less like the hard Causeway rock of Gilladubh's fortress. Ours are of traditional construction, earth moulded into timber lattice, rough-dashed with lime mortar, roofed in traditional manner, sods and rushes covering a framework of well-woven branches. Turf smoke escapes through a hole in the corner of the roof. The house has taken some serious beatings from coastal storms over the years. Always has survived though, well patched up where damage was done.

The victim lies unmoving. Stretched out on the rough settle bed. Senseless, silent, still as a corpse. Father McGlaim, his eyes closed, his hands clasped in fervent intention.

The kitchen where our prostrate guest rests is relatively bare, the atmosphere dark, despite an open half-door.

My family members gather there, looking down at the wounded figure. The younger sisters, Rosie and Meabh, shocked. Concern etched on innocent faces. Henry, the brown-skinned farm-boy, frowns, his hand pensively at his mouth. At thirteen he has my father's sturdy frame.

"Have you seen him before?" I ask.

My father is thinking. He has some idea who this might be.

"I believe him to be a McKay. The father passed away a few years back, God rest him. They have a place down near the Manor House, tenants of Stewart."

The priest interrupts his intentions. "Then we can't very well carry him down there and land him in on his mother. After losing the father it would be too big a blow for her, do you not think?"

"That's the truth," agrees my mother.

Rosie kneels close, checks his shallow breathing. "He is still alive anyhow. Where there's life there's hope," she says, "and such a fine boy he is too. Handsome as a prince."

"But it must have been a fierce blow he took to the back of his head."

I am instinctively running my hand over the top of my own skull. Maybe in sympathy.

"Why it didn't split him open I don't know."

"Must have a wile hard head, this prince," jokes Meabh.

"It's not funny," scolds our mother.

"And you think it was a stone, son?" asks my father. "The villain hadn't got close enough to attack him? How on earth did yous come on it when you did?"

My friend, the priest, puts flesh on the story. "Darach and I were coming down the mountain rodden from...you may know of it, Martin? An old grove of trees near the head of the glen, where the burn starts. We had been looking for timber, you understand; for his harps. The air was so still you could hear the swallows changing the course of their flight. That was why we were able to make out the sound of an axe falling on a tree somewhere, and it kept clunking and thumping as we walked. Someone was working very hard. After the work we had just been engaged in ourselves we were curious to see who else was felling timber. We veered off the downward path and spidered back up the steep hillside to see what was going on. And then we heard the scream. To me it sounded like, '*Maeldearg abú*', an angry shout of triumph, or maybe of threat, I wasn't sure, but it was close by, just up over the brow of the hill. We hurried forward and, as we did....and it's a good thing we did...we saw the red-headed figure of a man kneeling over something or someone on the ground. Out of instinct, or with Saint Michael's guidance, I know not which, I raised my hands and shouted. '*Stad, mo chara*! Stop, my friend!'"

"It is just as well you had that kind of authority in your voice," I tell him.

"Indeed it is," says my father. "You may have saved a life."

"The fellow had a *scian* in his hand and I hate to think what he would have done with it if we had been seconds later. This one would have had his throat opened for him."

"So the fellow just ran away?"

"He did, Martin," the priest continues, "but he wasn't alone. He had another with him who looked very much the same as himself; they could have been twins. The second one was hiding behind the wall, but he took to his heels very quickly."

I smile at the memory. "He was trying to whisper, but at the top of his voice. 'Come on Sean, it's a priest, it's a priest! Run!' So Sean was the name on the other one. We know that at least."

"Sean, you say?" My father thinks about this. Then he has it. "I have no doubt who it was. The two Reids from Knocksoughey. Sean and the brother, can't recall his name. A rough pair of boys. They have a bit of a reputation around here; seems they are determined to live down to it."

"Why would they be attacking this McKay fellow?" Henry asks.

"It's a long story," father says. "For a start, he wouldn't be of our faith."

"He's a Protestant you think?" I ask. "Surely that's not a good enough reason to be slitting somebody's throat? Everybody gets on the best around here."

"They do," agrees my father, "but this feud goes back to land ownership, and some of the happenings way back in the past."

The priest returns from the table with water in a beaker to wet the victim's lips. "In this land of ours," he says, "we have a habit of carrying the past around with us like it's a corpse that we can't bear to bury and be done with."

"How did you manage to drag him over the hill to here?" asks my mother. "He must have been heavy and awkward."

"He was," I confess, "but we managed to get him up on the mule. We draped him over its back, head hanging down on one side, legs on the other. One of us on either side to steady him if he started to slip off with the jigging about on that rough ground."

"Very resourceful, weren't we Darach," laughs Father McGlaim, "and my mule did a great job. But what are we going to do with him now we have him here?"

We look at each other.

"It might take him a day or two to rightly come out of this, if he ever does," says my father.

"Is there not a healer in the neighbourhood? Should we get the physician from Ballycastle," asks Father McGlaim.

"There's none locally," replies my father. "Not unless you go to Ballylough for Brian McLaughlin. He would hardly be much use though. He has the charm for a few ailments, warts and rashes and the like, but he is more used to working with cattle. Anyway, I don't think this fellow is well enough to move at the minute so we may just let him lie here."

"And I agree with you," says Father McGlaim. "But one of us will need to go down to Ballintoy, let his family know where he is, and that he is in good care. It is only right, for the mother will be beside herself with worry till he's home."

"I could do that if you like," I say. "It won't take me long."

"And we can keep him here till he gets better?" asks Rosie, a bit too eagerly.

"I suppose we can," father says, looking at mother.

"But where will he sleep," she asks. "We haven't a lot of room here."

"Would he not be alright on this bench?" my father asks.

"It is not a problem," grins Rosie. "He can sleep in our bed, in between me and Meabh sure. We'll take good care of him, won't we sister? He'll not come to any harm with us."

"Rosie!" my mother cries. "And in front of a man of the cloth! You are such a disgrace to us."

"I think she was only trying to lighten the atmosphere, Mrs O'Cahan," smiles the priest. "And she succeeded, didn't she? But now after that outburst of carnality, Rosie, I am afraid you'll have to promise me that you will come with me to Bonamargy Friary and take your vows to join a holy order with Sister Julia. She will fix you, for we can't have you being tempted by every handsome young Protestant you see, can we?"

Rosie looks stunned for a second. "But I was only joking," she mutters.

"And so was I, Rosie," says Father McGlaim. "I wouldn't kill your sense of fun for all the whiskey in Bushmills. Talking of which, Martin, maybe a wee dram before we go on our way, if you have any in the house?"

That is clever, I think, smiling in my mind.

"I do indeed, Father, and you shall have it."

The *uisce beatha* goes down the clerical throat with the ease of much familiarity. After the drink, and as he is about to take his leave, Father McGlaim turns to me with a suggestion.

"There is no point in you having to come to Ballintoy to try to find the McKay home and then have to retrace your steps to go back to Dunluce tonight. Ballintoy is not far off my route home so why don't I call and inform the lady myself? It may even come better from a clergyman than a stranger of the boy's own age, you know what I mean?"

"Even though he is a Catholic priest?" asks Henry. "Would that not be dangerous? You don't know these people."

"I believe the McKays are decent folk," my father says. "You'll not have any bother with them that way. Anyway, sure you would never know to look at him that he is a priest."

Father McGlaim struggles up on to his tired mule. We hesitate to help, out of respect. The whiskey may be dulling his senses a bit. He sets off, heads north along the rodden towards Ballintoy to find the family of our stricken guest. As I turn to spend some more time with my folks Meabh appears at our cottage door.

"He has opened his eyes, Darach," she says excitedly. "He hasn't said anything yet though."

I arrive beside the settle bed. Stare down into dull, uncomprehending eyes. No panic in them, no fear either; just an absence of light, of curiosity or sensibility. The room is quiet as we have instinctively become silent.

"He may be conscious but he hasn't come to his senses yet," whispers mother.

"How are you feeling?" I ask.

Nothing.

The response is a long time in coming. We watch and wait. Mother offers a drink but still no reaction. It is a fearful half hour before anything stirs in our guest, and then only because Rosie has had the impulse to kneel down beside him, stroke his face and sing gently to him, an ancient Gaelic lullaby that has been sung in our homes for generations.

Rosie, ever the soul of empathy.

The young man's eyes never leave her face as she sings. She finishes, waits. The music has indeed touched something deep in him. He stirs a little bit on the stuffed fleece below his head, looks around slowly at each of our faces.

"Where am I?" he whispers.

"You are safe. You are in our home and you are alright," my mother tells him.

"Whose home? Where am I? What happened?" His speech is slowed, slurred, as if by too much strong beer.

"You are safe with us," she says gently. "You're in Straid. You are not that far from your home, though you likely don't know us."

I sit myself beside him and explain the story, so far as I know it. "You must have got hit very hard on the head, for you haven't been with us for the last while. Do you remember anything about it? Being up on the hill?"

No answer to that question, just scared eyes now gazing around the room as if trying to connect with something they might recognise.

"Do you even remember your name?" asks Rosie.

"I do," he says after a pause.

"Tell us then."

"Alex McKay, of Ballintoy. Why am I here? What happened?" he asks again.

I try to explain things to him once more. He seems to have no memory of the past few hours. He even says that he knows he had had the intention to go up to work in the hill country. He had talked to his

36

mother about it, but he still thinks it is ahead of him, still to be done.

"I must get up there... get that place tidied up," he says thoughtfully to himself.

I draw attention to his hands. Both covered in peaty dirt. He stares a while at them, then at me.

"I suppose I must have been working up there, if you say so. But where are my tools? I must have had a spade or something."

"You did have. They are still safe up there, waiting for you. My father can go back up with you tomorrow for them, if you are able."

"Can we not go now? I need to be getting home...my mother...she will be worried," he says, struggling to sit up on the bed. His head must have a sudden spasm of pain though. He sinks back down immediately.

"I think you see yourself that you wouldn't be fit for it," my father tells him. "But you needn't worry about your mother. Father McGlaim has gone to explain to her what happened and to tell her you are safe."

"Father...who's Father...whatever you said his name was?"

"He is a priest, a friend of mine," I tell him, sensing a tinge of discomfort in his reaction. "He is the one who helped get you to safety, lifting you on to his mule and bringing you down here."

"Is that so?" he says thoughtfully. "But my mother. She doesn't know that I am alright, that I can speak. She will think I am still..."

"He's right," my mother says. "Father McGlaim doesn't know that he's come to, does he? We would need to get word to her that he is alright."

Alex raises himself again, looks at me. "Would you go down to her...I would be obliged," he says.

"I'd be glad to, if you tell me how to find her. But I would need to be leaving now for I have to go on to Dunluce after and it is getting late."

"I thank you for that," he says and explains how to find the McKay home.

I leave my timber with my father for collecting later. I run all the way across the bogland and over the hill to Ballintoy. It's a long way but I am nineteen and more than fit. I enjoy the challenge, tired and all as I am from the day's exertions. I don't break my steady stride until I can see the church. The McKay home should be somewhere near it so I go in that direction. There seems to be nobody around to ask. I approach the first house along the lane. As I arrive a burly figure of a woman appears from the vegetable garden beside the house; she stops to stare as I come towards her, worry creasing her craggy, red face.

"I am looking for the McKay house."

"You as weel?" she replies. "Lord but we are the favoured people this day. Yer maybe looking the priest that was here a while ago?"

"I am not but I see I must be at the right place. You must be Alex's mother?" I say. "I have just come from him and I am sent to tell you that he has wakened up and is fine. He is talking and he knows who he is and all, even though he can't remember what happened to him. He will stay with my folks until tomorrow, just to be on the safe side."

"Good news. I am naw his mother, I'm the aunt, but I will pass on the message," the woman says, all the while giving me an intense examination, from head to feet. "And who might you be when yer at hame?"

I smile at the hint of indecent interest from this elderly woman. I make a quick decision to keep my identity to myself.

"When I am at home," I say, "I am my mother's son. I must leave you now. Please pass on the message."

"I will," she says, "but will ye no come in? There's nay rush awa'. There's lassies here would love to get a luk at a fine figure o' a fella like yoursel?"

I can't help being amused at her foxiness. She is a bit of a character.

"Maybe another time," I say, turning to go.

"Ah, always the same oul story," she says, "but ye'll be mair than welcome."

I leave her and stride away out the lane, turning west towards Dunluce.

Chapter 8

A Welcoming Feast

Katie McKay

Alaster McColla McDonnell arrived, a brute of a man!

Only once in my life have I seen one of those Highland cattle. The occasion is etched in my memory, for it was one of the last adventures I had with my father. I must have been thirteen at the time and that walk to Ballycastle to the famous fair was the furthest I had been from home.

The Highland bull we saw that day looked so powerful and menacing as it was led up the street from the quay to the market square; people stepped well back in case it would swing its hoary head and catch them on the point of one of those long, curving horns. I had never seen such a shaggy coat on any beast; it was the colour of autumn bracken. I was puzzled as to how such a monster could be transported from Scotland to our shore. It would never agree to lie peacefully in a small boat. My father thought maybe it had been brought here as a calf and reared on an Antrim farm.

He also told me a tale that day that has stayed with me ever since. The story was that, many years before, a young man was celebrating some significant event…was it his coming-of-age or perhaps his marriage?….at the Ballycastle fair; he somehow got involved in the bull-baiting that was common then and got himself killed. I even recall that he was a McDonnell as well, by the name of Gillaspick. What a tragedy, to have your life torn out of you at such a young age by the horns of a bull!

And this Alaster McColla McDonnell reminded me of that Highland animal. He was indeed a bull of a man; he had the swaggering gait of a beast; his body was threatening, broad and thick limbed; his head was large, brooding and hairy; his whole character seemed somehow hidden. Perhaps it was because you could never quite see his eyes for any length of time, as his locks tended to veil his upper face. And tall! Surely no human being has the right to be as tall as that, the height of a corn-stack.

I noticed almost at once that my employer, Archibald Stewart, for all his self-assurance, was intimidated by Alaster McColla…indeed everybody was. He did not say much; he didn't need to, for his whole presence was so powerful. No doubt that is what made him the mighty warrior of his reputation. His very aura commanded attention and obedience. I watched those Highlanders, a dozen of them, as they straggled behind him through the gates of Ballintoy House; I thought they resembled a pack of exhausted game dogs, all following their master's every gesture. Even the one they said was his brother, the tall, thin man with strange eyes, seemed to be following after him with a hesitant air about him.

My immediate instinct was to gather myself into myself, hide my female figure, bow my head and hope to stay unnoticed by him. I know Jean had the same reaction as we stared at this McColla. He seemed to be surveying the courtyard, taking everything in.

"Heaven preserve us," she breathed and grabbed my hand. She had more to worry about than me as well, for while I was working mainly in the kitchen Jean would be serving food to these men. She had every right to feel the threat that we both sensed.

"You will be fine," I whispered back. "Just never meet their eyes."

"If I could even see his eyes," she said. "Did you ever see such a shaggy-headed man?"

"Never," I said. "That man standing beside him is his brother. Raghnall is his name, I think. He seems a lot more civil of himself."

"They don't look much like brothers, do they? What's wrong with his eyes, this Raghnall?"

"I don't know," I said, "but I did notice the same thing. Maybe he's got some sort of a squint or he's got something in them that makes them look wet and rheumy. All the same, I'd prefer him to the hairy brother."

There was something about how Alaster McColla looked me up and down that rang warning bells in my head. I made myself a promise to never be found alone in the many shadows around Ballintoy House and the nearby lanes while this big Scotsman and his henchmen were with us. I even asked Alex, once he had mended from his head injury and was well enough to be out and about, to come across to the yard in the late evenings to walk me home. To his credit my brother never missed a night. He even brought me a bit of a rebuke that I was so disconcerted by the arrival of these Scotsmen.

"Sure aren't you getting to earn a bit of money for the house out of it all? And me," he said, "I have been having to catch twice as many herring for Stewart, to keep them in food. It's been good for us, don't you see?"

"I do see that," I said, "but you have to admit that the whole atmosphere around the place has changed with those men about. I can't wait to see the back of them."

"That could be a while, sure they've only just got here," he said. "And they want me to play a welcome for them at this feast on Saturday."

"I didn't know that," I told him. "Are you nervous? There's likely a few master pipers among those gallowglasses."

"Are you saying I am not good enough?" he joked. "I'll play any of them under the table."

'I just hope McColla isn't a piper,' I thought to myself. 'His arrogance couldn't cope with anybody being better at something than himself.'

It was good to see Alex regain his confidence and humour. Whatever had happened to him up on the mountain that day had taken its toll on him and he had needed a while to get over it. The whole mystery of being attacked by some unknown assailant that he hadn't even seen, or at least couldn't remember, had changed him. There had been debate in our house, and among Alex's friends, about who might be to blame. We recalled my mother's earlier warnings regarding the Reid boys; Bruce McClure was inclined to suspect some of the young hallions who were known to hang about Dunseverick Castle; Manus O'Cahan's name was mentioned as a ringleader of these renegades. But no-one had any proof. We couldn't very well go to complain to the Provost of the area if there were any grounds to the suspicion that his son was involved.

****

The big welcome feast itself was about to pass me by. I had been busier than I had ever been in my life in that kitchen. Between plucking and cleaning pheasants and grouse, roasting mackerel, herring and salmon, boiling turnips and cabbage, baking sweetbreads and washing up after platters were brought back into the kitchen. I was run off my feet. My head was spinning with the bustle of everything, I was sweating like a pig and I thought I stank like one. My working gown was filthy, streaks of grease and splashes of dirty water. I looked a sight and felt even worse. But above all I was just exhausted. And the very moment I sat down for a few seconds of breath-catching I heard the master's voice at the door.

"Katie McKay? Where is Katie McKay?"

"Katie, where are you?" shouted Mrs Kerr, the cook. "She was here a second ago. Katie?"

I dragged myself from the pantry and stood before them.

"Sorry," I said. "I was just…"

"Never mind that," Stewart said. "You're wanted out here. Come on." He turned to leave.

"What?" I spluttered. "What for?"

"Come on," he repeated, turning to go, expecting me to follow him. "Need you to do a dance for us."

"Wait," I called after him, far too much boldness in my voice. "I can't dance tonight."

He turned with a scowl. "Why ever not? What's wrong with you girl?"

"Look at me. I am filthy. I have been working in here since morning. I am filthy. More than that, I am tired. I can't hardly move, let alone dance."

"You're going to dance anyway," he said. "Your Alex has just been playing the pipes, until McColla ripped them off him and showed him how. Now he is demanding that somebody dance to him playing."

"McColla is?"

"Aye, McColla is. So get yourself out here the now."

"I can't, Mr Stewart. I just can't. What about some of the other girls?"

"Aye, they've all been trying but they are not very good, are they? McColla just laughed at them; told them to sit down. 'Have ye no real dancers?' he shouted. Somebody said, 'Where's Katie McKay? She'd do better.'"

"I can't Mr Stewart. Can Jean not do it?"

"Jean has gone home already. Some Highlander tried to make a grab for her and she ran. I don't blame her. She refused to go back into the room. Kerr sent her home. But come on, Katie. You'll have to do it."

"Mr Stewart, I'm not fit for it, not tonight…"

"Do you want me to send McColla in here for you? Just come and do one dance to him playing, please. Help me out here girl. Take off that apron thing and you'll be grand."

"I can't take it off. These are my old working clothes. Look, they're old and torn. I can't be appearing in front of people in it, not in a hundred years. Can I not run home and put on my Sabbath dress?"

"No time dear. You know what he is like. Let's go."

He left me and I stood like a statue. I did not move a muscle until I felt Mrs Kerr's hands take the working gown off me and push me towards the door of the main hall.

"Go on, girl; just do your best," she urged.

I turned back though and gave my face a quick wipe with a cloth, then washed my hands. There was nothing I could do about what I was wearing but I did think to pull the clasp from my head and let my hair fall around my face. Maybe it would cover some of my embarrassment, maybe give me some hiding place. I forced myself to take the few steps along the passage way from the kitchen to the hall.

I will never forget that 'grand entrance'.

The blast of noise! Laughter, language, music! The nervous stares from local people that I knew who were pressing themselves against the walls of the room. The rank stench of a dozen half-drunk men in kilts; what had they been eating? I have smelt cleaner middens. And, in the middle of the room, that great bear of a man with my brother's bagpipes looking so tiny under his huge arm and the chanter pushed through the undergrowth to stick between his sneering lips.

"Good," he said in a loud, sleazy voice. "A fine looking lassie if she was cleaned up a bit. I am going tae play a reel if ye can manage the steps for that, a'right lass?"

I did something with my head, something between a bow and a nod.

"Fine," he said. "We hae had one or two bits o' Irish dancing here, but I think we need tae show them what a good quick Scottish solo reel looks like. Are ye ready?"

Another nod. Oh for the floor of Ballintoy House to have opened up right at that moment and swallowed me.

I kicked off my clumpy brogues. He sniggered at me.

"Right, and if I'm going o-er quick for ye, just keep up."

He blew violently into the chanter and filled the bag like it had never been filled before. A thump with his fist and the drones screamed for mercy. He fiddled with the tuning for a few seconds, then away he went into his tune. And aye, he was quick.

I decided that the only way through this ordeal was to forget about the audience and the circumstances and the fact that I was the dirtiest I had been since rolling about in potato mould when I was a wee lass; forget about the ripped seam down my left side under my armpit, forget everything but the music and the dance steps and just enjoy myself. I would see off this over-bearing Scottish bully and show him the verve and spirit of an Ulster girl.

My feet were flying. The leaps of me, and me so tired in the legs not many minutes before. My hands raised above my head, my hair streaming about and my body in fluid unity with the tune. I spun around that room oblivious to the crude calling and off-time clapping of those Highlanders, careless of the embarrassed looks of the local Presbyterians who likely thought I had drink taken. And I was enjoying my own performance…until!

As the piper neared what I judged would be the end of the set I did a lovely spin, close to the top table at the far end of the hall. As I completed it I happened to focus, for the first time, on the onlookers behind that table.

And I saw him! The stranger!

The young man I had met on the Causeway cliff-top path.

What, in the name of all that's holy, was he doing here?

You are not supposed to let anything distract you when you are in the middle of a traditional Scottish reel. You are supposed to finish it off properly, should the roof fall in around you. You are not supposed to do what I did.

The tune continued but I didn't. My legs seemed to freeze solid below me. The old tiredness returned and filled them with lead in an instant. My hand went to my mouth as I stared at him. Those eyes again.

Piercingly blue as the ocean, yet full of empathy for what I was going through at that moment. I was still standing, stock still. People were peering at me from all corners of the hall. I could almost hear the necks creaking, craning for a better view.

'I must look like an eejit,' I thought and my hand dropped from my mouth as my arm compensated for the tear under my armpit. The snort of laughter from a McColla soldier nearby told me I was too late.

In that split second before I tore myself away from the place and ran all the way to my mother's house, I imagined I saw a small smile in the stranger's eyes, around his lips. It wasn't a rebuking smile either, it had kindness in it, I thought. I also seemed to see that he was standing at the table and behind a musical instrument, maybe a harp. That was just an impression I had when I thought about it afterwards.

The harp didn't matter though. The eyes did.

I saw them all that night.

Chapter 9

'Who is she?'

There wasn't a pair of eyes that didn't follow Katie's flight from the hall. Only two figures made a tentative move to follow her. One was her brother, the other was the youth who had played so beautifully on his harp earlier in the evening. Neither took any more than a couple of steps, however, unsure of what to do and where their responsibilities lay.

McColla quickly finished his tune.

"She was good, wasn't she?" he bellowed. "Good while she lasted. What in Hades happened tae scare her aff like that? Women! Ye can niver be sure what they are going tae dae next." Then to a baffled Alex, "Here son, take these pipes. Get practising and dinnae try tae play them in public again 'til ye can handle a tune, ye hear me?"

Cowed by the Scotsman's bluster, Alex took his pipes and headed to a corner as the entertainment came to an end. He sat alone for a few minutes, licking his wounds, resentful of McColla's insult and at the same time curious about what had happened Katie. Soon he was joined by Darach who approached him with a friendly, enquiring face.

"It's good to see you again," he began.

Now Alex looked even more confused. He looked long and hard at Darach before replying.

"Thank you," he began, "but… forgive me, do I know you?"

Darach smiled. "You may not remember me but we have met."

"When was that?"

"Not long ago; you were injured, up on the hill near the Druid's Altar, remember?"

Alex still looked a bit blank. "I know about that, but I don't remember much of what happened. How do you know about it?"

"I was there," Darach smiled. "It was my parents' home you rested in before you recovered enough to be brought down to your own place."

"I am sorry, I don't really have much of an idea about those days," Alex confessed. "It's just a very foggy memory of what happened. I don't even remember who you are and how you…"

"Don't worry about that. I am Darach O'Cahan."

"Darach O'Cahan? I live here and I've never heard tell of you. You can't be of the Dunseverick clan? Tirlough Óge and Manus?"

"They would be my cousins, but I live over at Dunluce, beside the castle. That's why you haven't seen me about here."

"Ah, I see," Alex said.

"And your name is…?"

"Alex, Alex McKay.

"I enjoyed your tunes," Darach said.

"Agh, I'm not very good. But you can fairly play the harp, I'll say that for you. And how were you…you see, I can't recall much about that day at all. I seem to think I was in a house somewhere, some kind woman. My mother says it was two young girls that brought me back home to her. I don't even know who they were. Do you know them, for I would want…"

Darach smiled again. "I know them alright; my wee sisters, and believe me you were lucky the same girls didn't try to keep you locked up in our place. They are rascals, the pair of them."

"They may be rascals but they had a good yarn with my mother that day. They told her that it was their brother and some old priest that had come on me up on the mountain. According to them, that is what saved my life. Would you have any idea what they are talking about?"

"Not very much," lied Darach. "You would never know what stories those two would be making up. They likely enjoyed taking care of you that night. I was away back to Dunluce."

"Is that so?" Alex studied him closely. "But you are their brother, aren't you? Any other brothers that they could be talking about?"

"Just me and young Henry. Listen, I was enjoying your tunes until that McColla took the pipes off you."

"I have a feeling you are changing the subject here. I may be wrong but I think I probably owe you for whatever you did that day," Alex told him.

"We didn't do much, only what you'd have done for us," said Darach as Alex reached out to shake his hand. "But I have a question for you."

"What is that?"

"That girl who danced?"

"Which one? There were a few trying to dance tonight."

Darach smiled at the memory. "There were," he laughed, "but, that last girl? The tall one with the freckles? She was great. Until she ran away."

Alex paused. "What about her?" he asked.

Straight away Alex could guess exactly why this fellow was asking the question. He was thinking quickly, even before the next query came.

"Do you know who she is?"

It would be futile to deny it. "I do. Why do you ask?"

"Well, this is a bit embarrassing, but I think I have met her once before. It was just a chance meeting on the path above the Causeway. We didn't say a word to each other but I thought she was very…so you say you know her?"

Alex made an instant calculation and a quick decision. He had been wondering himself what lay behind Katie's astonishing behaviour and her uncharacteristic flight from the hall. He had followed her gaze when her dance had stopped and she'd turned into a statue. It had been fixed on the harp player. Her brother was not going to be entirely truthful with this Darach O'Cahan. The younger sister might just need to be protected here by a few little white lies.

"Aye, sure everybody knows Katie. She is the maid in the kitchen here. Very busy at the minute with all these men around the place," he said.

"I suppose she must be. She's a lovely dancer, that Katie, for a kitchen maid I mean. And you say she is busy with these Highlanders?"

Alex shrugged his shoulders. "You know what they're like, soldiers. Very demanding."

"And if I wanted to find her, how would I...where would I look for her?"

Alex waited as if giving this request serious contemplation, perhaps holding something back.

"If I was you I'd forget about trying to find her. You'd have to fight your way through all those Scotsmen. Just let her be. Leave her to her own devices, know what I mean?"

Darach was disappointed and a bit bewildered by this. "I am not sure I do know what you mean, but I will not take the subject any further," he said. "I just found myself thinking a lot about...but here, why don't you and I play a tune together before the night is out? We can show these Scots what music in Ireland is really like, eh?"

"Indeed. We should do that."

So it was that in the dying minutes of the evening as many of the Highlanders lay stretched out around the hall the worse for Stewart's generous supply of whiskey, and when most of the locals had gone home, Darach and Alex sat together in a corner and began to investigate each other's music. When they found a tune that they both knew they had a go at playing it together, be it a march, a dance tune or a slow air. Sometimes it worked, as in the case of an ancient tune called *'An Cath Gairbheach'*. More often than not it was a bit of a struggle, not least because the Irish harp found it difficult to make itself heard above the powerful shrill of the Highland pipes. More important than musical consonance, though, was the easiness of the relationship that the experience of playing tunes together brought to the two young men. It all felt very natural to be engaging in this exploration of their shared Gaelic cultural inheritance and, at the same time, both were aware of a new sense of excitement in unearthing some of the entwining roots of their traditional music.

Everything was going wonderfully well until the final few minutes.

As they were packing up their instruments in response to James Kerr's reminder that some people were trying to sleep upstairs, Archibald Stewart approached unsteadily from the kitchen area.

"Lads, yous were both terri…terrific. So talented. A credit to the provi…providence of Ulster," he said, trying his best to pronounce these difficult words while so inebriated.

"Thank you, Mr Stewart," Alex replied, more than a little surprised to see, for the first time, that the normally abstemious land steward was 'in drink'. "Glad you enjoyed it."

"And thank you, sir, for the invitation to play," added Darach.

"No, not at all…my priv-age, priv-ilege," Archibald said between small burps. "And to you for making the journey from Dun…Dunluce, young Master O'Cahan. The Earl is a good man, aye! What O'Cahan are you now?"

"I am Darach. My father is Martin, of *Sráid*."

"Darach is it? I see. Do I know a Martin O'Cahan?" Stewart said, thinking hard. "Maybe. But you work at Dunluce, do you not? Can you make a living playing this harp of yours?"

Darach smiled. "I wish I could, sir, but I try to make them as well as playing, and I do carpentry work around the castle."

"Good for you. Make sure to see Kerr before you go. He has a wee somethin' for ye," said Stewart, turning back to his tenant, Alex.

"But tell me, young McKay, what on earth happened to your Katie that she ran out on us like that?"

The atmosphere changed at that moment as if someone had opened a door and let in an icy breeze. Alex was immediately flustered; it showed in the turning away of his body and the reddening below his chin as he mumbled a response.

"I have no idea, Mr Stewart," he said. "Some notion came over her. You'd need to ask her yourself."

"It is not like her, is it? So bad mannered on this occas…cassion, and her normally such a sweet girl too," he said as he turned to wander off to find his bed.

At once a silence seemed to rise between the musicians like an invisible stone wall. Alex felt desperately embarrassed by his own deceitful behaviour earlier but he could not find it in himself to return to the subject and apologise. It would be too humiliating to own the reasons which, he was fully aware, were to do with his own prejudice as much as to protect his sister. The longer he let the silence grow the harder it was to break it.

Darach glanced at Alex, but his body seemed to have angled itself towards the wall. He was more bemused than anything else. What did this mean? In what sense was this girl 'your Katie'? Were the two of them walking out together? Was she family? But he found he could not

48

bring himself to embarrass his new musical friend by asking for clarification. In fact, so discouraged was he by the whole issue that he could think of nothing further to say.

The silence dragged on.

Alex cleared his throat but not a word came from it.

Darach gave him a sideways look, a brief one but one full of entreaty. 'Just tell me the truth; I don't want to affront you by asking and making a discovery I will regret,' he was thinking. But his questioning look brought no reaction. He took a couple of steps away, paused and stood still briefly, harp under his arm, head bent, scratching his nose, hoping for an opening.

Nothing came. He turned towards the door.

"*Oiche mhaith*," he said, his soft, lilting Irish resigned, even hurt. His steps away from his new-found musical companion were slow, as if begging for a call back, an explanation. Instead all he heard was a barely audible

"*Oidhche mhath.*"

Aye, goodnight indeed, he thought, but not as good a night as it might have been.

Alex wandered home in a deflated mood. He tried to explain to himself what he had just done, attempting to justify his deception. He told himself that he had been right to try to screen Katie from the interest of this O'Cahan, more than that, to protect her from herself and her own obvious attraction to this Irish stranger. He told himself he should be glad that he had been there tonight to witness those first signs of connection between them.

'Maybe it was meant to be,' he told himself, 'that I saw Katie being enticed by him, and then to be in the right place to hear him ask all about her. Aye, I am glad I was present there tonight, for now I can put a stop to it.'

An owl hooted from a tree somewhere on the hillside behind him, and bats flitted between the hedges by the lane. The sound of the owl comforted him but not the presence of the bats. He'd never liked them, always thought they had a dark, evil aura about them. Tonight they caused him a shiver of revulsion. He looked away to his left where there was still a blush of light in the northern sky above Islay.

As he arrived at his door he began to reflect on something he had witnessed in his home a few weeks before. It had been a Sabbath night. The girls had been out walking all day. He had been at the harbour with his friend Bruce. His sisters had been giddy that evening, especially Alice and Connie. Maybe because they were very tired after their exertions they seemed to be very lightheaded. They were annoying Katie, whispering, giggling and nudging each other and making such a nuisance of themselves that their mother had had to chastise them firmly.

"Will yous stop this nonsense and give my head peace," she had said. "If this is how you behave on a Sabbath evening after going a walk you will not be allowed to go again."

"And that would be such a shame for our Katie," Alice had sniggered, "after her meeting her handsome...."

Katie had not let her finish, interrupting her with a loud rebuke. "Alice!" she said, "Don't be letting your imagination run away with you."

Now it crossed Alex's mind that maybe what Alice was referring to was some tryst with Darach O'Cahan. Could that be it? He decided to quiz her about this in the morning. In the meantime he wondered whether or not he should be telling his mother about what he saw tonight at the feast, about Katie's attraction to this fellow, about the mutuality of the matter. The Irish fellow was obviously struck on her. Maybe it was his duty to discuss it with his mother. He decided against it though. After her anguish about what had happened to him up on the mountain he thought she needed to have no more to worry about. He had been shocked by how devastated she had been over that affair. It was obvious to him that the over-reaction was due to her vulnerability as a lone parent, not to mention her continuing grief over the loss of her husband. He understood that, while he had recovered quickly from the ordeal and had put it from his mind, her apprehension for him would persist and blight every waking thought where he was concerned.

'No,' he thought, 'I can handle this myself. I should just keep an eye on her as our father would have wanted. I'll make sure the affair goes no further. Katie will listen to me. Mammy doesn't need to know about it.

Chapter 10

Graveside

She knelt carefully on the long, late-summer grass, leaned forward and pulled some handfuls of it from around the grey tombstone. A few black beetles and grey slaters scuttled away to safer quarters. A curious robin came to perch on a nearby cross and watched her attentively.

"Sorry Daniel," she said, "this grass grows so quick with the heat, after the rain we've had."

The grave surrounds tidied up a bit, her fingers reached up and, in a touching manner, traced the name chiselled roughly on the slab of sandstone.

> **HEREIN LYETH**
> **DANIEL MCKAY**
> **DEPARTED THIS**
> **LIFE 30TH JUNE**
> **1637 IN THE 46TH**
> **YEAR OF HIS AGE**

"Daniel, Daniel, Daniel," she breathed.

The robin bounced unnoticed to another tombstone and cocked its head to the side, as if to better detect an unsuspecting spider.

"What am I to do without you, Daniel?" As ever, the silence offered no answer to this frequent and fervent question. The Scotch Kirk-yard at Templastragh, one of Ireland's most northerly graveyards and undoubtedly one of the most scenically situated, was no better than any of the others as far as offering resolution to age-old questions such as this. While Isobel McKay always took solace that her man was buried within sight of his native Islay, it was a desperately cold comfort. When the clergyman had remarked on this 'Islay view' after the burial service she had wanted to scream at him, "How is that meant to keep me warm at night?"

That was the cry in her mind. She hadn't uttered it of course. She had kept her dignity.

Even when the normally very sensitive Mrs Stewart was heard to mention that day 'the wonderful vista up here' and 'what a place to be buried' she had grabbed her frustration by the neck and squeezed her anger into dumb submission. The idiotic things that people say at times like those.

The silence was disturbed by a sudden outbreak of noise, the distinctive crex-crexing of a corncrake from the long grass of a nearby field.

"Do you hear that, Daniel?" she said. "*Tráonach*...remember how that sound used to drive you mad when you had worked hard all day and then thon wee bird would start in the evening and keep you from sleeping? It meant no harm but it always seemed to grate on your nerves, God love it."

Isobel did as she always did when up here with her husband. She told him everything, just as she had during his life. She asked him the questions he couldn't answer, just as he couldn't answer them about that fateful day when his heart had betrayed him out behind Sheep Island. He alone knew what had happened that afternoon. His final conscious thoughts, 'If those two fellows in that curragh had hastened to my aid when they heard my cries of pain, rather than offering scornful laughter and wise-cracks, I might have made it back to shore.' But all that was not something that anyone was aware of, anyone apart from those two Reid brothers, of course.

Isobel took a quick look around to make sure nobody had arrived in the graveyard behind her.

"The bairns, you'll be wanting to know how they are," she said confidentially. "Well, they are all fine. Alex had a bad experience a couple of weeks ago. Somebody attacked him up on Altmore when he was working at clearing bushes. He got hit on the head with a stone and it must have knocked him senseless, for he still can't remember a thing about it. There was some priest came to tell us what had happened. And then Biddy heard from some other young fellow that Alex had come to, and that he was talking. It was a very worrying night, Daniel, and I cried myself to sleep. I needed you so much, just to talk to and maybe to go looking for him. But it was alright in the end. Two wee Irish girls arrived with Alex the next day, one on either side of him like they were his guardian angels. They seemed well taken with him but, as for Alex, he barely seemed to be conscious of them, or of anything else. It has taken him a few days to come back into himself. Now he is back working away like the sound lad he is, just like you were training him to do. He does get a bit worked up about things at times, and I don't know what to be saying to him to calm him down. That's where I miss you, Daniel. He'll naw listen to me. He would've heeded you. He gets a notion in his head, maybe one of his friends tells him some strange story, or maybe the minister has put something in his head... and he is like a dog with a bone. He'll not give it up easily. But, apart from that, he is managing the farm like a man twice his age. Archibald Stewart keeps an eye on him from a distance and keeps him right. You'd be proud of him."

An interfering, cauliflower-shaped cloud passed in front of the sun, leaving her feeling a sudden chill in the air. She lifted her head to study the sky. This burgeoning cloud seemed to have reared itself up against her, threateningly, like a startled horse, pawing above her. Instinctively she cowered and drew her shawl protectively over her shoulders.

"Katie, she was here with me a wee bit ago but she's restless these days. I don't know what's come over her. She's not seeing any young fellow at the minute, not since she turned her back on young McClure. But there today, nothing would do her but she would walk on towards Dunseverick. I suppose I can't expect her to come here and talk to you the way I do. She has got a job in the Manor House, working with Mrs Kerr in the kitchen and she seems to be doing well. She hasn't a bad word to say about any of the ones she's working with, nor about the Stewarts. Mind you, she has no time for those gallowglasses who are about the place at the minute. She has lots of stories about them, an uncouth crowd of soldiers that are staying at Stewart's and other houses here. Don't ask me what they are doing in Ballintoy but they have certainly livened up the place. The rumours about them are flying around. Katie had to dance for them at some welcome party in Stewart's and I get the impression it wasn't a great success. Whatever happened, Katie is now very wary of them, and likely it's as well that she is. She has no need of any of those men coming after her. Maybe I shouldn't have let her go walking...."

Isobel paused, feeling a little nervous. She stood to her feet and, putting her hand to shade her eyes, peered across the table-flat fields into the distance in the direction of the Causeway. She saw no sign of Katie.

"I don't see her," she told Daniel, kneeling again. "Maybe she has gone down to the harbour. I'll go and find her in a minute. Where was I? Aye, Connie. Connie is just Connie, full o' craic and as daft as ever. But she's a smart one, for all her madness, and she has the boys queuing up to chat to her. She can handle them all the same. The latest one to be after her is young Smith, the Thomas one. He comes down from the village often in the evenings and hangs around the loanin. Sometimes she'll go out and talk to him; other times she tries to send Alex or Katie out to him. The poor chap doesn't know if he's coming or going with her. He must feel tortured, but that's just our Connie. "I'm testing him out, mother," she laughs when I tell her she needs to be a bit kinder to him, not keep him running after her if she has no notion of him. I was never like that with you, was I Daniel? I was never so cruel."

She paused briefly in her account as memories of her own courtship echoed back across the intervening years and across the water to Islay. "Agh but weren't those the happiest days of my life,' she thought.

"And Alice," she continued, "well, you know your wee Alice. Still just as sweet as honeysuckle. You should see how much she has grown these last couple of years. She can run near as fast as Connie, and she can work every bit as hard too, when Alex has us out at the hay. No, I have no bother with Alice. She has a wee pet lamb that she looks after; nothing is allowed to happen to that animal. She gives it so much attention. And she has so much patience with your Biddy, far more than the rest of us put together."

"Lord above, Daniel, would I ever have thought when we courted in Port Ellen that your heart would fail you and I would lose you so soon… and then end up with just your sister in residence instead! I know it was the right thing to do, to bring her with us when we came here. She had nobody else after your father and mother passed. That dour brother of yours, he was far too preoccupied with his business and that bit of a farm he had been left. It was the least we could do to take Biddy with us. Donald wanted nothing to do with her, nor her him!"

Isobel well remembered the family row that had proceeded her marriage to Daniel. The old grandfather, a cantankerous old fellow at the best of times, had had a fall-out with Daniel over some affair in which the family curragh had been blown out to sea and lost. When he passed away and his last will and testament was examined by the clergyman, hadn't he changed it! The older brother, Donald, was to get both the business and the land. Daniel had been disinherited. He, along with everyone else in the family and the community, had had an expectation of the farm being left to him; Daniel had been working the land since he was knee high, while Donald had tried to make a living from his joinery. So, not six months before he was due to get married to Isobel Gilchrist, Daniel found himself without a means to make a living. It had therefore been a Godsend when, not long after, they received word that Archibald Stewart was looking for tenant farmers across the channel in Antrim. The young couple had grabbed the opportunity at once. With Daniel's sister acting as unwitting chaperone, they had taken a boat across the water to Ballintoy, discussed the tenancy with Stewart and had been married in his newly-built church.

Relationships with the family back in Islay remained icy and, for a number of years, there had been no contact. Then Donald had turned up at the Lammas Fair a few times and things thawed as the brothers began to talk again. Indeed, after Daniel's passing four years ago, his brother had made a point of being at the fair in the August following and travelled to Ballintoy for the first time. He had stayed with the family for two nights before returning to Islay, and Isobel appreciated his kind gifts to her children. Biddy, however, had refused to be civil to him and had ignored his gift to the family, a token bottle of Islay's famous *uisge beatha*.

Isobel's reminiscences were interrupted as a figure moved into the periphery of her line of vision; she went very still and glanced surreptitiously to her right. Had she been heard earlier? A very tall man with a huge head of straggly hair and enormously long arms was walking slowly around the graveyard. He seemed to be preoccupied, reading the tombstone inscriptions. But then again, was he taking wee looks in her direction? She kept an eye on him and sure enough, at one point she caught his stare towards her. Her glance bounced away from him like a pebble ricocheting off a Causeway rock. It returned immediately though, back at this mountain of a man. The big man's kilt had caught a sudden gush of wind and swirled to the north, revealing dark tree-trunks of thighs. Astonished, Isobel took in the sight momentarily, but then jerked her gaze away, just in case anything else of a more personal nature should be disclosed. She made a quick decision. Even from this distance she could sense that there was something about this man, something powerful, but also intriguing.

'Goodness!' she thought. "This is the big Scotsman that Katie has been talking about, McColla or something. What on earth is he doing in our graveyard? And why is he looking at me?"

A shadow of dread rose in her, less for herself and more for Katie who might encounter this giant on her travels.

"Goodbye, Daniel my love," she said, getting briskly to her feet. "I have to go here. Katie is out along the coast and I need to make sure she is alright. I'll be back again some Sabbath as soon as I get the chance."

She slipped away around the front of the old kirk just as Alaster McColla McDonnell turned deliberately in her direction, leaving his greeting smeared to a halt on his coarse, curling lips.

Chapter 11

What to do about McColla

Dunseverick Castle was in the centre of a line of north-facing strongholds on the Antrim coast, a series which stretched from Dunluce in the west to Dunynie in the east, at Ballycastle. Probably the oldest of these castles, Dunseverick had been the main seat of power in the ancient Kingdom of *Dál Riada*. And like its sister castles, Kinbane and Dunluce, this small fortress was built high on a rocky promontory, almost an island, which jutted out into the ocean, affording a commanding view of the seascape of *An Sruth na Maoile*. That such a view was entirely necessary had nothing to do with scenery or aesthetics. It had everything to do with security concerns. The McDonnells of Dunluce and the McQuillans before them, the MacAllisters of Kinbane and the O'Cahans of Dunseverick not only had had to worry about each other in the recent past; for centuries the folk of the north coast had had to be ready for threat from a range of would-be invaders, from the early Vikings to the more recent Spanish and French.

Archibald Stewart was a seriously angry man as he rode along the last few yards of *an* s*lighe,* a primitive road that began a hundred and fifty miles away in Dublin. This ancient path connected the capital to the northern regions of Ireland. It wound its muddy way through historic sites such as Tara and Emain Macha, eventually ending at Dunseverick Castle. In legend, and maybe in fact, Saint Patrick had walked this way centuries ago on a pastoral visit to his followers in Ulster.

Stewart descended into the huge natural amphitheatre that lay in front of the castle, his black mare struggling with the steepness of the slope. As he passed along a rough lane through a straggle of stables, artisan's huts and poor-looking residences he couldn't help thinking how dilapidated this once grand castle had become. In part its demise was down to its exposure to the fierce elements it had had to endure over the centuries, but there had doubtless been human failure too; it had never been properly restored after the Vikings had reportedly made such destruction of the place. In more recent times an absence of diligence in maintaining the crumbling structures lay, he felt, at the door of the O'Cahans. The place gave the impression of being on its last legs.

He climbed again towards the elevated gate lodge guarding the three-sided promontory, trying to ignore the gruff barking of the castle's wolf-hounds and the sullen glare of the gate-keeper. He and Gilladubh

O'Cahan may not have been best of friends, but they had mutual respect for each other in their distinct roles. Gilladubh was a small, wiry man who looked older than he should for one in his middle years. He had a distinctive face; his shoulder-length grey hair and pointed little beard gave him the appearance of an untidy billy-goat. His body may have seen better days, but locally he was still thought of as an able and clever magistrate, though maybe a bit too fond of his liquor.

For all that, he was Randal McDonnell's appointee as Provost for the area, while Stewart had been manager of the Earl's estate since the death of John McNaughton ten years previously.

"I have this letter, this command," he told Gilladubh as they met in the castle yard. "You won't credit it! Dublin says I have to arrest Alaster McColla McDonnell. Imagine! And me just after throwing a welcome party for him! What sort of people do they think we are down there in the capital?"

Gilladubh, his face as wizened as the bark of an old yew tree, was equally puzzled. He swore quietly to himself. "It is true what they say," he said. "Those folk in Dublin Castle don't know their arse from their elbow when it comes to managing the affairs of Ulster. Will you come in and have a drink?"

Stewart nodded, in agreement with both the political comment and the idea of a drink. He followed his host through what had once been a stately-looking door into the hall.

"You are not wrong," he said to Gilladubh's narrow back. "Sure isn't it only a matter of months since they were recruiting an army here in Ireland to sail to Scotland to support McDonnell. One minute they are for fighting with him against the Covenanters, the next they want him arrested."

"I know," agreed O'Cahan, "and credit to you, Archibald. In spite of your Presbyterianism you were loyal to the Earl and played your part in that whole business."

"Little thanks I get for it now," responded Stewart, waving the Dublin letter in annoyance.

"This just came today, you say?"

"This morning."

"No mention of the brother Raghnall in it? Is it just Alaster they have issue with?" Gilladubh asked.

"Seems so. Nothing about Raghnall at all."

"Strange," Gilladubh said, reaching for the letter.

"How did they even know of McColla's arrival? Have they spies as far north as Ballintoy?" Archibald wondered aloud.

Gilladubh took the letter and surveyed it, scratching his head.

"Looks like they might well have their informants indeed," said Stewart, inclining his head in that characteristic way of his.

"Maybe not though. You informed the Earl that the McCollas were coming?" he asked.

"Of course I did. I wouldn't keep that from him."

"Well, maybe the authorities down there don't need spies in Ballintoy," Gilladubh said quietly. "I am thinking that Lord Antrim is not happy with the idea of his volatile cousin being in his backyard. The man is an infamous scoundrel after all, but, Earl and all as he is, Randal doesn't have the power to do much about it. So he warns Dublin. And they issue you with this impossible order. Our good master has cleverly shifted the problem to you."

Stewart gave this some quick consideration. "You are more than likely correct, Gilladubh. That is what has happened. But what am I going to do? Even if I wanted to I don't have the men to arrest him and his henchmen. They are proper warriors; my men are farmers and tradesmen at this point in time. Anyway, I can't be trying to jail a man I have just welcomed with open arms."

"No you can't," agreed O'Cahan. "You'll just have to think of a better plan."

The obligatory goblets of red wine were handed to the two men by a servant girl.

"*Sláinte mhaite*," O'Cahan said, raising his drink.

Stewart reciprocated and returned quickly to his immediate concern. "Have you any ideas yourself?" he asked.

"Well, you will have to reply to this," Gilladubh said, pushing the communication back into Stewart's hands. "You'll have to assure them of McColla's loyalty to the Crown; tell them that there's no hint of any ulterior motive in him being here; maybe explain that it's a temporary thing. This is just a time of sanctuary, after all his troubles back at home. He is no threat to anybody; maybe tell them something like…that he intends to return to the Highlands after he has undertaken some military training of your own men. Pretend it is all your doing, that you have it all under control."

"That seems like a sound course of action," Stewart responded. "Thank you; you always see a way out of things. I will write some sort of rebuff to this daft order and get it sent off today, before my guest gets wind of it."

"How are you going to send it? It is too late in the day for a courier to be leaving."

"Aye, you're right again. Maybe tomorrow," said Stewart.

"Look," suggested O'Cahan, "my young fellow is riding to Shane's Castle tomorrow. If you bring your missive to him by sunrise he could have it in Antrim by mid-day or soon after. O'Neill will have a service going to Dublin as usual so it could be taken on fairly quickly. Save your man the journey. I'm sure Manus won't mind."

In his mind Archibald Stewart was slightly hesitant about this plan, but he did not feel he could refuse an offer which, at face value, appeared to be a genuine and generous gesture. His hesitancy came from the suspicion that Manus was the less dependable of the O'Cahan sons; although the elder of the two, he didn't have Tirlough Óge's aura of sober-mindedness. Manus had a reputation all over the Route area for gambling and other debaucheries. Still, he was the Provost's son and heir, and this was just a simple matter of delivering a letter; surely Manus could he depended on to carry out that mission and, if he was going to be travelling to Antrim anyhow, it made sense to agree.

In the courtyard as Stewart was about to take his leave he and Gilladubh were joined by the younger son, Tirlough Óge. Not unlike his father in his rather slight build, Tirlough had a confidence about him that belied his twenty three years. His eyes had a steely quality and his quiet, sincere persona conveyed a strength of character. He stroked the nose of the land steward's lovely mare and waited to take part in the conversation. When that chance came he had an interesting question.

"So I hear your big banquet went well, Mr Stewart," he said.

"It did; who was telling you?"

"Cousin Darach mentioned it to me," Tirlough Óge said. "He slept here afterwards you see, so he was telling me all about it in the morning. He thought his harp playing went down well enough."

Stewart had to think about this to work out the connection. "Ah, of course. Darach, the harper. He played a few tunes alright. Aye, it did seem to go down well with the visitors."

"He's good at it for sure. None better around these parts."

"Indeed," Stewart agreed without much enthusiasm.

"Darach was telling me about the girl who was dancing...something about her disappearing half way through her reel?" Tirlough continued. "Who was she?"

Stewart looked at him, trying to recall the details of the evening. It had taken a full twenty four hours for his headache to clear up, and his memories of the banquet were coloured hazily by that unfortunate reality.

"Aye, that was a strange affair, so it was," he said guardedly. "I don't know what came over her. Maybe a woman's problem or something. I haven't set eyes on her since it either, come to think of it. She has been working in our kitchen while the Scots are here."

"Who was the lass anyway? He seemed to think she was a grand dancer."

"So I am informed; I wouldn't know myself how good she is, young Katie McKay. Nice child though."

Tirlough Óge smiled with a hint of lasciviousness. He winked at his father. "I am not sure Darach was thinking of her as a child, from the light in his eyes," he said.

"Ah, I see," mused Archibald. "So that is how the land lies, is it? I am not so sure that would go down well with her folks, so maybe better warn him off that idea."

Tirlough Óge said nothing to this, just looked at his father, a surprised and puzzled expression on his face.

"Sheep and goats and all that, you know," Stewart said by way of further explanation.

There was a space of silent processing of this remark by the father and son, and a further sharp glance flicked between them. The younger man cleared his throat meaningfully.

"No sir! I will not be warning him off," he responded eventually, his tone and countenance changing towards a scowl. "I hope you are not suggesting that an O'Cahan isn't good enough for one of your flock?"

"Not at all," Stewart protested. "I just meant that…"

"I know what you meant. You meant the purity of the tribe," Tirlough Óge said with rising sarcasm. "No looking across the fence."

"I didn't mean to…"

"Sheep and goats! My God! You Protestants forget so easily that a generation or two back you were every bit as popish as you think we are. And now yous would try to make us all turn into nice wee Episcopalians, go to your wee church in *Baile an Tuaigh*, and only speak in the English."

"Tirlough Óge, that is enough," his father scolded.

"It's the truth!"

Stewart went red in the face and squared his shoulders.

"Now wait there, my young friend! I do not have to listen to a lecture from you, Tirlough Óge O'Cahan. Nobody around here has ever tried to convert you. That may be the way of things in other parts of Ulster, but you will never be able to say that any proselytisation has happened on my watch in this art of the country. None whatsoever. The Earl wouldn't stand for it, for one. Mass still happens in his castle, I hear, and in Ballycastle and other places hereabouts as well. So you need to retract your false accusation and your father needs to insist that you do!"

Gilladubh nodded his head. "He will. I don't think he meant any harm, Archibald. He was only saying what is the official position of the authorities. Your Lord Wentworth may be gone out of Ireland, and he has received his just rewards for his folly, but his policies are still in force across the land. That is what is so galling for us all. Tirlough Óge and his generation feel it, being treated as aliens in their own country unless they anglicise."

"Not around here, Gilladubh," responded Stewart. "That is my point. Nobody has ever tried to insist that any of you speak English, have they? Here we are today talking in Gaelic to each other, with a letter in my head to be written in English, and there is no issue with it. Tirlough Óge is deliberately exaggerating the situation and I beg his apology."

Tirlough Óge had cooled down a bit. He raised his head and looked the taller, older man in the eye with just a touch of retraction. "Mr Stewart," he said evenly, "I do apologise. You and your people here have been fair-minded and have not treated us with any disrespect in your doings, I agree that is mostly the case. But in the country at large it is a different story and resentment against the English is growing by the day."

"I accept that much of the policy that comes out of Dublin Castle is deeply flawed," Stewart said, "but it does not make its way into our local affairs here on the north coast. We have remained as we have always been, neighbours and friends… and fellow Gaels."

"Fellow Gaels you say," Tirlough Óge retorted. "you see, this is what I am talking about. We are 'fellow Gaels', we are 'neighbours and friends' you say, but you could never bring yourselves to countenance the notion that one of us, a fine young man like my cousin Darach, could ever be allowed to wed one of your Protestant girls if he wanted to! It would be some kind of contamination! Do you not see that such thinking is an insult to me and my religion? We are made to feel inferior citizens in what is our own country?"

"I am sorry you feel that way but I cannot be held responsible for how you respond to the realities of the situation in the country."

"Maybe not," Tirlough Óge said as he turned to go, "but somebody will be held responsible at some stage for the division you have all created in my country! And I mean 'my country'! Not yours!"

He stomped out leaving his father examining the distant horizon, and Archibald Stewart open-mouthed, even wider-eyed than usual and frowning deeply.

"Well! I never expected to be lectured like that by one so young. You need to take these boys in hand, Gilladubh, both of them, for I hear Manus can be a right hell-raiser around the country."

O'Cahan responded with his usual diplomacy. "It's just youth talking. You know what we were all like when we were young, believing we could set the world to rights. He will regret his outburst when he calms down and thinks about it. Don't let it bother you."

"I must get away home and write a reply to this," Stewart said, waving the Dublin letter. "I will be back in the morning. Please ask Manus not to leave before I arrive. And tell him I want him to deliver it for me. I'll pay him the usual fee when he gets back."

He mounted his mare and rode back to Ballintoy, shaking his head reflectively about what he had just experienced with young O'Cahan.

"I do hope that was indeed only youth talking," he thought. "If a fellow as reasonable as Tirlough Óge has resentment building up in him, how bad might it be in places like County Armagh and Londonderry where English laws are being much more rigorously enforced?"

Chapter 12

The Fair in Ballycastle

Katie McKay

I never did understand why my brother Alex failed to ask me what had happened at the banquet for McColla. He showed not an ounce of concern or curiosity about my flight from the hall; not that night, not at any time over the next few days. It was not like him. Maybe the blow he received to his head a week or so before had somehow changed him, left him confused. He certainly did not seem to be himself.

    I had heard him arriving back into the house following the big night, ages after I did. Often he would have looked in on me but on that occasion he didn't bother. Maybe he thought I would be asleep but I was not asleep…indeed I slept very little that night. I could not get the stranger's stare out of my mind. What was it in his face this time? Shock? Pity? Disgust at the state of me?

    Aye, of course I had wanted to see him again. I had thought about little else. But I did not want to meet him like that, not when I was so frayed and unkempt, the dishevelled dancer at her disordered worst. In my head I had told myself a romantic tale of finding him on the Causeway path again, on some balmy evening, the sun setting over Donegal's Malin Head away to the west, blue-bodied dragon-flies darting off the bogland, midges swirling grey like ash-smoke in the shafts of light. Deep in his mind he would have sensed that I was going to be there and would be sitting on a big lump of coal-black rock, waiting, staring out to the horizon as I came up behind him. I had tried to imagine what I would say, how he would react, how the conversation might develop between us, how he would look at me. And, of course, how we would touch for the first time.

    Instead I had made this spectacle of myself. What a fool!

    But it was not at all my fault, I told myself. I had been working, working very hard. I was the lowly maid. What I was wearing was suitable for my role, not for dancing in front of all those people. I was a sweating mess because I had been doing my job well all evening. I should not have been anywhere near the Great Hall, let alone dancing. I should never have been exposed like that by Mr Stewart. It was completely unfair. It was not my fault. Oh why, why, why did he have to be there and see me like that?

What was he doing there anyhow? Who was he that he was so important as to be a guest at a welcome feast for Alaster McColla McDonnell in Ballintoy House? I still had no inkling of who he was or where he came from. The mystery man. And was I correct to remember that I saw, beside or behind him, a harp? Was that my imagination?

I thought of asking Alex about him. Had there been anybody playing harp during the earlier entertainment? But I sensed that that would not have been the wisest thing to do. Alex would have seen through my request. He would have interrogated me about why I had abandoned my dance and fled the hall…and I did not want to raise that subject. So I held my wheesht on the whole matter.

I had asked Jean the next day about him. She didn't know what I was talking about. Nobody had played a harp while she was in the hall, she hadn't seen a harp either, but then, as she explained, she had left early. I wish I had had the excuse to leave early too, well before I had to dance, but, at the same time, I was glad I didn't have to go through what she had had to endure when that lewd Highlander pulled her down on to his knee and groped her all over before she could get away from him. She did right to flee.

It was too late to be regretting my own flight when I was lying in my bed that night, but I did almost wish I had not been so hasty. If I had been able to control my reaction and finish the dance I could have talked to him. I could have explained why I looked in such a state. I could have found out something about him, anything. Instead, here I was, two meetings later and still as much in the dark as ever. I should put him from my mind. It clearly wasn't meant to be, so just forget him.

****

The Lammas Fair in the small village of Ballycastle on the last Tuesday in August was an annual excursion for our family. It had actually been something of a pilgrimage for the McKays from many generations back, when the family had lived on Islay. *An Sruth na Maoile* was no barrier to those people, the opposite in fact. It had been easier to travel on the sea than on land in times gone by. As sea-faring folk, the Straits of Moyle was what joined them, rather than divided them. My father, when he used to take us to the fair in my younger days, often repeated this piece of knowledge, this part of our ancestral custom. The tradition was partly to do with trade, but also very much social…the community of the islands of the ancient kingdom of *Dál Raida,* from Kintyre and Arran, Jura and Rathlin, would assemble often in specific places, as if to salute their cultural heritage; the Lammas Fair in Ballycastle was one such opportunity. You could watch from the cliff-top above the quay as a variety of boats from those islands tied up there to unload their sheep and cattle. They had crossed contrary currents and tidal races, rolling journeys of twenty five miles and more on the open sea, to bring produce and crafts to the fair. But mainly it was about the coming together of fellow islanders and Antrim folk; folk from the nearby glens, mountain folk and sea folk. It was about catching up with long-lost cousins, the gossip and conversations, the whisky and beer, the revelries and rivalries, and the craic of long evenings chatting about old times in the drinking houses around the market square.

This year was no different. Early in the morning we saddled up our old donkey, loaded and tied a couple of ewes into the rear of the cart. My mother had a sack of vegetables to try to sell, and Biddy had a few *geansaithe* that she had knitted. They climbed into the cart as well. We set off on the six mile jaunt to Ballycastle. The girls and I walked along beside the rickety old yoke, as did Alex. Sometimes we had to lend our shoulders to the wheel to help it up an incline; the steep climb up Knocksoughey hill was a tough haul for the animal.

The weather was fine, but feathers of wispy cloud high in the morning sky were a sign of a change, according to my mother. "You could see rain in the afternoon," she predicted. I saw more than rain, as it turned out! It was to be an afternoon I would remember for a long time, and nothing to do with the weather.

The normal affair of negotiating a price for the ewes took an hour or two; buyers don't like to make a purchase too early in case prices drop. Aunt Biddy and my mother fussed around the various market stalls examining the things they couldn't afford to buy, and finding fault with them so as to ease the pain. Connie and Alice were hanging around the adults, trying to put pressure on to get a few halfpennies for some trinkets they wanted. The atmosphere around the market square was busy, noisy and boisterous as markets generally are; hawkers selling their wares and trying to be heard above the general hubbub; men arguing loudly, haggling over prices, spitting on their hands before the traditional slap to seal the deal; the laughter of women meeting old friends; the yapping of the local dog population; the baaing, roaring and squealing of the farm animals, not to mention the strong smells that were so familiar to us as rural people; the danger of a sting from a curious wasp; the buzz of frenetic blue-bottle flies and their quieter cousins, the blood-sucking cleggs that you had to keep an eye out for…it was a familiar scene for all of us.

In the middle of all this pandemonium didn't we bump into relatives from Islay, uncle Donald and his wife, Mary. We had no idea they would be there. It was four years since we had seen them, but here they were this afternoon, having sailed with a fair wind and friendly tide early this morning. We spent a good while catching up on their news and answering their questions. Not having any children themselves, they seemed very taken aback by how much we had all grown up, so they said anyhow, Alice and Connie especially. Four years does change things of course, but it hadn't changed Aunt Biddy's regard for her brother. She barely smiled at him. It was all a bit strained and, after the first five minutes of the conversation, Biddy seemed to get bored and made her way off to look at a few nearby stalls. My mother, on the other hand, had lots of questions about her home village, the place called Port Ellen. She had many queries about her remaining cousins there, and concerning the friends she had known in her youth. We listened as politely as we could, glad to see some emotion other than worry in our mother's face.

Eventually we were able to drag ourselves away from what was becoming a repetitive conversation. Donald and Mary were heading for a hostelry, so we left them to it and returned to the business of the fair. It was all getting a bit crowded so, as soon as Alex had made his sale and pocketed the money, he and I walked together from the market area all the way down the path to the shore, the area known as Port Brittas. I suppose we were curious to see what vessels were still arriving, what sort of people were landing at the quay, and what sort of produce might be on sale down there. As we approached the bottom of the long street, where the town meets the sea, we saw ahead of us a group of folk standing in a rough circle; they all seemed to be focused on something or someone in the centre. Through the gabble of the fair-goers I began to hear the faint sound of music. It seemed to be coming from this gathering, right beside that house at the corner, the one that I had always thought had such a perfect view out over Ballycastle Bay. Alex and I moved closer in its direction, and it wasn't many seconds until I recognised the clear, ringing sound of a harp. I couldn't make out the tune yet, but it was being enthusiastically played, a quick hornpipe type of melody I thought.

We arrived at the edges of the crowd. I was too far back to see over the tall folks watching so I tried to find a small gap to see through. Alex, though, could see into the centre of the circle straight away; his reaction though was not what I expected. He is a musician himself so you might have anticipated that he would be keen to stay a minute, to listen and watch whoever was producing such lovely sounds. But no! As I pushed my head in between a couple of big farmers I felt his hand grab me roughly by the elbow and pull me far too quickly back out from the audience to the middle of the street. I was taken aback by his sudden change of mind.

"What are you doing, pulling me like that?" I asked, annoyed by this action. I noticed a strangely intense look about his face, one I did not recognise and could not understand. He had been changed, my brother, by whatever had happened to him up on the hill when he got wounded.

"No time for that. We're going to the pier remember. Come on."

He was actually pulling me away from the music! This was just very weird behaviour from him; I couldn't account for it. I did struggle with him, trying to break free from his grip, to no avail. He was a couple of years older than me but that was no excuse to man-handle me so forcefully.

"What is wrong Alex?" I said. "We could take a minute to hear the music, for goodness sake. There's no rush. What has come over you all of a sudden?"

"Nothing has come over me," he replied. "Just come on Katie. Nothing there for you to see."

Something about how he put that, how he emphasised this last point, made me all the more determined to see whatever this 'nothing' was that I was not being allowed to witness. For a second I pretended to go along with his will, just long enough for him to relax his grip on my arm and step around the corner to our left and towards the quay. As he did I sneaked another look around again at the music watchers. I was so glad that I did, because just at that moment a couple of them moved away leaving a gap in the circle. Through that space I got a fleeting glance at the musician.

Sitting on a black stool and strumming on that harp was someone I recognised, even from that distance. I could never mistake that face. It was him again!

My heart skipped a beat and I stopped dead in my tracks for a second until Alex turned and shouted again. "Come on Katie!"

He was too late though. I had seen the harper; the third time in the past few weeks, after having never set eyes on him during the entire seventeen years of my life. I didn't have a notion whether or not he had seen me this time.

I dragged myself after Alex and, as I did, the gnawing question in the back of my mind was, 'Why is Alex so determined to stop me even seeing this fellow? Why drag me away so adamantly and hold me so tightly? Had Alex somehow connected my embarrassing departure from Stewart's feast with seeing the stranger at that same moment? Was that why he had never asked me for an explanation?'

I could not work out what had happened, nor what this recent change in his behaviour meant. I was not about to ask him either. My mind had started to work in another direction. How was I going to escape from my protective brother so that I could see the dark haired one again?

We wandered around the sea-front for a while, just taking in the sights and the sounds, wasting time really. I had always loved the view from the quay across the bay to that imposing headland they call Fairhead and, beyond it, across the sea to the tall, grey cliffs of Scotland. Today Fairhead was looking its magnificent best.

I chewed dulce; you have to have a poke of this salty dried wrack if you're at the Lammas Fair. I watched a couple of excited black-headed gulls do a long, curious dance together, their mad squawks echoing each other and their thin red feet tapping furiously in unison on top of a stone wall. Oblivious to the crowd of noisy fair-goers, they seemed to be enjoying the excitement of the day as well. It was all very nice, but there's only so long you can enjoy looking at scenery or dancing seabirds when you want to be looking for a particular somebody else.

There were a couple of traders that Alex seemed to know, but he showed no inclination to engage with them, much to my consternation. I was hoping for an opportunity to slip away and follow my own head. We spent too long down there at the shore doing absolutely nothing of importance. By the time Alex decided to make our way back up to the market the music session on the street had ended. The harp player had disappeared. If only I had been on my own; I could have joined the crowd, I could have stood and listened, waited until he had finished his performance, maybe had a first conversation with him, found out his name for a start. If only my silly brother wasn't so domineering. I was so annoyed, so discouraged. How I resented Alex's rash interference.

As we neared the market place we paused to watch a juggler performing in front of the castle wall, the residence of the Countess Alice McDonnell that dominated the centre of the town. This juggler was clever with his hands, even more clever with his words, telling jokes and taking a rise out of those who were standing around watching.

"Did ye bring that snout wae ye for a day oot?" he asked a farmer who happened to have a very large, reddish nose, a man who obviously loved his strong drink, I thought.

The poor victim of his abuse took it in good heart and laughed back at the juggler. "Go on, you ham-fisted bugger! You're going to drop one of them," the farmer shouted at him, but divil the one did he drop. To a big country woman the juggler was downright rude. "And here comes the Countess o' Ballyclabber, Lady Muck hersel'! I see you got a new bonnet, m'lady. It luks even worse than last year's one. Did ye steal it aff a scarecrow somewhere?" She must have known the rascal for she just laughed at him, taking the insult in good heart. All this while he was keeping half a dozen painted sticks rotating in the air. As the applause faded at the end of one of his tricks and just as we were about to move on I heard a soft voice that I didn't recognise behind me. It spoke in Irish, but sounded very much like our normal Scots Gaelic greeting.

"*Cad é mar ata sibh, Alex agus Katie?*"

I turned to the voice and found myself looking up into the gorgeous blue eyes of the harp player.

Finally!

Alex seemed to pause, then turned and mumbled a brief Gaelic response. I said nothing, just smiled inanely, my heart jumping so wildly in my chest that I thought he must see it through my clothing. He would certainly notice the blush of embarrassment around my neck, my usual reaction to anything like this.

But he had called us by our names. How did he know them?

There was a moment of awkward silence. I should have spoken but my tongue had become somehow entangled with the rush of thoughts whirling through my head, and I couldn't think what to say. I hoped Alex would bale us out here, but my brother seemed agitated, impatient to move on again.

The stranger saved the day. "So how have you enjoyed the fair?" he said, his voice every bit as musical as the sound of his harp, and his dialect of Irish easy enough for us to understand.

Alex and I looked at each other. Why was he not showing some manners and making conversation? He had half-turned away to stare at the passing crowd. I took over, dry-mouthed.

"It's great, isn't it? We always come. To the fair I mean," I croaked.

"Aye, and a big crowd too," he said.

"Indeed it is, even bigger than usual," I replied. "Was it yourself playing that harp?"

"It was," he said. "Did you listen?"

"Just a wee bit. It sounded lovely." Then after a wee space of silence, "How come you get to play in places like this?"

"Mr MacNeill sent for me. He wanted music in the street during the day, and I have to play in his great hall in the evening for some party."

Alex was impatiently listening to all this, but still looking away to the Diamond as if to find our mother and sisters. He shuffled back and forward uncomfortably.

"Did you sell anything Alex?" the stranger asked. How I wished I knew who he was. And how I wished I understood how he seemed to know Alex.

"I did, a couple of ewes," my brother said. Dourly, to the point.

I could not contain my questions any longer.

"How do you know our names? Have you two met before?"

He and Alex met each other's eyes, the briefest of glances from Alex as his bounced away to stare down the street again. Why was he so uncomfortable, so hidden? The harp boy was being more than friendly. He seemed to be waiting for a response from my brother. When none came he spoke. "We were chatting after the gathering that night in Ballintoy."

"Oh," I said. "You never told me, Alex."

"Why should I?" muttered Alex. "Sure hadn't you just made a fool of yourself in front of the whole gather-up?"

This was harsh. It was also uncalled for, to be drawing attention at this moment to my whole mortification on that dreadful night. He was deliberately trying to humiliate me in front of this stranger. I gave him a dark stare, but I couldn't think of any words to defend myself. I needn't have worried. The stranger stood up for me, against my own brother!

"I don't think you are being fair," he told Alex. "Her dancing was lovely. She wasn't the one who made a fool of herself that night, as I recall it!"

I did not have a notion what he was getting at with this comment. Neither, it seemed, did Alex but, whatever it referred to, it fairly annoyed him.

"What is that supposed to mean?" he growled sourly. "If you have something to say then say it!"

"If the cloak fits," was the stranger's reply. "Anyway, like I told you that night, your family is very talented. You on the pipes and her at the dancing."

Alex had gone into such a sullen mood during this conversation, uncomfortably shifting from one foot to the other. He clearly wanted to put an end to it.

"Enough of this," he said, moving away. "We should be finding the rest of them. Come on Katie."

I hesitated. This was not going to be the end of my first proper meeting with the harp player. I had to know his name at least. I found the courage to stand my ground.

"You go on and find them sure," I said quietly.

"You should come with me," he said. "We need to be getting home."

Once again I had some support from the stranger. He smiled at Alex. "Give her a minute, Alex," he said. "You surely owe me that at least. I promise she will be safe, I'll see that no harm befalls her. No ambushes! Not a soul will touch her."

Alex stared back at him for a second. There was something unspoken between them here, but what the underlying story was I did not know. Whatever it was, the stranger seemed to have come out on top.

"I will be back in a minute," Alex said, turned on his heel and stomped away towards the Diamond.

We looked at each other, suddenly wordless, tongue-tied. Happily so, though. Then we both spoke at exactly the same time. He laughed, the eyes sparkling with August evening light.

"Go on then," he said.

"I was just going to ask how you know our names, but I suppose if you talked to Alex that night he must have told you?"

"That's right; I'm surprised he didn't mention it to you."

"Not a word," I said. "What happened after I left?"

"Everybody cried," he said through a broad grin. I loved his humour. Generally he seemed quite a serious, thoughtful sort but then there would be these lovely smiles, and the eyes would be lit up from behind by whatever he was thinking.

I knew when my leg was being pulled.

"You're funny," I laughed. More silence, just looking, just drinking him in.

"At least we won't have to walk past each other at the Causeway the next time without speaking," he said.

"No we won't indeed," I said. "But what will we say? We've run out of things to say here already."

"You think," he laughed. "I haven't. I just don't know where to begin."

"You could begin by telling me who I am talking to."

"That would be a grand place to start," he said. "I am Darach O'Cahan. That's all you need to know, isn't it? Now you can go back to Alex and the rest of the McKays. And the next time we meet you can say, 'Hello Darach'."

I smiled at his easy-going manner. And I wasn't going anywhere. "How come I never heard of you before if you're an O'Cahan?" I asked.

"Because I am not one of the Dunseverick crowd," he said. "They're relatives but my folk live at Straid."

"Straid is near us," I argued. "If you live there I would surely have seen you before?"

He smiled away at me. "I am getting the impression that you spend your time wandering around Ballintoy looking at all the handsome young men about the place, trying to decide what ones to charm."

"No, it's not that," I answered, flustered. "It's just…I am sure I would have met you somewhere, or heard of you…the great harp player, you know. There aren't a lot of you harp boys around."

"Alright, fair enough," he said. "I live in Dunluce, at the castle; well …in the village beside the castle. That's likely why we haven't met before. And I haven't been around the countryside much till lately you see."

"Why is that then?"

He pondered that one for a second as he took my arm and led me to a low wall. We sat down together, but he swung his long leg over the stones and sat astride the wall, looking at me from the side. The fair-goers passed us by, the hawkers continued shouting, but they might as well have been on Rathlin Island for all the awareness of them that either of us had that afternoon. Cattle came charging past, horses neighing and sheep jostling along the road, but we didn't notice them. We had eyes only for each other. I have never felt so apart from everyone else in Ireland than at that moment.

"Well, you see," he began, "I am a shy sort of fellow. I haven't been in company very much."

I laughed in protest but he insisted. "It is the truth. You don't know how much courage I had to find in myself to come forward to speak to you and Alex there. But I am glad I did."

"Me too," I smiled back into his eyes.

We were quiet for a bit then, just enjoying this beginning. Wondering.

"Have you been to the castle?" he asked.

"Where? Dunluce?"

He nodded.

"No, I've never been any further than Portballintrae. That's where we were coming from the day I…What's it like, the castle?"

"It's very grand. You should come and see it."

Was this an invitation? While I was wondering about that he continued.

"Will you go walking on the Causeway sometime again?"

"Are you asking me?"

"I don't see anybody else," he laughed.

"Alright," I said. "If you are asking me, I will."

"When?"

"I don't know when. I have a job now, in the big house in Ballintoy. I never know when I am needed, or when I have a bit of time to myself."

"Aye, I do remember that," he said. "Sure I saw you there."

"You did! In all my finery," I said. "Don't remind me. I was so affronted that night when I saw you. I wanted to disappear into a hole. I couldn't believe you had seen me in that state."

"I saw you, and that is what matters. You danced very well. Then you panicked for some reason and fled."

"You know the reason," I told him.

"Maybe," he said, smiling, "but anyhow, I'm not complaining. At least I knew you weren't just some dream I had had. There you were in flesh and blood…"

"Dirty as a pig," I reminded him, "so the dream turned into a nightmare."

"No nightmare," he laughed. "It's a pity you can't stay around till later this evening. You could've come with me to this party. I have to play tunes for the guests. You could have done a dance or two."

"I could not," I said. "I have to go home with my mother. She would be thinking I had gone mad. And Alex is very protective of me."

"I noticed. Rightly so. When will you go walking, do you think?"

"I don't know," I said. "But I will try to get away on a Sabbath afternoon sometime."

"Sabbath?" he said. "Is that *Dé Domhnaigh*, our Sunday?"

"Sorry, aye….Sunday. But it might not be for a week or two. And I have to work my way around Alex and my mother."

No sooner had I mentioned their names than I saw my family coming towards us up the street. I stood up, as did Darach. Unconsciously we moved a bit further apart as they approached. Thankfully my mother was away behind them, chatting to someone down next the market. Alex, though, had that resentful air about him. Connie and Alice on the other hand couldn't take their eyes off Darach, sly smiles on their faces as they recognised the boy they had seen at the Causeway.

"It's him," I saw Connie mouth.

But it was Biddy's reaction that really astonished me. Shortsighted as she was, it took her a minute to come close enough to focus on Darach. She seemed at ease at once, smiling even, as if this was someone she was familiar with. She couldn't have known him though.

"Agh, it's yoursel'. I won'ered who Alex was talking aboot. Well son, ye see yoursel'," she said to Darach as she nodded towards Alex, "he is well mended, isn't he?"

Darach smiled. "He is indeed." That was all he said. We all stood looking at each other, mainly at Biddy, and her gawking and grinning at Darach in that dopey way she has.

Not a word of sense could I make of any of this. What was Aunt Biddy santerin' about? Had she had a drink or two and lost her reason? There was no way she could have known Darach, I thought, so this was just a piece of typical nonsense that she sometimes comes out with, her being the way she is. She was embarrassing us all here, but Darach, to be fair to him, seemed not to be bothered by her ravings.

"Did you enjoy the fair?" he asked Biddy. That seemed to be his stock question.

"I did surely," she said, "but we would need to be starting for hame, for it is a quare oul tramp to Ballintoy. Are ye coming our way yersell? Ye could walk wae us. Keep us in chat. The lassies wouldnae say no tae that, would yous girls?"

Goodness, I thought, Biddy is the right oul blether when she starts.

Out of the corner of my eye I saw Connie and Alice nudge each other; I also caught Alex shaking his head and turning away in annoyance.

"That is kind but no, for I still have things to do here," Darach said.

At that point my mother joined us. Her eyes went from Darach to me, to the girls and Alex, as if waiting for an explanation. I was saying nothing.

"Right, let's go and get the donkey," Alex said, easing the tension and moving away. "Come on girls. We need to start before this plump of rain hits us."

Aunt Biddy and my mother moved after him straight away, mother giving me a commanding nod of her head to follow. Reluctantly Connie and Alice joined them, but with several backward glances and giggles. Slowly I began to sidle in their direction, Darach taking the first few steps with me before we both stopped and looked at each other one more time. My heart was doing its fluttering again.

"I'll bid you goodbye, Katie," he said, all very mannerly, and began walking backwards away from me, but still focused on me, his eyes gleaming like a sunset on the rippling sea.

"Goodbye," I said, the smile inside me matching the one on my face.

"And don't forget…the Causeway."

"Don't worry yourself," I called after him.

I couldn't forget if I tried, I thought.

It had been a lovely day altogether, but Alex was determined to ruin it for me. Up ahead I watched him in a serious talk with my mother. I knew what was coming. There would be a reckoning regarding my innocent conversation with this Irish stranger. I didn't have to wait long.

Mammy slowed down, turning back to walk with me.

"This boy you were talking to?" she said.

"What about him?"

"Yous seemed very friendly?"

"Did we?"

"Aye, too friendly, Katie. He's not the sort…"

I interrupted. "Mammy, I have never spoken to him before in my entire life, so how could I be too friendly?"

"You know what I mean."

"I don't."

"You've never spoken to him before but you're looking at him like he has just dropped out of heaven on to your lap."

'Maybe he has,' I thought.

"Just you be careful, daughter," she said. "You don't know him. We don't know him. Your father wouldn't be happy about this."

"That's not fair, mammy," I said. "Daddy isn't here to ask, is he? And anyway, Aunt Biddy seemed to know him."

"Aunt Biddy! Aunt Biddy is away with the birds." We walked on in tense silence for a while. Then she started on a different tack.

"There are plenty of nice lads in our own kirk at Ballintoy. Bruce McClure had his heart set on you, didn't he?"

"Mother, don't talk to me about Bruce McClure! He scunnered me with his pestering."

"Alright, but there's Matthew Taggart, what would be wrong with Matthew? A fine hard-working chap. Even that Patterson fellow from Lisnagunogue seemed to be setting his cap for you last year. He's from a good Presbyterian family, well-doing folk."

"Agh mother!" I said. "Just let me live my own life. You have enough to be worrying about."

"Don't I just," she said. We left it at that.

The promised rain had just started to splatter on us.

'Do your worst,' I thought. 'You'll not dampen my spirits today.'

Chapter 13

An Unfortunate Meeting

Darach had climbed the steep hill from Ballycastle town to Dunynie Castle. The view from its cliff-top position to Rathlin and Kintyre was stunning that evening after the fair, and he had paused outside for a while to let it fill his senses. Now he sat in the corner of Hugh MacNeill's hall, playing his tunes more to himself than to anyone else, for no-one seemed to be paying him much attention. As a result he kept his verses safely in his head and only played airs. No point in wasting words when no-one was paying him heed. He enjoyed the chance to practice, all the more so as the harp he was playing was one he was particularly proud of. Made from cherry-wood but with an alder sound-box, the 'puffin' harp, as he thought of it, had been made to order for the lady of the house. Darach had asked if he could use it for tonight's meeting to save him having to carry his own instrument all the way from Dunluce, a request which Mrs MacNeill had willingly agreed to. The harp's tone was wonderfully bright; the brass strings he had used had come in from a new supplier, a harpsichord string-smith across the water. They lent themselves to the aggressive, finger-nail plucking style that he had mastered and so enjoyed.

The room was spacious with a high ceiling. It had excellent acoustics for musical performance, helped by the amount of oak panelling covering the walls. Several flickering candles provided a hazy light. Hanging from a picture rail were a couple of large oil paintings, portraits of past members of the MacNeill clan. Hugh had been appointed as Constable of Dunynie Castle and granted a large portion of local land by the first Earl McDonnell, thirty years before. He was not averse to displaying his prosperity to whoever wanted to see it. A whole wall of this room was given over to shelving which displayed vases, ornaments, a range of old weaponry and, of course, a few books and scrolls.

As the evening wore on Darach witnessed the usual coming and going of important local men, each paying their respects to the master of the house, having a cup of sherry and talking loudly about current matters in the region. Several wore kilts, denoting that they had come from mainland Scotland or from its islands for the fair. He did not recognise any of the visitors until later in the evening when he was surprised to see his Uncle and cousin, the Dunseverick O'Cahans, make an entrance. They acknowledged him in his corner with a lift of their heads but paid him no more attention, instead fawning around the host and his elegant wife.

It was getting late and Darach had just begun to play what he thought should be his final piece, a slow air he had composed himself as a lament for the destruction of so many groves of trees all over Ulster, when the door burst open with a crash that made him pause in his performance. Into the room stepped Alaster McColla McDonnell, closely followed by his brother, Raghnall, and a perplexed-looking Archibald Stewart. Darach saw the look of surprised annoyance on the face of his host. MacNeill's eyes opened wide as he stepped forward. Stewart's hands, he noticed, were held wide as a gesture of resignation and apology for the uncivilised intrusion, a sort of 'This is not my doing; I tried but I couldn't stop him'. Every head in the room turned to stare at the two Scotsmen, the larger Alaster especially.

"What is this?' MacNeill asked in an unimpressed tone.

"My apologies, Constable," Stewart said sheepishly, as McColla surveyed the room in his arrogant fashion. "This is Raghnall and Alaster McColla McDonnell, my guests at Ballintoy. They insisted on meeting you, so here we are."

"Hmm, very irregular," said MacNeill coming towards the two McCollas, his face anything but friendly. "We haven't met sir," he said to Alaster. "I am Hugh MacNeill. You are welcome, whatever your business."

While Raghnall nodded and took MacNeill's hand in a mannerly fashion, Alaster was slow to reply, even slower to extend his huge hand. He stared his host in the eye with something between curiosity and a downright sneer.

"You're a MacNeill then? One o' the pirates o' Barra?"

The 'r's of Barra seemed to trip off his tongue in a fashion that made it sound like he wanted to rid himself of a mouthful of foul-tasting phlegm. To his way of thinking, to be called a 'Bar-r-r-r-a' man was obviously one of the baser forms of insult.

MacNeill pulled his hand away with a jerk. "I am a Ballycastle MacNeill, I will have you to know. My people may be from Barra originally but I am here, I was born here and I'll have no aspersions cast against me, nor indeed my ancestors."

"I don't think he meant any mischief," Stewart interjected, but McColla ploughed on.

"And would ye be a Covenanter, tell me? A supporter o' the Campbell cause again the King?" Listening to McColla's tone Darach wondered how so much derision could be packed into one short question.

MacNeill rose to the bait with intense indignation in his voice. "I would not, but what I am in my religion and my politics is my own business, sir, and if your business in my house tonight is not of any immediate relevance I will beg your departure."

McColla ignored this and, losing interest, turned away from MacNeill to shake the hands of Darach's uncle Gilladubh and Tirlough Óge. He was followed in this by Raghnall and a muffled conversation began between the four of them.

MacNeill remonstrated quietly with Archibald Stewart who did his best to calm his anger. Darach, who had not resumed playing due to all this commotion, found himself caught between the two conversations.

From Archibald Stewart he heard, "Calm yourself, my friend. He is not meaning to cause you offence. It is just his rough Highland manners."

But MacNeill was hopping mad and it was all Stewart could do to pacify him. "I have never been so insulted in my whole life," he was saying, "and in my own home, and by a scoundrel who entered uninvited. I feel like taking down my sword to him."

"Be advised," said Stewart, holding his host by his shoulders, "that would not be a wise course of action. This man has a fearsome reputation with the sword, as you will no doubt have heard. He would be best left alone to cool down; it is only the strong drink talking. Just let him be, that is my advice. And I apologise again that he entered your home uninvited….I must take the blame for that, but as you see, he is hard to turn."

McColla's conversation became louder, so Darach tended to hear more of what was being said in that corner of the room. He was able to distinguish that the conversation was all about the Randal McDonnells, Lords of Antrim, and how their loyalty to the Crown had been bought by the Earldoms they had received from the English kings, both James and Charles.

"And you haven't even met the Earl since you arrived?" Gilladubh asked. "You haven't been to Dunluce yet?"

"We haven't," confirmed McColla. "Sure Randal never seems to be aboot the place. From what I gather, his bonnie widow-wife has little taste fer the draughty oul castle and the cowl winds o' the north Antrim coast. They spend as much time as they can in the company o' various other landed gentry in this God-forsaken country…in Armagh and Dublin and every county seat in Ireland. Randal could always ken the richt people to be big wae."

As Darach watched he noticed fairly quickly that young Tirlough Óge was clearly fascinated by this notorious soldier, hanging on his every word. He heard his cousin ask something about a recent campaign in Islay that McColla had led against the Campbells, the traditional enemies of Clan McDonnell. Tirlough Óge was to be disappointed though. McColla didn't seem to be inclined to talk over past battles as might have been expected. Instead he appeared to get bored of the conversation and started to look around the hall. As he did, his gaze fell on Darach.

"Ah," he said, coming to stand before him, "it is the harp laddie frae Ballintoy. What happened tae yer tunes the night? The wee harp is silent? Has it been offended by my presence maybe?"

"No sir, I had just finished my repertoire as you came in."

"Your repertoire, is it? Very grand words for such a paltry set of airs, if yer last performance is anything to go by."

"Sorry sir," said Darach, taken aback but reacting with a humility that was expected of him in such a situation.

"And what do ye do when you're naw wasting your time playing that thing?"

If he wasn't riled before, this comment did annoy Darach. He paused for a second to calm himself and measure his response properly.

"When I am not playing the harp, sir," he said softly, "I am making them."

"You are making what?"

"I am making harps."

"You actually make these instruments?"

"Indeed sir. This is one I made for the wife of Mr MacNeill."

"Well, guid for you," McColla said with a still slightly mocking smile. "A maker o' harps. Just what Ireland needs, eh?" He looked at the other O'Cahans as if to entreat their backing, but Gilladubh stepped forward to defend his nephew.

"Darach is a young man and new into this profession," he said with that serious, magisterial look on his face, "but he is very well thought of in the area as a young bard. He's also an O'Cahan, a son of my brother."

"Is that so?" McColla looked like he was losing interest in this conversation, but he turned back for a final thrust at the musician. "And thon wee lassie o' yours? Who would she be?"

Darach was shocked by this and his face reflected his confusion. "What wee lassie...I don't know what you are talking about," he stuttered defensively.

"Oh come on laddie, dinnae play the innocent wae me. Ye ken richt weel. The lassie who disappeared half way through her dance thon night in Ballintoy," said McColla, an unpleasant leer on what could be seen of his sallow face.

Darach was stunned into silence. How could this man know so much about him? Was he a mind reader? Darach had not told anyone about his interest in Katie; not a soul knew a thing about his secret infatuation. He said nothing, just stared the big Scot in his teasing eyes.

"I watched ye that night. Ye were drinking her in like she was sweet mead. Your eyes never left her for one second when she was dancing. Ye were virtually slobbering frae the mooth for her."

"I am sure everybody in the room was watching her," Darach whispered.

"Nonsense; I didnae watch her, for one. Mind you, she is a pretty bit of a wench. But nobody looked at her the way you did, did they? And when she eventually happened to spy ye through the crowd what did she do? She fled frae your sight. Noo why would she dae that?"

"I have no idea."

"Hae ye naw, lad? My guess is that the last time she saw ye, ye were lying between her thighs, enjoying al' she was offering you. Would I be richt in that wild guess, would I? That's the only wae I could explain her embarrassment. I presume ye were as big a disappointment to her as ye are on this instrument?"

Darach's anger simmered under his calm response. "Sir, you have no right to say such a thing to me. You do not know what you are talking about. I bid you goodnight!"

And with that Darach left the harp and strode past the burly figure to the door. He nodded to MacNeill and Stewart who were standing open-mouthed at the altercation that they had just witnessed. Both men followed him into the hall. MacNeill caught him by the arm and began to fish in his pocket for some money.

"I am so sorry you had to experience that hostility, my young friend. Please accept my apology and please take double what I had promised you by way of reparation. We enjoyed your music very much."

"Thank you, sir," replied Darach as he took the coins. Archibald Stewart stepped forward supportively.

"Don't mind that rude fellow," he said to Darach. "He is in drink and is well out of order. You handled that situation very well. Goodnight to you."

Darach left them. As Stewart followed MacNeill back towards the hall he asked his host a question.

"What do you know of this harp player, Hugh? I am concerned about this possible connection with one of my tenant lassies."

"I wouldn't know anything about that, Archibald," MacNeill replied, hiding a smile at Stewart's prudishness. "To my mind he is very capable. That lovely instrument he was playing tonight? Made it himself."

"Aye, we had him play at Ballintoy and I think he said that he made that instrument too. A good craftsman then but what sort of fellow is he?"

"I think he is a sound young man," MacNeill continued. "He has learning too. He was one of the Bonamargy students for a while, I believe."

"Is that so?" Stewart said.

As Darach wandered the streets in the drizzling rain, his mind could not dampen the worry that Katie was working in the big house at Ballintoy where this McColla was resident. This thought preoccupied him half the night until he found an unoccupied corner of a barn and curled up in the dusty hay to try to sleep until morning. His dreams included scenes in which he was standing between the big Highlander and this girl who had so quickly become his fixation; he jerked awake several times in dread at the confrontation with McColla that he imagined he was about to have. He found himself trying to think of a way that he could somehow send her a warning to be on her guard against McColla, indeed any of those kilt-wearing gallowglasses, but he had to console himself with the thought that her overly-protective brother, who was so obviously wary with regard to himself, would be watching out for her. It wasn't a great night's sleep he had in that Ballycastle barn

Chapter 14

Bog Oak

Katie McKay

It had not been easy to get sneaked away from the family for a Sunday dander, my mother's loyalty to the strict Sabbath observance of her Presbyterian background being the main obstacle. We had never been allowed to do anything that looked like work or pleasure. Meals had to be ready from the night before, same with cleaning your footwear and any other household tasks. Attendance at kirk was an unwritten rule, and not just once in the day; if the clergyman hadn't too many other congregations to service he would have you back for evening worship as well; if you were a child you could find yourself in the kirk during the afternoon for Sabbath school. We were always instructed that church attendance could never save a soul but, with three meetings on a Sabbath, they gave it every opportunity, just in case it helped.

During those early September weeks it was even more difficult to get away, mainly due to my suspicious brother. A very disagreeable bee seemed to have taken up residence in his bonnet around then. Every time I ventured out in the direction of the Causeway I had to take Connie with me just to quell Alex's fears; he had a way of throwing me a questioning look that made me uncomfortable. He knew right well, I am sure, what was going on in my head; he could read my motivations. He had witnessed my eagerness to talk to Darach in Ballycastle. He didn't say very much about it but I could sense his distrust. He hovered above me like a hungry hawk watching a field-mouse.

The thing was that back then I had no way of comprehending this strange connection he had to Darach; he had made no further mention of our meeting that day at the fair when Darach had somehow known us. I was in the dark for a good while after that.

Connie was great though. She didn't mind the long walks; we both enjoyed the bracing sea air, particularly because the weather around then had improved from the earlier storms of July. Such a bad year it had been. All the farmer folk were complaining, warning that there would be food shortages in the hungry months if there was any more disruption to the autumn harvest. None of this could dampen Connie's spirits though. She was the eternal optimist, full of energy and laughter.

Although only fifteen, she sometimes could appear to be older than me; maybe it was her build, in that she was a bit bigger-boned, sturdier than I was, but she also had a way with her that spoke of confidence. Where I seemed to have an inbuilt shyness, Connie covered whatever insecurities she might have with a readiness that at times verged on the brash. Certainly, as far as relationships with boys was concerned, she could have bought and sold me. Fellows found her openness of character and her quick humour to be irresistible. When I watched her interactions with the local lads I often saw that look in her eyes and that sideways tilt of her head that almost seemed to offer a challenge to them, a sort of 'take me on if you think you're up to it lads!'

As we walked west that afternoon, the fourth venture since the Lammas fair, Connie was not behind the door in questioning me about Darach. Up until that day she had made quiet jibes in passing about my 'secret lover' but we had never really discussed the matter in any depth. The curiosity had been building up in her. This was her chance and she took it. To be honest I did not mind…in fact I quite enjoyed the opportunity to talk about him. Her main issue was the expected one.

"What will mammy say when she finds out?"

"Finds out what? I have only ever talked to him once, and that was for a very short time."

"Aye, but you're struck on him, aren't you? I can tell. And it won't stop here, will it?"

"How do I know where it will stop, Connie? Might never even get a chance to go anywhere. Might never set eyes on him again, let alone have the chance to…"

"But you want it to, don't you? I don't blame you mind. He is a bit special, from what I can see anyway."

"He is special, I'll not deny that," I said, "but maybe it is just an impossible dream. It's not something I can do anything about, is it?"

"Apart from going walking in his direction every chance you get?"

"Well, he asked me to."

"And that must have made your day."

"It certainly didn't spoil it. But it's been nearly a month. No sign of him on those other days."

Connie laughed at me. "It's a big area. He could have been walking on a different track, maybe waiting for you above Ballintoy, maybe in with his cousins in Dunseverick when we were walking past."

"Could be…but he did say the Causeway. We're just so far apart. It's a five mile walk for both of us. I keep thinking it's all just a bit impossible."

"Well, what I am thinking is that, if we do run into him, it's going to be me that's in the impossible situation…stuck like a sore thumb between the two of yous," laughed Connie. "I should be getting paid for this service; how much do you think it is worth?"

"Not a penny," I said. "Sure you're as keen to see him as me."

"Away on with ye! He's all yours."

'If only,' I thought.

We had reached the path that leads from those placid green fields around Templastragh old church down to the little natural harbour at Dunseverick. The black rock below us glistened in the sun; I always thought it looked like its maker had spewed it out in an angry tantrum, great ugly turds of darkness that were so irregular you could barely walk on the surface. Such a contrast to the even neatness of the meadows that ran right to the cliff edge. We raced down the path like a couple of children, skipping and leaping and laughing at how quickly our sophisticated conversation had dissolved into girlish rumbustiousness.

"I can still beat you, Connie," I called over my shoulder.

"You cheated. You started first."

"Never did!"

"Just wait till I get you on the flat ground," she yelled.

"You think? You'll never catch me."

But catch me she did. She fairly flew over the deep autumn grass below the cliff, arms and legs flailing and her whooping like a seagull.

And then my foot went down some sort of hole and I fell, head-first to the sandy earth. Connie had no sympathy, landing on top of me, tickling me like we were back ten years ago as children.

"Get off me," I said in annoyance. "I might have hurt my ankle."

"It can't be very sore or you would be howling."

I pushed her off; she rolled to the side and, as she did, a tall shadow fell across me. I squinted up into the sun and there, standing above me and grinning from ear to ear, was Darach.

Yet another disaster of timing. I gave myself a second to think before I spoke. "Is there ever going to be a time when I don't make an eejit of myself when we meet?" I said.

"Hopefully not," he laughed, reaching down to pull me up. That first touch! Only his hand and only for a split second, but it felt just so perfect, full of meaning…him lifting me up. "Are you hurt? You were flying there when you tripped."

"Think I am alright," I said, testing my weight on my ankle nervously. It really was a bit sore but I didn't want to admit to it, not straight away anyhow. "Where did you come from?"

"I was walking the Causeway, just hoping. When I didn't see any sign of you, I thought I would keep going…."

Connie interrupted at this point. She had been standing back observing us and, to be honest, I had sort of forgotten her presence. "Hey you two, I am going to go back up to Daddy's grave above, so give me a shout when you are finished Katie."

Darach moved towards her, his arms out in a gesture of entreaty.

"No need for you to go," he said. "Stay with us."

Connie hesitated, looking from one to the other, her boldness gone. I felt for her at that point, her awkward otherness. She hadn't even been introduced to this man who had so taken over my thoughts in the past months. I felt it only right to introduce her, and I didn't mind if she stayed or went, at least that's what I told myself.

"This is my wee sister Connie," I said.

They smiled at each other, nodding, silent for a second. Connie backed away slowly.

"Nice to … meet you," she muttered sheepishly. "But I will leave yous to it, whatever it is you're for doing, not that I…."

She stopped before she dug any deeper.

"Seriously," Darach said. "Please stay. We don't mind, do we Katie? It would be nice to get to know you as well…"

He faded off in his persuasion as Connie turned and ran a few undignified steps before turning and embarrassing me even more.

"Sorry but I'd only be in the way; and anyway, Katie's told me all the lovely things she wants to say to you."

With that she fled as I began a pointless protest.

We looked at each other.

"What things would that be then?"

"I never told her any such…she's just being a silly wee sister, teasing me."

"She seems a lively one?"

"Aye, that's our Connie. But she has a good heart. She looks out for me. That's why she comes along with me on all these walks I have been…"

"So you have come walking a few times?" Darach asked. "I am sorry. This is the first chance I have had to come to look for you. I was away travelling with John in Derry."

"What took you over there?"

"We were trying to find timber for a new build inside the castle. John is my foster father at Dunluce you see. I am his apprentice."

"And you've been gone for three weeks?" There was just a small taint of disappointment in my tone; I hoped it wasn't coming across as a rebuke. I had no right to lay any of my secret expectations on him.

"No, it's not like that. We go on our searches at weekends when he is not working and whenever we can borrow a couple of horses from the stables. You wouldn't believe how hard it is getting to find the right sort of wood. John gets very annoyed."

"Really? Why is that?" I asked.

He grimaced. "Do you really want to know?"

"Of course I do; why else would I ask?"

"I suppose it is because with all the new settlers arriving into the countryside over the past thirty years, you know the government's plantation thing; these people have just cleared all the forests in front of them. It's a disgrace what has happened. Completely thoughtless they are."

I wasn't sure what he meant and it must have showed in my expression.

"I wouldn't expect you to understand Katie," he said, "but the groves of trees that used to cover much of the district from Coleraine to Garvagh have mostly been cleared. That's where John used to get most of his timber. But these English folk needed it for their new towns, so they took down huge areas of trees. Then they sold hundreds, maybe thousands of trees, for building ships and the like. And what they didn't exploit for gain they cut down to make way for new farms."

"That is tough for yous," I said.

"It's great for the English, but those forests were part of our heritage. We Irish put great value on trees. They are in our legends and they have been part of our landscape for ever. Now they're all going."

It was some speech and I couldn't help noticing how ardent he was about the subject. We had only just met and already he was drawing me in, emotionally, to one of his causes. I admired his passion, even if it was not the romantic type of conversation I had been hoping for.

"Are you not able to get timber for your harp making?" I asked naively, trying to bring the conversation around to him.

"Agh it's not about me and my harps. I will always be able to find the wood I need. It is more to do with what people value. To the English a grove of trees is in the way of the plough; either that or they're there to be chopped and sold for profit. That's the English way. Not our way."

"Go on; I can see you love your trees," I said.

"I do. You see, each type of tree has a story behind it, a legend. Some are used in charms, so it may be to do with the tree's healing properties, or maybe it's a tree that has to be handled right in case it brings bad luck; or like having an elder tree beside your house keeps the devil away. Or maybe it has a special religious significance…like the blackthorn, you know? It was used to make a crown for the head of Jesus."

"How do you know it was the blackthorn?" I asked. "Could have been a hawthorn or a bramble even."

"We don't 'know', we just believe," he replied more slowly. "Now we are losing so many of them that it's hurting us, hurting nature itself."

"Lord but aren't you the passionate Irishman," I said; I was only half joking too. His speech had shown me a side to him that I found quite a shock, not an unpleasant shock but one that I needed to think about.

"Sorry," he said, "I shouldn't have got carried away on my favourite theme. Come; we'll go down to sit by the harbour. Can you walk alright or do you need me to carry you like I did with…"

He stopped short and I wondered who or what he was referring to.

"I think I am fine," I said but as we made our way to the edge of the water I did notice jabs of pain in the right ankle. Darach's solution was to have me dip the foot into the icy cold water for a while; it didn't take long for the pain to disappear, likely because after a while the foot got so cold I couldn't feel it any more. The kelp swirled around my toes as if determined to tickle me into submission. Shoals of tiny fish came close for a look, darting, inquisitive, but the green shore-crabs thankfully kept their distance down among the rocks. I held my ankle in the sea as long as I could bear and, when it became almost completely numb, I lifted it out. My galant friend took my foot in his hands and massaged it gently, bringing some heat back into it and all the while looking me in the eyes, both of us smiling at the strange intimacy of this moment. Darach was holding my ankles in both his hands, caressing the sore one. I was loving it. No fellow had ever touched my ankle before, let alone stroked it. I thought I was going to pass out from excitement. I breathed in the sweet, earthy scent of his hair, filling myself with his aroma; it aroused me. So fresh, so virile.

I happened to notice the length of his finger nails.

"Your nails are very long," I whispered.

"They are. You know why?"

"No idea. I can't think straight at the minute. You tell me."

"All harp players have long nails," he said.

"Ah, of course. Silly of me."

"Not at all. Is it starting to feel any better?"

"It is but…maybe a wee bit more."

I didn't want this moment to stop. His gentle touch again. It was doing things to me in the pit of my stomach, feelings I had never experienced before. I couldn't have taken the smile off my face, not if you had offered me a piece of silver.

"That's enough now," I said eventually, the first words between us for a good while.

"Are you sure? Are you not enjoying it?"

"Don't tease me," I said. "You know I am enjoying it but I feel like I should be shouting for my wee sister to come back and protect me here."

He laughed again. "Don't do that, or at least not yet."

We didn't talk all the time we had together. We were comfortable enough with each other just to enjoy the other's presence. We didn't touch any more. We didn't need to; the bond was growing in the quietness.

Darach broke the silence.

"I need to tell you about what happened in Ballycastle that night after the fair." I waited, just a wee bit anxious as I watched a shadow of unease behind his eyes. "I had a bit of a row with that McColla man."

"Oh no? He was there at your music thing? He's not a good person to be making an enemy of."

"Maybe not, but I couldn't let him away with what he was saying."

"What sort of things?" I asked.

"It's hard to describe them; he was just in a very insulting mood."

"He insulted you?"

"Aye; not just me. Maybe he was drunk but his talk was very coarse and aggressive. With everybody; not me alone. I can't stand the man."

"What did he say to insult you?"

"Agh, you know; things about my harp playing, things about you."

I was shocked by this. "Why, what did he say about me? Sure he doesn't even know me."

"He has seen you, that was enough for him to think he could make a sarcastic comment about the two of us."

"The two of us? What does he know about the two of us? He couldn't know anything for there was nothing to know?"

"Aye, but it doesn't stop him surmising. He saw you dancing at the feast and he noticed me watching you. He puts two and two together and gets seventeen. He's a dirty scoundrel, so he is."

I put my hand on Darach's arm. "Don't let him bother you then; don't pay any heed to his insults."

"I couldn't help it; I stood up for myself. I stood up for you too and I am proud that I did."

"So you should be," I said, impressed. The very thought of Darach, my youthful admirer, standing up to that brutal beast of a man was almost as ridiculous as it was admirable. He probably saw the smile I was trying to hide behind my hair at that moment.

"But Katie," he continued, "I want you to promise me that you will stay well away from that man, alright? Have nothing to do with him. In my opinion he is dangerous; I got him mad I think, and he might try and get back at me by hurting you. He is capable of anything, so you watch him."

"I will watch him, you needn't worry."

This was an unexpected revelation; McColla had obviously got under Darach's skin, whatever he had said. Secretly I was thrilled that Darach had defended me in that altercation and that he was making a point of bringing me this warning now. It had obviously played on his mind.

"Thank you for being concerned for me," I smiled.

"That's alright," he said. "Here, I have something for you."

He put his hand in his pocket and produced a small object wrapped in a few sycamore leaves.

"I made this for you," he said with a smug little smile of pride.

I opened the leaves. A small black cross lay in my hand, a simple but striking carving in some kind of dark wood. It was about the length of my smallest finger and shaved so thin it seemed to weigh nothing. I was almost scared it would break if I held it too firmly, so delicate was it.

"It is beautiful," I breathed.

"See at the top; it's got a wee hole pierced…that's in case you want to hang it around your neck. I have a thin strip of leather here. Do you think you would want to wear it?" he asked, slightly hesitant.

"Maybe. But would it not break if…"

"It won't break," he said. "It's *Dair dhubh*."

"*Dair*? Sounds like your name."

"Same word. Means bog-oak, or dark oak. It has been lying in peat for hundreds of years since the tree fell over. The moisture down there protects the wood from decay, you see. So it's sturdy, even though I carved it so thin."

"You made this for me?"

"'Course I did." Then after a little silence between us as I feathered the smooth surface of the little cross on my cheek, he said shyly, "You understand why, don't you?"

My heart gave a strange wee flutter. I didn't know what to say to this. It was a different level of query, one that was about to take my relationship with this boy to a new place of realisation, that bit higher up the mountain to a height from which it would be difficult to descend. When you try to put words on a feeling it can create too much of a hard shell for it, casting it in stone before its time. But the time felt perfect for this admission. My heart was racing like a runaway pony; it did that at such moments; could I rely on it to guide my answer?

"I think so," I breathed, "but I want you to tell me."

He glanced away briefly. Was it embarrassment, shyness? When he looked back his eyes were full of gentleness; he reached for my hand and we held the bog-oak cross between our two palms.

"I am no good with words. That's why I hoped this gift would say what I wanted to say; but if you still don't know? Alright," he said softly. "You and me, whatever this is, it is special. I know it is. I know in my spirit that it is…Look, since I first saw you….Aaagh, words! I am hopeless."

We were back to silence. I hadn't helped him at all in this moment. I had just been willing to let him flounder along and watch him get his tongue tied in knots. I needed to let him know that I understood.

"It's alright Darach," I said. "I do know."

His smile said relief. I continued.

"And this cross says it all. It is very special and I love it; I love that you made it for me; and I wish I had a gift for you."

"You don't need to. Sure aren't you the best gift ever," he laughed.

"Thank you," I said, "and will you do one more thing for me?"

"What is that?"

"Tie it around my neck. I want to wear it."

So he did, another intimate moment; my neck blushing; the cold of his fingers footerin' against my skin, exciting me as he tied the cross in place. I laughed as he wrapped me in his arms for the first time. I drank in his scent, the scent of wood, I thought…or was that just because he had been speaking so much about trees? Maybe, but it was a smell I loved. A good smell; homely; mine.

"There," he said, "that's the place for it. From six feet down in an Antrim bog to hanging around the neck of the prettiest girl in the county."

"And you tell me you are no good with words," I said, my head pressed tightly under his chin.

Chapter 15

The Brother

Alex and Connie waited at the top of the path. They had been standing there watching, seeing everything that happened in the past few minutes between Katie and Darach. After her brother found her at Templastragh Connie had had to persuade him to stay with her and not to hurry down to the shore to confront the couple.

"Sure what good will it do?" she had argued. "You will only cause Katie terrible embarrassment."

So he had listened, waited and seethed quietly.

Katie gripped and lifted her long skirt as she approached the last few difficult steps on this, the steepest section of the climb. She was being slow and careful, conscious of the vulnerability of her ankle. Becoming aware that she was being watched from above, she paused and stared up against the sky.

Alex! The warm glow of that idyllic day just went cold for her. 'Oh no,' she thought. 'Where has he come from? Why can't he just leave us in peace?'

The final steps gave her time to think how she would handle his challenge, but then she was not aware of how much he had seen. Had he witnessed that final embrace? She was suddenly able to dismiss the disappointment that Darach had stopped short of kissing her down there. That could wait until later, a next step to look forward to in the future path of the romance, if indeed next steps were going to be possible after Alex had had his say.

Before she even reached his level he spoke.

"What was all that about?"

"All what about?"

"You and that O'Cahan fellow? I saw him hugging you. How foolish can you be?"

"Why would he not hug me? We are friends; it was a perfectly harmless hug," she argued. "You have no right to be questioning me anyway. It is none of your business."

"It absolutely is my business. I am your older brother. You have no father. Let me remind you that he is lying across there in that graveyard and he would be turning in his grave if he could see the sort of girl his daughter is becoming. Have you no shame?"

Connie was champing at the bit to get into this confrontation. Katie needed her support.

"What are you talking about, Alex? Why should she feel shame? She is nearly eighteen. Darach is a nice lad. They like each other. What's wrong with that?"

"I'll tell you what's wrong with…" Alex began, but Connie wasn't finished what she had intended to say.

"Just because the sap hasn't started to rise in you yet," she added, turning from him dismissively. Alex paused while this criticism filtered into his consciousness.

"What is that suppose to mean?"

"Sure you never look at a girl, and you nineteen. Jean Kennedy did her best to get your attention and you just ignored her. Worse than that, when she used to come about our place you treated her like dirt. You always had to disappear out to the cow or something, rather than face talking to her."

Alex was hurt by this outburst, but he hid behind bluster rather than show any vulnerability. "This is not about me! It is about Katie so just you shut up and mind your own business!"

"And you take your own advice, big brother! You mind your own business, not Katie's! I am going home!"

Connie stomped away in disgust and Katie followed. Alex wasn't giving up however.

"Look Katie," he said from behind, "I am not saying you shouldn't be seeing boys. There are plenty of good lads around Ballintoy. There's more than one would be delighted if you showed any interest in them."

Katie had the advantage of being ahead of Alex on the path. She trudged on, head down, not feeling she had to reply to this. Her silence annoyed the older brother.

"What would be wrong with our fellows in Ballintoy? Good sound lads, same background as ourselves. You have no call to be thinking you're too good for them and you have no need to be looking for somebody over the fence, especially an O'Cahan."

The last comment couldn't be ignored. Katie spun around, the black cross swinging from her neck and instantly drawing Alex's attention.

"'Especially an O'Cahan'? What do you find so offensive about the idea that I would be friendly with an O'Cahan?"

"You know what they are like, Katie. That crowd in Dunseverick Castle have been thorns in our flesh since our family came over here. Daddy always said never to trust them…some dealings he had with Gilladubh back in the day, I can't recall exactly what is was."

"Well, even if you are right about what Daddy said, I'll have you to know that Darach isn't one of them."

"He is one of them. He is a cousin. They're all the one sow's pigs."

"Listen to yourself, Alex! You are talking about them as if they were animals. You insult them, and you insult me with a comment like that. 'All the one sow's pigs'! God forgive you."

"I didn't mean it like that, you know I didn't. It's just an expression. I am just saying…"

"Well don't say any more. I will not listen to you insult my… Darach is a gentleman and nothing you say will turn me against him. You should get to know him and you would start to appreciate him. That reminds me. How does he know so much about us?"

"I told you. He and I played a tune after McColla's feast, that's all."

"He knew my name?" Katie persisted.

"He must have asked who you were."

"And you told him? You told him I was your sister?"

"Maybe. Something like that. It doesn't matter. What does matter is that you need to stop seeing him. Stop it now before you get any more spell-bound by him."

"I am not spell-bound. Lord above, you'd think he had bewitched me or something. Is it not possible that he likes me for myself and I like him for himself? It feels very natural. He didn't have to put a spell on me."

Alex's eyes fell on the black cross again.

"You mightn't see it but that is exactly what he has done. And this cross thing is part of it. It's pagan."

Katie fingered the cross, shaking her head in disbelief. "That's a new one. A pagan cross! You're in sinking sand with that argument."

"No, I'm not. It's as dark as sin. You need to take it off your neck and throw it over that cliff. It is already starting to be a bondage to you. Remember the Scriptures? It's there in black and white. No graven images. No false idols."

"Oh brother! You are talking nonsense. It is a cross, a symbol of christianity, not paganism. It is Darach's gift to me; he carved it from a piece of bog oak. He wanted to show me that we have a common loyalty to our faith. It has nothing to do with pagan."

"It is black, that's the first thing. If he wanted to give you a cross he could have made it from a bit of an ash tree or something, something clean and white, not this dark bog oak. Sure wasn't the oak the most sacred tree of the Druids? It is a pagan cross, Katie."

Katie turned away from him and looked out to the horizon, as if for inspiration. The green-tinged sea met a clear, cold-blue sky in a very distinct line today. Islay, though, was indistinct, a misty greyness in the north. The crash of waves foaming against rocks below was in her ears.

Inspiration did come to her and she smiled inwardly at the power of this thought, an idea that had just seemed to land in her mind from a source she didn't comprehend.

"Has it never occurred to you that it was a pagan cross that Jesus was crucified on?" she asked him.

Alex pondered this. "How do you mean?"

"I mean that the cross didn't begin as a nice, clean, christian symbol, did it? It was all about blood and pain. It was about cruelty and death. Likely it was dark too. What do you think? Surely it had to have been a pagan tree?"

Alex thought about this, a notion that he had never come across before. Katie judged that his silence might signal agreement with her argument. She grasped her little cross and held it towards Alex.

"Darach gave me this out of love and respect, and because we are both christian, not because he wants to somehow trap me into paganism. Don't you see that, Alex?"

"But at the end of the day he is still Catholic."

"He is, and so was our grandfather and all those early relatives across the water. Are we to be ashamed of our ancestors? I will not be ashamed of Darach. In fact I am proud of him as my friend."

"You can he proud of him as a friend, but have you thought about the future? What are you going to do if this friendship gets any closer? You can't be thinking…"

"I am not planning a future. I am living one day at a time."

"And one day leads to the next day and the next day and so on, until you are in love with this fellow and there'll be no stopping you then. You'll be in too deep."

"You talk a lot of nonsense."

"This is not nonsense, Katie! Do you never listen to Reverend Blare? He is always warning us about marrying outside the faith. What is he going to think when he hears that you are meeting this O'Cahan?"

"He can say what he wants; it's not as if Darach is a heathen."

"Have you told Jean? She'd surely talk some sense to you."

Katie hesitated. "No, I haven't said anything to her yet."

"You see? You'd be scared of what your friend would say. Look, whether you like it or not, that fellow is one thing, you are another. It is like oil and water, black and white. The two can't mix."

By this stage the couple had reached the rocky shore approaching Portbradden, Katie still ahead of her brother. She paused and looked round at him, waiting. "Do you see where we are walking?" she asked.

"What we are walking on?"

"'Course I see it. What of it?"

"Look at that cliff face. What do you see?"

Alex cast a quick glance to his right. "A pile of rock. Why?"

"What kind of rock is that top layer?"

"I don't know what kind of rock it is. I am no expert. Hard rock?"

"Aye, it's hard alright. What colour is it?"

"It's dark, black. What are you on about?"

"And the rock below it? The bottom layer? What kind of rock is it?

What colour is it?" Katie persisted.

"It's that chalky sort of rock. Softer, mostly white."

"It is. Two completely different kinds of rock, lying together. One black, one white."

"So?"

"Well, God made them both and he must have thought it was alright for them to lie together, black and white. He could have kept them apart if he'd wanted to, couldn't he, but he must have thought it was a good idea. In fact he probably thought that they looked well together, you know? The contrast, the design. All along this coast it is the same, black and white rocks together in layers. See what I am saying?"

Alex did see the point she was making and he resented it. He wasn't about to be schooled by his little sister.

"You are twisting creation to suit your own ends. There's lots of arguments the other way round. You never see a horse mating with a cow, or a dog with a cat, do you?"

"'Course not. But we are talking about two human beings here, not two different kinds of animal. Darach and I are not cat and dog, are we?"

"Maybe, but you're from two different faiths, you can't deny that."

Katie held the bog-oak cross towards him triumphantly.

"He gave me this cross, Alex. Do you not think it's maybe a sign? He believes in the same dying Jesus that we do. We aren't all that different."

Alex seemed to be defeated. He was quiet for a second before firing his final shot. "We'll just have to see what Reverend Blare says about it then, won't we? He'll put you right."

Connie was waiting for them as they reached the strand. She smiled as she came towards Alex, head to the side, an air of contrition seemingly written all over her face.

"I am sorry for what I said," she told Alex.

"Alright," he said.

Connie wasn't finished though."But seriously Alex, you need to take life a bit easier, spend less time working your guts out on our farm."

"You think? Who else is…"

"And more than that, you need to spend less time worrying about our Katie. It's me you should be counselling. I have eight different fellows running after me and I haven't enough days in the week to handle them all. That's before I start counting those Highlanders! What would you advise me to do?"

Alex couldn't help but laugh at yet another of Connie's diversionary tactics, nor could he resist putting an arm around her playfully and pulling her struggling towards the small waves breaking on the white sand. The acrimony of their earlier arguments quickly dissolved as hot tempers met the cold, clear water of White Park Bay and Connie's laughter turned into shrieks.

Chapter 16

Discussions in Dunluce

Darach and John McSparran were sawing lengths of well-seasoned ash in the yard in front of the brewhouse when they heard the yapping of the castle mongrels, followed by the first clattering noises of horses arriving on the cobbles at the entrance above. Not an unusual sound in itself, but it was the accompanying clamour of raised banter, swearing and unruly laughter and, above all, the unmistakeable intonation and accent of one particular voice that put Darach on instant alert.

The voice was that of Alaster McColla McDonnell.

Before the arriving company turned the corner into the yard Darach followed his first instinct. He moved swiftly to hide in an alcove between the stable and the barn. Surprised by this retreat, McSparran observed the action of his young apprentice but said nothing, focussing instead on three horsemen as they approached down the slope and drew their mounts to a stop beside him.

"Here man," Alaster McColla called roughly as the three swung themselves stiffly on to the dismount platform, "make yoursel' useful and stable these horses for us. They'll need fodder an' water. See tae it, will ye!"

McSparran had no choice but to obey; there seemed little point in trying to explain to these visitors that he was a carpenter, not a stable boy. He took charge of the horses one at a time, resisting the temptation to call for Darach to help him as the Highlanders muttered impatiently.

"What are ye working at today?" asked Raghnall, seemingly a bit more aware than his companions that McSparran was no yard-hand and was being interrupted in his task.

"Just some roof repairs in the MacQuillan tower, sir," McSparran answered briefly without making any further eye contact. As he led the second horse towards the stable the bigger Scotsman called after him.

"Where is your harp-maker today? Naw workin' wae ye?"

There was the briefest hesitation in his walk as McSparran contained his surprise that this guest should know anything of his apprentice. He continued into the stable and tied the horse to a rail; it gave him time to think how to answer the query and, considering Darach's reticence to be seen by these men, he decided to provide a bit of a smoke-screen.

"Not working with me at the minute," he said, coming back for the third horse. "He must be about somewhere. Who should I tell him was looking for him, sir?"

"Nae matter," Alaster McColla said, ignoring the implied insult and turning away towards the funnel and the entrance into the castle itself. McSparran watched them go and soon was aware of Darach's head peering surreptitiously around the corner of the building. As the trio stomped their way into the shadows of the gate-house he emerged cautiously to explain his apprehensive behaviour to his mentor.

****

The Earl of Antrim, Lord Randal McDonnell, sat opposite but well apart from his three kilted guests in the great hall of the castle's Manor House. His rather dainty hand massaged the flaccid features of his face. On his countenance, a rather haughty expression looked as if it had been freshly painted on and was now suitably framed by a magnificent wig. With feigned boredom, he glanced languidly out to sea through the room's bay window. Randal was fairly confident that this grand building, the Manor House, constructed by his father some twenty years before and refurbished more recently by himself and his new wife, was the most opulent these three warriors had ever set foot in. The floor was of perfectly prepared oak, partially covered by a Persian carpet of the most elaborate design; the floor-to-ceiling wainscoting panels completely hid the rough stone walls; the tapestries which hung were the most lavish and colourful to be found in England; they showed mainly hunting and woodland scenes. Each piece of furniture was London's best; the fireplace design and dimensions spoke of an eye to style and proportion; no better stags' heads could be found in Ulster than those which graced the stonework. Two Irish harps stood on either side of a grand chaise longue, one handsome, with ornate etchings, the other a smaller instrument with a swan's head cleverly carved on the end of its neck.

The Earl had called for wine and waited in silence for its arrival. His sad-looking eyes, following the faces of his visitors, saw what he judged to be a sense of awe as they took in their surroundings. This initial stillness, he thought, would give him an edge when it came to the awkward conversations that were bound to follow.

"Cousins," he began as the butler left, "let us begin by drinking to Clan McDonnell."

"Clan McDonnell," they echoed, raising their goblets. While the Earl sipped his with an affectation he had observed at court in London, he noticed that his relatives guzzled their drinks with rustic abandon, draining their wine in one long gulp. A wry smile played about his lips. These Highlanders! His ill-famed cousins were just as crude in their manners as he had been led to expect.

"So, to what do I owe the honour of this visit, gentlemen?" he said, his accent an interesting blend of raw Ulster intonation and continental cadence. Randal had enjoyed a most unusual educational experience. It had begun in boyhood, in traditional Gaelic manner at Dunluce, had included spells studying in France and several years in English high society...and the melding of these various strains had never been properly realised. At times the joins showed.

The three looked at each other. "Ye asked us tae come," said Alaster, puzzled. He glanced at his brother for support.

"Aye, ye sent for us," repeated Raghnall. "So Stewart said."

Randal appeared to be trying to remember, brow puckered, running his finger across his well-shaven upper lip, all in his silly little game.

"Did I now? Ah yes, maybe I did mention to Archibald that you hadn't bothered to grace Dunluce with your presence since your somewhat surprising arrival several weeks ago. How long is it now since you made the crossing?"

Raghnall answered while his brother stared intently at the Earl, as if trying to understand his tactics in this discussion. "It must be six or seven weeks."

Murdo, the third member of the trio and a distant relative, added his support. "Seven weeks and three days, to be exact," he said nodding his untidy head vigourously.

Randal smiled at his precision. "Seven weeks and three days? Really? So long? I find this difficult to comprehend."

Alaster opened his mouth to begin a defence, but Lord Antrim wasn't finished his chastisement just yet. He had to take this opportunity to remind these cousins just who they were talking to.

"I am sure," he continued in his most pompous-sounding voice, "it has not escaped your attention that, since the unfortunate flight of Hugh O'Neill and his friends, O'Donnell and the rest of them, the Earl of Antrim is now the last remaining Gaelic lord in Ulster; I am certainly the only one with any clout. As such, I think I might have expected you to pay me a courtesy visit long before now, gentlemen. You think not, Alaster?"

"We had every intention, cousin," replied McColla, his disdainful look only partially hidden behind his facial hair, "but our information was that ye were seldom here at Dunluce. We had it on good authority that ye travelled to Dublin and Antrim and Carrickfergus on various occasions during our sojourn...so what woulda been the point in us visiting the castle in your absence? Unless perhaps to meet and get to ken this new wife ye hae? The famous Lady Katherine. Where is she anyway? No portraits of her on your walls yet? We were al' looking forward to haeing a gleek at her. From what I hear she is a bit of a beauty, Randal? And naw withoot ither...ither assets as weel?"

The Earl opened his mouth, about to answer. Two portraits of his wife did hang in his house; the one by Rubens normally graced this room but had been removed temporarily. The other, a Van Dych, hung halfway up the grand staircase. Sensing the sarcasm in McColla's tone, however, he closed his mouth and said nothing. His cousin wasn't finished.

"And a widow, I hear? A high-born one, it seems? Ye got yersel' one of the wealthiest women in all England, albeit I hear she is a wheen o' years ouler than yoursel'. Can we get to meet her maybe, before we leave…. today, I mean?"

The Earl had almost visibly sunk back into his armchair at McColla's inquiry. He judged it to be tinged with unwelcome lechery and spluttered to answer. Already the attitude of detached superiority he had decided to adopt with these men was being seriously undermined. What was it about Alaster that so aggravated him? He was fully aware that he was not alone in this feeling; his cousin's charismatic power was legendary.

He bluffed it out, his voice spluttering as he had to clear his throat before responding. "My wife, sir, is no concern of yours at this time. I will thank you to leave her out of our converse today."

"As ye wish," smiled McColla. "I shoulda begun by gaein' congratulations on…on the 'catch', I suppose. *Math dhut*, and lang may your love for each other last, even efter the late Lord Buckingham's funds hae run oot." As he spoke he reached for the wine, poured himself another generous helping and raised his goblet in Randal's direction. "To yer guid sel's, the Earl and Countess of Antrim." 'Countess' sounded like a hiss, as he intended it to.

The others joined in warmly but only a fool would not have noticed the faint whiff of mockery in their toast. The Earl had little option but to receive the congratulations and move the conversation on without further acrimony.

"Now, cousins…to your sojourn in my estate. Do you have a plan? Do you have business calling you back to Colonsay, or to Scotland? I suppose I am asking you how long you are intending to foist yourselves and your friends upon the hospitality of my generous land steward in Ballintoy?"

Alaster McColla was quick to answer, having expected this query. "We hae nae fixed plan, tae be honest. Soon as we hear that things hae settled doon across the channel we'll return tae Colonsay. Argyll has been hard tae shake aff, typical Campbell that he is."

"Not like you to run from the challenge of a fight," observed the Earl provocatively.

"Whiles retreat is the canniest policy, don't ye think?" Raghnall McColla said.

"We'll get back at him," Alaster continued, "and reclaim our McDonnell birthright in Kintyre when the time suits us. Argyll is gan tae be vulnerable if he aligns himsel' o'er close wae the Covenanters and takes on the King. That'll be the time tae strike."

"I don't disagree there as you know. The King has my full support, as always. It is just a shame that recent plans came unstuck….and I am not blaming you for that, Alaster."

Alaster McColla looked him directly in his cunning eyes for a few seconds. "Aye," he said, "it is a strange creature ye are, Randal. Loyal tae the Crown an' loyal tae the faith o' the Gaels at the same time. Dae ye naw see that as an impossible path tae be troddin'?"

"I do not, sir!" the Earl blustered. "It is my hope to see the free exercise of the Roman religion, which I am devoted to and am engaged to maintain in duty to God, and for my own salvation. That does not impinge upon my loyalty to the interests of his majesty's honour and power."

The three Scots exchanged a doubtful look.

"There'll naw be many will understan' ye, I'll wager," Alaster said.

The Earl resumed his query.

"But what I want to know, gentlemen…are you returning to the islands or not? And if it is your intention to winter here in Ulster what are your plans for these next months? You cannot presume upon the kindness of our friend Stewart for so long?"

As McColla was about to answer he was interrupted by his brother.

"Would ye hae a garderobe aboot? I could dae wae a piss efter the journey, and then al' that wine o' yours, Randal."

"Certainly, Raghnall. Through the door and straight ahead to the end of the corridor, it is on the left."

"I'll come wae ye," said Murdo, his hand clutching at and pressing his sporran as he scurried across the room, a sight that suggested that Raghnall's request was well-timed. Alaster McColla waited until the two had gone.

"I understan' your concern an' I wouldnae wish tae put Archibald Stewart tae any mair trouble or expense. Would it be o'er much tae presume on our kinship, cousin, tae consider offering us some employment in your service here at Dunluce? Is there a role that we could fulfil here, short-term of course? We wouldnae expect tae be kept for free."

The Earl was completely wrong footed by this notion. 'Why hadn't I seen this coming?' he thought. 'He has me over a barrel here, especially after me raising the subject of him over-staying his welcome at Ballintoy. I have to try to respond positively to him but, in all honesty, having this gang of Scots about the place is a step too far, especially given the unpredictability of this volatile cousin. It will all be so unsettling to the tranquil pattern of life that Katherine and I have become accustomed to. And if we are travelling away, as we hope to continue doing, I cannot envisage a situation where Alaster and brother Raghnall are residing here with such autonomy. I cannot see Captain Digby or my other officials being comfortable with their presence in those circumstances. What can I answer at this moment to buy me some time?'

He hummed and hawed for a bit and McColla let him stew in his own ruminations, knowing that to deny the request pointblank was not an option. He decided to play a further card to add to the pressure.

"Could Raghnall and I, for instance, offer tae engage your men in a trainin' exercise? I'm sure ye would judge us able for such an undertakin'?"

It sounded an excellent idea but the Earl still hesitated. What if the two McCollas had a secret plan to train the McDonnell garrison and somehow attract them away from their service to him? Perhaps that had been his long-term goal all along and he had come to Antrim for that very reason. He was fully aware that Alaster McColla had always been on the lookout for mercenaries from whatever source to join him in his various campaigns against Archibald Campbell and other clan lairds across the water. Still, he was in no position to challenge his cousin's motivation, since he had been the one just now to suggest that the Scots were out-staying their welcome.

"That does sound like an attractive idea," Lord Antrim mused, "and I will consider it. Give me a few days to talk it over with her Ladyship and some of my staff here…we would have to consider questions of accommodation and kitchen and the like, not to mention what kind of military training you have in mind. Will you let me think about it?"

"I will."

"And while we are on the subject of military manoeuvres, what is this new tactic that I have been hearing about in connection to you and Raghnall? 'The Highland charge', I have heard it called. Tell me about it."

McColla smiled temptingly. "Certainly I'll tell ye aboot it, once we hae come tae an arrangement, a'right? In fact, ye can be witness tae yer garrison being the very first group o' soldiers in the whole o' Ireland tae practice the strategy. Noo that would be a feather in your cap. Phelim O'Neill would be sick wae jealousy."

From the quickened look in the eyes of Lord Antrim McColla knew he had offered a temptation which could not be resisted. Randal forced himself to nod thoughtfully, while his mind was racing with delight at the idea. His troops perfecting a new military tactic on the northern fringes of Ireland before any of his rivals had even heard of it! What was there not to cherish in the very imagining of it?

"It is a possibility," he said in measured tones, "and, as I say, I will get back to you when we have considered your proposal. Now, cousin, will you come for a tour of the castle with me? I have introduced some improvements that will impress you mightily."

McColla followed him outside where they were joined by no less than three castle wolfhounds, and eventually by Raghnall and Murdo. Randal led the way towards the most northerly point of the complex, the part which seemed to jut perilously on the precipice above the waves far below.

"This is the inner ward," he said, "and you will notice here that I have converted this building which had been used for storage into a sort of temporary chapel."

"A chapel? For Mass for yoursel's? Away frae prying eyes, I suppose?"

"Not only for ourselves; there are many devout Catholics in the surrounding area, indeed in our village here. They come too, whenever we can get the services of a priest."

"And ye dinnae feel any threat frae…"

"Not so much threat, now that Wentworth has been deposed. The Crown knows that the Duchess and I are loyal; my people here, both Irish and Scots, are decent, peaceable citizens. They also know that my friend Charles is no zealot; he doesn't really give a damn how people worship in the far north of Ireland, so his officials in Dublin know to leave me alone."

'My friend Charles!' thought McColla. 'The King is my best friend! Pah! What a pompous bragger this man is, him an' his blue-blood wife! Duchess, my arse! A few generations ago his people were squabblin' wae their neighbours o-er a stolen donkey.'

He kept his assessment to himself though; no point in antagonising anyone.

"Lang may Dublin let ye be," he said. "But storms can always blow up, even on the calmest day in these political waters. Ye're best tae aye be on your guard, cousin."

As they were leaving, the Earl took his guests through a fashionable loggia, showing them two brass cannons which his grandfather, Sorley Boy, had salvaged from a sunken Spanish galleon nearby. As he did so, Randal could not escape the suspicion of faint warning in McColla's conversation. Kinsman or not, he would keep a very tight eye on the two McColla McDonnells during whatever time they were going to be in Ulster. Men worth watching, he thought.

Chapter 17

Calm Before the Storm

Katie McKay

None of us saw what was coming.

We were all happily going about our business, oblivious to the ferment and change that was about to be unleashed on us. We could never have believed the devastating effects on our neighbourhood of what we were to experience over the next few months, events that would shape the rest of our lives.

My own normal life around then was very much illuminated by the whole thrill of falling in love for the first time. To the outsider looking in I was going about my daily work in the kitchen of Ballintoy House, all in my usual diligent fashion. I had nothing to do with the growing crowd of Highlanders about the place and I stayed well clear of them. I saw little of either Archibald Stewart or his wife. My friend Jean and I had manys a yarn behind the backs of those who were in charge, but not even Jean could have guessed the inner bliss that was glowing in me. I don't know if she ever suspected anything. Obviously I could not be telling her about Darach; it wasn't that I thought she would disapprove of me seeing an Irish Catholic boy, but at that stage I had to guard against the courtship becoming common knowledge. I would not have wanted news of it to reach the ears of the more devoutly religious in our Ballintoy parish, particularly the elders and the minister himself.

Reverend Blare's sermons had continued to be full of warnings about the contaminations of our present world. We needed to stay separate from almost everything that would give us any kind of earthly pleasure. Our way of life had to be blamelessly pure, a shining beacon of wisdom and serenity for the darkened sinners in our midst to follow. That seemed to be God's purpose for us here in Ireland according to his thinking…bring the heathen nations to His grace, save them from papist folly, show them the proper way to salvation and true faith. At least that was what I gathered during the times I was actually listening to him and not dreaming of my handsome harper.

And while I laboured in Ballintoy House my mind was far above the smells and dirt of that kitchen. I relived every moment of the times I had spent with Darach. We had been together on three occasions now since our introduction at the Lammas Fair; once at Dunseverick harbour, once at Knocknagalliagh, an ancient cairn in the sand-hills behind the strand at White Park Bay and once when I took him up to the Druid's Grave on Altmore.

The Druid's Grave, or Druid's Altar, as some people called it, was a strange pile of rocks high in the hills above Ballintoy, not far from our own bit of bogland, an area known as Altmore. Three huge rocks acted like giant legs, supporting one massive flat rock on top. My father had taken me to see it when I was just a wee lass, so it was doubly special to be there with the person that I believed would become even closer to me than my daddy had been. I treasured the memory of that visit years ago, but it faded a bit from my mind, overtaken by the experiences of that day with Darach.

First of all, the way he lifted me up to sit on top of that rock, his hands holding me in a very intimate manner, lingering longer there than they needed to, and me enjoying it too much to be even thinking of objecting. Later, the blackbird that came and sat in a twisted thorn bush just a matter of feet away from us; we were sitting so still, me leaning into his arms, that the bird stayed for ages and sang beautifully, just for us you would have thought. We talked so deeply then....now that was a memory that I would cherish forever, no matter how our love would develop from that point.

And that was one of the subjects we talked about that day on Altmore.

The thing about all my conversations with him was that there was never a second when I was wondering what he was really thinking. Everything was so open, so frank. We said exactly what we meant. That day was no exception. To me it was an incredible thing that, with this my first serious courtship, I had no doubts; Darach was mine and I was his and that was all there was about it. We had spoken these words to each other. Yes of course I was only seventeen and he nineteen...so how could we possibly have known? My answer to that would have been that when I was with him I felt a strange emotion of being in light, being in a special kind of brightness that made every shadow of darkness and doubt disappear. It was a wonderful feeling and it gave me confidence for the future. I recalled that our clergyman had read in the Bible the verse that says that there is no fear in love, words to that effect anyhow. That was how I felt about Darach...he made me feel the safest girl in Antrim, and the luckiest.

For such a quiet, serious boy Darach had great ambitions and he wasn't behind the door in sharing them with me. He wanted to become the best harper and the best harp-maker in all Ireland. He had made a vow to himself that he would do whatever it took, learn the secrets of the trade from whatever master craftsmen he could find and go wherever he needed to go to find them. He was driven by this need to perfect this art.

Would I go with him, he wanted to know. Of course I would, I would follow him to the ends of the earth.

"Even Dublin?" he asked.

"Wherever you go, I want to go too," I told him.

We were so naive, so full of hopes and dreams and ideas and, above all, of blind innocent love.

"What about your family?" he asked.

It wasn't an easy question to answer straight off the top of my head. "I think they will be happy for me," I said softly.

"Alex?"

I hesitated; I could not imagine how this might play out with my older brother and there was no way I could pretend everything would be easy with him.

"If he sees that it is best for me he will come round to the idea. My mother too, once she meets you and gets to know you. She will still have Connie and Alice at home, and Alex is doing a good job as the man of the house. And I'm fairly sure that Aunt Biddy will be on my side for she seems to like you, doesn't she?"

"She does, aye. She's a funny one," he said.

"She is. How will your family take to the idea of you being with me?" I asked, taking his hand and trying to divert attention from the problems I might have to face.

"Because you're Scotch, you mean?"

"I'm not Scotch. I was born here, not in Scotland," I argued.

"I know," he said, "but Scotch is just the name we have for yous."

"Alright, but how will your ones feel about us?"

"They'll be grand. They will likely be completely surprised that I have found such a fine looking girl, even more shocked that she wants to be with me."

"Will they not worry that I'm Presbyterian?"

"I doubt it. Why would they?"

"Because…because we are so…different in that way."

"That is not how I see it," he said. "But sure, if they think anything like that I'll tell them that it's just like when I am making a harp and I have to use two different trees. I might make the frame out of a wild cherry tree and the box from a willow, know what I mean? They hold together well if I do a good enough job with the joints."

"I don't follow you," I said.

"It'll be the same for you and me," he said. "Well jointed together."

"You and your harps," I laughed. "So who will we get to make the joint? I can't see my minister agreeing to it."

"Leave that with me," Darach said. "I think I know just the man."

He told me of a priest from Ballycastle that he knew, a thoughtful, caring man who had been at Dunluce Castle at times to serve Mass. This man of the cloth had obviously impressed and encouraged Darach.

"I hope you can meet him some time, and get to know him," he told me. "You will love him. He is such a gentleman, and full of lovely thoughts."

"Lovely thoughts about what?" I asked, a bit puzzled by the notion. Priests of the Catholic faith were not really held in much esteem within my community, indeed a sort of fear of them was instilled in us from an early age. I suppose every group of people needs a bogey-man, someone who embodies all the negative traits of the people who are not 'our-ones'. For a lot of my Protestant friends the priest seemed to represent a set of beliefs and rituals that we weren't comfortable with. Indeed it was fair to say that many of them had a dread of priests; they were thought to have a sinister darkness about them that was verging on black magic. So for Darach to speak so warmly about this priest was a bit of a shock to me, certainly a challenge to the type of thinking I would have been used to.

Darach must have noticed the hint of skepticism in my question, for he rolled over and up on to one elbow to look down at me.

"Do you find it strange that a priest could think nice wholesome thoughts?" he said. "You shouldn't be surprised. Not all clergy are so driven by the dogma of their church."

"Mine is," I said.

"Well, Father McGlaim talks a lot about the beauty of nature; he loves the natural world; he sees God in all of it; he loves every sort of animal, and what he doesn't know about birds and plants and trees isn't worth knowing…he would agree with you about that blackbird, the one that arrived on the fairy thorn just to sing a blessing on our love."

"I never said that."

"No but you thought it, didn't you?"

I couldn't help smiling at his intuition. "You're right," I said. "How did you know? Imagine me and a priest in agreement."

He wasn't finished telling me about his mentor though.

"He writes wee poems and things about all sorts of subjects. They are lovely to read."

"You can read?" I said, surprised. I didn't know any young men of Darach's age that had that gift.

"I can, and I can write. I am not great at the writing though. Father McGlaim has tried to improve me in that, give me more words and ways of putting things."

"And what do you want to write?" This was a new revelation to me; it almost scared me, to think that my fellow was so educated.

"Write poems and stories and songs, especially songs."

"Goodness Darach," I said. "Is there anything else I don't know about you? How did you learn letters?"

He laughed. "Well, my mother and father thought I was a very serious sort of child. They must have imagined I had some ability in that direction. They even had the idea that I was cut out to be a priest myself."

I could not help laughing at the idea of Darach as a priest. He let me giggle and then continued.

"So they thought I should be given the chance of learning. They took me to Bonamargy Friary to learn from the monks there. I think I was ten or eleven at the time."

"And what happened?" I asked.

"I didn't really settle. At the start it was alright. I learned my letters well enough and I could hold my own with the other boys, but after a couple of years I became unsettled. We would be walking on the beach near the Friary and I started to notice the girls from the village."

I pretended to be annoyed with him for this admission but he had a good answer for me.

"Maybe it is just as well, or I wouldn't be here with you now."

"True," I said, "but go on with your story."

"I wanted to leave and eventually my father came for me. Then I was at home for a while, but my father thought it would be better if I learned a proper trade. So he got me fixed up with these relatives, the McSparrans, at Dunluce, beside the castle. John could teach me his woodcraft and I could still get the odd lesson from some of the learnéd folk who would be about the place."

I was amazed at this side to him, amazed and impressed. I was also a bit concerned about his mention of being a priest. Again Darach seemed able to read my silence. He grabbed me and pulled me close to him in a jokey but very amorous way. "And in case you are worried Katie, do you seriously think I could ever give up this? You are too big a temptation."

I enjoyed his kiss to the full.

"And what sort of things might you want to write a song about?" I asked after he gave me back my mouth.

"I wouldn't have the language to write about that kiss, so you are safe there," he smiled.

"Good," I said, "so could you write about anything? Take that thorn bush for example? Could you write a story about it? Or a song or something?"

He thought about this challenge. "Maybe I could," he said. "I never thought of that before. There is a lot of history and mystery in these fairy trees. I must remember to ask Father McGlaim what he thinks about them."

Him again!

"He seems to know everything," I said.

"It's not like that," Darach said. "He knows because he is curious. He is always asking questions, even to me. He is trying to find out how I think, what I feel about things. That's just the way he is, curious."

"Is he curious about us?"

I was fairly sure Darach was so close to him that he would have talked about me.

Darach laughed. "You know me so well," he said. "Aye, I did mention you to him. He was surprised but… You'll just have to meet him. You'll like him, I know you will. He has a way of making you feel as if you matter to him."

"And do you think he would maybe marry us?" I asked. It was out of my mouth before I considered how bold the question would seem. My heart went skipping along at a great rate as Darach looked long into my eyes.

"Maybe he will. Whenever you meet him you can ask him," he joked. "Sure it's all your idea."

We couldn't have known it at the time but that wonderful day we had together at the Druid's Altar on Sunday 17th October 1641 was to be the last for a very long time; indeed it might well have been the last ever for our relationship, had it not been for a number of very fortunate happenings and had it not been for the compassion and bravery of a number of good people, Darach and his friendly priest among them.

Chapter 18

The Fairy Thorn

*There's a Fairy Thorn on top of the hill
It has stood for years and it's standing still
By the Druid's grave, by the old stone wall
By the blackbird's song and the curlew's call
By the curlew's call and the mountain mist
Where the ocean and the land have kissed
Like an ageing man in the bending wind
There stands the Fairy Thorn*

*There's a Fairy Thorn and it guards the cliff
And its twisted trunk is old and stiff
By the scented breath of the yellow whin
It's branches stretched by the western wind
By the curlew's call and the mountain mist
Where the ocean and the land have kissed
Like an ageing man in the bending wind
There stands the Fairy Thorn*

*There's a Fairy Thorn and its roots go deep
In the minds of the people who love to keep
All the old traditions of history
Of the Fairy Thorn and its mystery
By the curlew's call and the mountain mist
Where the ocean and the land have kissed
Like an ageing man in the bending wind
There stands the Fairy Thorn*

Chapter 19

Rumours - October 1641

Darach O'Cahan

A week since I spent the day with Katie.
    I tried again this morning to put poetic words on her. *Amhrán grá*. A love song. On my feelings for her. These words do not take shape. The truths are in my head. They don't seem able to survive when I force them from my quill, shrivelling and dying on its tip. The song of the fairy thorn came easily to me. The lyric followed the tune…naturally, without effort of thought, already half-formed at my hand. They appeared on my page as if prepared in advance. Or loaned to me from beyond.
    But not so for the song of my lover. All words are a disappointment, worse…a sacrilege. They tarnish the grace of this bonding. When I say them in my head they are out of tune, like a poorly strung harp. Or like a thought that refuses to be carved.
    Since that first sight of her, that summer's day vision above the causeway, I think of no other. Her loveliness has enchanted me.
    That smile, a shaft of sparkling sunlight through half-stripped branches. Those eyes, the colour of autumn grass, with a dusting of gold and brown flecks, like fallen leaves. Her hair, hanging long and straight, rich chestnut with some lighter strands, like the grain of an old apple tree. Her face, delicate but strong, open, curious, bronzed with a scattering of sun-freckles. Her lips, enticingly perfect in form, set on the edge of laughter. And she is tall at seventeen, slender, her shapeliness perfectly sculptured, matched only by the surprise of that ready humour she shelters.
    I am entirely beguiled by the person behind this beauty.
    We must be together. I want her entirely, not in lust, not in greed, more in the sense of completion. Without her I will live as half a human. With her we will be infinitely more than two.
    But such thoughts defy the limitations of song.
    As words smudge themselves on my lips, so my fingers stiffen on the strings. My music fades to quietness.
    I embarrass myself. I surrender and stop.

****

It is a Sunday, 24th day of this month. I have walked early on the long strand beyond the chalk cliffs. We call this place the 'White Rocks'. Beside me the furrowed ocean. Low, gentle waves, rustling, dissipating, surrendering to the rise of the sand. A mile or two out to sea the sloping Skerries. These are a string of small, green-coated islands which have always looked to me as if they were battling against the swell of the Western Ocean, striving to escape out to sea, to get away from our north Antrim shore.

I have marvelled, today as always, at the dark profile of Dunluce Castle against the honeyed glow of sunrise in the October sky. Towering above that tall stretch of cliff, it has always managed to look impregnable and vulnerable at the same time. I have often wondered at the courage and skill of its builders. They must have had to cling to the sheer rock-face, creating foundations on the very edge of disaster, laying stone upon stone to build this striking edifice. Dunluce is a work of audacious art. A building of breath-taking beauty. A statement of Gaelic Ulster power on the most northerly fringe of Ireland.

The purging sea-breeze above the White Rocks has enlivened me as I return. What a place to live!

When I reach the entrance to the castle I am surprised to meet my uncle Gilladubh and some companions.

They have journeyed from Dunseverick this morning. They expect to hear Mass. I have to tell Gilladubh that the sacrament will not take place here today. He is disappointed, as is his son, my cousin Manus. No priest has been arranged. They did not know.

The Earl is not in residence today.

"Somebody should have let us know," my uncle grumbles. "A bloody waste of a journey."

"Not yet a waste, father," says Manus. "A drink maybe?"

"Aye. We'll try the public house of the Protestant. Jimmy Stewart will not turn away old friends with big thirsts on them, Sabbath or no."

"True. He likes his shilling too much."

In the absence of Mass, a more earthy diversion will have to suffice.

They turn from the castle gatehouse. Make their way to the village tavern around the corner. I follow. Nothing better to be doing this day.

Jimmy Stewart's place is a short walk. He opens a room for the Dunseverick visitors. Outside I meet with young Thomas, son of the publican, a curious, pale-faced ruffian of a lad who loves nothing better than to chat. Through the open shutters I see beer poured. Over the next while it is poured very often. The sounds are of increasing drunkenness. I turn away. Thomas nudges me and laughs knowingly. "Bleutered they will be," he says.

Later I walk alone towards St Cuthbert's Church just beyond our village. Once of the old faith, of course, now converted to Anglican, whether it wants it or not. It services the folk who settled in this new village, the Scotch who came some thirty years ago. So I am told by John and Eilish.

In the distance I hear the thunder of hurrying horses. Coming closer though. Dust rises to the south. They come quickly into view. Cloaks furl out behind like flags. A dozen riders at full gallop pass me and into the castle's outer ward. I do not recognise them, so fast are they travelling. Only one mount is familiar to me, the great chestnut horse of Archie Boyd, a Dunluce neighbour in our village. The frothing stallion has galloped a long way, and very quickly.

Why the urgency? I wonder.

By the time I get to the yard most are dismounted, all but three.

Horses lathered in foaming sweat, straining against their reins for the water-troughs. They are allowed to drink.

A shouted command from one rider, the leader it seems. Shouting in English to those still mounted.

"You go on to Dunseverick and Ballintoy. Inform Gilladubh and Archibald Stewart. Do it in haste."

Three horses turn from the troughs, too slowly for the leader. I know Captain McPheadress' voice; he is loud, agitated, impatient.

"I said in haste!"

Back out to the road they trot. Then kick up gravel and into full gallop. Too late I realise… but Gilladubh O'Cahan is here at Dunluce. I move towards McPheadress timorously. His mood is gruff.

"Captain," I say, "Gilladubh is here. He is in Dunluce at this moment."

McPheadress looks hard at me for a second, as if doubting me.

"Gilladubh is in the castle?"

"No, he and Manus are drinking in the village. Have been for a good while," I tell him.

"Humpt," he grunts, "just what we need, some drunken Irish. Do you think you can persuade them away from their liquor and bring them to the castle, Darach? Tell them it is a matter of the greatest importance and urgency. Drag them here if necessary."

"I will do my best," I say, more confident in word than in spirit.

Word of the irregular arrival is spreading through the narrow lanes. I hear muttered comments. Veils of worry on faces as people glance up and down the village street.

I enter Stewart's tavern. Confront the three drinkers.

"Uncle. Cousin Manus! You are summoned to the castle. You must come at once," I say, astonished at the tone of authority I have managed to conjure up.

Never before have I told my uncle, the provost of the Route, what to do. He is equally aware of this fact. Looks at me as if the world has gone mad. The company is speechless at my audacity.

"The order comes from Captain McPheadress, gentlemen. He sent me and with urgency. Some news of importance. He just rode in at great speed with a detachment. He has sent to Dunseverick and Ballintoy…so you must come, now."

"My God," said Gilladubh, struggling up from behind the narrow table, "what can this be about? We better go and see what news he has."

The younger men are more reluctant. They down the dregs of their tankards in long gulps. Rifting wind from the deep of their bellies they steady themselves against the wall as they wander after Gilladubh.

I follow behind them myself. Several other onlooking villagers do as well. Back to the outer ward. McPheadress is standing on the dismount step in front of the stables, talking behind his hand to Captain Digby. A crowd has gathered. Some Irish, but mainly Scotch from the village. Nobody knows what this is about, but already the two groups are giving each other suspicious looks. The apprehension here could be sliced with a knife.

Digby calls for quiet. "Captain McPheadress has an announcement to make," he tells us. "It is not good news, but I ask you all to bear with us till we know the ins and outs of everything. There is to be no panic."

But panic there instantly is, in the minds and faces of all my neighbours, and that before we even hear these tidings.

McPheadress steps forward.

"The news I have been given to tell you today is that a rebellion of the Irish against the Crown has broken out in Tyrone and other parts."

A rebellion? What rebellion?

Gasps and hands to mouths, mainly of the Scotch among us. But some Irish too.

"It is being led by Sir Phelim O'Neill. There has already been slaughter of English settlers in parts of those western counties. So far they have not reached the river Bann, so we think they are not in Antrim or Coleraine as yet. But I believe that we must prepare for all possibilities in case they do cross. Captain Digby is to take charge of these preparations until we hear from the Earl."

Digby holds up his hands against the growing clamour.

"Pray listen, citizens," he says. "In these circumstances the standing order is for the men of the village to assemble here in this outer ward with our own soldiers from the castle garrison. We will be forming companies and issuing what few weapons we have."

"Do you mean just the Scotch?" calls a sarcastic voice. I turn to see that the question is from my cousin Manus. The look on his face is insolent, mocking, aggressive. I cannot understand this. It is the drink talking, surely.

Digby stares at him. "No, I don't mean only the Scotch. We will all be in this together, Manus O'Cahan. Lord Antrim would say the same if he were here."

"If he were here," mutters Manus, loud enough for those around him to hear. Murmured agreement and nodding heads.

Digby continues. "So gentlemen, I will give you until the next bell to go to your homes and put your things in order. Then you must reassemble here for further instructions. Alright, go; be quick now!"

People do as they are told, nervously in the very tense atmosphere which has descended among us. I watch my neighbours, both men and women. Countenances are stoney grey as the castle's walls. Uncertainty and dread written clear on every face.

Every face except those of Manus and some of his antagonistic friends. Grinning, they lean against the stable wall to take a piss.

I watch them like a hawk; either the beer has excited them or they find the news of O'Neill's rising very much to their taste. There's a glint in their eyes. I cannot hear their whispered conversation, but I have no problem discerning their response to these tidings. Their enthusiasm for this rising is clear to see. They can barely contain their anticipation.

Meanwhile I watch Gilladubh as he wanders back to his friend Jimmy Stewart. Doubtless another few beers to drown out anxious thoughts of what might be about to befall our lovely land.

****

Such days as this are like winter's worst snow storms. Flurries of rumours come thick and fast and blur our vision, our judgement.

Mid afternoon. I hear that my uncle has somehow slipped past the guards at the foot of the funnel. People say he has entered the gatehouse and raised the drawbridge behind him! Now he is ensconced in the upper ward. Alone there but for some servants, he is refusing entrance to all others. I think that his sense of self-importance has been fuelled by the amount of wine he has had today. He is a small, drunken magistrate.

Digby is frustrated. His spluttering arguments fail to make it through the bars of the main gate and into Gilladubh's befuddled brain.

"I will not come out! I know what youss are sssc..scheming. I am Lord Randal's pro...provossstt," he slurs, his head bobbing like driftwood in the tide. "I have it on good authority, this scheme."

"Oh, come on, Mr O'Cahan," Digby pleads. "What do you have on such good authority? Who is this good authority?"

"Good authority is who he is!"

A local man steps forward beside the Captain.

"It was me," he says humbly.

"What was you? Who are you anyway?"

"I am Doole McSparran of Bushmill, kin to John McSparran here at Dunluce."

"And what have you told the provost that has him in this state?"

"It was what I heard in the toon."

"What toon? What did you hear?"

"A man in Bushmill toul me that there be five hundred of Argyll's Protestant soldiers comin' this road."

He looks over his shoulder towards the lane above, as if expecting their arrival any minute.

"And when were you told this? How long since?"

"I dunno… a while anyways."

Digby is torn. Gilladubh, hopelessly intoxicated, has over-reacted to what is likely a false tale and shut himself in the castle, locking everyone else outside. But might there be truth in the report? Should he heed this rumour? A crowd gathers around him at the raised drawbridge. Tension and uncertainty spread like the stench of a rotting whale carcass.

As the rising tide of fear swills among us we hear the sound of horses in the distance, coming from the east, from Bushmills direction.

Some of the crowd, convinced of a counter-attack by Argyll soldiers, begin to cry to Gilladubh for admission to the safety of the castle. The clamour increases as horse-hooves clatter closer, now on the cobblestones at the outer gate. Heads turn to see who is arriving. Relief on many faces. No tartan-clad warriors this time.

Instead, familiar figures…Archibald Stewart, followed by Tirlough Óge and then, the reassuring presence of Earl's much younger brother, Alexander McDonnell.

It strikes me to wonder if Alexander has ridden all the way from his home at Glenarm, the other McDonnell castle which sits in the Antrim glens.

I am glad to see them. Alexander will bring some much-needed authority in the absence of the Earl. Archibald Stewart will bring wisdom and order to our disarray; a strong and calming man. Tirlough Óge will be able to talk sense to his father if Manus can't. Or won't.

"What is happening here?" asks Stewart, confused at the sight of a yard full of idle Scotch and Irish, and the castle drawbridge raised against them. Captain Digby appears a bit sheepishly and begins to explain this ludicrous situation to the new arrivals.

Suddenly we hear a shout and see a wild-haired Gilladubh looking down at us from high on the battlements of the gatehouse. Swaying up there like a withered thistle caught in a strong breeze. Archibald Stewart addresses him brusquely.

"What was it that had you so worried, Gilladubh? A foolish rumour about Argyll troops? Come on down now. Open the gate and let us in."

"I'll no come down," shouts Gilladubh, fighting manfully to articulate the words, even as he speaks them. "T'is gate is staying shut! I see what…what is happening here. Them Argyll ones…going to take control of the castle. They will join all you Scotch ones 'gainst us… we will be left out…outside to fend for ourselves."

"That is nonsense man! There are no Argylls within a hundred miles of here. What would bring them to Antrim, for God's sake?"

"I dunno, they are likely… looking for their old eminy, McColla."

Alexander McDonnell steps forward to win the argument. Not as towering as his long-limbed brother, he still carries an air of authority.

"Mr O'Cahan," he calls up. "Put your mind at ease. There are no Argyll soldiers in Antrim. McColla is safe in Ballintoy House. All is well. Content yourself man and come down from that tower before you fall down. Nobody is going to harm you…you have my word."

I see Gilladubh back away from the embrasure and I imagine he will descend the tower now, one way or another.

Stewart addresses Digby and McPheadress as the drawbridge is being lowered.

"How on earth could you let this happen? Where were your guards? You have a garrison of trained soldiers here! But a drunken magistrate can lock himself in the castle with access to what weaponry is stored there, and the good people of Dunluce locked outside? And all this fiasco at a time when we are facing serious threat from the Tyrone rebels. It is madness, Captain. Utter madness!"

"I can only apologise…"

"Wait till the Earl hears of it!"

"I know how it must seem, Mr Stewart, but honestly…"

"The Earl and his castle are loyal to the King! See to your duty, sir."

Mr Stewart, impressive yet again. His anger fades. He goes to reassure those watching from the yard.

I have a fleeting query. Where is McColla all this time? It seems everyone else of importance is here in this debacle at Dunluce. Not the bold warrior though. I have not exactly missed his sarcasm, but if he is still at Ballintoy I find myself hoping, praying that Katie is well protected from him.

As the evening wears towards night I sit alone on a stone wall at the edge of our village. I watch the wine-red sunset pouring itself over the Inishowen hills, colouring the sea, glinting off the chalk-white cliffs. I need to talk to Katie. She needs to hear that, whatever commotion this conflict throws against us, whatever division it threatens, she and I will not be divided.

Chapter 20

A Defensive Plan

Darach O'Cahan

Four days later.

Gilladubh and Tirlough Óge are still ensconced at Dunluce. What fear is on them that they think it wiser to stay in Dunluce? Their own castle at Dunseverick must not inspire much confidence in them. Manus seems to have disappeared.

Alexander McDonnell appears to be in command here now, in the continued absence of his brother, our Earl.

On the Thursday Archibald Stewart returns to us from Ballintoy. He looks preoccupied, busy, his burly figure striding importantly down the cobbled yard towards the gatehouse, cloak flapping behind him like a rook's wings.

I watch from the open door of our carpentry workshop beside the brewhouse. It crosses my mind to ask him if he has seen Katie. Briefly only. I desist. The man has far bigger fish to fry.

Surprisingly he greets me as he passes my door. I am amazed that he remembers me from the few times we have met, at McColla's welcome feast and in MacNeill's at Ballycastle.

"Still making instruments?" he asks, pleasant of manner.

"No, no," I say. "That is a spare time pursuit. This is a cabinet door."

"Ah right. Good work lad."

He passes on down the funnel to the drawbridge below.

Katie. What is she doing right now?

It is such a pity she cannot read. I would have written some words for her and entrusted them to Mr Stewart when he is leaving. I feel I could trust him. I would love to have sent the lyric about the fairy thorn; she has not heard that one yet. No point of course, but I promise myself that at some stage in our future I will teach her to read and write. I know she will be fit for it. She is a smart one.

Can I escape Dunluce this coming Sunday to visit her? It is my fervent hope that I won't be hindered from these visits by these new uncertainties. I can't envisage being involved in the conflict myself. I will be happy to avoid everything to do with it, to remain here doing my usual menial tasks.

By midday some new arrivals have landed here and entered the castle. Not ones I welcome either. Alaster and Raghnall McColla McDonnell with their band of kilted Highlanders. A dramatic and colourful sight.

Since their coming to Ballintoy nothing has happened by way of hair-cutting or beard-trimming, but they do look as if they have been cleaned up. Perhaps a few soakings in the harbour. Invigorated, their eyes seem to shine out from under their helmets like points of bright light. Smiles on every face. Their dialogue as they dismount is boisterous. Ribald jokes are bouncing around between them. These men are doing what they love to be doing…perhaps, more to the point, what they anticipate to be doing in the near future.

The scent of skirmish is in their nostrils. They are a pack of wild dogs sniffing a quarry.

I hunker down behind my half door, so as to avoid conversation with Alaster. Too late. He has seen me from the moment he came into the courtyard.

"Harpy," he calls as he strides past. Giant steps for a giant man, I think. "Sing us a welcome there."

I stay where I am, keek over the door when I sense they have moved on. I watch their backs disappear through the gatehouse.

This man! Why am I so intimidated by him? His brother seems less threatening, but what is this instinct in me that wants to avoid Alaster McColla's glare, his disdainful tongue?

****

They are back out of the castle. The bell has rung to summon the locals. Archibald Stewart stands high on the dismount step in the outer yard. He is clearing his throat as others from the village, almost all men, meander hesitantly in from their daily activities. Behind him stands Alexander McDonnell, Alaster McColla and Raghnall McDonnell, the two Captains, Digby and McPheadress, uncle Gilladubh, Tirlough Óge and the men in kilts. It is an imposing line up. No-one is going to argue back against the land steward today, that is for certain.

"People of Dunluce," he begins, a bit too grandly I think, "these are perilous times; you don't need me to tell you that. Some of you will have heard the rumours. Phelim O'Neill continues his mutinous insurrection against us. His forces have moved into the county of Londonderry and advance towards the Bann river. We have no intelligence that they intend to cross into Antrim, but by the same token we have no reason to suspect that they will not. We are therefore in a very serious situation. Already rumours of atrocities abound. There can be no under-estimating the dire straits we are all in!"

A rumbling of suppressed anger at this statement from the majority of those listening.

"The good Earl is fully aware of the predicament of his people here in the Route and the Glens."

I detect a small muttering of what I take to be resentment at his absence. If Stewart is aware of it he doesn't let it show, continuing.

"He writes to me," he says, holding up a scroll for us all to see, "and he bids you all to be of good courage. He promises to return to Dunluce at the earliest possible opportunity."

More shifting of feet, quick glances between neighbours, the sounds of sucking through tight, cynical lips.

"This is another part of the letter that I feel I want to read to you all." He holds up the scroll and begins. "'To my great consternation I learn', says Lord Randal, 'that my relative, Sir Phelim O'Neill, has risen in rebellion, while at the same time proclaiming his allegiance to King Charles; and furthermore, O'Neill wants us to believe that apparently the King is completely in favour of this military campaign here in Ulster. He assures us that there shall be no harm done to the loyal citizens of the King who live among us, in other words he intends no harm to the Scottish and English.'"

Stewart breaks off from the letter briefly to comment. "O'Neill must take us all for fools! How can he claim allegiance to the Crown but attack its loyal citizens, then imagine no harm shall come to them during this rebellion? He is speaking in riddles. It makes no sense whatsoever! My feeling on this, and it is shared by my colleagues here present," he says, indicating those lined up behind him, "is that this is just a ploy to try to get others of the Irish Lords to lend their support to his rising."

All this talk of distant politicking is leaving the audience a bit restless. What we need to hear is information of a more practical kind, such as what we are expected to be doing here at Dunluce in the meantime. We are just about to find out.

"Lord Antrim is in Meath, at Slane Castle," continues the land steward, "but he orders us to organise in the following manner. We are to form a defensive regiment of three companies. One will be of his Irish tenants in the Route; the second will be of his Scotch tenants; the third will be a mixed company from Dunluce, tenants and garrison troops. It will be led by Alaster McColla and his Highland troops. I am sure some will be only too glad to do so, learn from McColla, and get to experience some of his battle strategies."

"Who'll command the other companies?" someone asks, not unreasonably.

"The Irish will be under the command of Tirlough Óge O'Cahan, and I myself shall lead the Ballintoy folk."

"Lead us where?" pipes up a nervous voice.

"Not to any particular place at this present time. Just to be prepared and well trained and ready should O'Neill become a threat in this area. To begin with it will be about defending our own areas. Later we may be called on to fight in other places, you understand."

"And is this the sum total of us?" asks another villager.

"Not at all, sir," comforts Stewart. "There are already others, from Ballycastle and Ballintoy. There will be men from Coleraine, Ballymoney and the local villages. Many will flock to our flag once the word gets out."

Much conversation now erupts among those gathered in the courtyard. Questions bounce around between the groups of people and, cleverly I think, Mr Stewart allows a few minutes for this reaction to subside. He then shouts for silence again and he gets it.

"I hear some queries, but let us do it in an orderly way. John…you go first."

My step-father looks surprised to be invited to speak, but he rummages around in his bag of doubts to find an appropriate question.

"What about the older folk like myself? The bones are very stiff. I doubt I could march very far."

"Nobody will be forced to join if they are too old or if they have an infirmity, you have my word, but this must not be used as an excuse by those who would prefer to be minding their cattle," answers Stewart. "Next there?"

"I'm not one o' yer garrison soldiers; I have no experience of fighting," says someone, "and I drag a leg. Do I have to fight?"

"I see him taking that leg out for a drag over to big Ellen's place every night," comes a voice from the middle of a group of younger men. Laughter relieves our tension.

"There's naw a hate wrang wae his middle leg anyways," says another.

"Men like yourself are still needed," says Stewart as the joviality subsides. "There will be horses to mind, cattle to be driven with us, other food to be found, cooking to be done."

"God love us if you are cooking for us, Billy! We'll all be poisoned."

"And here's an important point," shouts Stewart. "There may be long marches in this campaign. It may well last through the winter months, so you all need to have plenty of decent clothing, sheep-skin and the like to keep you warm at night. And make sure your brogues are going to last."

"Brogues?" somebody calls. "Where are we going to get brogues?"

Stewart looks at Digby and McPheadress. They look at each other.

"Who is the cobbler around here?" Stewart asks.

Ezekiel Brown shuffles forward through the crowd. "That's me," he says shyly.

"Just yourself? Nobody else?"

"Aye, just me…but I have had a couple of apprentices. They're working not that far away," says Brown. He knows what's coming. His skills are going to be needed.

"Right," says Stewart. "Find them today. You're going to need them for you'll be working round the clock for the next while making sure all these men have decent brogues, new ones or repaired ones. McPheadress, I am putting you in charge of finding as much leather as you can. There must be some in the castle stores, but, if not, you are to scour the countryside for it, starting today. Digby, you are responsible for making sure the weapons are all in best working order."

He continues barking out instructions to various people.

I am starting to realise that I am not going to be able to avoid involvement in this military campaign, like it or not. This will be a first. The thought is not easy to accept. I do not see myself in any sense as a warrior. What role might I end up playing in this war, if indeed a war it becomes? Nobody has any use for a harper, or a harp maker…maybe a joiner at times, I suppose. And whose company would I be most comfortable being part of? Certainly not McColla's. Probably not Stewart's either, so most likely I will end up under my own cousin, though doing what I cannot guess.

I need to know when we are expected to join up for this military training so I venture a question above the clamour that has begun. Stewart hears it but so too does McColla. He scoffs in my direction, as if to say, 'You are not a soldier, boy. We will not be needing you.'

Mr Stewart answers though. "Tomorrow morning. If not then, within the week. The sooner the better. You all need to get your things in order and be ready for it."

Get your things in order!

Sounds a bit terminal.

What I hear in his words is this…make sure you say goodbye to those you cherish.

I have a number of folks I need to see. The McSparrans, my own family at Straid, and Katie of course.

I cannot leave it any longer. I must go to her tomorrow. She deserves that.

Chapter 21

Fear Rising

Katie McKay

The atmosphere in our kitchen changed after we got the news about the rebellion in Tyrone. We were all praying that it wouldn't come here, our fingers crossed up to our elbows that our peaceful wee neighbourhood wouldn't be disrupted.

Alex was the main worry though. He and his friends were all for joining up with Archibald Stewart's militia to defend Ballintoy. Why anybody would be interested in attacking such an insignificant wee village with its simple kirk and manor was beyond me. But according to Mr Stewart that might just happen, hence the Earl's instruction to get the men ready and prepared to fight. My mother and Aunt Biddy were beside themselves with worry. Biddy spent most days with the big tears running down her cheeks. And that was before Alex had even joined up, let alone fought anybody.

"He'll be kilt altogether," she kept wailing.

Alex was only determined to do what everyone else who was able would be doing, and nothing my mother could say would stop it.

Her argument was that Alex should be excused from such service because he was the only man left in our house. I could see her point but Alex refused to listen.

"Can't you see that is all the more reason for me to join up," he argued. "I have to do my bit. Daddy would have done his bit, wouldn't he? And he's not here, so it falls to me."

"And if anything happens to you what becomes of us, you ever stop to think about that?"

"Agh mother! Nothing is going to happen to me."

"You think not? There must be thousands of grieving mothers who have heard those exact words. There are plenty of other men about the place who haven't the same responsibilities that you have. Let them go."

"How would I look them in the eye when they come back, tell me?"

"If they come back. And if they have eyes to look in," she said. "You have no idea what sort of bother you might be in if you join up. Those Irish could get very angry; it could be a terrible time."

"You expect me to just sit here and watch Bruce and Tommy and the rest of them march off to fight to protect us? Think again, mother."

My mother was exasperated with him, I could tell that, but Alex had always been very headstrong. When he got something in his mind he was nearly impossible to move on it. I knew that from how he had refused to take to the idea that Darach and I could be together.

Darach! Immediately I thought, "He must not get involved in this proposed army. No, he couldn't possibly be thinking about it. Violence is not in his nature, indeed it is the very opposite of him as a person. He is a craftsman and a bit of a dreamer, never a military type. I just hope he keeps safe if it ever comes across into Antrim."

Over at Stewart's place I had noticed men working at various parts of the house; if anything they seemed to be turning it into more of a fortress than the Manor House it was usually thought to be. The building had always looked imposing, but in a small-scale, modest kind of way, as if it didn't wish to be considered as too haughty of itself. Archibald had never been a great one for appearing high and mighty, or above his station as a land agent; that humility had always been shown in how he had built and maintained his house. It did have a fairly daunting wall around it, but that day in late October some heavy loads of what look like causeway rocks had been arriving. I could only think they were to raise the height of the wall, maybe even buttressing it where it was weakest.

The house itself was a solid looking building, four-square in shape and almost as tall as it was wide. If a stranger arrived over the hill and saw it standing there in the middle of those lovely, flat fields he might have thought somebody had started to build a traditional tower house, but got fed up, stopped half-way through and just stuck a roof on it. The corners of the building were outset at the top and built in a semi-circular fashion so as to provide better sight of the areas below. This idea was called a turret, I had gathered, and was for defence purposes. On the ground floor there was the main hall stretching from front to back; beside it were the kitchen, pantry and buttery, with other small rooms on the other side. On the floor above were five bedrooms, not all of which were used. The oak staircase was very grand and had always struck me as too big for the hall. A smaller set of simple steps led up to a third floor where servants' quarters were crammed into the attic space.

We Ballintoy folk were proud of our big house and quite proud of its owner and his wife. Many places lacked this kind of devotion to their leader, but he never had any reason to doubt our support…and it was this loyalty that he knew he could rely on in times like these.

One evening Aunt Biddy had gone for her usual evening dander over by Larrybane. She had always loved to sit by those gleaming white cliffs and watch the workers mining blocks of limestone, their shouts mingling with the screams of the sea-birds in the still autumn air. She always arrived back in just about sunset, ready for a sup of buttermilk and a bit of soda bread to take with her to her bed in the lean-to. That day, however, she arrived back much earlier, some sort of scheming look about her. I didn't know if anyone else noticed it, but every time she caught my eye she was making the strangest wee signals, nodding her head towards the door and making quick pointing motions with her hand. I nearly asked her outright what had come over her, but as I opened my mouth she gestured with her finger to her lips; I stayed silent, but her strange performance went on…until I finally began to suspect that she wanted me to go outside. Maybe she wanted to follow me out; perhaps she was up to some prank; or could she be bearing some mischievous message? Eventually I rose from the settle-bed and sidled towards the door. Another glance at Biddy and I saw that tiny nod and smile, so I knew I had guessed right. She wanted me to go out into the evening. Thankfully it wasn't teeming rain as it had been earlier in the day. I stood just beyond the door, hesitating, waiting for Biddy to appear behind me with an explanation about this mischievous behaviour. She didn't come. I was about to turn and go back in when I heard a sound over to my right, behind the side wall of our byre.

"Katie. It's me."

My heart knew that whispering voice even before my ears had registered it. "Darach? Good lord, where did you come from?" I said as I ran to him. He grabbed me and held me close for a second.

"We better go somewhere a bit safer," he said and I followed him along our back lane towards the steps down to the harbour.

"Your aunt did a good job for us there. She's a decent lady," he said as we stopped to sit on a rocky outcrop.

"Don't think she's ever been called that before," I laughed, "but she seems to like you, for whatever reason."

"I couldn't think of any way to get you to come out until she came wandering along. I was about to knock your door."

"What? Glad you didn't do that!" I said.

"She stopped me. So she told you that I was here?"

"Not in so many words…she gave me enough signals to get me to come outside. I didn't expect to be seeing you though. It's a nice surprise…but how come you arrived tonight? I wasn't expecting to see you till the end of the week."

He was silent for a moment and drew me close to his chest so I couldn't see his eyes. It was comforting and worrying at the same time. I sensed fear in the slight shudder his body gave.

"What is it, Darach?"

"This trouble, this rising."

"I know. It is horrible, isn't it…but it won't affect us? You won't be going anywhere sure?"

Again the silence, the tightening of the hug and this time his face comes down on my shoulder. I knew now.

"You can't be? You are not a soldier, Darach. You can't be joining this defence thing?"

"I'm not a soldier, you are right, but that doesn't mean I won't be involved."

"Why not? How will you be involved?"

He told me all that had taken place at Dunluce.

"Whenever it was all over," he said, "and people had been put into their different companies…your Mr Stewart came to talk to me. I had sort of volunteered myself with Tirlough Óge's soldiers. He is my cousin after all, and most of the men I know over there were joining him."

"But you are not a fighter, Darach. I know you. You are the sweetest, most gentle boy at all. How can you even think of learning to use a musket or a bayonet? It's not you! It's not my Darach!"

I was becoming quite emotional, a mixture of anger and fear and helplessness. I was far more worked up about this than I was about the idea of my own brother going to battle. At least Alex had a belligerent side to his nature; he enjoyed a good fight with a bull or a boar about the farm. He even had a bent nose from when he picked a fight with a dour old ram we used to have. Alex was the sort of person who could look after himself in a conflict. Darach was more likely to be thinking about how to play some tune or other than planning how to stay alive in a fight.

He smiled weakly at me. "I like that," he said. "'It is not my Darach'. I agree, I am not a fighter… so what I was going to tell you is that Mr Stewart gave me a special sort of job."

"What job?"

"Well, I won't have to be fighting as such. He wants me to be a courier, sort of a messenger between the different companies and the different headquarters. It's an important role."

"I would rather you weren't going to be involved at all, but at least that sounds a bit safer. How come he picked you for that job?"

"I don't really know. He asked me if I could read and write. Said something about how if he needed a message taken somewhere when he is busy, or he's not able to write it he could tell it to me and I would have to write it down, then deliver it."

"But how will you know where to go?"

"Well….I suppose I know the area as well as anybody; I have been all over the Route with John when we go looking for timber."

"So you are a message boy?" I didn't mean it to sound so dismissive but it did cause Darach to give me a look.

"It is better than killing folk," he said. "Anyway, as well as messages he said that I might have to observe what is happening and write notes on it, sort of as a witness. I think he must trust me for some reason."

"And will you be working under him?"

"Likely. Maybe under all three of the colonels. It might actually be an interesting thing to be doing. I will get to have a sort of overview of everything. It beats looking after horses, or making weapons for them."

"How did you get here tonight? You didn't walk all this way?"

"I didn't. I asked the Captain if I could take a horse from the stable and go for a long ride. I told him that I needed to get used to riding and the horse needed to get used to me. He thought it was a good idea. Gave me a lovely grey mare to try. She's called *Liath*. So here I am."

"And where did you hide her?"

"She's tied to the rail over behind the church."

"Aye, but aren't you so clever. You are surely not going to ride back all the way in the dark?"

"Ah no. I was hoping I could maybe stay with you. Would that be alright? I am sure your mother and Alex wouldn't…"

I had another of those strange flutters somewhere near the bottom of my stomach…but, even in the twilight that had fallen I could still see the twinkle in his eyes. I played along with him though.

"That's a great idea. I am sure aunt Biddy wouldn't mind at all, sharing her bed with you like! Or maybe you'd prefer to climb to the loft and slide in beside Alex?"

He laughed and drew my head close to his. "You are some craic, Katie McKay. No, I have another plan. You see, I haven't seen my parents for a while so I put that idea into my request to the Captain and he agreed. I'll ride inland to Straid, it's not too far through the bogland. I will stay there tonight and ride back to Dunluce in the morning."

"Very thoughtful," I said, "and thank you for coming to see me first. Are you sure you don't want to snuggle in beside my brother though? I could make you breakfast in the morning."

"Sound very appealing…all except who you want me to sleep with."

We were enjoying the tease and the unsaid messages that were travelling between us. Then he put words on what we were both feeling.

"Someday we will, Katie…and the sooner the better."

I smiled into his neck and whispered, "Well, you'd better make sure you look after yourself in the next while. I don't want any part of you to be hurt or damaged, you hear me?"

"I hear you," he laughed.

We talked a little while longer, our courting getting far more impassioned than ever before, likely prompted by the fact that my lover was about to be going into dangerous situations. Then as he kissed me so long, so wonderfully, I heard the sound of impatient shouting from back up the lane. My brother!

"Katie! Where are you? You are to come back in. You hear me?"

Darach and I looked at each other.

"Go," he said. And I did. Quickly.

Chapter 22

Family Treasure

Darach O'Cahan

John McSparran needs me in the Manor House. I am being pulled in every direction. Bone-tired from the gallops of the past few days I follow John along the cobbled pavement. My backside hurts as I walk. Was it worth it? Of course, to see my folks a couple of nights ago, and earlier, to talk to Katie, to hold her! Aye, it was worth a hundred painful joints. I will become accustomed to these horse-back jaunts I imagine. I must.

I glance left through an embrasure in the wall. Today the White Rocks cannot be seen. A thick fleece of sea-mist has been dragged in over the Skerries. It wraps itself around the coast, a damp blanket on the sand-hills and the strand. On my mood as well.

We skirt around the men working at weapons in the yard, their bodies angled to the task, eyes down, elbows pumping. Sharpening-stone grates hoarsely on steel, like the sound of a dozen corn-crakes. Keen bayonet blades glisten against the dripping black of the curtain wall.

John would not explain this task to me. Last night he came to my room before bedtime. I was carving a piece of old sycamore that I had come across on a forest path near Bushmills. The grain had yielded nicely to the shape and the neck was starting to look graceful. I was moving on to the shoulder, hoping to finish it before I leave with Tirlough Óge's company.

All John had said was, "A job in the Manor House in the morning."

"What's that?"

"Ah... you'll see." That was all he said.

So now I follow him, wondering.

Entering the upper ward in front of the Manor House I am amazed at the bustle of activity. Servants have obviously been mobilised for some important task. They scurry around like ants. A few carry large chests which, by the looks of the strain on their backs and faces, are really heavy. I watch as one fellow trips coming down the main steps. He almost falls under the weight of the box he is bearing. MacArthur, the castle clerk, seems to be in charge. While some of the Antrims' key household servants have travelled south with the Earl and Duchess, MacArthur has been allowed to stay at Dunluce. Now he sits splay-legged by the doorstep, peering short-sightedly at a list in his hand, a quill in the other for checking off items.

What on earth is going on, I wonder. It looks like someone is moving house.

"What is this, John?"

"Never mind," he whispers. "Just come with me."

He has a quick word in passing with MacArthur who now creaks himself to his feet and follows us. We mount the steps, standing aside at the top to allow two servants struggling under yet another chest to descend the steps.

I follow John into the entrance hall. It is a good while since I have been inside the Manor House. Surely there used to be more items of furniture then? Had there not been some sort of wall tapestries hanging here? The huge paintings? Where have they gone?

We climb the staircase. Into the great hall. John approaches one of the harps. Not my swan harp though; the ornate, expensive one which Randal had brought from London.

"This one," he says.

"What about it?"

"We have to make a box for it."

"A box for it? Is he storing it?"

"He is sending it to England. Or maybe 'she' is, to be more exact."

"What? Why? What's going on?"

"I don't know," says John. "All I know is that he sent instructions from Dublin for everything of value to be packed and ready to be transported to a boat at the harbour in Portballintrae."

I am astonished by this. It has me speechless for a minute.

"At least he is leaving my harp in Ireland,' I tell John in a whisper.

I think back to his grand arrival here in the castle three years ago. Randal had been living at the court of King Charles for a few years. He was used to everything rich, smooth, cultured. At court he met and married the elegant Lady Katherine Manners, widow of an English aristocrat. Then his father died and he had to make the decision; 'Do I stay here in the comfort of the London palaces or do I persuade my wife that we should go back to my father's old seat in cold, dreary Antrim?' For whatever reason they chose here.

What am I seeing now? A reneging of that decision? Could he and his lady be about to abandon us? What a time to be doing it, if that is his intention!

"Does that mean he is not coming back to Dunluce?"

"I have no idea, son," says John, measuring the harp's dimensions. "I am not in his mind. I only know what we have been told to do."

"So all that pile of stuff out on the yard is being carried to some ship? How come he has a ship?"

"Maybe the King is going to help him out again and send the navy like before," says John. "It was the King's navy that brought most of these possessions here in the first place, you know."

"I just can't believe he would abandon Dunluce, leave all his people here in the lurch. He has us all organised to go and fight to protect the place! While he sits in Dublin and writes letters of instruction."

"Doesn't look well, does it?" John agrees. "Maybe it's herself."

"Maybe he knows something we don't. Maybe he can see ahead that Phelim O'Neill is going to win. Places like Dunluce will fall into his hands. Aye, that will be it," I say. "He is cutting his losses. If the Irish win and drive the English out they will have all this stuff to fall back on in England."

"You could be right, Darach, but would you stop standing there with your two arms the one length. There's a pile of things to be done."

"What should I do?"

"See these paintings? These ones and the ones on the staircase. They are likely worth a fortune. They need to be taken down and packed in some way that stops them getting damaged. Maybe make some sort of light crate for them, could you?"

"I could, John. I could…but all the time I will be thinking of the idea that I am protecting the Earl's paintings, while in a week or two a whole lot of his subjects are maybe going to be at the wrong end of some mad Tyrone man's musket. It is just a strange thing to be thinking."

MacArthur has been standing by the window, trying to read his inventory of the Earl's possessions. As I work I watch him struggle with some of the words. He wipes his eyes as if they are tiring from strain. I sidle up to him and offer to help. This way I get a close up look at what is being assembled in front of us.

"Where is this all going?" I ask him.

"Some place called Chester," he tells me off-handedly. "For its own protection."

For its own protection?

I examine the list of possessions. Huge! Half the stuff leaves me scratching my head for I don't even know what the words mean. Like these things;

'Arm chair in blue damask with gold lace and silk fringe';

'One saddled cloth of black velvet, bridle and trappings richly wrought with silver lace;

'Sixty-six pairs of curtains in three chests'; ('Sixty six?', I think. 'Why would anybody require sixty six of these things which nobody else even needs?')

There were chests of fabrics, silks, velvets, gold and silver lace, damasks, satins, fifty nine table cloths, (fifty nine!) a library of books, ornamental cabinets, a telescope and something called terrestrial globes…whatever they are. I see several large mirrors with carved gilt frames, very ornate looking miniature caskets with insets of what looks like ebony and ivory, a number of Persian carpets…the procession of possessions goes on and on! I am astounded by the wealth.

Most of this stuff has obviously been hidden away from view, out of sight of the locals. Of course it has!

And now it is to be stored more safely across the sea in the Lady's homeland.

I always knew that the McDonnells were well off….but this degree of riches is surely an injustice, a madness of greed!

My stomach has sunk and I feel sick.

John has left me on my own for a bit. I take the chance to rest briefly, sitting on the smooth floor-timber, my back against a gilded pillar. I find myself staring up at the substantial oak beams that run across the ceiling. They are huge. I wonder where they were brought from. And how on earth did the builders even get such weighty timbers up there and into place?

The thought of our tiny clay-and-wattle houses, one-roomed abodes, thatched with branches and sods and straw, an open hearth in the middle of the floor and the peat smoke drifting up through a hole in the roof. Farm animals sharing the dark space with the family…we get their warmth, but also their smells and noises. Basic possessions you could count on one hand. These are the homes of our native men and women and their hordes of children. They are the people who in their own land are paying tenancy to land stewards and therefore to Lord Antrim. Paying to this chieftain who already owns far more than all of these people put together will ever own in their entire lifetimes.

Fair enough, the people who live in the new village of Dunluce have good homes; one or two are stone and mortar built, though most are well constructed in timber. The First Earl, Randal Arranagh, planned and built this village from the ground thirty years ago. The residents are mainly Scotch. One or two, like the Boyd family, are very well off and can afford to pay the lease on their homes. That would not be true of the native Irish folk who live in the hills and bogs around my parents' area.

Later John betrays some similar disquiet at the situation. Out of the grim silence at table he says to his wife, "I wonder how his grandfather would feel about this if he was still with us?"

"Aye," says Eilish. "For all his faults Sorley Boy was always thought to be a man of the people. He wouldn't be abandoning us like this."

"No indeed. He would be at the front of his men, waving a claymore," says John.

I know little about the famous founder of this Clan McDonnell, but I hope he would have the decency to be turning in his Bonamargy vault at the state of affairs in Dunluce today.

Chapter 23

A Plan of Action

The church meeting house in Ballintoy was at its coldest on this early December morning. Faithful parishioners shivered on their rough timber pews and hoped for an early end to the service. Teeth chattered as the final Psalm droned too slowly to its close. The clergyman's benediction came in misty wraiths as his warm breath hit the frosty atmosphere of the kirk. He signalled the congregation to be seated.

Archibald Stewart didn't sit. He shuffled soberly to the altar at the front. Reverend Blare descended the pulpit steps and stood aside to allow him to climb up. The land steward paused and gripped the sides of the lectern in his two hands. Beads of sweat seemed to be trickling slowly forward on his broad, hairless crown. His large round eyes looked solemnly down at the congregation. Apprehension coloured every face.

"Thank you, Mr Blare. Friends, believe me when I say I would rather be horsewhipped than to have to bring you these tidings today. You have all been aware of the rumours over the past few days concerning the rebellion that has broken out in parts of our province, indeed in the whole country, it would seem.

Our present information is that the forces of Sir Phelim O'Neill are on the march through the new County of Londonderry. They are under the command of one, John Mortimer. They are headed for Kilrea on the river Bann and it is our belief that they will try to cross into County Antrim in that vicinity. There is a ford of some kind near there, or so I am told. Lord Antrim has sent instructions that our troops should muster there as quickly as possible.

This was not what we had anticipated. We believed that we would simply have to defend the Earl's lands here in the Route. Now we are commanded to go further afield and take on an enemy we know little about."

He went on to describe the nature and leadership of the three companies of defenders, and outline the plan to march to Coleraine for weapons and supplies.

"Then we go south towards Kilrea," he continued. "Many more good loyal men will join us en route to help defend their homes and lands against these insurgent Irish.

My message to the men is to be ready by first light, assemble in the yard in front of my house with your supplies and weapons. And to you who remain behind, be brave and steadfast in your faith. We will need your prayers. Thank you all."

There was not even the hint of a sound when he had finished. Never had the atmosphere of the kirk been so hushed, so tense. Heads were tilted forward, eyes bored into the floorboards, many of them glistening with un-wiped tears. Wives silently slipped work-worn hands into the firm grasp of their husbands' big fists, and children's heads hid themselves under mothers' arms. Eventually a small stifled sob was heard from the back row, no-one quite sure who had broken the spell. It was the signal for the clergyman to rise and try to bring some comfort.

Reverend Blare joined Stewart who had remained in the pulpit, head bowed like so many others. The minister put a hand on the land steward's shoulder and launched into a long impassioned prayer for the mission, for safety for the soldiers and for God to give victory to 'His people'. He had already preached his sermon from the Gospels. Now he resumed his exhortation, this time alluding to the miraculous victory that God had given the children of Israel over the walled city of Jericho.

"Father in Heaven," he prayed, "we remind ourselves that 'if God be for us who can be against us.'"

Afterwards there was not the usual congregating of gossiping families outside the kirk. Most folks left the churchyard and hurried homeward, their dark-clad bodies bent into the south-western breeze that had blown up overnight. Above them, purple-grey blobs of cloud seemed to want to rush over this curséd countryside and escape out to the safety of the sea.

Only a few younger people remained by the building's eastern wall; almost all the males among them would be meeting again in the morning by the Manor House to march with Stewart. Sisters, girl-friends and old mates gathered around them, Connie, Katie and Jean among them. The usual banter was almost entirely absent but inevitably some gallows humour brought a few strangled laughs.

Alex stood slightly apart, staring north towards Islay. He did not take part in the conversation, understandably preoccupied. Jean Kennedy noticed and stepped over beside him, sensitive as was her nature.

"A penny for your thoughts, Alex?" she said.

He grimaced, still looking towards the ocean and sighed.

"Not really thinking at all," he mumbled.

Jean waited quietly, trying to be considerate and supportive. Then took him by the elbow. "You will be grand," she said. "You're too good a man for anything to happen to. Somebody up there will be looking out for you."

He didn't answer. It was as if he hadn't heard a word. But he didn't pull away either.

After a bit he said, "Do you ever notice how flat the sea is? There's nothing in the world any flatter, is there? We live beside it, we see it every day but ... look how level that line is, where the sky and the sea meet. It's never been any different...always the same flatness, that line."

"I know," Jean said, hiding her bemusement.

"And us here on the land, looking down on it all the time. Standing up here on the top edge of the world, you would nearly say. Do you ever think that the sea and the land are in a sort of battle with each other? The blue against the green. It's a fight that has been going on since creation. The waves batter away at the coast, but the cliffs are far too strong for them, so the land keeps winning."

"Aye, I know," she said, not knowing at all.

Alex lapsed into silence again, seemingly oblivious to Jean's continuing physical touch. She still held his arm, shivering slightly with cold, drawing a little heat and protection from him. Some feminine instinct deep inside had drawn her into a bodily closeness to him, a comforting intimacy that was intuitive, rather than something she had planned or even understood. This lad, her friend, was heading into danger. She might be the last girl to ever take his hand...so she did, boldly, kindly.

If Alex noticed he didn't show it. His gaze remained fixed on the ocean, the rumble of its movement humming in his ears, punctuated by the occasional squeal of a gull overhead.

"I seem to have spent half my life looking out to this stretch of sea," he said. "Never was much bothered until now about what was happening over my shoulder... inland, I mean.   That is all about to change, I suppose."

"Inland isn't so bad....I hear that anyway," she said lamely. "You'll not be away that long."

"Maybe," he said quietly. Then, clumsily drawing her closer and resting his chin on top of her head, "But this is some place to live, isn't it Jean? It's our own place and we take it for granted. Couldn't be a lovelier place in the whole of Ireland. I just hope..." he tailed off into silence and Jean, pulling away, glanced quickly up at his weather-tanned face with its slightly bent nose and the shadow of rough stubble on his cheeks. She saw tears well in the blueness of his eyes.

'What?' she thought, 'Alex McKay can't be for crying?'

"I know," she said aloud, "It is God's country alright...and you'll be back to it in no time, you hear me now, Alex?"

"Please God," he said. Releasing her abruptly he walked away from her, down the path towards Ballintoy's tidy little harbour.

Chapter 24

Ready

Darach O'Cahan

I've not known such feelings before. A stirred soup of emptiness and regret, anticipation and dread, worry and detachment. I shake inside, yet I see a stoic face when I look at my reflection in still water. And I do look long at this face. Is this me? Have I wakened up today in someone else's body?

How will I survive this new responsibility? Rather, these responsibilities…because, as time has gone on since Stewart's entreaty, my roles seem to have increased.

Take messages…that had been the first job. Be a dispatch rider.

"You know the lie of the land," he had told me. "After travelling with McSparran in the inland regions you know the whole area, don't you?"

Maybe.

"Ballymoney? No? You have been through Coleraine? Of course. What about Clough…the McDonnell castle there at Oldstone? The Kennedys live there."

No sir. I'd never heard of it, let alone been there.

"I'll draw you a map of the whole area. You'll be able to find your way no bother. And if you are stuck you can always ask…but you'll have to be very careful who you ask, remember. These times you can't just ask the first person you come across. They might not be friendly to our cause, might want to hear what your business is."

A nod of understanding.

"And you got on alright with that horse they lent you from the stable here?"

"Aye, *Liath* was fine. Lovely quiet mare."

"And you remember what I said about maybe having to write down messages yourself? I'll have to get you a scroll of parchment so you can make notes about what you see. Make observations. Let me know anything you observe or hear that you think I need to know about. Bring me all relevant information. Alright?"

"Alright, surely."

Alright surely? Be like a spy for the Colonel? Now wait…but no, don't wait; I'd already said alright. He was moving on. Leave it.

"And there are a few things you will need to carry for us, so the horse will have to have good saddle-bags."

Saddle-bags? A few things?

"What things?"

"Well, I'll get you a few medical things. You and a couple of the other officers."

"Medical things?"

"Aye, just stuff…a bottle or two of brandy and likely a few…"

"Brandy?"

A condescending look at me.

"Aye, brandy. Maybe wine too. Not for drinking though."

What then?

"More for wounds. If somebody gets slashed with a sword or a bayonet and it's not too bad…you would know what to do, wouldn't you?"

Now as it happens, I would actually. Eilish has me well trained in that area. Working with saws and chisels and the like, you inevitably cut yourself. Or, as happened on one occasion with poor John, you cut your foster father! I do know about cuts, how to clean them with wine, how to poultice them with crushed nettle leaves or dog-daisies or vetch, whatever you can find that works to keep the wound clean…but where would you find such plants at this time of year? I know about using spiders' cobwebs to bind a wound but those are easily found around a place like Dunluce Castle…not so easy in countryside I have never set foot in, I imagine. And yes, I am well aware of the healing properties of honey, but it is going to be some job to find any in December's County Antrim.

I don't bother to spill all these doubts out to Mr Stewart though. I just nod again.

"We will have some nicely washed bandages for you to have handy, just in case. And I'll dig out a supply of honey for you. There must be some dried herbs to be found in the castle as well."

Great, he knows about honey. And medicinal herbs. And clean bandages.

"Have you ever had to stitch a wound?"

What! My mouth opens and closes again as my mind races.

"Don't worry about it," he says with a smile. "It most likely won't be needed. Just as long as you can do a good tight tourniquet and stanch any bleeding. You'll be fine. You will know as much as any of the rest of us. If it is grapeshot or a musket ball there's not much you can do anyhow. I am hoping your cousin will have that McLaughlin man with him. He has been known to do an amputation. He has a lot of experience on the medical side of things. Very good with cows and sheep too; he's done me a favour manys a time. If you get a chance watch him. You'll learn a lot."

I am sure that I will indeed learn a lot, but I am hoping that how to cut off someone's leg is never part of it.

The way he is speaking to me is very interesting, almost confidential I would say. This man hardly knows me. Why is he putting so much trust in me, an Irishman? I am mystified. I am also confused about who I am going to be responsible to. I had thought I was going to be in Tirlough Óge's company but the way Stewart is talking to me seems at odds with this. I want clarification.

"Mr Stewart," I begin, "are you sure you don't want me to be in your company rather than Tirlough Óge's?"

"No. Why do you ask?"

"Well, it's just that you are the one giving me my instructions and all. And you want me to write down what I see and hear... sort of be an ear for you, as well as take messages for you."

He stares me out for a second, then a brief smile of acknowledgement.

"You are a clever lad. I think I have picked the right man for this job. Aye, Darach...you are to be answerable to me, but how can I stay abreast of everything that is going on with the other companies if you are with mine all the time? So I want you to move around. Be as free as a bird. You're a carrier pigeon after all." He laughs at his own wee joke. "Be with the O'Cahan group and the Highlanders, McColla's men, and with my men and keep me informed of all you see, any discontent, any rumblings or rumours."

"But will Tirlough Óge and the McCollas not object to me being this carrier pigeon, flapping around between the three camps? Will they not see through it?"

"They might, but it's up to you to do it without the flapping. Do it without attracting attention. You have a good aura of integrity about you, and you are his cousin. That is what first made me think of you for this job. I know it is a big ask of you but I believe you are up to it. I don't think you will let me down."

"I don't intend to, sir, but I have no experience."

"You'll soon learn."

I will have to, won't I.

****

My rear end has hardened up a bit over the past few weeks as I have taken to riding everyday on this placid mare. *Liath* and I are becoming good friends. The next while could be a lonely experience so I will be glad of such a friend. I just hope *Liath* has a good sense of direction.

In my emotional lostness I expect that thoughts of Katie McKay will be my constant northern star.

Have I said everything to her that I needed to say, wanted to say? Yes and no; maybe never could. But she knows. We both know. I am not sure how to explain exactly what it is we know but, whatever it is, we both know it. That we are for each other. What we cannot know yet is how our future will unfold.

Not for one second do I have any doubt about the rightness of 'us'. Nor does it enter my head that I may not come back from this military venture. I simply must. I believe I will. I have faith enough in God to be my proverbial high tower and to protect me from disaster. I think Katie does too. Still, it strikes me that on this final evening with John and Eilish before I depart I need to leave some token for her, some tangible sign for her to hold on to. I have given her the bog-oak cross, of course, but it lies on me to do something more. One idea is to try again to write a poem or a song for her. She would have it should the worst happen…but there is no point; she cannot read as yet.

The other idea is one that she will like. I come to John and Eilish in their kitchen to explain the plan.

"I have some things to say to you, before I go," I begin.

They both stare at me with some intensity. This is not a usual kind of utterance from me. I don't do much talking to them, sadly…more listening. I should have done. I take them so much for granted, but I really value them. How do I tell them? I decide not to. Like Katie, they know.

"What is it you want to say, son?"

A pause for a deep breath.

"I have a girl."

I notice the quick glance between them and John's sly smile.

"We know," he says.

"How do you know?"

"You have changed in the past few months," says Eilish. "We hoped maybe it was to do with a girl."

"Who is she?"

"She's a girl from Ballintoy. Her name is Katie, Katie McKay."

"She sounds Scotch?"

"She is. Her father is dead."

"Agh, I am sorry to hear that," John says. "Was it recent, his death?"

"Half a dozen years ago. It happened at sea. She has a mother and an aunt and a brother and two sisters. They farm near the Manor House there."

"Well, at least you won't have to worry about the poor father chasing you off with a big stick."

"No, but her brother wouldn't be too keen on the two of us seeing each other," I tell them. "It doesn't matter anyway. We won't be put off by him."

"So that's the way of it, is it? You're in over your head?" Eilish is grinning, enjoying this. She would have been a great mother, I am thinking. What a pity she and John never had any wains. I have been the beneficiary of that unfortunate reality.

"Maybe I am, alright," I agree. "But the thing is…"

I pause. This next sentence has to be said, no matter how morbid it will sound.

"If anything happens to me I would want yous to find Katie."

Another glance between them, a pained one this time.

"Nothing is going to happen to you, son," Eilish whispers. "You are going to come home to us and to your family and to this Katie girl."

"I have every intention," I say, "but just in case…I need you to promise me this."

"Alright," John says softly, "but promise you what?"

"That you will find her."

They look at each other, then back at me, Eilish smiling.

"We promise we will," she says.

"And take something to her that I would want her to have."

"What's that?"

"My eagle harp."

"Your new harp? Is she a player too?"

"She's not, not yet anyway, but it would be a piece of me for her to keep."

"That is a very nice thought, Darach, and we will do what you ask… but don't worry yourself, you are coming back to us."

"And I might write some sort of verse for her too."

"That's alright. You do that," John says, clearing his throat half way through.

He stands up abruptly, turns away quickly and stalks stiffly out into the cold of the night. Maybe he is just going to the turf stack for more peats. Eilish gives me a long stare.

"He will miss you, so hurry back to Dunluce as soon as you can."

I have to say more. I owe these great people.

"Eilish, thank you both for all you do for me… and make sure you tell that to him too," I say.

"I will that, son," and she rises to stand behind my chair and give me a first-ever hug, a strangely awkward one from behind, a hug that presses too firmly on my Adam's apple and near enough chokes me.

Chapter 25

The March to Cross

Darach O'Cahan

There is no beating drum on our march.

I say 'march'. It feels more like a shuffle of the begrudging.

There is no sense of eagerness among us, no enthusiasm, no call of destiny. Dank December drizzle envelopes us, drenches us as the day wears on. Our bodies, numbed by this damp chill. Our minds equally numbed by questions; diverse and bewildering questions.

We are a strange raggle-taggle band of mainly unwilling soldiers. Men complain continuously of aching feet. Feet unaccustomed to the ill-fitting brogues that many of them have been instructed to wear. They swear at toes and heels that have blistered early, damning the jagging pain of every step. Older knees and backs creak and jar increasingly as day creeps towards its closing. Loads on shoulders weigh more heavily. Eyes water in the cold sleeting wind. Groans and curses, suppressed in the earlier hours, escape chattering lips without reticence. Some of the more dishevelled of my fellow travellers stop frequently to readjust; they fall further behind, bringing guttural oaths and rallying calls from officers, and countering truculence from the ranks.

"Alright for you bastards up on your horses!" the muttered response on more than one occasion. I hear it directed at myself on those times when I ride on *Liath,* so for much of the journey I walk beside the mare. I lead her, chatting encouragement as she pulls a cart heavy with supplies.

The first part of the journey to Coleraine hasn't been too bad. Mr Stewart seems to be in overall charge. It surprises me that the Earl's brother, Alexander, doesn't have that role. He seems to have disappeared from Dunluce in the past week or so. The rumour is that he will lead his men in defending his own castle at Glenarm against the local Irish.

Stewart's company of Scottish settlers had left Ballintoy early. Tirlough Óge's smaller group, local Irish from Dunseverick, had not managed to catch up. The previous day McColla's Highlanders had travelled from Ballintoy to Dunluce, so they could join forces with our soldiers at the castle. I had been witness to their night of revelry in the castle's outer ward after drinking Stewart's tavern to its last dregs. The resulting hang-overs slowed down our departure this morning, so this, the largest of the three companies and the most diverse, is the last one to arrive through the gate in the earthwork ramparts that protect Coleraine.

The regiment's transport carts and sledges rumble noisily along the cobbles of the main street. They halt in the open space before the town's market hall. Residents have gathered in curiosity by the roadside to watch, to show their appreciation of these volunteers. Enthusiastic shouts and applause. Our soldiers pay little heed, dour, withdrawn. Some flop down wearily against the new buildings which line the broad thoroughfare. Others jostle for heat around bonfires. Wood-smoke drifts low through the grid-planned streets. It fuses with the misty drizzle, distorting my view of the place as I try to see through this heaving greyness.

Shortly the men are devouring vittles served up by the women of Coleraine. The Mayor of this new plantation town has been determined to rise to the challenge and has had his townsfolk provide a substantial meal for the soldiers. Huge vats of stew have been boiled up in the open space where the market is held, a tasty mix of vegetables, beef and pork. You can see the mood of the men lift, hunger satiated. Dozens of animals must have been butchered in the preparation. I imagine streets running red, blood flowing down to the river.

Thirst is slated by a continuing supply of tankards of brown beer. Made here in the town, this comforting brew is greatly welcomed by everyone. Standing close to Stewart's volunteers at this point I hear some banter between the men.

"I doot the drouth bate yeas, boys!"

Laughter at the expense of a few sheepish-looking Presbyterians, their heads bowing to hide reddening faces. Seems like their abhorrence of strong liquor lost out in the battle with exhaustion and thirst.

"Ye weren't lang o' gaein' up yer teetotallin' the day! Yeas were aye wile staunch aboot the drink 'til yeas needed a sup!"

What a richly earthy sound, the dialect of these lowland Scotch. It hasn't taken long for it to be woven into the texture of languages here in the Route, just a couple of generations. I wander among these men and listen intently, to them and to the local folk. I can easily pick out threads of English, of Scots and Irish Gaelic, and of this lowland dialect. It's a tapestry as colourful as the landscape itself.

It is on my wanderings that I meet Alex McKay. It hadn't struck me that he might be in Archibald Stewart's company. It should have, of course it should, but perhaps I imagined he would decide to remain in Ballintoy. His mother and the girls need him, maybe for protection at some stage. He is the only man in that house after all. But here he is, with a couple of friends. We almost bump into each other as he rounds a corner from a side street, so he has no chance to avoid me.

I speak to him. "Hello Alex, I didn't expect to see you here."

He looks a bit embarrassed, put out in front of his Presbyterian friends because a stranger has addressed him in such a warm manner.

"Well, of course I am here," he says coldly, quietly. "What made you think I wouldn't be?"

No smile of recognition. No admission that he knew my name. No hint that we have a connection from before. I would love to ask him about Katie. I dare not though. Instead…

"How are things in Ballintoy?"

He is slow to answer, edging away from me. "Things are alright," he mumbles.

"And what about the journey this morning?"

"What about it?"

"Your feet hurting at all?

"My feet are grand."

I sense that he wants to tell me to mind my own business, but I try one more approach.

"Did you bring the pipes with you?" I ask, only half-joking.

He looks at me as if I am boring him. "I did. Why are you asking?"

"Agh you know…just wondering. You'll be able to stir up the men going into battle. All that."

"You're talking nonsense," he says, turning away to his friends, abruptly, dismissively.

What is it in him that cannot engage with me? Not even pretend, superficially, out of basic manners? Is it embarrassment that he feels somehow in my debt? Is it to do with his failure to speak the truth back in Stewart's party all those months ago? Is it his opinion about my courtship of his sister? His dour rudeness is so unlike her. I would love to tease this out with him; it will have to wait though.

It is during our mid-day sojourn in Coleraine that I have become more aware of hostilities underneath this veneer of contented feasting. I catch glares of sheer enmity. I overhear discontented conversations. This regiment is anything but at peace with itself.

"We were toul we were to be defending Ballintoy. Noo we are ga'n tae a place we hae nivir heard o', nivir min' been tae!"

From others, in their native Irish, I hear similar complaints, similar but with an added flavour…one of conflicted loyalty.

"B'fhearr liom bheith sa bhaile i mBaile an Tuaigh arís," from someone who would rather be back home in Ballintoy. And then from another, a question about which clan leader has their best interests at heart.

"B'fhéidir gurb é Mac Domhnall ár dtiarna talún ach d'fhéadfadh sé gurb é Ó'Néill ár slánaitheoir."

The Earl of Antrim may indeed be our landlord, but might Phelim O'Neill be the hero who delivers us from the hands of the oppressor? It strikes me that some of these troops would be as happy fighting with O'Neill and his rebels as fighting against him. I can sympathise with their dilemma.

****

I travelled from Dunluce with McColla's company this morning. It had crossed my mind then that his group is composed of men from three very different backgrounds.

There are the rough Highlanders with their pikes and long-bows. They stuck by themselves; maybe hangovers are to blame but these men seem to be missing their normal exuberance. The spark is absent, eyes are glazed; no laughter, just a sourness of attitude.

The second group, the sober settlers from Dunluce village and the surrounding farms. Some of these men are neighbours of mine. I know one or two of them fairly well. We have talked at times, mainly about matters to do with the running of the castle. While they are friendly enough to me it would be wrong to describe them as any more than acquaintances. I doubt very much if any of them even know of my interest in the harp. I notice that they appear a bit wary of the kilted warriors. Is it a case of age-old animosity between Lowland and Highland Scotch? Maybe. Perhaps more significant is the fact that these settler folks are largely Presbyterian, unlike McColla's men.

Then the Irish, people like myself. This third group would have a degree of antipathy to both of the other gangs. The Scotch had displaced them over the years.

It's fascinating to watch these disparate groups interact with each other. They sit on opposite sides of the Diamond, their backs resting against the mainly stone-built walls of the newly constructed homes. The Highlanders hog the middle of the broad thoroughfare, nearest to the vats of stew and the long trestle-table where the beer is served. There is a lot of staring across the street, much sizing each other up going on here, I think. And that's before everyone comes under the unified command of Archibald Stewart. And before any rivalries emerge between the three company leaders.

A ruckus seems to be breaking out in front of the church building along the street. From a distance I see men scuffling, punches being thrown. The row, whatever it is about, is getting noisier by the minute. Inquisitive, I move closer, just as one man gets wrestled to the pavement, a scrawny red-headed fellow. Someone comes to his aid, pulls him to his feet, another red-head. A bell rings in my brain. I look more closely. Is this not the same two men I saw on the mountain that day, the men who had attacked Alex McKay? The more I stare at them the more convinced I am. What were they called? I try to recall my father's comments, without success. I wish Father McGlaim was here to confirm my suspicion. But I don't need it confirmed. I watch as Tirlough Óge wades in through the melee. He grabs the two of them by the scruff of their necks, drags them out in my direction. I hear his rebuke.

"One drink and you two go off your heads! You disgrace my company again and I will horsewhip you within an inch of your lives, you hear me Sean Reid? You too, Michaél. No more of it!"

The Reids! The two hallions who tried to kill Alex. And the thing is I don't believe that Alex has ever been told that these were his attackers. Now they are in the same army, probably sleeping in the same camp, armed and supposedly fighting the same enemy. It all strikes me as a very incongruous situation.

Do I try to warn Alex?

His attitude to me galls so much. I think he can look after himself from now on. I have my own role here and it can't be compromised by looking out for Katie's thrane brother. I decide to put him out of my mind.

What lay behind this fight I have not been able to discover. Tension between the companies? More likely an aggressive outburst of temper fuelled by the beer.

Now there is much shouting of commands and even more mutterings from the confused troops. Stewart is trying to get the three companies to re-form into marching order so as to resume the journey. I watch as he turns to McColla for support. The booming Scottish accent reverberates around the walls of the Diamond. This time the soldiers seem to understand what is required of them. Gradually they formed themselves into proper company order. Men do what McColla tells them, I note.

Mr Stewart now stands high on top of a cart. I see someone being hoisted up beside him. It looks like some kind of priest, clergy of some sort anyhow, a tall man in black flowing garb. He holds up his hands for quiet and, after a wave of shushing that sweeps across the assembled men, Archibald Stewart clears his throat and speaks. To be fair to him his voice carries well across the space.

"Men of the Route, of Dunluce and Ballintoy, soldiers and friends from across the water! Before we make the final march today to quarter in the village of Cross, I want to thank the Mayor and the people of Coleraine for the hospitality we have been shown this day."

A ripple of applause, some shouts of appreciation swell and die again as Stewart holds up his arms.

"And before we leave now, the vicar of St Patrick's church here wants to say a blessing on our journey and our endeavours. Please bow your heads for prayer. Reverend Patterson."

Most men do indeed bow their heads, but, as the tall clergyman steps forward, I am conscious of murmurs of objection around me.

"Let us pray," he shouts at the top of his trebly voice.

As he begins, the mutterings around me grow into disgruntled discussions that in turn become protests. It becomes so noisy in sections of the crowd that the clergyman seems to stumble in his prayer. In the gaps I hear calls from the Irish.

"What about us Catholics?"

"Get us a proper priest to pray for us!"

This heckling is countered by men from the other company, mainly Ballintoy. They are joined by onlookers, Coleraine residents I guess.

"Be quiet and let the Reverend say his prayer! Have you no respect at all?"

It shows the tension that soldiers are swearing at each other in the middle of a prayer for our protection. I look up at the face of Archibald Stewart to see how he is reacting. I think I see his head shake slowly from side to side, as if despairing of this task he has been called to.

The prayers fade to a confused finish. Stewart wastes no more time with speeches or formalities. He shouts the order, "Forward march!"

Out of the centre of the town we go, down towards the wooden bridge over *An Bhanna*. We turn left, taking the path beside the river towards our base for the night, a village called Enagh Cross, (or Cross, as the locals call it), several miles to the south.

We are not far off the winter solstice now. Only a couple of hours of daylight are left, though it is being generous to call today's conditions 'daylight'. The officers have the tough task of hurrying the sore-footed men along, otherwise the final part of our journey will have to be completed in darkness. At the rear of the procession are many horse-carts and mule-drawn slipes; some are stacked high with fodder for our animals; some have piles of tents and sheepskin bedding; there are crates of weapons and ammunition, while other carts have supplies of water and food, mainly vegetables and some dried fish. Their progress is very slow where the ground is water-logged, which, given this route alongside the river, is very often.

We pass the ancient site of Mountsandal, a remarkable looking fort on a very high promontory overlooking the river, so broad at this point. I have seen this mighty river before on my journeys with John, heard all about the legend Mananánn Mac Lir and his lust for Princess Tuag of Tara. I feel fortunate to have had John tell me these legends. Not all my fellow-travellers would have been to Coleraine. Fewer still, I imagine, have ever seen anything like Mountsandal fort. The sight causes much curiosity and speculation among them.

I too wonder about the people who built such places. What were they like? Why the idea to make such massive earthworks? Were these religious places or were they simply living spaces that had to have an eye to defence? Who they were, these ancestors of ours? Do I carry their blood in my veins? The diversion soon wears off; our weary trudge continues along this high embankment.

Below us, a long ledge of rock called the Salmon Leap juts out across the river, creating a natural weir. A number of years ago a cut had been opened in this obstacle by the new planters. Its purpose, I had been told by John, was that timber from our native forests could be brought down river without impediment for the construction of Coleraine town. Later many more trees have been floated down to be used in building ships for the King's fleet.

"Nothing that we owned is sacred anymore," I remember John saying. "Imagine, the Crown stripping out our ancient oaks and yews to build the English navy!"

At this place salmon leap heroically over the weir during their journey upstream. Nothing leaps today. The sound of water rushing through the cut fades as we leave it behind. After that, all that breaks the silence is the sound of feet squelching on the sodden path. Then, from way up ahead, I hear the sound of bagpipes drifting back to us through the riverside mist. Alex, I presume, has finally found the courage to play a few tunes. Whether or not people can or want to march to his rhythms is a different question but at least the sound lifts our spirits a bit.

Soon we pass Loughan Island, site of an historic ford, once controlled by my own tribe. The O'Cahans had had a wooden castle on this island, right at the eastern edge of their territory which stretched all the way to the Foyle in the west.

The atmosphere among the marchers is as bleak as the weather. At no stage have we seen the sun today, nor do we see it set this evening. By the time we reach Cross the foggy light of the afternoon has thickened through gloaming grey to oppressive blackness. In this darkness a few hundred tired, dispirited soldiers have to be allocated to various barns and dwellings in the locality.

The chaos in Coleraine was nothing compared to what I witness on this murky evening in the churned *clábar* of Enagh Cross. We are in muck to the ankles.

This small settlement has grown up tight to the shore of the Bann. Its normal population, I am told, is less than a hundred. Tonight it has grown to four times that. The troops that have arrived from Coleraine have found that there is another large contingent from the nearby town of Ballymoney waiting to join us. I have a feeling many of us are not going to find a bed of any description. The ground is so water-logged that we are going to have to develop the skill of sleeping while standing up.

I will tie *Liath* to a tree somewhere nearby. I may have to try to get my rest leaning against the mare!

Chapter 26

Camp at Portnaw

Darach O'Cahan

The misery of Christmas at bleak Portnaw.

Not a stable in sight, not an inn for miles it would seem. Actually, nothing is in sight, apart from stands of tall sycamore, beech and ash behind us and, beyond a line of spindly salley bushes, the sluggish flow of the broad Bann. Wise men stay well away from a damp hole like Portnaw.

Our regiment stretches along a few perches of the river's eastern bank. Furthest to the south is Stewart's Ballintoy company, augmented by some stout citizens from the Ballymoney area. Away to the north, Tirlough Óge's Dunseverick men, with McColla's Dunluce fractious mixture in the middle.

I have only come across Alex McKay once or twice since we camped here. I had heard the squeal of his pipes a couple of times and followed the sound. He and his mates seem to be camped in a stand of bare trees furthest away from the river, on the outskirts of Stewart's company. A good choice I thought when I noticed this; the driest site in the encampment, and directly underneath a couple of huge trees. Alex has continued to ignore me but I made a point of quietly wishing him season's greetings during our Christmas morning meal. It was just a quick comment in passing, though I did so much want to talk to him about Katie and how much we both are missing her, and how Christmas would be in the McKay house in Ballintoy without him present. I didn't though and, to be fair to him, he did return a festive compliment, albeit having checked to see if any of his mates were listening or observing first.

I have not seen the Reids since we set up camp. They may be keeping a low profile, staying well away from the Scotch up among the trees. I imagine they are in Tirlough Óge's company. Perhaps they have deserted, maybe even crossed the Bann to join the enemy.

I flit between the three areas, sometimes with messages from one colonel to another, more often just to try to keep myself interested in living. The change of scenery is barely noticeable and hardly interesting, but the different strands of gossip are.

Nothing much seems to be happening on the opposite bank. We have seen some of the rebel army among the trees on the western side, but it has been well nigh impossible to detect how many, or what their intentions are. They are aware that we are here; we hear cat-calls and obscenities shouted across the stretch of water. Our parentage and religious persuasion are frequently impugned. The trouble that Mr Stewart has is that there is a substantial rise of land just beyond the river, close to its western bank. So he has no idea how many rebel troops might lie hidden behind it. He could be facing a few dozen Irish, or it could just as easily be thousands. Apparently the Irish-held town of Kilrea is just beyond this obscuring ridge. We see the smoke rising from this settlement. At times it blows our way.

The grumbling has continued among our ranks, and not alone from the Irish conscripts. The weather is wintery, with hail showers often forcing us to shelter in the trees. Hunger is a constant issue. We have been in this camp for nearly two weeks and our food supplies began to run low half way through that period. Some of Stewart's drovers had been supposed to drive cattle from the areas around Coleraine and Ballymoney but these have not materialised yet. As a result he has had to send troops into the surrounding town-lands to commandeer cattle, oats and vegetables. This has met with angry resistance from both Protestant and Catholic farmers, especially the latter. I have witnessed this anger first hand.

"Does your Colonel Stewart not know that this has been the worst year ever for our crops? We are already in the beginnings of a famine, and he sends looking to steal whatever animals we have left? Tell him to go to hell!"

This outburst from an apparently well-to-do farmer at Movanagher Bawn, a plantation of English and Scots settlers a few miles north along the river. Not a lot of sympathy for the military who have come so far to try to protect the likes of these folk.

I can understand the resentment that these people are feeling. So, I believe, can Stewart, indeed all the men. But soldiers must be fed. Pigs arrive and are butchered amid screams that would wake the dead. Hens, ducks, geese and of course a few skinny cattle…these form our diet for the Christmas season. Even the whooper swans on the river are not safe. A few fish get pulled from the Bann as well.

Fires burn constantly, both for heat and for cooking. Wood is not scarce here. The trouble is getting the wet branches lit. Again we have to steal dry timber and bits of turf for kindling from the local farmsteads.

So morale sinks lower by the day. How long are we going to be here for? Could this take months? Are we wasting our time? Will the Irish rebels even bother to try to ferry themselves across this river? If they do, can we hold them off? They will be vulnerable to our musket fire and our cannons as they cross the open water, if we can see them at all. If they attack at night we will be the ones exposed, silhouetted against the light of our fires. They will be camouflaged against the dark shadow of the western bank. The uncertainty creates great nervousness, from Stewart down to the cooks and cattle drovers.

Myself, I am in reasonable spirits, although the uncertainty of everything and the endless hours of waiting in this limbo do take their toll. There are certain things I miss from my normal life in Dunluce. I would love to have one night in the secure family atmosphere of John and Eilish's cottage. I miss the normal routine of castle and village life. I think I probably miss the sea air and the seabirds cries more than I imagined I would. I do think a great deal about Katie. In my mind I have an ongoing conversation with her. I catch myself believing that when I have a sudden flashing memory of her features, or when in my mind I say something to her out of the blue, that this is because at that exact moment she is thinking of me as well. I would love to be able to satisfy myself that this is actually true. In the meantime I do have faith that it is so.

I also miss my music and my harp. Tunes are constantly playing in my head; my fingers curl to imaginary strings. When I next play the eagle harp I believe I will enjoy it ten times more than I have ever done before.

There is some music here in the camp. Apart from Alex's pipes I have heard someone play a rapid reel on some kind of whistle; I am guessing it is a homemade one as the tuning was awry at times. Then there are occasional bursts of song. One or two of the Scotch folk begin to sing a religious piece, a psalm or canticle of some sort. Others join in until it sounds like hundreds of them are singing together. I say 'together', but in truth it is anything but together. The cadences of the tune seem to surge in waves along the shore of the Bann. A line will start somewhere far upstream in Stewart's camp and, just like the river itself, gradually ease its way down past where I sit and progress to the ranks of the Dunluce folk. It is a beautifully haunting sound, a rippling echo of long notes and slow drawn-out lyrics. Even more awe-inspiring is when the tune has a natural harmony and some men add this counter melody. The overall effect is the most mesmeric noise I have ever heard. I will never forget it. Those Presbyterians can sing. It is a deeply mystical experience. Spiritual and moving. It has the added side-benefit of breaking up the monotony of our long wait here.

****

In the end, a couple of unforeseen events move the situation forward.

A message reaches Archibald Stewart from Walter Kennedy of Clough Castle. A tenant of the Earl in the estate there, he and his people are coming under attack from the local Irish who have been causing unrest, even before O'Neill's troops have been able to cross into Antrim. Kennedy begs military support at once, otherwise his garrison will be over-run and his family destroyed.

It is a dilemma for our leader. Can he afford to send a small platoon of soldiers to rescue and defend his friend? In the absence of immanent attack from O'Neill's forces he agrees, and fifteen soldiers leave us to travel to Clough, a distance of some ten miles, I am told.

I sense no disagreement from anyone about Stewart's decision.

But then another cry for help arrives.

It is the first day of January 1642.

A letter comes in the hands of a very brave but very anxious labourer. By fortunate coincidence I encounter this man when I am out exercising *Liath*. He almost collides with the mare as we meet, half-blinded by sweat, half-running, half-staggering along the river bank, totally breathless and in a terrible state of panic.

"Where can I find Archibald Stewart?" he rasps.

So I lead him back to our camp. On the way he tells me his story.

He has come from the Agivey, across in County Derry, from a small bawn there under the command of a George Canning. Like Clough, Canning's demesne is being besieged, this time by rebel forces, 'led by an O'Cahan', he thinks. This man says that he escaped the attackers by the skin of his teeth, slipped through them and made his way to the Bann. He commandeered a small boat, rowed across and has run for several miles to deliver Canning's plea for help to our Colonel.

"How did you know where to find us?" I ask him.

"I crossed the Bann at a place they call the Vow. I made my way to the nearest house, a big important looking establishment. It was owned by a Sir James McDonnell. He knew about yous; he said that Colonel Stewart was a friend of his. He had watched Stewart's troops pass along the side of the river a while back. So he pointed me in the right direction."

Back in our camp Stewart sends me to get Alaster McColla and Tirlough Óge for a discussion. I rouse the two men from their board games and they follow me back to the forest clearing where the visitor is being revived with some hot liquor. The three Colonels go into discussion. I cannot help but hear their deliberations. I cannot help but see the looks between Tirlough Óge and McColla when Stewart isn't watching. And I cannot help but see the shock, the resentment in my cousin's eyes when Stewart gives the following order.

"Tirlough Óge, I want you to select a dozen of your best men, more if you like but not too many more. Travel with this courageous man down to where he left his stolen boat and cross over with him. We need to give whatever support we can to Canning and his good folk at

Agivey."

Tirlough Óge and McColla look at each other intensely. I sense the unspoken dilemma going through their minds. It is one thing to travel east into Antrim to help at Clough Castle. It is an entirely different matter to cross the Bann into rebel-held territory, led by a stranger you don't even know, never mind trust, find the homestead of an unknown settler-farmer at a place you've never heard of and deliver him and his people from God-knows how many Irish rebel troops.

McColla probably wisely tells Stewart that this excursion needs a period of thought and preparation.

He addresses the recovering messenger. "How far is it tae this Agivey castle that ye speak o'?"

"I wouldnae be guid at the measurin'," the man confesses. "It took me a guid while, maist o' the efternoon… and it woulda taken me langer if I hadnae come on thon boat."

"It must be about six or seven miles down river," Stewart confirms.

"Look Archibald, it is late in the day," McColla says. "By the time Tirlough Óge and his men would get tae this Agivey it'll be pitch dark. What dae ye say that we leave it tae the morning? What dae ye think Tirlough Óge?"

Tirlough Óge is nodding his head, relief and puzzlement on his countenance. Stewart nods too.

"You are probably right, Alaster, but come first light you must be on your way, Tirlough Óge. See what you can do for this Canning. And when you've accomplished your mission get yourself and your men back here as soon as possible."

Everybody agreed, the two of them leave Stewart's camp and wander off towards their own quarters again.

Chapter 27

Treachery

Darach O'Cahan

Tonight is to be one of the most momentous nights of my life so far. I will struggle to do proper justice to the course of events but, though it might sound arrogant, I may be the only person present here who actually knows what truly occurred. It is a 'privilege' I would very willingly have foregone.

I am unable to sleep. It is a strange and doubly unfortunate affliction on this particular night. Perhaps the fish I had eaten earlier had not been properly cleaned; maybe not sufficiently cooked. My stomach cramps painfully. I make far too frequent visits to the latrine pit by the river bank to relieve my bowels. During one of these visits, while I am squatting in the reeds, I become aware of a whispered conversation which seems to be taking place not more than ten paces from my position. I am about to finish my business and rise to escape the stench when I start to hear the gist of a conversation, softly-spoken, secretive.

"How did you get this intelligence? Is it credible?"

"I believe it is."

I recognise that voice straight away. The strong accent, the Scots Gaelic. It is Alaster McColla. By virtue of the kind of man he is, McColla is not a great whisperer. His voice continues, increasingly audible.

"It comes frae my brother, Raghnall. He has just got back frae Rasharkin. I had sent him tae our kinsman there, Donnell Gorme O'Donnell. I wanted tae fin' oot what wae the wind is blowin' wae his folk. It was Donnell Gorme who toul him that some o' the Protestants in our army are planning tae turn on us, here at Portnaw."

"How did Donnell Gorme know about it?" says the other voice. I now realise it belongs to Tirlough Óge.

"I think he heard it frae James McDonnell o' the Vow. We should take it seriously," McColla says.

"I agree, but what are we going to do? I have Stewart's order to go defend these folk at Agivey. I can't obey it! I can't be attacking my own brother!" Tirlough Óge has become more vociferous, emphasising his point.

'His own brother?' I think. 'What has Manus got to do with this?'

"'Course ye cannae! It's an impossible situation," McColla agrees.

In the silence that follows I realise that I have, in complete innocence, put myself in the shittiest of situations. In so many senses. My breeches are around my ankles. I cannot easily crawl out of this sagging trap. If I try to rise and sneak away I will most likely be discovered and accused of eavesdropping, spying. Nor can I crawl in this state, half-undressed. If I stand up and speak, letting them know of my presence, I might find myself under the exact same suspicion. McColla already despises me. He will show no mercy. I'll find myself drowning in the dark flowing waters beside me.

If I continue in my present squatting position my knees may freeze in place and I may never be able to arise; they could be talking here for hours. But I have no choice. I must remain still. Hope that I am not discovered.

That is what I do.

And, in so doing, I become party to their discussion and to the laying of a most terrible plot.

Having listened to the conversation from half-way through I can only guess at the earlier course of the discussion. I have gathered that there are two key items of news here...the possible plot against the Irish in our regiments and the conjecture that the O'Cahan who is attacking Agivey is none other than Tirlough's brother, Manus.

I had known that Manus had disappeared from Dunluce after the announcement concerning Phelim O'Neill's rising. There had been an unspoken suspicion among those of us who knew Manus. We were aware of his penchant for roguery. We did suspect that this was the opportunity he had been waiting for and that he had fled west to join the O'Neill. Now the chickens had come home to roost for Gilladubh's clan. A son on either side of the conflict. And he himself, the peace-keeping magistrate for the Earl!

The Bann flows serenely beside me. Listening. Not a sound does it make. There is total night-silence here.

Tirlough Óge is speaking. I hear his words quite clearly now that I am attuned to his voice.

"This is a most ill-conceived campaign, McColla. There are already Irish men in this county who have risen to support O'Neill and the rising."

"You mean at this place called Clough?" McColla asks.

"Aye. There and elsewhere."

"An' you hae sympathy for them, don't ye?"

"I do; of course I do." Then after a pause I hear Tirlough Óge continue, irritation growing in his voice. "How have I managed to find myself stuck here in the dead of winter, trying to defend the interests of the bloody Earl who cannot even be bothered to stay with his own people?"

"It's madness," McColla says. "Raghnall and I can fight on whatever side of this argument, ye ken. We hae nae great loyalty tae Randal, even if he is kin."

"I have no loyalty to these Protestant farmers that we are supposed to be defending, especially the English settlers! My sympathies lie with the Irish over that river. They are the ones who have been dispossessed by these foreigners."

"Foreigners? Ye're naw saying that men like Archibald Stewart are foreigners surely? They are Scots. Gaels like yoursel'. They speak your language, or at least a version of it."

"I know, I know, but these English who have been planted on our lands don't speak our language. They despise it. They want to squash the Gael out of us, destroy our ancestral way of life. You can see that yourself."

"So what are ye saying?"

"I am saying that I have no longer any loyalty to the Earl if he asks me to choose him and his thieving settlers over my own people, my own brother, for God's sake. You understand that?"

"Aye, but it has tae be your ain decision."

There is a long silence. I think maybe they have moved off. I raise myself so my head is above the reeds, but in the moon shadow of the trees I cannot make out a single thing. I am about to pull up my breeches when I hear McColla cough raucously and clears his chest of phlegm. I sink slowly to my previous position.

Tirlough Óge's voice again. "You know what is so strange in this whole thing?"

"What?"

"This company of Stewart's, half of them are living back in the hills, looking down at the fertile farms in the valleys that their fathers used to farm. And here they are now, fighting alongside the very men who displaced them. Fighting against an army that wants to free them and restore them to what they had before!"

"It is the height o' irony, isn't it?" McDonnell agrees.

A further silence. Then the gruff voice of the Scot again, his words forcing things to a moment of crux.

"I think we are baith talking ourselves into a terrible decision here, Tirlough Óge, dae ye agree?"

"We are."

"The thing is, if ye refuse tae obey Stewart's orders he will ask ye tae lay doon your arms, an' he'll maybe even try tae arrest ye, an' your men. I would hae tae help him in that. If I refuse then our two companies are going tae hae a bloody fight right here. It is a hopeless position tae be in."

Then I hear Tirlough Óge say the dreaded words. "It is not hopeless. We cannot wait for some hot-headed Protestants to attack us. There is only one course of action to be taken."

"Go on."

"I have to support my Irish brothers. You too, McColla. They are your Catholic brothers. We must change sides. Do you agree?"

I hear a slapping sound. Either McColla has punched him or he has clapped him on the back. I don't have long to wait to find out which. The Scotsman's words send an icy chill through me.

"So we switch. We dae it the night. At first light…which, looking at that sky, is naw very lang aff I think, maybe half an hour…we rouse the men and we attack Stewart and his Scotch. We'll naw kill many o' them. We'll just do a guid oul-fashioned charge, make a lot of noise, fire a few cannons and muskets. Stewart and his company will scatter and flee. They are a bit under strength at the minute, wae thon wheen away tae Clough. Are ye agreed?"

"I am, but don't forget that there are some of our Irish brothers quartered in Stewart's company, and with your Dunluce gang. You don't want to be killing any of them or scaring them off. It could be chaos. So how will we know who is who? And how can we warn the Irish of what is going on?"

"Ye make guid points, but hae ye taken note o-er the past few days that the Scotch and the Irish hae tended tae quarter in different places, in their ain groups?"

"I have seen that alright," Tirlough Óge agrees.

"The Scotch hae taken the drier ground, up frae the riverbank, un'er the trees, whereas the Irish are closer tae the water, more exposed. So we dae twa things. We attack only those areas near the trees and we shout Irish war-cries at the top of our voices, so the Irish there will ken that this is an attack against the Protestants, not against them."

"I see what you mean." Tirlough Óge's enthusiasm seems to be growing as he understands McColla's scheme. "What about Raghnall? So you think he will agree."

"He will completely agree, I hae nae doot. Noo," the big Scotsman continues, "the first thing is tae ready our ain troops. We must dae this quietly and quickly, we only hae a very short time tae get readied. I'll rouse my Highlanders. They can prepare the gunfire and lead the charge. The other Scotch in my company, the Presbyterians, they mus'nae fin' oot! Ye must go quietly aroun' your men and inform them. Get them up as quietly as ye can. Get them armed and ready."

"I'll do that," says my cousin.

"But listen Tirlough. Make sure that nobody attacks or harms Archibald Stewart himsel'. He is my host and he is a guid frien'. So he must naw be harmed, you understand?"

"A good friend? But what if he…?"

McColla interrupts. His leadership is very decisive already, ruthless in its clarity.

"Stewart will naw be harmed! Make sure o' it!" he says emphatically. "And mair than that, nae needless killing! There are many guid men in Stewart's company who hae been very kind tae my Highlanders o-er the past months. Scare them aff certainly, but dinnae be butchering everybody in sight. That is an order. We are naw savages tae our fellow Gaels."

Their voices become more faint as they move off to put their treacherous plan into action. My heart is thumping so hard and so fast in my chest that I notice I have put my right hand against it to press it into some sort of more normal order. It is not the only part of my body to be malfunctioning.

If my bowel has been giving me problems before this episode, now it is in explosive mood. Thanks be to God I have been able to control it when those two were close by, otherwise I would have been discovered in the most embarrassing of circumstances.

Now it is not only the river Bann that flows!

Eventually matters come under control. I rise carefully, adjust my clothing and slip silently upstream to wash my hands and refresh myself by splashing some river water over my face.

What am I to do?

Tirlough Óge makes sense to me. Like him, I have begun to feel that I am on the wrong side of the river here. I have ignored the feeling. Suppressed it. Now it gnaws at my belly again.

Like many of his men, I have watched our traditions being undermined by the prevailing regime. I have nothing against the ordinary individual citizens. The Scotch are the best of folk. As McColla has just said, many are generous neighbours, good men and reliable friends. But the system that has them here in our country, destroying our forests, fishing our rivers, farming our land, that is just wrong.

If that was all that was wrong you could maybe try to live with it. But it is not. Living and working around the castle at Dunluce I am privileged to witness two different ways of looking at the world. Randal McDonnell rides two horses at the same time. He is a Gael, of course he is, and yet he is very enamoured with the English ways. Clearly he does value our customs. He promotes our stories, our legends, and nothing pleases him better than to have a bard or a *seanchaí* or a singer of our ancient songs around the place. He has always encouraged me in these pursuits. He loves the harp. He plays our tunes himself and speaks our language. He has a chapel for Mass and brings in a priest when he can, against the government's edicts. But, for all that, the Earl is also working the system, the English system. He is loyal to the king. He pays his dues to the Lord Lieutenant in Dublin. He is surrounded by English-style luxury. He entertains the elite of the kingdom while his tenants scrape by and are often hungry. The McDonnells may have had no part in the new plantations of English folk in other parts of Ulster, Derry and Tyrone and Fermanagh, but they have been bringing Scottish settlers on to our land for decades. And, as Tirlough Óge said, all we can do is watch from the hills.

Nothing else to do about it.

This is what I am thinking as I go back to my station. It is a spinning torment of thoughts and emotions. I am undecided.

I will not change sides, however. It is not in my nature to do this. I cannot abandon my role in this affair just because I have heard the logic of what I have always felt, now so clearly argued by Tirlough Óge.

Why do I find myself in this position anyhow? Simply because Mr Stewart 'volunteered' me to be his messenger, his scribe.

And that is what I am. But I am not his spy.

I did not sign up for betrayal.

Should I be sneaking off through the trees to find his tent and warn him about this treasonous plot? That is my big question.

I rise to my feet again and start to wander uncertainly up-river in the direction of the Ballintoy encampment.

I don't get very far. Doubt sticks out a foot and trips me.

The doubt comes from a certainty. Either way this is not going to end well.

If I find Archibald Stewart and waken him, tell him of the impending attack, what is he going to do? Would he even trust me? I might have difficulty actually convincing him to believe me. Whenever he does catch on to my meaning he is going to raise the alarm at once. Two things can happen then. One is that the sound of this alarm warns McColla and Tirlough Óge who then abandon their plan and send their men quickly back to their blankets. Stewart will then look at me like I am mad, a conspirator, a troublesome stirrer. And that will only be half my problem. McColla will, I have no doubt, find out what I have done and my life will be in grave danger.

I wander back towards my bed, distraught. Another thought thread begins to run through my head. If I hurry I can still report this thing to Stewart, but if he rouses his men and they take up their arms there will be a free-for-all of shooting and many will die, maybe even more than if I just stay silent. The strain of the whole thing makes me want to vomit, and I do! I can't help it. My stomach is in a mess of painful convulsions. My head is spinning. I feel faint with the dread of it all.

There is one thing I can do that might count for something.

I make a sudden decision!

I begin to run. I am heading flat out towards the Ballintoy camp to the south. It is maybe ten or fifteen minutes away if I can keep up this speed but I am weakened by the diarrhoea and the sickness. I have to slow down soon, otherwise I will pass out, I think. I stagger on. Do I have time to do this before the hullabaloo breaks out? I hope so but I cannot be sure. I may find myself in the line of fire if I can't get there in time.

I must try to rescue Alex McKay.

I have been more conflicted in the past few minutes than at any time in my life before now. But this? I know this is the right thing to do. If I cannot save the company, if I cannot save Stewart and his defence of Antrim, I can at least try to make sure Katie's brother survives. I don't really have a plan, other than to find him. I have a fair idea where he sleeps. I am hoping that he is alone and not surrounded by his friends from home.

The full moon which had been high in the southern sky earlier has moved around a little to the west. It now examines me, one eyebrow raised, from across the river. My impression is that it is not entirely approving of my actions here. It hangs unhappily just beyond the town of Kilrea. I am thankful though; this frowning moon may yet prove an ally in the next while.

As the sky begins to lighten in tone above the tree-line away to the east I reach Stewart's camp. I slow and stumble into the clearing beneath those two ash trees that I recall from earlier, tall, ghostly-white skeletons in the pale light. There are a few rough looking shelters and tents here to choose from. Alex is in one of them. No clues outside. I must take my chance and look inside.

I pull aside the first flap of cowhide. Two sleeping bodies. Thankfully neither awakes as I peer closely at their faces in the semi-light. A shaft of moonlight could not be better directed. I do not recognise either face; these are strangers to me.

In the second tent, which is some sort of sheet tied between a couple of poles and a tree, I have the same disappointment. My luck is holding though. These men are dead to the world; nobody wakens.

As I lift the sheep-skin flap of the next tent two things happen simultaneously.

I notice Alex's pipes resting on a box beside his mat, right by his head. And at the same time I hear the crackle of musket fire to the north.

The attack is on.

I place my right hand firmly over Alex's mouth. My head goes down right beside his ear.

"Alex!" I say quietly but urgently. "Wake up. It's me, Darach. Listen to me! Don't make a sound. You are in danger."

As I speak he gradually stirs, comes slowly awake at first, then jerks violently against my hand, eyes wild. I hold him down firmly.

"Listen to me, Alex! I'm Darach O'Cahan. You are in danger. I need you to come with me to safety."

He mumbles through my fingers and struggles. The other man in this tent stirs and turns on to his side. He is not far from being awake, I think, given the disturbance beside him and the distant musket fire which is now getting louder.

"Stay quiet," I whisper firmly. "You are under attack. You must come with me. Right now, and quietly. You hear me?"

My hand is still holding his head down on his mat, but I need to get a move on if we are to make good an escape.

"I am going to take my hand away, Alex, but don't cry out. We have only seconds to get away from here, alright? So when I take my hand away just get up quietly and follow me to my horse. Right, I'm lifting my hand."

I do. Alex sits up with a jerk. He looks at his mate. I put my finger to my lips. He stays quiet, looking very scared, disorientated. The boom of a distant cannon sounds through the camp. I hear loud swearing, men starting to shout, both in this immediate area and from further away. The Highland charge may be seconds away.

Alex gets up. "What the hell is going on? Why are you…? What are we to do?" Then to his still sleeping mate, "Bruce, get up!" he shouts and kicks out at him. As Bruce starts to struggle awake I grab Alex by the arm and pull him as strongly as I can out of the tent. He doesn't fight against me. I am awake, he is only half-awake.

"My brogues," he says, showing some presence of mind.

"Get them quick," I tell him.

He dives back inside. I hear him shout something at his mate, I didn't hear exactly what. A warning, no doubt. He re-emerges seconds later, brogues in hand. And strangely he has brought something else, his pipes! Imagine having the thought to bring his music with him when his life depends on being quick here, quick and quiet.

Again I grab his arm and we lurch together through the undergrowth and away from the encampment. Alex wants to stop, to ask questions, maybe to put his footwear on. I don't want to give him time for that. We are still too close. We can both hear the blood-curdling yells of the Highlanders and the firing of muskets and pistols a matter of yards behind us. I have a fear that a stray musket ball could rip through these bushes and take one of us down. I keep pulling Alex by the arm, running, falling. He is cursing the thorns in his feet, the unseen branches that swing back and slap his face, the cold stones he stubs his bare toes on.

"Where are you taking me?" he pants. "What is going on?"

"McColla has turned sides, that is what," I tell him.

"My God!"

"I have a horse back this way, if I can find her."

I am almost out of breath.

"I can get you to somewhere safe," I wheeze.

Conversation is difficult on this rampage. Alex must have so many questions. Can't take time to answer now. Out of breath.

Just need to get away.

I am weakening again.

The spirit that has been flowing hotly through my veins is beginning to cool down, slow down. So am I.

Can I find *Liath* in time, before I pass out?

The pain inside is hurting bad again.

"Are you alright?" I hear him ask from behind. "Would you not let go of me instead of pulling me after you like I'm a pig on a rope? I won't be running back there, believe me."

In some relief I let him go. In doing so I stumble, fall over. Maybe the tiredness. Sudden pain…like a lightening bolt to my eyes.

My head! It's hit a tree stump.

I lose the light.

He is pulling me. Lifting me now.

"Get up, for God's sake," he is pleading.

The stars stop flashing.

I can still see the big primrose-coloured moon above a thin layer of mist that seems to float on the river.

'What is the moon doing over there? It's not usually in that direction… I be seeing it often over Portrush… Is it even the same moon?' I wonder aloud.

"Are you alright?"

Probably not, but…

"I'm just tired," I say weakly. "Dead tired. There's a horse…"

Somebody pulling me. Cold grass at me.

Sliped over mud.

Slithering wet like a new-born calf.

Must be at a stream now, I find myself thinking. Because water is running down my face. Why is it?

"Drink it," he says, his hand to my mouth. Whoever he is. I drink. Very cold. But good. We rest a minute. I start to come to my senses, a bit. More water. I suck it in off his hand. More thrown at my face. Very cold water for the time of…but it is winter, of course it is.

"We need to get moving again," he says. "Find this horse you spoke of. Do you think you can walk again?"

"I could always walk," I tell him. "Why do you ask?"

My voice sounds far away, echoey.

"Because for the last while I have been carrying you, whatever the hell is wrong with you. Can you try to get to your feet now?"

I try. It's no bother, I think. I find I can stand…in a manner of speaking; wobbly though; light-headed and dizzy.

Stomach still feeling very disordered, but I take a step and it seems to work, if I take it slowly enough.

"Right," he says, "Let's try and find your horse. What colour is it? We are just east of Tirlough Óge's camp, if that is any help in working out where you are."

"She's *Liath*," I tell him.

"A grey," he says. He understands my Irish of course.

We fight our way through some salley bushes and reeds in the direction of the dimming moon, the sky behind us lightening from charcoal black to smokey grey. Ahead I can make out an encampment, the quarters of the Dunseverick troops, I believe. There's no-one around. Of course there's no-one around. They are all away to the south with Tirlough Óge, chasing Stewart's men across the county, those still alive to be chased.

Liath remains here where I had left her, thanks be to God, tied to a low branch of an alder. She whinnies a welcome. I think I see a nervousness in her wide eyes. Maybe it's no wonder. I get her saddled up while Alex keeps a lookout.

Poor *Liath*. She turns her head and gives me a look, as if to say, 'What? Two of you getting on my back?"

We trot away along a narrow track towards Movanagher Bawn.

"Why did you waken me?" he asks, after a silence between us.

"To warn you."

"Aye, but why me? Why not warn Stewart?"

"I didn't have time to find him," I lie. "You heard the guns going off. The attack was under-way. They were about to charge."

"How did you even know about it?"

I can be honest this time. I tell him about the overheard conversation on the riverbank, a bit embarrassed about the circumstances.

"But surely you should have gone to Stewart? Why didn't you think of that? If you had warned him first maybe he could have..."

"Maybe I should have done that," I interrupt. "Maybe if I had done that you would be lying dead back there with a musket ball in your chest. Maybe I was thinking that your family back in Ballintoy would like to see you alive again. Maybe I was wrong, but it's too late to change it now."

That seems to have him thinking for a bit. Then he has another question.

"Where are we going?"

"I'm not sure," I tell him.

We try to keep a lookout for any rogue troops. All we see, though, are a few very sullen looking soldiers scurrying away from the horrors of Portnaw, one or two clearly injured, trying to stay out of sight among the bushes.

"I will take you as far as I can, maybe all the way to Coleraine," I say over my shoulder. "You'll be safe there in the meantime. We'll just follow the river north, the same way we came."

"But I need to get home to Ballintoy. I need to see that they're alright. And they need to see me too."

"They do…and if you get there, when you get home, will you…"

"Will I what?"

"Will you tell your Katie… tell her you saw me and that I am fine?"

He sits silent behind me. I can't see or guess how he is reacting to this awkward request. I wait.

"I will tell her anything you want," he says quietly.

That's great, I think. He sounds a bit less stressed about things.

"Tell her…" I can't say it though, coward that I am

I stop. Wait.

"I'll tell her," he says, his hand briefly, lightly, on my shoulder.

Chapter 28

Conflicted Loyalties

Darach O'Cahan

How I wish it was me that Archibald Stewart is sending to Ballintoy rather than Alex. Instead I have been told to take a message to Clough Castle, wherever that is. Alex has the more enviable role, to journey to his home village. Tell his people to be prepared for an attack from the rebel forces.

How has this all come to pass?

Alex and I had made it back to the safety of Coleraine two days ago. It took a longer time due to my weakness; also because it wasn't good to be expecting *Liath* to carry us both all the time. To his credit Alex let me ride. He walked alongside, his head down for much of the journey. His depression was understandable. There was little conversation between us. He had left behind his friends, his commander, his regiment. What was happening to them back there while he was fleeing for his life?

On our journey we met many scared people. Rumours had started to fly around. Some too gruesome to be repeated. While Alex was becoming increasingly angered by them, I was reserving my judgement. You cannot believe everything you hear at such troubled times. Nevertheless, as we entered the gates at Coleraine's rampart, there were dozens of families funnelling in there with us. It was like a plague of fear.

The following day Archibald Stewart rode into town, several of his officers on horseback with him. Not far behind were what was left of his Ballintoy and Dunluce regiments. A sorry sight! Many were carrying injuries, faces gaunt from hunger, fatigue and down-right terror.

Stewart stood on a cart in front of the Market House and made a speech to us all…his troops, the townsfolk and the refugees. It was a sober but a passionately irate address. He told the sorry story of the betrayal at Portnaw. He had some details wrong of course, but I was the only one to know that, having listened to the planning. I wasn't going to stand up here among all these people to clarify his facts.

Between thirty and forty of his loyal Scotch volunteers had been slain by the Irish and the Highlanders that morning; some were still missing, maybe escaped, more likely thrown in the river.

Alex gasped at this and immediately said to me, "Have you seen

Bruce or Tommy among the soldiers?"

I shook my head. "I don't think I would recognise them," I said.

I kept listening to the speech, but Alex left me and started looking everywhere for his Ballintoy comrades.

Stewart said that he himself had escaped when he fought off a couple of rebels in his quarters. This I doubted, having heard McColla's instruction that he was to be allowed to escape unharmed, but maybe he was telling the truth. He said he had rallied what was left of his company and marched them back here to protect Coleraine. On the way they had seen black smoke mushrooming into the air as they approached Cross. The village was completely on fire, torched by the Irish. He had spoken to bereft residents who had told him that the burning was not done by the rebel troops, but rather by some local people emboldened by the rising across the river. He spoke of dozens of Protestant families, men, women and children, roaming through the countryside looking for shelter.

"I hate to have to inform you of this," he said, "but they were nearly all naked except for under-clothes. Some didn't even have a rag to cover their decency. The Irish had spared their lives but stolen their clothes. I have been told by some survivors that they were only reprieved because they could speak Gaelic. But then they had been stripped, turned out on the road, and had watched their dwellings burn behind them. It is barbaric what is happening in this county, and not here alone. News has come in of a massacre at a river in County Armagh. Protestant women and children, dozens of them, thrown alive from a bridge into a freezing river, speared to death if they tried to crawl out. I have to tell you, good people of Coleraine, that we face a horrendous foe, a very ruthless one. You must prepare yourselves for the defence of your town, and be ready to receive many more good people who will flee here for safety. They will need food and clothing from us all."

The atmosphere in the market square after this speech was like nothing I'd ever witnessed before. People were wailing, and not just women. Arguments had broken out among some, curses and judgement shouted down on the Irish. Mothers were pleading for food for their children. Horses unsettled, neighing and stamping at the uproar. It was like a scene from some ancient legend of hell. As an Irishman, I was feeling more than a little uncomfortable.

Alex came running through the crowd towards me, another soldier trailing after him, a big lump of a fellow. This, I discovered, was Bruce.

"Tommy is killed," he said in an agony of spirit. "Tommy is killed!"

Bruce was trying to calm him down, without much success. Alex was in a terrible state. "He didn't even get to die in his own place," he cried. "He'll likely be thrown in that bloody river."

"Maybe not," I said. "Maybe someone will give him and the others a decent burial."

"Who?" he shouted at me. "Who is left to bury them? The Irish won't be bothered burying them."

"Maybe somebody will. They're not all cruel," I suggested, more to try to distract him than out of any genuine hope.

"They bloody-well are!" said Bruce angrily. "We saw bodies hanging off trees on our way here, not a stitch of clothes on them. These people are savages, every last one of them." Then to me, suspiciously, "Who are you anyway that you are trying to stand up for the Irish?"

It was an awkward moment. With him looking at me so crazily, if I said my name he would know that O'Cahan is Irish. In this atmosphere it might be the last thing I ever said. Thankfully Alex came to my aid.

"He is a friend of mine from Dunluce," he said. "Leave him be, Bruce. He's the one who helped me escape back there."

"What do you mean? How did he help you escape?"

I gave Alex a fleeting frown, just the merest hint of a shake of my head. He understood my signal.

"After I heard the cannon go off and woke you up, remember? I was scared. I took to my heels. I thought you would be following me," he told Bruce. "And as I was running Darach caught up with me on his horse. He offered to let me ride with him. That's how I got to Coleraine so soon."

It was a clever alteration of the facts. It gave me some cover.

"You say his name is Darach? I don't recognise him from our crowd? How come he is in our ranks?"

"I work for Mr Stewart," I told him.

"You work for Mr Stewart? Doing what, might I ask? You don't sound like somebody he would be employing."

Alex spoke again in my defence. "He is a courier for Archibald; he knows the whole countryside. Just leave him alone, Bruce."

In the middle of all this a woman had sidled up to us. I say 'woman'. On a second look I realised she is very young, just a girl really. She stood waiting, thin and gaunt, bent over like a broken tree. I will never forget her appearance, the pathetic look on her face. She was skin and bones. You could see that, even through her very bedraggled clothes. Barefooted despite the winter cold. Long matted hair. The poor girl hadn't washed for ages. She stank terribly, God love her. She could barely raise her head to speak to us.

"Sirs," she said in a brittle whisper, 'I have a small place. You want to come... to me?"

We look at each other, puzzled, shocked. Had we heard her right?

"You can have me, all of you...if you can get food, for my wain."

We were all very taken aback by this brazen invitation, stunned to silence. It was not something I ever expected to encounter in a model town like Coleraine. This girl was desperate.

"Your wain?" I said.

She lifted her head to me. She was startling to look at. She had probably been a very pretty girl, and not long ago, I could see that....but her sickly-white skin was drawn so tightly over her face and skull that she looked like she was a corpse talking. A skeleton, still breathing out of habit. Eyes that seemed too large, too vivid for her face. Her mouth too wide. When she spoke her lips stretched open over damaged teeth, the few that she still possessed.

"I have a girl," she said, big tears standing in those hollowed eyes. "She is starving."

She may have been a hopeless case but she still had the instinct of compassion for her child...and she moved me near to tears just to witness her plight.

"Where is she?" I asked. "Where can we find you if we get any food for you?"

Bruce cleared his throat noisily. He looked at me as if I was daft.

"Down to the river, turn this way," she said, indicating to her left with a boney hand, "beside the old abbey wall, I have a place where I sleep... where my girl is hiding. You can stay with me...it's so cold..."

"No need for that," I said. "We will see what food we can get and try to find you. What's your name anyway?"

"Nellie," she said.

Mother of God! I must try to help this girl, I thought.

She seemed to bow, as if in thanks, then wandered off.

We looked at each other in stunned silence.

"What are you doing, falling for that story?" Bruce said cynically. "She's just a hoor, pure and simple."

"She's just a girl," I tell him. "She needs care. Anybody can see that."

"Anybody can see what you're after," he smirked.

"Don't be ridiculous, Bruce. He is only trying to help her," Alex said firmly.

"Aye right!" Bruce said, giving me a knowing grin.

I felt like giving him a thump in the face. Still, this wasn't the time or place to be starting a row with this fellow. I was in the sort of position that I should not be drawing too much attention to myself. I let it pass. I knew my own motivations. I did not have to be answering to Bruce's suspicions.

This girl's predicament was symbolic of what was happening in the whole area now. The food shortage in the country was already starting to hit the poorer of the citizens...and this town wasn't even under siege, except from the influx of displaced country folk.

At that moment Stewart himself came wading through the crowd in our direction. People were hanging on to his arms, pleading, crying. He was highly agitated, breathless and red-faced.

"Alex! Darach! I have been looking for you two. I thought you had perished at Portnaw. I didn't see you on our march here? What happened you? How did you escape? No matter now. I have more urgent business at present!"

He shook off some of his tenants with more violence than I expected of him.

"Let go of me and begone!" he cried. "Alex, I want you…. and Bruce can join you just in case one of you doesn't make it, two might be better than one in this case….I want you to take a message to my two men in Ballintoy. Thomas Boyd is a good reliable fellow, and Reverend Fullerton is there. He's Captain of Yeomanry for the area. I will write exact instructions for you later tonight. It is essential that we convince them to fully prepare the Manor House and the kirk so that they can withstand an immanent attack from the Irish. Tell them to leave nothing to chance. Our lives and our homes are in extreme danger."

Alex and I glanced at each other disbelievingly. Ballintoy might be in trouble soon? That little church attacked? Even after Portnaw and Cross, this was hard to take in.

"When do you want us to go, sir?" Alex asked.

"Tomorrow at first light. Sooner the better. I will make sure two horses are left ready for you. You should travel quite a distance apart, in case one of you should fall. You must be very, very vigilant out there. This is no country for carelessness, you hear me? And you'll need to take the news of Thomas Smith's death to his people."

"Of course, sir!" Alex said, Bruce nodding in agreement.

"And you, young O'Cahan; I hope you are keeping detailed notes on all you have seen of these proceedings?"

I nodded and told him that I have been. It was a bit of an exaggeration.

"Good," he said. "A true account of what happened will be vital. Later I want you to take an important letter to Sir James McDonnell at Clough Castle."

I had heard of this man before, from McColla, and from the Agivey messenger at Portnaw. Had he not said that this Sir James was a friend of our Mr Stewart?

I remarked on this point to our Colonel. "Ah," I said, "a message to your friend, Sir James? Does he hold this castle at Clough for the Earl?"

Stewart shook his head ruefully. "My friend?" he said grimly. "A few days ago I would have said that, yes, he was a friend of mine…until now. Unfortunately he has come under the influence of his kinsman, Alaster McColla, and has decided to throw his lot in with the Irish. Another traitor!"

He paused to catch his breath, his throat dry with nervous energy.

"After those turncoats completed their dirty work at Portnaw they sent across the Bann, to Mortimer and your cousin Manus, inviting their army to cross the river safely. Such treachery. So not a shot was fired to prevent the O'Neill flooding into Antrim. Sir James, it appears, welcomed them as well."

I could see Bruce staring at me, working this out. A look of disdain spread on his broad, spotted face.

"You are an O'Cahan!"

His lips formed the soundless words, his face astonished, full of dark enmity. If looks could have killed at that moment I would have been a certain victim of that Bruce fellow. Alex took him by the arm, firmly, consolingly, turned him away and whispered in his ear. I would have loved to hear what he said, but Stewart was continuing.

"My information is that the Irish have split up into various groups. Some have gone south towards Antrim, some to Ballymena and perhaps on towards Carrickfergus to attack the castle there. Some will no doubt be on our tail here to Coleraine. But McColla and Sir James McDonnell did go to Clough Castle, I know that for sure, and the information that I have received from there is quite dreadful."

"What information is that, sir?"

"Well, I hear that Walter Kennedy refused to surrender to the Irish at first. After all, he had that dozen men I had sent him from Portnaw. He should have been able to hold out. But Alaster McColla played his Scottish card, promising Kennedy's women and children safe passage out to Scotland if they would surrender, which they did in good faith. But no sooner had they left the confines of the castle than they were ambushed at the Ravel river and massacred, every last one of them. Disgraceful! Fiendish! This is the man I have given succour to! I am appalled by his behaviour and I must appeal to him through Sir James to desist. James may be a bit more reasonable. Will you take the letter?"

"I will, if I know where to go?" I said. At the same time I was hoping that I wouldn't have to have any dealings with Alaster.

"I will have someone who knows prepare a map for you. And you will probably have to wait and bring back a reply."

So it was that Alex and I, our relationship having been reconciled, received very different missions from our Colonel. Alex, with this Bruce person, to go to Ballintoy; me to a distant village called Clough.

Tonight I must take time to scribble some notes on the day's happenings. More importantly though, I will give some little word-of-mouth message to Alex to pass on to Katie. I know she will pray for my safe return.

I will also scavenge around to see if there is any scrap of food available to take to that haunting girl and her child.

****

I slip away from Alex as he counsels his darkly suspicious friend. I think they barely notice me going. I have a mission of mercy to fulfil this evening. My heart will let me do nothing less.

I join dozens of others scavenging around the town looking for food. The granaries and little shops are all securely locked up. I think I must leave the town and travel in the wider area. The scarcity of supplies in Coleraine is just too great. As soldiers, our own meagre food supply is always strictly controlled. I can get nothing from that source.

I take *Liath* and gallop a few miles to the east. This is a risk, I know that. I have no idea where the Irish forces are. But I have a great advantage over most other folks about here. If the Irish stop me to ask who I am I can rightly say that I am an O'Cahan. I have the language to prove my Irishness. If any of the Scots accost me I can say I work for Archibald Stewart. In less troubled circumstances I might laugh at my immunity. Not tonight though.

The early half-moon gives me some light when the evening drains the colour from the sky. I have reached a substantial looking farmhouse. Do I risk going up to the door to beg for food? Or should I just have a look around to see what I can find in the outhouses, perhaps risk rousing a few dogs, maybe having to dodge a farmer's musket ball?

It strikes me that it's unlikely that any man here will have a firearm. If they had had one they are probably in Stewart's regiment by this stage. So I will try thieving.

I tie the horse to a bush and begin my search, squelching about in glar and manure, feeling my way around darkened outhouses.

No dogs disturb the night calm. There is no sign of life about the place. Before long I have a hen under my arm and four eggs in the cup of my hands. I am delighted with myself, until I reach *Liath*. Then reality hits me. How do I transport four eggs and a live hen while riding a horse through the dark of night? The hen must die. I pull its neck and it splutters into its destiny. Into the saddle bag it goes. I'll need to find a fire somewhere when I get back.

The eggs? Eventually I solve the problem. I take off the thick socks that Eilish had knitted for me and put two eggs in each, wrapping them as carefully as I can and tying the tops of the socks together. This delicate parcel I hold in one hand while the other takes the reins.

I ride back more sedately along the track, asking myself the question, 'Why on earth are you doing this, taking this risk for a girl you know nothing about, a girl you only met for a minute today?'

I do not know the answer. It is just an instinctive thing. If I don't try to give her some help I can't complain about others not helping; if I turn away from what I feel is my duty I have no right to get angry about the circumstances that have brought her down to this level of depravity.

Somehow I get back to Coleraine unscathed. The eggs survive, not a crack. My next problem is the cooking of this food. I find a private corner and pluck the hen without too much bother; my *scian* does a great job of gutting it. A mangy-looking mongrel arrives to feast on the entrails. I tolerate it. But how do I get the hen roasted? With all these poor hungry people crowding close to the fires in the market square I will never get away with cooking the hen in public. It will be ripped from my hands. The raw eggs will be down somebody's throat before I could say '*Fionn Mac Cumhaill*'!

I decide that the safest thing to do is to somehow find Nellie, give the food to her to protect, while I find a way to build a wee fire somewhere. Once I have the horse stabled I go looking for her. The hen and eggs need to be hidden as I walk through the busy streets so I make a bag out of my coat and place them inside. I shiver my way down the street to the riverbank, turning left along the path between the water and the abbey wall. Dotted along this wall are lean-to shelters where the destitute huddle for protection. Mostly these are made of branches, with a few leather hides and sheep-skins to keep the rain off. Up ahead I see a low fire flickering, bodies gathered to it for heat. Perhaps Nellie is there, or maybe someone can tell me where she is, because the chances of finding her in these shadows seems remote to me.

I approach the group and look around the faces. No sign of her among these sad-eyed folk. I decide to risk an inquiry.

"Do any of you know where I would find a girl called Nellie?"

A couple of pale faces turn my way, wordless, dismissive. I repeat the question. I add that I have good news for her. More interest this time.

"You're the first of the night," a woman scowls. "That lassie!"

"You know where she is?" I ask.

She points back the way I have come. "Somewhere down there. Just shout for her. If she's free she'll appear."

So I retrace my steps. This time I am walking into the shadows and I have no hope of seeing her. Eventually I get the courage to say her name aloud. "Nellie? Nellie, are you there?"

My calls are unheeded. I return along the path. I am about to give up and go back into the town when something catches my arm from behind; it feels like the sharp claw of a bird. Then a feeble squeak of a voice.

"I'm here," she says.

She leads me so slowly to a pathetic shack propped against the high stone wall. I can make out few of its features in the dark, but enough to wonder how anyone can live in such a place, never mind rear a child in it. The one thing in its favour is that at least there are sufficient cow-hides and sheep-skins attached to a low timber frame that the rain and wind don't seem to penetrate too badly. Still, it is cold, very cold. One flickering flame shows me a sort of bench covered with old tattered cloth and more raggedy sheep-skins. It doubles as a seat and a narrow bed. Beside it sits a low timber cot. My attention is drawn there at once. Sleeping inside is a tiny child, a fair-haired girl, happed up in a few old rags of cloth. She must be foundered, I think. It is hard to work out what age she is, so I ask.

"She was born… summer solstice, I think two years back," Nellie tells me.

"And what's she called?"

"Her name is Kate."

"Kate? Did you say Kate?" I splutter.

"Aye, Kate. That's the name I gave her."

A strange emotion washes over me. Kate! I feel my throat tighten. Would my own Katie understand why I am here with this street-girl, in this dark hovel, alone together except for her sleeping baby? I know my motives are pure; I hope they stay that way; I believe I will be true to Katie but I also would be foolish to deny that I have put myself in the way of temptation tonight. It may be out of mercy, but there is also a hint of fascination. I am drawn by this girl's vulnerability. I am curious to understand how someone like this can find herself in such dire circumstances. She is studying me. Gauging what I expect of her. Wondering about my silence. Wondering even more, I imagine, if I have brought her any food. Still she stares. Her skull seems to shine out through her skin like some kind of internal ghostly light, so poorly is she.

I would need to get my tongue moving and explain to her.

"I am sorry," I begin. "You say your child is Kate. You see, Katie is the name of my girl. That's why I was quiet."

"You ha'e a girl?"

"I have. We are together now since the summer. She is in Ballintoy waiting for me."

"Ah, fine," she sighs, her head bows and those huge eyes drop towards the gravelly floor.

"But I brought you some food. It's here in this bundle…if I haven't smashed the eggs," I say, carefully opening up my coat.

"Eggs? Eggs you say?" Nellie says, her voice rising above a weak croak for the first time. This news excites her. Her thin lips stretch open in amazement, her teeth a broken gate. "Where you get eggs?"

"I went to a farm somewhere," I tell her, delighted to see that all four eggs have survived. "I couldn't even take you back there. And look, I got you a hen."

Nellie starts to cry. I am a bit dumbfounded by this. Her boney hands are up at her face and she is bawling her eyes out. It's the most energy I've seen from her. I touch her shoulder, as if to say, 'It's alright.' She leans against me.

"Why you help me?"

"Because," I say, hardly knowing the answer myself. I allow her to lean, give her a brief hug before standing back; the hug is very gentle but even then it felt dangerous, so incredibly thin is she. She is like a sack of dried sticks. The smell of her body is like nothing I've ever experienced before, God love her.

"Right, how can we cook it, or do you want to wait till tomorrow?"

"Now," she says. I catch a flash of a fleeting smile, another first. It strikes me again just how desperately hungry she is. It must be nearing midnight, but her pain drives her to eat, despite the difficulties.

"Eggs or chicken?" I ask.

"Maybe eggs the night," she says, scrabbling around under the bed. "I ha'e a wee tin pot. You get water frae the river… take it up to thon fire…they'll maybe let you boil them. Just take two. If you take all… those folk'll rob you. Just one for us; you, me."

This long whisper seems to exhaust her. Nevertheless I smile at the idea that she still has the instinct of generosity to be sharing the eggs with me.

"I won't eat one," I tell her, "but keep it for Kate in the morning."

So it is that I find myself on the banks of the dark-flowing Bann in the middle of a chilly mid-winter night boiling two eggs on the remains of a dying fire of damp sticks for a girl I barely know.

"What happened to you, Nellie?" I ask later as I watch her lick the inside of the shell for the last crumb of her boiled egg.

"Nothing."

"Have you nobody belonging to you? No mother or father who could help you?"

"No."

"Surely someone knows you, someone could help you?"

Her eyes slowly lift up to meet mine and I see the rush-candle reflected briefly in them.

"I am alone," she says.

"But why? Where is Kate's father?"

"With wife," she says so quietly I have to tell myself that those are the words I actually hear from her.

"I'm sorry," I tell her.

"Me too. Daddy put me out."

"Your father put you out? When you had the baby coming, he put you out? Is that what you are telling me?"

"Aye, he did. He strict, you see. Pres-ba-ter-an," she confides. "He couldn't be doing with me… having a wain…'specially to Tadhg McAleer. Him with a wife an' a whole litter o' wains already."

What a tragic story, I thought. This girl with her two year old child, cast out because of her indiscretion and now starving on this freezing cold January night in a pathetic hovel outside the walls of Coleraine's deserted Dominican Abbey. I wish I could do something more to save her, like take her to Dunluce for Eilish to look after. Maybe I will do that, if I get the chance when I come back from this mission to Clough.

She lies down, exhausted.

"Thank'e," she says, closing her eyes.

I can't help myself. Before I leave I put my hand on her head, stroke her hair for a bit, as if she is a child needing comfort.

Because she is.

Chapter 29

Alex Comes Home

Katie McKay

I could not believe it. Alex had come riding into our loanin on that frosty afternoon in late January. There was pure joy in our house. Aunt Biddy cried…we all did, a bit, but nothing like as much as Biddy!

Then we noticed Alex's face. Aye, he was pleased to be home, but his happiness lasted only a few seconds. I watched the pleasure in his eyes fight with some other emotion that couldn't be contained. A look of pain quickly replaced his smile. It was like when a thundercloud blows in across the sun on a muggy summer's day; everything suddenly became sombre; a quiet pause as the warmth faded from our hearts and a chill of foreboding blew in to replace it.

He sat by the fire, soaking up the heat and sniffing in the smell of the burning turf, while gorging himself on soda-bread, a mug of buttermilk in his hand. It looked like he hadn't eaten in days, which he hadn't of course, not properly. How worn-out he looked, as if he had added twenty years to his life in the space of that few weeks since he left us. Biddy's tears of joy turned to ones of concern.

Through a full mouth he explained to us that he had been sent from Coleraine with an urgent message from Mr Stewart for Thomas Boyd and Reverend Fullerton, the men now in charge of our village. According to him, we are all in danger, even here in our quiet wee Ballintoy. It was hard to take in. One minute you were feeling fairly safe, well distanced from the trials people were suffering in far-away areas of the country, the next minute you were fearful that this trouble will come right to your own doorstep. It suddenly had become even more real!

It seemed we were going to have to take refuge in the church while this uprising lasted, just in case the rebels marched on the north coast and tried to drive us out. Mammy was distraught, not just about what the future might hold, but especially about the thought of her son out there in the countryside, riding around with secret messages in areas where he could be seen as the enemy.

What Alex told us next did nothing to ease her worries.

He described the experiences he had had since he left us. It was very hard to hear all this. The story of the treachery at Portnaw especially. We were heart-broken to hear of the death of poor Thomas Smith, Connie especially. While she had always protested that his affection for her was not returned, Connie grieved the news of his death long and deep. Bruce McClure had come with Alex to Ballintoy that day and he had gone to Tommy's folks to tell them the sad news. What a tragic home the Smith's must be from now on.

Then to hear of all those poor people who had crowded into Coleraine, and so little to eat in the town. What was to become of them?

And to think that the O'Cahans and the McColla McDonnells were the leaders of the ones who had betrayed their friends! That they had slaughtered innocent men as they slept, men they were supposed to be fighting alongside! What sort of world were we living in when neighbours turn on neighbours? Those were terrible things to hear about the very men I had been cooking for over the past six months, men who had been staying here in our community with local Presbyterian families.

And Tirlough Óge! His father, the man who was supposed to keep law and order in the route on behalf of Lord Antrim! Everything was shaken that morning, everything I had believed in, it seemed.

Naturally my mind wanted to go to the subject of my lover. Where was Darach? How was he in all this trouble? Was he safe? Was he lying in a ditch somewhere, bleeding to death from a wound? Worse still was the terrible question; had he turned sides as well? But these thoughts could not be expressed. I had to lock them up in my mind, in a room beside all the other fears. I couldn't ask my brother if he had any knowledge of my love. The fate of Darach would have been the last thing in his mind, even if he was the first thing on mine. It was a terrible position to be in, the desolation of not knowing. Might I never know? Might I never see him again? It was all I could do to keep this turmoil from spilling out into floods of tears. I thought that Connie was reading my mind. She was watching me very closely through her tears. At one point, while we were distracted by Biddy's wailing, she sidled over to where I was standing and slipped her hand under my elbow supportively. This despite her own loss. We hugged. For all her frivolity, my sister had always had a lovely sensitivity for reading how someone was feeling and being able to make the most appropriate gesture of support. How I wished I could think of my callous-hearted brother in the same terms.

There he sat, taking every last bit of heat from the glowing hearth, wiping the crumbs and the smear of buttermilk off his unshaven face with the back of his hand as he finished his hasty meal. He stood up and spoke to us, sort of in a fatherly way, as if he realised the weight of being our only protector in the absence of our daddy.

"Look," he said. "This is going to be a very tough period of time in all our lives from here on. If daddy was here he would be saying a prayer for our protection and he would be telling us all that God will see us through to the other side of this. You all have to be strong, for the memory of him if for no other reason. Don't do anything that he wouldn't be proud of, don't do anything foolish. Stay safe in the church when the time comes to take refuge. We will get through this if we keep strong. Stay in hope for our future here in this beautiful place."

We were all silent at the end of his homily.

'Lord above,' I thought, 'that's me rebuked.'

The callous-hearted brother had just shown a side to him that I hadn't seen before. He was taking on our father's mantle…at last. It was a lovely speech, and a thoughtful thing to have done for us all. Mammy went and hugged him and shed tears on his shoulder. Biddy couldn't contain herself and scurried off to her lean-to at the back. We all joined in with mammy and sort of family hugged. It was a special moment.

But Alex could not stay long with us that day. He said he had another letter to deliver, this one to Mrs Stewart from her husband, and that then he must return to Coleraine without delay.

"Katie, I need to speak to you alone," he said quietly when no-one else was paying attention. "Slip out after me in a few minutes when I am leaving, alright?"

It was clear that Alex was being secretive. I wondered straight away was this to do with Darach. My heart started thumping in my chest at the thought that he might have been one of the casualties at Portnaw. Alex must have seen the blood drain out of my face for he put my mind at ease immediately.

"It is not bad news," he said with a glimmer of a smile in his eyes.

But I was desperately curious. I could barely wait to follow him up the loanin when he was leaving. I pretended that I wanted to lead this lovely bay mare that he had arrived on, but Connie saw through my guile and followed us at a distance. As soon as we were out of earshot of the others Alex began his story. And what an incredible tale it was.

He and Darach had become friends! Unbelievable. After all that strange antagonism my brother had shown towards him, my Darach was now his friend. He had helped Alex escape during the attack by McColla's soldiers, and they had ridden together to safety at Coleraine. More than that, Alex confessed to me that Darach and the priest McGlaim had been the ones who had rescued him from the Reids that day last summer when he had been attacked on the mountain. What a thing to hear, so long after the event.

"Why did you keep that from me?" I asked, completely astonished at this news.

"I don't know," he said. "I suppose it was because I could see that you both liked each other and I didn't want you to…"

"To what?"

"To be falling in love with an Irish fellow, a Catholic. It's just that…" He shook his head despairingly. "Look sister, it is not allowed, you know that already. It's not permitted at any time, but all the more so at the minute. At times like this it is never going to work, Katie. It's too hard for yous to make it work. Everything is against it, mainly the minister and the kirk."

"And do you still think that?" I asked.

"Maybe I do, but what I think doesn't matter. I have a good opinion of him as a person. I have seen a lot of terrible things recently, really evil people doing cruel things to folk of the other religion, things I couldn't repeat. I have nightmares about some of it, I honestly do. But Darach is so different from all that. He has a light in him, a sort of genuine thing about him."

"That's nice," I said. "And I agree, he does."

"Mind you, Bruce wouldn't share my opinion of him. He doesn't trust him."

"Bruce? Why, what does Bruce have to do with it? I hope you didn't tell him anything about me and Darach," I said.

"No of course I didn't. He just takes a different view of things, more black and white. But I told him that Darach has a good side to him."

"A good side? I hope it's more than that," I said.

"It is. He has been more than kind to me…and I despised him for it. I thought it was just because he was trying to impress me, as your brother, as if to bring me around to accepting him. But I saw him do something the other night in Coleraine, something very generous and caring, something that he didn't have to do."

"What was that?" I asked.

Alex seemed to think about whether to tell me the details or not.

"Well," he started again, "he went out of his way to act very kindly to a poor beggar, just a young street girl…and I realised that he acts because he has a good heart and a good conscience, not because he wants to get something out of it."

"What did he do?"

"She's starving, she has a wain and he went out at night into dangerous country to try to get her food. He didn't have to. She wouldn't be a very respectable girl, if you know what I mean, but he was kind enough to take the risk, just to get a few eggs for her and the wain."

"A street girl, you say? With a wain?"

"Aye, and he seemed really taken by her; felt sorry for her like."

"Oh dear," I said, "I wish he wouldn't put himself in such danger. Is he alright? He's not hurt or anything? Does he seem well?"

"He is fine, and he told me to tell you that," Alex said with a smile as we reached Stewart's Manor House.

"Is that all he said?" I asked.

"No, it's not all," he laughed. "He said a lot of things, far too many for me to be remembering."

"Oh Alex, tell me!"

"Just that he thinks about you all the ..."

Unfortunately Alex did not get to finish the message. At that moment, just as we arrived through the gates of Stewart's bawn, the front door of the Manor House burst open and Reverend Fullerton appeared, striding out urgently towards his horse, his beard thrust forward and his trademark black cloak billowing out behind him. He became aware of us and turned.

"Are you still here, young McKay?" he said, a bit irritated.

I was of no account here.

"I have a letter for Mrs Stewart," Alex said.

"Alright, give it here and I'll make sure she gets it. Now, away on to Coleraine before it gets any darker. You don't want to be out in open country at night-time. It is not safe anymore. Go lad!"

"I have to go to find Bruce," Alex said. "He came with me."

"All the more reason to be on your way now," Fullerton instructed firmly. "Give me the letter and away ye go!"

"Mr Stewart told me to give it into her hand."

"And I will do exactly that," Fullerton said, holding his hand out impatiently for the letter.

Reluctantly Alex handed it over.

"Now away ye go lad, and travel safe!"

Alex jumped on his horse with barely a 'goodbye', galloping off and leaving me to wonder about Darach. What was the missing part of his message to me? What should I make of this story about his kindness to a street-girl and her wain? Why had he become involved with her? I just wish I could have him here, to hold, to talk to, to hear him tell about everything he had seen. Maybe I am just being selfish and fretful. I should be rejoicing that I have heard from him at all, that he and Alex are safe and, above all, that they are friends.

I turned to find Connie back along the loanin, conscious that, while I had just had some of my worries eased, she was bound to be in need of comfort tonight.

Chapter 30

A Letter from Clough Castle

Darach O'Cahan

"Your Mister Archibald Stewart seems very angry," James McDonnell says, his voice sounding like a purr, "and I can understand why. Can ye understand why yoursel'?"

My immediate thought as I stand before this man is, 'What are you asking me for? I am just the message boy here.' I dare not antagonise him though, so I think quickly and come up with a diplomatic answer.

"I haven't read the letter, sir, so I can't really comment."

He glares at me. "But ye have an opinion, have ye naw? Ye say yer an O'Cahan…but ye are still loyal to Archibald Stewart. What sort o' Irishman are ye at all?"

This riles me.

"The sort that sticks by his friends….sir!"

"What is that supposed tae mean?" James' temper changes at once.

"Are ye trying tae suggest that I am an inferior kind o' human being because I have taken the Irish side in this infernal row? Count yoursel' lucky that I need ye tae take a reply letter back tae Stewart, otherwise a cheeky comment like that could hae ye thrown in the dungeon wae Kennedy and the rats down there."

"I meant no disrespect, sir," I tell him. "It's just that he gave me a job and I am trying to do it. I am taking no sides in this. I am bringing messages as I was employed to do."

"Very well. An' ye read these messages?"

"No sir."

"But ye can read?"

"Yes sir."

"And write?"

"Yes sir."

"Very well. If ye can write, that will save me the bother, for I struggle wae the letters in poor light like this."

While this sounds like a lame excuse I am in no position to argue. I myself find the evening light in the hall of Clough Castle to be very dull at that point. Sir James guides me to a solid-looking oak desk, sticks a quill in my hand and rummages around for parchment.

"Ye will have tae stay here the night," he tells me, selecting a tattered sheet that I think has already been used for another purpose. "This'll dae. Ye can take my response back tae Stewart at first light. And try tae impress on him that neither me nor Alaster McColla are his enemies. We wish him nae harm…but he must think hard before he decides tae oppose us…will ye make sure he understands the import o' this?"

"I will try," I tell him, "but maybe you should tell me what to write before the light disappears entirely."

'Very well,' McDonnell says; he clears his throat and begins.

Cousin Archibald,

I received your letter and, to tell the truth, I was ever of the opinion that your own self has no guile in you. All of us gentlemen on the Irish side agree with this. But if they had not acted as they did at Portnaw, and acted when they did, we would have been utterly destroyed, our wives and children as well. I myself had had intelligence of attack by your men from one who heard the plot being laid.

Those captains of yours are not honourable. They are, to be honest, a completely different breed to yourself. (They would be better called cowboys). They vexed us every day and picked quarrels with our men, which nobody could endure. I vow to the Almighty, had they not forced me (and many others of ours with me who would rather have hanged than do as they did), I would have stuck to your side as strongly as any of yourselves.

To tell you the truth, Cousin, the whole country has now come to us. Drogheda is under siege and people are reduced to eating horses. The folk of Ballymena and Antrim are fled to Carrickfergus. Your side must lose this war. It is folly to resist what God hath pleased to happen here.

You and your people in Coleraine are doomed. I wish no personal harm on you. In fact I will myself send boats from Rathlin Island to ferry you down the Bann and to safety, for believe me, if you wait there for Sir Phelim O'Neill to arrive at your gates you shall all most certainly be killed.

As for the killings of women and children here, none of my soldiers are responsible for such, but the common people are not under rule and did it in spite of us. In good faith we released the women and children of this place with the promise of safe passage to Scotland. We were not responsible for their deaths.

It is only fair to point out that some of your own side killed three score of women, children and old people. I have sent word of all this to our Lord and Lady who have gone to Slane.

Do not stir out of Coleraine until I come, otherwise you may perish. We do not wish to go against the King, nor indeed against the Earl, but our only aim is to have our religion settled and every one in his own ancient inheritance.

I rest your very loving cousin still,

James McDonnell

From the Catholic camp at Oldstone, Clough Castle;
11th January 1642

****

I lie in the draughty attic of this unfortunate castle. It is hard to sleep in these circumstances. This, despite my relief that Alaster McColla does not seem to be here at present.

Through a small opening in the gable wall I can see no less than three flaming beacons blazing on nearby hilltops. Their glow is reflected on the underbelly of the low-hanging sky. I cannot decide whether these are burning homesteads or bonfires set by rebels, an ancient ritual in our people, either as a call to arms or a publication of victory. It is an unsettling feeling in any event.

Before I came up these winding stairs tonight I happened to witness a very loud and angry conversation between Sir James and a distressed priest who had arrived at the castle. In hysterics, this priest…I did not catch his name…was inconsolable about the butchery of many of his parishioners at a place called Castle Upton. This cannot be far from here. In what seems to have been a reprisal for the murders of Protestant women and children nearby, many of Captain Upton's Irish Catholic tenants were slain without mercy by a rampaging mob of vengeful men. The Captain did not, or maybe could not, act to protect them. Yet another vile act to add to the many I have been hearing of. The clergyman had other examples; he had heard a rumour of a massacre at a place called Islandmagee where a large number of Catholics had apparently been butchered. McDonnell tried to calm the clergyman with promises of justice, but I got the feeling that authority over proceedings had been lost by these military commanders. It is now mob rule, beyond anyone's control.

As I try to sleep I am thinking that some distance below me the castle's occupant, Walter Kennedy, one of the Earl's loyal tenants and supporters, is probably trying to stay awake so as to scare off the hungry vermin in the dungeon. A few weeks ago he could have been wining and dining Sir James McDonnell, the same man who now sits in his seat of power and sends warning letters to loyal servants of the Earl. I wonder how long it will be until my home place at Dunluce is under siege, or under the control of these Highland McDonnells. How quickly things can become unstable in the strange and complex world of Irish politics.

Things can seem calm on the surface; the river flows quietly towards the ocean. Then something triggers a rupture of the normal and in no time the river has reared up and is flowing back towards the mountains.

I think about Katie. I wonder how she reacted to the message I sent with Alex yesterday. I wonder did he tell her of our reconciled relationship, indeed of our mutual friendship. I hope he did. I think he probably did…and I imagine she is very happy about that. I wonder what sort of panic is going on among the Protestants there in Ballintoy? I hope she is feeling safe.

She and I. What future can we have in this place where you cannot be sure of the course or direction of the river? We have each other, and I know that nothing will change that. But we also have the histories and memories of our peoples running deep in our blood-streams. Will things run smoothly? Or are there even worse rapids up ahead that could throw the course of our life together into even deeper chaos?

And I think about that poor girl and her child on the banks of the Bann. What chance has she had in life so far? Abused, taken advantage of, abandoned with her bastard baby, little Kate. What sadness there is in people's lives. So many now fleeing in fear and desperation towards the strongholds of places like Coleraine. They are like sheep, trying to take protection in each other's company, not really understanding that, as in the days of wolves in Ireland, the flocking together instinct is the worst thing they could do. It makes them an easier target. The wolves don't have to scamper around searching them out any more. Now they have them cornered.

I wonder what I will find when I ride through this boggy terrain tomorrow on my return journey to Archibald Stewart. I know he is going to be livid when he reads this letter, that is the one certainty.

I lie here listening to the whistle of the wind in the eaves of this old castle. What I would give right now to be walking on the strand at White Park Bay with my girl, sniffing the scent of the wild flowers and the clean sea air, and hearing the relentless swish of the waves. The melody of my own music rises in me and I hum the tune of the sea quietly to myself. Tonight the minor keys prevail and the piece takes on the feeling of lament, a dirge of hopelessness.

When will I hold my harp again?

When, if ever, will I hold my girl again?

Chapter 31

Survival

Darach O'Cahan

Back in the comparative safety of Coleraine I am thankful for my survival on that return journey. North Antrim is now a landscape polluted by violence. Wild men dance in a carnival of revenge. They target anyone 'other'. Failing to find a clear enemy, they choose to take out their retribution on easier prey. I was such a target. A target for both sides.

Near Dunloy I was dragged off my horse by three gulpins who leapt down on me from the branches of a couple of wayside trees. Trees used to be my friends; now I am going to have to start looking at them with suspicion.

These were dangerous men. Half drunk on *poitín*, half mad with hatred. What was I, a stranger, doing in their country, they asked in English. I replied, in English, that I was only a messenger on a journey and was about to show them the letter to Mr Stewart as proof of my bona fides when I heard one of them, a dagger-wielding older man, say, *"Maraigh é!* Kill him!"

"Ná maraigh mé!" I replied urgently, going easily into Irish and setting the tone and language for the rest of the conversation. They had been about to kill me on the basis of a guess that I was a Protestant, with no Irish.

Not long after I was on the outskirts of Ballymoney travelling through a boggy area of reeds and salley bushes. This time a whole mob of about twenty, both men and women, surrounded me. There was a lot of anger in their eyes, anger and fear. They swore revenge for the burning of their homes at Cross. It didn't seem to matter to them who they took their revenge on; I had strayed into this swamp where they seemed to be taking shelter in hovels made of little more than turf and branches. I was in severe danger of being lynched there and then, regardless of who I was. The conversation was all in their local Scottish-sounding dialect of English this time. I quickly realised that a word of Irish here would have ensured that it would have been my last. As would mention of my surname. By this stage 'O'Cahan' had become as devilish a name as that of Satan himself.

This time the letter to Mr Stewart was my saviour and, after a period of questioning, to which I replied with only the minimum of words, and in as Scottish an accent as I could muster, I was allowed to go on my way.

Not far from there I witnessed a sight that will stay in my memory, but might well have been my fate, had I not possessed that letter. As *Liath* brought me through a pleasant grove of tall oaks and birches, something away to the side attracted the mare's attention, disturbing her usual calm. She gave a snort of panic and made a sudden shy off the path. I looked to see the cause of her scare. Hanging from a branch were the naked bodies of three men, their flesh slashed all over so that wounds lay open and entrails hung out. I retched and spurred the poor horse forward away from this scene of butchery. What savages we have become in this God-forsaken country. What had they done to deserve death in so cruel a manner? Likely nothing at all. It was enough to be of the wrong faith; perhaps enough to have no word of Irish or to be clothed in garments that were needed to protect someone from the winter cold. Or perhaps this was a revenge killing, meted out on some vulnerable Catholic neighbours. Either way, it was a grotesque sight.

It feels much better to be inside the ramparts of Coleraine. This, despite the growing crisis of hunger in the town. My mind goes at once to the plight of Nellie and her child. I badly want to find her and make sure that she has been all right in the three days since I brought food.

I wonder has Alex returned from Ballintoy; what news is there of Katie? Is there a message for me from her?

But first I must find Archibald Stewart and pass on this response from McDonnell. He is nowhere to be seen in the market hall. I wander around searching for him. As I do, I witness the sad sight of bodies being carried through the gates for burial just outside the ramparts. I count four such hasty funerals in quick succession. The corpses are covered by filthy looking shrouds. Stretchers weigh heavily in the hands of solemn-faced older gentlemen who, I presume, were not considered able-bodied enough to be in the regiment. From a distance I watch as the shrouds are removed and the naked remains of these poor people are tipped into a huge pit. No time for individual graves in these fraught circumstances. A very tall, sharp-faced clergyman holds his nose as he intones the burial rites. The stretcher carriers do not even wait until he is finished, dragging their stooped figures back past me to find more cargo, biers and shrouds in hand for further use. I turn away, steeling myself to be faithful to my particular duties.

When I find Mr Stewart and share the letter, his reaction is one of fury. He shouts his rebuttal of every point in the letter, laughing sardonically at the offer of safe conduct out of the town on boats from Rathlin.

"If, as he says, he respects me and my integrity, why is he siding against me? Why is he with the rebels? If he hates to be disloyal to the King and the Earl why is he choosing to be so? The man is a mess of contradictions. And as to his demand that we stay safe in Coleraine until he comes...does he not understand that we have many thousands of people here who are starving and will perish if I cannot secure them food? What is to become of them if I take one of his imaginary boats to Scotland? They will be slaughtered like pigs in a pen. What nonsense he writes!"

I do see his point. I admire his commitment to these his people, his feeling of duty to feed them and protect them. I cannot see how he will be able to manage this though. Where is he going to find the food supplies for this multitude when so much of the country is in Irish hands, and so many cattle have already been stolen or slain?

He asks me who and what I saw at Clough? Was Alaster and Raghnall there? I tell him that I saw only Sir James. I have no idea where the brothers were.

I decide to ask him if he has any news of his home village.

"Has Alex McKay returned from Ballintoy, sir?"

"He has, and Bruce McClure too. They must be around here somewhere. You'll excuse me now...and well done on your exploits, even if I don't like the message you brought."

So I wander around the town, becoming more and more disturbed by the sights I am witnessing. Thankfully I find Alex before too long, for the loneliness of being so helpless here is starting to distress me. I need to be talking to someone about more normal things.

Alex and his two Ballintoy friends, Bruce and another young man called Matt, are warming themselves beside a blazing bonfire. I see their distorted faces through the rising heat and blowing smoke. I go to join them. We start to exchange stories; it is what men do in these grim circumstances. They listen closely to my tale concerning my travels to Clough and back. Even though I do not feel comfortable enough to share the gory details of the massacres at Glenravel or Castle Upton, I notice their grave reactions to the experiences I do recount. Bruce is studying me very closely, especially when I mentioned the hangings in the grove of oaks.

"Did you not stop to see if there were any of them still alive? You might have saved a life," he says, his tone accusing.

Before I can answer, Alex does so for me. "Hardly likely, Bruce. Anyway, he'd have been putting himself in danger if he'd stopped. You can't be doing that when you are carrying an important message, can you?"

Matt supports him. "No sir," he says, "you can't be doing that. He's right Bruce. He is surely."

I move on to ask about their trip to Ballintoy.

Their news is mixed. The Smith family, Bruce tells us, are in deep mourning, understandably so. The loss of Thomas, their only son, is a massive blow. Bruce had had to stay with them until a clergyman could be found to bring them some solace. Alex had delivered his messages safely to Fullerton and Boyd, and then a letter to Mrs Stewart. They had encountered no dangers on their trip, they say.

I am less interested in that information, however, and it probably shows in my impatience. Before Alex has properly finished the detail of his tale I can wait no longer.

"And did you get to speak to Katie?" I ask, far too eagerly, then realising what I have done, I add, "and your mother and all?"

The pained reaction in Alex's eyes tells me that I have spoken unwisely here. He flicks the briefest of glances at his friends. I follow his look. Bruce's face is a dark picture of surprised indignation.

"Aye, everything's grand," Alex says dismissively. He then rambles on about Aunt Biddy and some story about her goat getting lost, but I am not really listening. Neither, I notice, is Bruce. He is staring daggers at me. I am not sure what ghosts my question has stirred in him but, from the hostility I feel from him right now, I am guessing that he suspects my relationship with Alex's sister…and objects to it.

"You know Katie?"

His question comes out as a rough rasp, his throat tightened by some ill-disguised emotion. I cannot but answer the truth.

"I do," I say as casually as I can muster. "She and I are friends."

"Hmm, you have a lot o' friends," he says. "There's that lass with the big eyes that you fell for, last time we were here. She was your sort of friend, wasn't she? Now you tell me you are friends with Katie McKay as well. You're spreading yourself around, aren't you…. O'Cahan?"

I could tell him to mind his own business but I don't think it would go down well. I decide to ignore his barb. To my mind he is just looking for a fight. I am not going to oblige.

I wonder about his motives. Is his antagonism here simply to do with my religion? My Irishness? Or does he have feelings for Katie himself, perhaps some prior claim on her from before she met me?

I will ask Alex later about this reaction. In the meantime I think I will steer well clear of Bruce. He is not going to get over this easily, I am thinking. I make some excuse and leave the three of them to their bonfire.

****

Thinking about Katie, even admitting to my friendship with her, and braving the reaction I have just witnessed, is all very fine, but it is no substitute for being able to be with her in person. I need to see her face again. The sights I have seen today need to be counter-balanced by the sweet loveliness I see in her. My depression needs to be tempered by the sense of wholeness and contentment I have when I am with her. How I miss that…and yet the absence of her, the deprivation I experience when I am long without her, makes me realise just how deep is our connection, our oneness. She is the soft welcoming sand to my crashing waves. Whatever template God used when he created Katie, it was the mirror image of how he constructed me; the two of us fit together so perfectly, like a well-made mortice and tenon joint.

I am about to leave the town's market square to go to search for Nellie when Archibald Stewart reappears leading a procession of his key soldiers. Something is happening, I can sense a mood of action. Gradually I gather that a large company of soldiers is being assembled to search the surrounding countryside for food. It will be a dangerous mission should these troops encounter a column of the Irish, I think, as I watch them ride out through the eastern gates of the town, Alex and Bruce among them.

I am not required for Stewart's scavenging escapade, so I take the opportunity to go to look for Nellie and the child, to see how they are. Going down towards the river I notice that the level of the Bann has risen by a few feet; I don't know whether this is because of heavy rainfall upstream or if a high tide at sea is holding back the river at the Barmouth.

Soon I arrive at Nellie's makeshift shelter. I call from outside but there is no response. Nellie must be somewhere in the town. As I turn to search elsewhere I catch the faint noise of what sounds like a child whimpering weakly. It seems to be coming from the shelter so I approach and lift the hanging cowhide which serves as an entrance. I immediately see that Nellie is there, stretched out asleep or at least resting on her rough bed, her face turned towards the wall. Little Kate is awake in her cot, making a weak gerning sound. She turns and sees me through that mop of tousled fair hair; the cry becomes louder and she stands up, stretching out her skinny arms to me in that familiar gesture of wanting to be lifted. I look at Nellie, but she hasn't wakened. Should I lift the child to give some comfort? My natural reaction is to do that, perhaps take her for a bit of air or exercise, or to find some milk in the market square if there is any, but I would not want Nellie to wake up and find her child gone. I look at her again, her head tucked away under a shawl. She seems so sound asleep that I think I can risk lifting Kate. Her arms still reach up for me, her innocent eyes pleading. So I take her up and give her a cuddle.

I wonder how long since either she or her mother have eaten. I must take Kate and try to find some more food.

I walk into the market square again, into that sea of anxious faces. I am carrying the child. She has stopped crying, thankfully. I search for any sign of vittles. Even a small cup of milk would help give some nourishment to her. But there is literally nothing I can find for her to eat. Dare I give her a mouthful of beer, the weak brew that is still being produced in this town? I go in the direction of the brewhouse just beyond the east gate, and I am thankful that I do. It turns out that the brewery owner has just organised some sort of a kitchen and his workers are handing out small bowls of gruel, perhaps using the spent grain left over after mashing. I have coin enough to buy two bowls, one for Kate and one to staunch my own hunger. I use my fingers to feed the child; this isn't easy as the gruel is so thin and I have no utensil. It's a case of dip and suck on my fingers. Still, Kate gets some nourishment into her, although it would not be true to say that she enjoys the taste. Neither do I; we could do with some flavouring, a pinch of salt or something. The two wooden bowls we must leave for the next folk in the lengthening queue. Now to go back, waken Nellie and bring her for some of this gruel.

Back in her hovel I see that she still sleeps.

I put Kate back in her cot.

I speak to Nellie, but she doesn't make any response; she must be so tired, I think. I touch her arm, lightly. She feels…

Horror rises in me! She is so cold.

I shake her.

"Nellie! Nellie! For God's sake Nellie…waken up!"

Cold as a fish.

She will never waken up again. Nellie lies still on her bed…I turn her head up towards me. Huge, darkly blank eyes! Her skin a cloudy white, her lips bluish.

Dead to the world. In every sense.

I am struck into a terrible wordless freeze of disbelief, realisation, confusion. My hands clasp tightly behind my head. My chest hurts sharply.

The poor, tragic girl! How could this have happened? What to do? What have I done? Why did I let this happen? How long has she been dead? Why did I not realise this when I first saw her lying there so still? How am I going to handle this? Will anyone help? Does anyone else care? I don't even know her second name.

And above all…what am I to do with Kate, this unfortunate child?

I have experienced much anguish in the past few weeks, but this horrible lonely death of one so undeservingly destitute, so very young, shakes me to the core. What has our innocent world descended to?

Slowly I come to realise that I must get those men with the stretchers to come and carry Nellie's body away for burial. So once again I walk through the town centre, looking for help, carrying Kate in my arms. It is a useless search. I can find no pall bearers. By a piece of good fortune the one person I do run into is the tall clergyman, the one I had seen burying bodies at the mass grave earlier. He is busy outside his church in the main thoroughfare of the town. I wait and watch as he and a couple of women are caring for some very needy-looking families. It is not easy to interrupt such admirable efforts, but eventually I catch his eye.

"Can you help me?" I say.

"If I can. What can I do?"

So I tell him the story of Nellie's death, and of this child.

"Nellie was Presbyterian," I say, "so if I can get her body round to the graveyard could you give her a proper burial? In her own religion?"

"What is she to you, young man?" he asks sympathetically, but with just a hint of a suspicion. "Is this your child?"

"Not my child," I tell him. I am not convinced that he believes me.

"Are you sure? How come you are so interested in it then?"

"Look Father," I say, a bit annoyed at his doubt and forgetting that this is not how I should address a Protestant priest, "I have only just met its mother. She is just someone I saw begging. The child has no father. If one of your women here could look after her for a bit while I bring Nellie's body please?"

"All right, I think I can arrange that," he says a bit more kindly, "but you must promise to come back for the child?"

"Of course I will."

"And what do you plan to do with her?"

I hadn't really worked that out yet, so I tell him honestly my dilemma, and that I am engaged as Archibald Stewart's messenger at present and therefore at his whim. I explain that I don't know the whereabouts of Nellie's family, not even their name.

"Don't you have family yourself, someone who could take care of her?"

Those thoughts had run through my head as well. Should I take Kate to John and Eilish at Dunluce? How would they feel about me landing this wain in on them, they who never reared a child of their own until they fostered me? Maybe my own family at Straid would be a better choice. Rosie and Meabh would love to be trying to rear a child, I have no doubt. I am sure my parents would not turn her away. So I tell the minister that I have a plan, even as it is forming in my head.

Kate is taken from my arms by a kind-faced, cooing lady. She hasn't the energy to resist, her small face a blank stare of acceptance.

"I will be back for you," I tell her, "when I have…"

No point in trying to explain any more. I arrange to meet the clergyman at the grave site shortly and drag myself back to Nellie's hovel.

Her final journey through her adopted town is something I will remember for a very long time.

She weighs nothing in my arms. Her head hangs over my elbow on one side. The long dark hair that was once her glory now a withered wreath. Her dark eyes stare up blindly at the low, purple-grey sky. Her thin blue lips stretch around a gaping bog-hole of a mouth. Skinny arms flap from her like strips of tattered cloth. Her long legs swing and clatter together like a pair of corn flails.

Smoke from a few fires in the middle of the market square drifts across my path and adds to the wateriness of my eyes. People move aside, turn their heads away. A few pitying nods as kinder folk meet my gaze, but I hear one or two curses of mindless contempt. A madness has swept through this place, a mania fuelled by hunger and hatred, destitution and despair. I have seen the worst of human-kind in the past month. I have also witnessed much mercy.

The minister is one of the merciful. Standing below me in the shallow pit, he actually takes Nellie from my arms himself and lays her down on the sodden earth with great gentleness. He calls her his daughter, talks to her with such kindness, tries but fails to close her open eyes before the soil is shovelled over her face. Then he reads his funeral rites in a voice that is ceremonial but full of compassion. There is no sprinkling of holy water as would likely have been done by one of our priests, just a few verses from their Bible and a couple of prayers. Nellie is committed to God, and to the earth from which she came.

I stand there for ages afterwards, after I have thanked him. He had taken both my hands in his and mumbled a prayer for me.

"Make sure you come back for the child now," he had said. "It is going to need someone of your caring nature to rear it."

Staring into that huge grave, at the thin layer of soil that now blankets the body of the girl whose name was Nellie, whose surname I never discovered, I speak a silent promise to her.

"Your child will be all right, Nellie. I will do my best for your wee Kate."

Chapter 32

Shelter

Katie McKay

How strange it felt to be leaving our home and moving to take shelter in our kirk. I had felt secure in our cottage. I could sense the fear and panic that my elders were possessed by, but it had not really taken hold on my own imaginings. I could not quite believe that we were in any danger in the home that had been ours since my parents set it up so many years ago. Our haven under threat from the people we had grown up beside, our neighbours? It was not easy to understand, never mind believe.

Yet there we were, sleeping on the rough wooden floorboards of the church, wakening up to the rude sounds of other families as they rose and especially as they used the buckets in the corner behind the pulpit. The stench from there was bad enough without the noises! The building was very small of course; I had never really counted, but probably only about fifty people could be seated for a Sabbath service. Even with most of our men missing there were over forty of us crowded in there most evenings during that time of waiting. Privacy, it seemed, was a memory.

All openings apart from the main door had been built up with stone against the possibility of attack. Only thin slits had been left for ventilation. As a result, the interior of the building was even darker than normal. The children did not enjoy this dull atmosphere. With the general fustiness and gloom of the unusual surroundings they cried and coughed a great deal. It was anything but warm in the kirk. Outside, winter frost lay on the land, and the icy cold atmosphere inside had us huddling together in families for some comforting heat.

In those early days of the crisis at the start of February we only went to the kirk at night to sleep. We were allowed to leave the building during the daylight hours to tend our animals if they were nearby. Reverend Fullerton gave us firm instructions not to go any further from the protection of the building than necessary. Although normally the vicar in Derrykeighan, Fullerton seemed to have taken control of things in our kirk of late. I hadn't seen much of him before, but according to my mother he had some official position in the Route yeomanry. He was an interesting looking man, elderly and very traditional with his flowing black clothes. He had the greatest beard I ever saw on any man. It must have been a foot long! Like Joseph's coat, it was a beard of many colours. He walked with a noticeable stoop, his head stuck out in front.

Our Connie joked to me once, "Fullerton's beard looks like it's leading him; he is just trying to keep up."

Mr Fullerton told the people who lived up in the village that they were not to venture there; it was too far away to be able to return safely if the church-bell was rung to sound an alarm. The McKays were all right in that respect, our home being only a matter of a short walk from the Manor House and the adjacent church. We could spend the day at home as normal, except that someone had to be on watch, ready to call us back in response to any sign of danger. No danger had arisen…until!

The day that the church bell rang! We froze in what we were doing, then ran, hearts pounding, pulling our door closed behind us.

But the bell stopped after a few clangs. We were halfway to the church, running. The bell stopped? What did it mean? Had it been a mistake? We weren't sure whether we should continue or go back home. Was it a false alarm or a genuine threat? The uncertainty was nearly worse than the initial dread that had arisen in us at the sound of those first peals. Mammy said we should go on to the church anyhow, just incase, so we followed her, more slowly this time, all of us looking around and especially staring up towards the rise of hills to the south and in the direction of Dunseverick to the west. If danger was coming it would likely appear from there. It wasn't likely that any threat would come from the sea, although Mr Fullerton had taken the precaution of posting a look-out on top of the white cliffs above the harbour. Our Connie had had to be the watcher a couple of days ago. Fullerton had organised a rota of sharp-eyed young folk to scan the horizon for possible attacking ships coming in our direction. None had as yet.

Connie was behind me as we reached the church. I went in after Aunt Biddy who was beside herself with fear. For some reason Connie didn't follow me. Other folks from the local houses were crowding in at the door, joining the people already inside, but there was much uncertainty.

Thomas Boyd was agitated himself while trying to calm us all down. "It may be a false alarm," he said. "We got a signal from the look-out on the hill, might be nothing but we can't take any chances."

I looked around for Connie. Where had she gone? What was keeping her outside? I moved towards the door to see where she had gone. As I reached it she appeared, a strange look in her eyes; she had seen something out there, but what? She was definitely not alarmed, nor in any dread. The opposite if anything.

She beckoned me outside. "Katie," she said, "come and look. It's a stranger, but I think it's all right."

I joined her in the churchyard and followed her gaze up to the hill. Someone coming down from there on horseback.

A grey horse. My heart leapt.

"I think it's him," Connie said.

Alarm or not, I was running towards him. Could it be true? I wished the wind would take me up and carry me, maybe even land me on that horse as well.

Darach! What on earth was he doing here? I could barely contain my excitement; his horse went down into a hollow and disappeared from my view. When it reappeared, much closer now, I could see for the first time that the rider had something in front of him, something or…someone? It stopped me in my tracks as I tried to focus more carefully. It was definitely a 'someone', a tiny child by the looks of things. But my attention went straight back to Darach's face, locked on to those intense eyes and his broad smile as he came closer, beautiful as ever; my heart raced with delight as he arrived beside me.

We didn't have to say a word to each other.

He reached the child down to me so he could dismount. And then I was in his arms, turning my lips up to his mouth, trying to stifle a sob that had begun as a giggle of joy. It was just the most wonderful feeling, to be with him again, to feel my lover back close against me…except that the child I was still holding was between our bodies and was starting to protest as the breath was being squeezed out of it. I drew myself back a little for the child's sake, but Darach still held my head between his hands.

"I love you, Katie," he kept repeating.

Eventually I got to ask the obvious question.

"Who is this?" I said, stroking the tousled fair hair of the little girl in my arms in an effort to comfort her.

"This is Kate," he said.

"Kate? And who is Kate?"

"She's just a child I found…it's a long story. Can we go down to your house, do you think? We could do with some food if you have any, and something to drink? Do you think your mother would mind?"

"No of course not," I told him, "She is in the church anyway, so please come."

We talked on the short walk back, Darach leading his horse. As I carried Kate I began to hear the strange story of her unfortunate mother. I soon realised that this is the child of the beggar girl that Alex had told me about. What had he said about Darach and his connection to that street girl? I did recall that my brother had been impressed by Darach's kindness to her. But who was she and how had my Darach become so concerned with her plight?

It felt strange to be entertaining my secret lover in my own home, the first time he had been inside there…and it is just him and me, and the child of course, and me making something for him to eat, and getting some milk for the girl, a proper wee family, of sorts.

But this wain?

She seems to be a couple of years old. I did not know Darach back then, nor anything about him. How well did I know him now? Could he have known this girl in Coleraine at that stage? What was it Alex had said exactly? A stranger, wasn't she? I hoped so. I told myself so. I put it from my mind as I looked at him across our table and we ate together.

Mammy and Aunt Biddy arrived in from the church, soon followed by Connie and Alice, and a whole set of explanations began. It was an awkward time for us as a family, very hard for mammy. I was ashamed and annoyed at myself for never having properly told her of my courtship with Darach. I knew that from long before she had probably guessed something had still been going on, but I had shied away from telling her about it. It had suited me to keep it hidden from her. Now, in the rawness of this situation, with the threat from the Irish, including those Irish who shared the name and lineage of this stranger, this O'Cahan, it was a terribly difficult situation for her. Poor Darach was caught in the middle. The presence of this wain made the whole affair even more of a problem. I was still trying to understand what Darach had been telling me about her and her mother. Now mammy was trying to come to terms with the existence of a suitor in my life, a young man she had very little notion of, who had somehow materialised in our home from nowhere… and bearing a little girl that he was somehow responsible for.

Aunt Biddy added to the confusion. At first I noticed her smiling at Darach in that gormless way she has, far too familiar. I thought little of it, Biddy and her simple-minded adoration of anything with breeches on it. Then I noticed her reaction change; as she became aware of the wain in Darach's arms she seemed to become more perplexed.

I don't think I have ever been in a more uncomfortable position. My mind was in turmoil and my heart torn between Darach and my mother and my family…and it was all complicated by this Kate whose existence I could not quite comprehend.

Initially there were long silences. Questions, when they got the courage to be asked, were gentle, mannerly. Then it all seemed to change, as the pressures of the external world seeped under the door and into our kitchen.

"Isn't this the same fellow you talked to last year at the fair?" mammy whispered to me.

"It is; I am sorry, mammy."

She shook her head slowly in bewilderment, deep hurt and disappointment on her face.

"This is a terrible time to be doing this to me," she moaned. "In the middle of all this…"

"But he and I, we love each other. You'll like him when you get to know him, honestly you will. He's a good person, mammy."

"A good person he may be, but what would your father think of this, eh? What will the neighbours think?"

Aunt Biddy joined in, supporting her, tutting. "And him bringing his wain into our house. Next he'll be wanting to take you away from us."

"I don't want to take…" Darach tried to say.

"He has a wain," Biddy mused, chuntering on to herself, half-heard.

"You're being very cruel to us," mammy said. I noticed she was on the point of tears. "He is not one of us, he's a complete stranger, and he walks in here…"

"It is not like that," I began, "the child has…"

But it was hard to be heard. Too many voices were speaking at once, the tone and volume raised. I looked at Darach, wondering what he was making of all this, and he at the centre of the fuss. I was scared he was going to get up and leave us in disgust, but he just stood there, quietly waiting for some resolution.

Thankfully our Connie stepped up and took on the challenge of settling us all down. She stood forward and spoke firmly to us all.

"Listen everybody, let me speak a minute."

People took heed of her when she spoke like that.

"Look," she said, "Darach is not a stranger. You remember mammy, we saw him at the fair in Ballycastle? I have been with Katie when she was walking out with him; she hasn't done anything wrong. She would have told you about him mammy, I know she would, especially after our Alex getting friendly with him."

"Alex is friendly with him?" mammy said. "How does he even know him?"

"Because Darach is the one who rescued Alex when he was attacked on the mountain!" I said.

That brought a long, confused look to mammy's face. She stared at me, speechless, but Biddy, I noticed, was nodding wisely in agreement.

"Aye, he is the one," Biddy said. "He's the one brought the message that Alex was all right that night. It was you, wasn't it? Same laddie we saw at the Lammas Fair? And then you came one night to see…."

"It was me, indeed it was. I met you on the lane," Darach interrupted, sparing my blushes. "And then, as you say, in Ballycastle…"

"There's proof of it," Connie said, "And that is not the only time he rescued Alex. He saved his life at that place when the Irish turned on our ones. Alex said all this himself. He owes Darach. We all do. Alex used to be against the idea of them courting, but it seems he has changed his mind a bit. Isn't that right, Darach? Katie?"

Darach looked at me and I nodded for him to speak.

"It is the truth. Alex and I are good friends. We both work for Archibald Stewart."

Mammy turned away silently to the door of her room, the weight of all these revelations visibly burdening her. She paused there, head down, wounded, bewildered, then spoke a gentle rebuke to me over her shoulder.

"Katie," she said, "I am hurt that you never told me of your secret. You should have trusted me. You should have told me about all this."

"I am sorry," I said, "but I didn't know how to explain it all to you. I didn't want to worry you. And Alex was against it, as far as I knew…up until recently."

She turned back to face us all and asked a question to Darach that I needed to hear an answer to as well.

"Be that as it may, but how does this wain fit into the picture? Is it yours?"

"Her name is Kate, and no, she is not my child. I promised her mother I would take care of her," Darach told her.

"Her mother? What is her mother to you?"

Darach looked pained. His head went down and I had another pang of fear… aye, maybe of jealousy too.

But he has just told me a dozen times that he loves me, I thought.

"I wish I could explain to you what is happening in Coleraine," he said. "Out here on the coast everything is still peaceful. You have food. You feel safe. But a morning's walk from here the country is in chaos. I know it's hard for you to credit; here the sea looks as calm and beautiful as ever, everything looks the same but believe me, this country is being torn apart and people are suffering terrible things. I have seen more dead bodies than I could count. I have seen people, women and children, almost naked, wandering about the countryside looking for a scrap of food. In Coleraine dozens of people have died with hunger. I wish Alex was here to tell you what we have seen. He knows about Nellie."

He broke off and became silent, his head down as he tried to control his emotions. I thought he was in some kind of shock, of despair.

This reference to a 'Nellie', the first time he had mentioned a name, surprised me, concerned me. She wasn't just a street girl, she was Nellie.

I found myself asking the question, "Who is Nellie?" even though I knew he was referring to Kate's mother.

He looked at me sadly for a moment.

"Who was Nellie, more like," he said. "She was just a girl, just like you, Katie, Connie. About the same age. I don't even know her second name. She was starving. I got food for her, and for the child. But when I came back from one of my journeys I found her dead in her shack. The child was crying beside her. Hunger likely killed her. I had to help."

He stopped and we waited in silence for a bit.

"You did," mammy said. "You had to help. Go on with your story."

"I got a priest to bury her. There are so many bodies they put them all in the same grave. He was a good priest, that man. He told me to take the child to someone to look after…because, you see, I made a promise to

Nellie, and her lying dead in front of me. I promised to look after her baby, but I don't know how, for now I have to go back to work for Mr Stewart."

"Of course," mammy said.

"So I thought I would take her to my family, over at Straid. My mother and sisters could sort of foster her, the way I was fostered myself. They would love another wee girl. But when I got to their house it was empty. My family are gone. I have no idea where. No sign of them."

"Your people have left?" I said. "Did you ask anyone about them?"

"I tried," he continued. "I asked neighbours, but they....well, first they ignored me. They seemed a bit embarrassed, awkward about me finding my house empty. Then when I became more demanding they chased me. I had to get out of there fast. One man fired a pistol after me. He missed of course, but it was strange to be hearing the sound of a gun firing and know it was pointed at my back and thinking that any minute now I will feel a tearing in my flesh. But it missed, thank God. My horse was great, so quick. So I escaped, and here we are. I could not think of anything else to do."

He looked at me, a long pleading look. I gave him a slight nod of approval. "Katie, do you think…you see, when her mother told me her name was Kate I sort of felt a connection. I never imagined then that I would be bringing her to you."

Mammy spoke for us all. "You did right and I commend you for it. We would take care of her until this is all over, but there's a problem. You see, we are all having to take refuge in our kirk at the minute. It's a Protestant one, you understand."

Darach paused to think about this for a second, trying to understand my mother's hesitation.

"Ah, I see what you mean," he said eventually, "but sure as long as it is a christian church? Weren't most of the Protestant churches around here Catholic churches before….before it all got changed on us."

That took the wind out of mammy's sails a bit. What he said was true, even if people of my religion did not like to be reminded of the fact. I could see that the barb in Darach's comment had antagonised my mother, but she let it pass and didn't let it put her off her point.

"That's as maybe," she said after a tense moment, "but not our wee kirk. The child would have to come with us…and if she is Catholic… well, maybe her mother wouldn't have wanted that, you know what I mean?"

"I do, but Nellie wasn't Catholic."

Mammy looked hard at him. "But you said you got a priest to bury her?"

"I did, but he was one of your priests. Nellie had told me she was Presbyterian you see. That's why I got one of your clergymen to bury her."

My mother thought about this for a second.

"So you promised that poor girl that you would take care of her wain, and she isn't even one of yours? She is a Protestant?"

"I suppose I did," Darach said. "I never thought about it like that. She was just a girl."

"Just a girl indeed," said Aunt Biddy. "You're a good boy,".

Then to me she whispered behind her hand, "I like him, Katie."

Everybody heard her, including Darach. He gave me a little wink. I couldn't help smiling at Biddy's benediction.

"What do you think, Katie?" Darach said, looking at me with a plea that I could not ignore. This man, my man, had a depth of love and kindness in him that I recognised as special. I felt privileged to know him, let alone be his girl. I smiled into his asking eyes. Then I crossed the floor to him as he sat there, Kate on his knee and, in front of mammy and Biddy and Alice and Connie, I took his hand.

"She can be our first, Darach," I whispered.

Aunt Biddy tutted in amazement at my brazenness, and Connie's face nearly burst laughing at her. My mother's face, though, was solemn and tight-lipped in doubt.

Darach stayed in our house as long as he dared. It was very interesting to watch how quickly he seemed to become one of the family. He had another bite to eat at our table, though the fare was very limited.

"Do you think we will be in danger here?" I asked. "We have the kirk to take refuge in, but maybe it won't be necessary?"

"I honestly don't know, but from what I have seen I would say that you will need to shelter there," he told us. "The rising is all over the country. It's just a matter of time before the Irish army makes it this far. And even if the soldiers don't come a lot of my own people seem to have a blood-lust boiling in their veins; nobody is safe."

It was not what we wanted to hear but none of us doubted him. And so, after I said goodbye to him and watched *Liath* gallop from view, I joined the rest of my family as we made our way over to the kirk for another night of uncertainty and discomfort. There were going to be questions when we arrived in with this wain. I didn't want there to be any mention of Darach and I said this to mammy. She nodded in agreement and called the girls and Biddy together into a family huddle.

"People are going to be asking who the wain is, and how she has landed in on us," mammy said. "So what we all say is that Kate was brought to us from Coleraine by a friend of Alex, all right?"

"If anybody asks just say that she is an orphan. Don't be saying anything about Darach," I added.

Connie and Biddy got the point, but Alice wanted to know why.

"Because Darach is working secretly for Mr Stewart and nobody is supposed to know about him. You can keep a secret Alice, can't you? You don't want to put him in danger."

Biddy grabbed Alice playfully, putting her hand over the child's mouth. "Aye Alice. You an' me can baith keep secrets, can't we."

Kate felt warm and content as she snuggled into me and fell asleep on my bed of straw that night. Sleep didn't come so easily to me though; my mind wouldn't give me peace at all.

Chapter 33

Black Friday

When they left the safety of Coleraine on that February morning of 1642 Alex McKay and Bruce McClure could not have imagined the disastrous events that they were to witness before their return.

On the first few days it had been a matter of searching for livestock. The troops spread out across the countryside, listening and looking for any sign of cattle, then seizing them from their resentful owners with the vague promise of recompense whenever circumstances permitted. The scrawny beasts were then driven back to the town for slaughter. On some farms the soldiers were able to acquire sheep, pigs and a few poultry. The convoys of food had to be well guarded in case of attack from rebel forces or hungry Irish. It was a huge operation.

Finding any other source of food was next to impossible. Corn supplies had been low all winter after the terrible weather of the previous summer. Vegetables were also in short supply. Many farms had been abandoned as fearful settlers had fled to the protection of the towns. Houses on these farms were raided for any remaining food and, indeed, for any clothing that could be used back in Coleraine to give to those who had been stripped of their garments. Other farms were still occupied by tenants of the Earl, mostly Irish who had nothing to fear from the rebel forces.

Alex listened to the strongly voiced complaints of one of these, a prosperous tenant, Coll McAllester, who farmed near Derrykeighan.

"You have stolen one hundred and twenty cattle from me, Archibald Stewart! When am I ever going to get compensation for these?" McAllester had yelled.

"You will get your compensation," Stewart told him.

"I will believe it when I see it," McAllester continued. "You think you are so high and mighty. Nothing has changed! You Protestants have the idea that you own this whole place. You are entitled to everything. You can steal whatever you like whenever it suits you. What about me and my people? Do you not think we need to feed ourselves too? We don't live on fresh air, you know!"

He was a brave man, Alex thought, to be shouting this while the blade of Stewart's sword pushed lightly against his stomach. To be fair to the land steward, he had been apologetic and had tried to explain to the angry man the famine conditions that existed in Coleraine.

"Nothing to do with me," McAllester argued. "I haven't caused it."

"Maybe not," Stewart replied, "but your people have risen against us and have committed such atrocities as to drive our people into Coleraine for protection. Our folk are starving and will die unless we take them food. You will be compensated, I give you my word."

Some time later a messenger arrived with urgent news for Stewart. Alex and Bruce watched his face change colour as he read. Apparently the rebel forces under the two McDonnells had left Clough Castle, marched north and made camp near the town of Ballymoney. The citizens of that town, already in dire straights after the burning of many of their buildings earlier in the conflict, were pleading for assistance. There was little choice for Stewart. He abandoned his quest for food and began to lead his troops on a quick march south across the broad expanse of the Garry Bog to offer support.

Baile Monaidh, as its name implied, was a settlement that had grown up on an area of bushy moorland. Its castle was a relatively insignificant shell, but its church was newly built and more consequential. It stood on higher ground, overlooking a winding burn and, beyond it, a sweep of rushes and low salleys on rising bogland to the south.

For reasons best known to themselves, the men of the town had made the decision to leave the confines of their damaged streets and take to that swampy landscape across the burn to engage the Irish in an area known as the Laney. Perhaps their motivation was to try to protect their women and children in the town; perhaps they thought they could surprise their approaching enemy from behind those bushes before they attacked the town; perhaps they imagined that their local knowledge of the area would give them an advantage over the strangers. Whatever their reasoning, it was to be a fateful choice.

Stewart and his company joined them too late to correct the decision. Alex watched the Colonel's disgust as he took in the situation.

"There is nowhere to hide out there in that open moorland," he said. "What have they done, other than ensure their obliteration? We don't stand a chance here."

The McDonnell Highlanders were, of course, well used to fighting in bogland. So were the Irish troops, their number now swollen with hundreds of angry volunteers from the surrounding countryside. Alaster McColla McDonnell despaired of these recent recruits. They were completely without military discipline and showed themselves to have not a shred of conscience. He despised them for their needless cruelty and brutality, and insisted that they be held in reserve, allowing his own Scottish troops to engage Stewart and the Ballymoney defenders using his well-tried and trusted tactic…the notorious Highland charge.

McColla's scouts soon ascertained the 'hiding places' of the Protestants. Once the enemy's position was known, the Highlanders drew closer and, on McColla's command opened fire from a set distance, provoking return fire from the defenders. Using the smoke of the discharge as cover, the Scottish warriors made an immediate charge, pikes poised, claymores and daggers drawn, their blood-curdling yells putting terror into the hearts of the Ballymoney citizens. The Highlanders were without match in close combat and soon their razor-sharp swords were slicing into these ill-equipped part-timers. It was a massacre.

There was little Stewart could do to salvage anything from the situation. He watched in horror as the Ballymoney men and a large number of his own soldiers were decimated in front of his eyes.

"We must try to save as many of our Coleraine defenders as possible," he shouted to his lieutenants. "Sound the retreat!"

Those who could fled west across boggy countryside, trying to escape McColla's soldiers. Dozens of them perished in a skirmish at a place called Bendooragh, half way between Ballymoney and the ruined village of Cross.

While Bruce had been held back in the reserves, Alex was among those escaping from the melee. He had very mixed feelings as he ran. It felt cowardly, but, at the same time, the instinct to survive over-took him with a vengeance. Looking behind him across the little river he had just waded through he could see a carpet of mutilated bodies of fallen men; from some he could still hear cries of pain. Some were wailing, screaming. He watched as a tall Highlander wandered among them plunging his *miodóg* into their breasts to put them out of their misery; they might as well have been squealing pigs in the butcher's yard. He saw a couple of young fellows skipping over the corpses in a mad frenzy of dark delight, collecting up whatever weapons they could find, waving them high and whooping like crazy savages.

"Who is going to be left to bury all those bodies?" he heard himself say to an ashen faced Bruce when they met on the outskirts of the town.

"I know. There must be hundreds of them," Bruce replied. "God help us if we don't get revenge on the Irish for this massacre!"

Bruce was right in his estimation. They later heard that of the nine hundred soldiers of Stewart's regiment that had set out from Coleraine only a couple of hundred returned. And, if that was true, then most of those hopeless men from Ballymoney had certainly been killed as well. Something between six and nine hundred lives were lost on that Black Friday, 11th February, at the so-called battle of the Laney. It was a day that would scar their memory for a very long time…and not their's alone. The town of Ballymoney was set alight and many of the buildings completely destroyed. Even the church, built not many years before with money given by Countess Katherine had been severely damaged.

Nearing the safety of Coleraine Alex was called forward to speak with Archibald Stewart.

"You do not need me to tell you that we are in a desperate situation here, Alex McKay. We are already severely out-numbered and I hear now that a hundred bowmen have arrived in Ballycastle from Rathlin to support the rebels. When we get back into Coleraine we will need to turn it into a very secure fortress… because those Highlanders we just escaped from will be hot on our heels."

"What can I do to help?" Alex asked.

"I want you to find Darach O'Cahan at once," Stewart told him. "I need to send you both on a very dangerous and difficult mission. In circumstances like these, two are better than one. The message must get through, so if one fails the other has a chance to make sure it is delivered."

"A message to where?" Alex asked.

"To Kintyre."

"Kintyre? In Scotland?" Alex was startled by this command.

"Aye, but you may not both have to go the whole way. If you both make it to Ballycastle safely one of you can take a boat to Kintyre and deliver the message, preferably yourself. The other can return to assure me that the message is on its way. I will supply you with good coin for the journey, for you will have to hire a boatman."

"Very well, and can I ask, sir, who is the message for?"

"It is to beg Archibald Campbell, the Argyll, to come to the aid of his fellow Protestants. We are in severe danger of being annihilated here in Ulster if we don't get assistance from our brethren across the water."

"What about Dublin? Don't they know what is happening up here?"

"Dublin is of no help to us. They have their own troubles trying to squash the rising in the south. The Earl is of no use to us, holed up in Slane Castle as he is. Campbell is our only hope, in spite of the antagonisms we have had with him in the past. He will at least understand our desperate need when you tell him of the treachery of his old enemies, the McColla McDonnells, at Portnaw."

"When must we leave, sir?"

"As I say, find young O'Cahan straight away. He has a good horse. I'll get you one as well. Leave within the hour, once I get him to write the message down. There is no time to waste because, like I say, our enemies will be quick on our heels to take advantage of that rout at Laney. If you get away fast you will not have the problem of having to somehow slip through their ranks."

"And when we get back, if we get back?"

"Aye, that will be a problem for you, I understand, but just do your best not to get caught… at all costs avoid that…but try to get word to me inside the town as to your success."

It was a tall order and such an important mission. As soon as the company dragged themselves back inside Coleraine's ramparts, he went looking for Darach.

Chapter 34

Back to Ballycastle

Darach O'Cahan

How strange to be entrusted to carry such an important message. Even more so, to be doing it in the company of Katie's brother. Here I am, an Irish O'Cahan, helping a Scotch settler in a bid to bring troops from Kintyre to defend these Presbyterian folk in Antrim. Defend them against my own kind! The irony of the situation I find myself in is not lost on me. I question myself continually.

A recurring dilemma has faced me since the Portnaw affair, a question I struggle to answer. Am I being a traitor to my own race? In the grand scheme of things I think I must be. Yet the faithlessness of what happened that morning on the banks of *An Bhanna* when my kinsmen changed sides has soured much of the sympathy I might have had for this rising. I content myself that my calling remains clear; to carry out my duties as I promised, and to do my best for the people I find myself in contact with.

I keep having a dream. A dream, as distinct from the nightmare I have had a few times, in which I am carrying Nellie's body to her grave, but can never find it. No, this is a different kind of dream, a very strange one which distresses me in my sleep and even lingers on to taint my waking thoughts. The circumstances surrounding the events in the dream can be different, but the essence of the thing is always the same. I find myself playing one of my harps, the swan one now owned by the McDonnells, before an audience. It might be to a group of the Earl's dignitary friends at Dunluce. Once it was to the monks at Bonamargy, although, as happens in dreams, they all seemed to be sound asleep. In the most bizarre circumstance, I have even been playing to some of Katie's family in a hayfield surrounded by noisy hens and ducks. The frustrating thing, common to all these dreams, is that the harp is not in tune. The lower notes seem to be fine, but when I begin to play a melody I notice that all the treble strings are too loose or too tight; I try to tune them; I have to use my fingers because I have lost my tuning key somewhere. I can get the pegs to turn, but they refuse to stay securely in pitch. So I try to play anyhow, but it is as if I am playing two different tunes, one with either hand. It is never a success. To my consternation, however, I seem to be forced into continuing to try to get a decent tune out of my harp. The whole thing builds up a level of misery in me that is unbearable. I get more and more thwarted and angry until something seems to jerk me into wakening up. I am always in a sweat at this point. The dream is so vivid that I am looking around to see who has noticed my embarrassment. I almost have to persuade myself that this hasn't been real. Getting back to sleep is next to impossible.

Last night I dreamed the same story again. I wonder should I tell Alex about it as he and I begin our journey.

But I have so much more important stuff to tell him… about Nellie and Kate, about my own family's disappearance, about my trip to Ballintoy and of meeting his family. To be honest, though, he does not seem to be all that interested. His mind is elsewhere. Initially I think it is preoccupied by the gravity of this task we have been given. It is only after a few miles of travel together that he seems to rouse himself from the veil of his thoughts and tells me all he has witnessed at this place called Laney. When he explains the intensity of the slaughter and the scale of the casualties I can understand his distraction.

I let him talk himself out before I bring him news of his own village, particularly about the refuge his folk are taking in the church. It is another wave of worry for him. The thing about this insurrection is that you think you are getting through one chapter of it only to realise you are already having to turn the page and brace yourself for the next one. It is relentless and very wearing. I can see that it is already beginning to have a profound effect on Alex's mind. I do not know him very well as yet, but what I am realising is that he doesn't seem to have been blessed by any great depth of resilience. He is dwelling on the images that have been etched on his mind over the past few weeks. They are not pleasant memories. He needs some sort of break from it all for a while.

When we get around to discussing the nature of this current mission I begin to see a possibility of providing him with such a break.

Alex must be the one to take the boat to Scotland, travel up to the north of Kintyre, find the Campbell fortress at some place called Inveraray and bring the message to Argyll. As the son of an Islay man, he and Archibald Campbell will have something in common, as Campbell has of late been given the laird-ship of Islay. They are both Presbyterian; they both speak Scots Gaelic. Alex is clearly the one to travel through this unknown territory of Kintyre. He will fit in, whereas my Irishness would stick out like a sore thumb. Even my name will cause suspicion. I could finish up hanging from a tree somewhere, accused of being a spy for the McDonnells.

I raise the subject with him, wondering if he will have the courage in himself to take it on. I shouldn't have had any fear. When I express the idea, concentrating on my own inadequacies for such a task and talking up his suitability, he is easily persuaded.

"But what about here?" he asks. "Do you not think I need to be helping to defend Ballintoy, if it comes under attack? With all due respect to you, Darach, how do you think you can be of any help to my folk and the other families there? I know you want to help Katie, but you will be without the means to do so. I could at least fire a musket through the window of the kirk."

I am ahead of him in this argument though. I have thought this out.

"That is where you are wrong," I say. "I will be of so much more use outside the church than inside it. I can maybe try to undermine the besiegers, maybe bring help to your folk inside….for the very reason that I am on the outside, whereas you would be totally stuck inside."

"Maybe," he agrees. "But what sort of help could you bring them from outside?"

I haven't quite thought that out as yet, but I make up an idea.

"Food. Let's say they run short."

"Aye, so what can you do about it? Persuade a few seagulls or pigeons to fly in through the windows or what?"

"I will think of something, don't worry; but as I say, you will be more likely to get this message through to Campbell than I will…and I can at least try to help at Ballintoy."

He thinks about this.

"Alright, maybe you are right. But help me find a boat tonight, and someone to sail me over tomorrow before you leave, will you?"

"Of course," I tell him.

It's a good decision, I think. For Alex, of course, but even more so for me! I cannot countenance the thought that I would be the person who brings Argyll's Protestant army to this my homeland. How would I ever live with myself thereafter? If Campbell should come to Stewart's aid, hundreds of my fellow Irish will be killed. Their blood will be, to some extent at least, on my hands. I have had enough trouble trying to reconcile in my mind my Irishness with my role in Stewart's army. I suppose in some measure my dilemma stems from my loyalty to the Earl, the man who is probably even more conflicted than me. I ask myself the question, 'Could I as an O'Cahan ever see myself fighting alongside my cousin, Tirlough Óge? Could I be part of the army besieging Ballintoy or Coleraine?' I do not believe I could. I was recruited to serve Lord McDonnell's cause. I will never be a turncoat, like those at Portnaw. I will never do anything to hurt Katie or her people. But will I take the further step of delivering a message begging for help from a notoriously anti-Catholic army from Scotland? Never. Yes, I will help Alex with what he has been asked to do by our captain, and I suppose I am, to that extent, a traitor to the Catholic cause. It feels like I am walking a narrow cliff-top path, with raging winds blowing at me from either side, and I am struggling to hold on to my wits, never mind my sense of direction.

****

We have had a straight forward journey to Ballycastle. Thankfully we saw no sign of the Rathlin bowmen who were rumoured to be in the area. The horses have covered the ground in quick time; as the evening falls we are descending the little valley that runs down towards the town.

Ballycastle. I love the place. It was at Ballycastle that I first talked to Katie when I saw her at the fair. That was a special day. The musical performance that night in Dunynie Castle, on Mrs MacNeill's puffin harp…an evening ruined by McColla. And of course, my friend, Father McGlaim, that I haven't seen for such a long time. He lives here in the Friary.

Suddenly I feel a strange inclination that tonight I should try to find him, just for a chat. This is an ideal opportunity. Perhaps Alex and I could stay with him overnight. Perhaps he could help us locate a suitable boatman, and Alex can be ready to leave first thing in the morning. It would certainly beat sleeping rough in the open air, or in some barn, as we had imagined we might have to do.

"Alex, I have an idea about where we might stay."

"Where's that?" he says.

"Bonamargy Friary, with my friend Father McGlaim."

"Did you say Father McGlaim? In a Friary? You don't expect me to stay…."

"If only you could remember, Alex, he is the one who rescued you on that hillside last summer. I think you'll be fairly safe with him tonight. Nobody will try to convert you, I promise."

"It's not so much that…" he says doubtfully. I sense a deep concern in him.

"What then?"

He grimaces, then responds slowly, carefully.

"It's just that, for me as a Presbyterian…well, staying in Bonamargy…it's a very Catholic sort of place."

I smile at this. "Of course it is. It's a Friary, for God's sake. What would you expect? And yes, McGlaim is a priest, but that didn't stop him helping you when you needed it."

Alex at least has the grace to smile. "Sorry," he says, "that was just me being…" He tails off and we exchange an understanding look. "Still," he continues, "I won't feel comfortable in such a place."

"Why not? I used to live there; didn't do me any harm. What are you afraid of? What do you expect?"

"I don't know what to expect. It'll be all religious and creepy. Chapels, and statues of the Virgin Mary…and crosses and tombstones."

"There's all those things, I agree. That's normal. I'm sure you already know that Sorley Boy McDonnell is buried there? And Randal, the first Earl. It is very much a McDonnell shrine; they sort of own it, so you'd expect their graves to be there. But I never heard of any ghosts about the place, not in all my time there. You'll be safe enough," I tell him.

We travel on in silence. I can tell he is not convinced. After a bit he raises another objection.

"What if these priests or friars or whatever you call them…what if they ask us what we are doing? They're not going to like it if they find out we are working for the Protestant cause, are they?"

He has a point, but I counter it. "We are both in the Earl's employ though. That is what we say. They all respect Randal McDonnell here. He is very good to them. The friary wouldn't exist without him."

"Aye maybe, but it isn't the Earl who has sent us on this journey, is it? It's Archibald Stewart. And it's to get a Protestant army."

This silences me for a while. He is right. We need to think this through before we go to stay there. If we do, it strikes me that no-one in there must find out the nature of Alex's mission, not even Father McGlaim.

"Alex," I say, "if we stay in Bonamargy we have to be very careful to keep the true nature of this business secret. Nobody must suspect that you carry a message asking the Argyll for help. He must never be mentioned, not to a single soul."

"I understand that," he agrees, "but what reason do I have for travelling so urgently to Kintyre? We must agree on a story."

"We must indeed. Maybe you are taking a message to some relative?"

"Aye, could be. How about if one of my neighbours has passed away, maybe leaving her invalid husband in a hopeless state? And before she died she made me promise to go to Kintyre to try to bring his sister to look after him?"

"That sounds as good a story as any other," I tell him.

Before long we reach the Friary. The old chapel is looking lovely in the low evening light, sunbeams the colour of buttercups casting long shadows across the flat meadow that separates the abbey from the river. At the entrance gate we ask of Father McGlaim's whereabouts and are guided to his humble cell.

"Is it yourself? Young O'Cahan, the harp-maker?" McGlaim says when he eventually answers our knock. I must say he seems unsure of himself, very timorous. Then, turning to study Alex, he asks, "And who is this? I seem to recognise the face?"

I introduce Alex as the young man we helped that day on the hills above Ballintoy.

"Of course it is," he says, "but looking a whole lot healthier than that day, thanks be to God."

"I owe you a debt of thanks, I am told," Alex says.

"T'was our pleasure," the priest replies. "You are welcome to my home."

We have only been together for a short time, but already I am noticing a change in Father McGlaim. There is a weary greyness about him, a shrunken feeling as if perhaps he has not been well. His eyes don't have the light that shone from them when I last saw him six or seven months ago. He has aged, in spirit if not in years. He pours a little wine for us.

"You are very brave," he says, "venturing out in these troubled times."

"We have both seen our share of violence and tragedy in the past few weeks," I tell him. "It is nice to come to a peaceful place like Ballycastle, especially Bonamargy. It feels safe…"

"This place? Peaceful?" he interrupts me, a certain bitter tone of regret in his voice. "I am afraid you have been misinformed if you think that we are peaceful here in Ballycastle."

Alex and I look at each other, then back at the priest.

"You clearly have not heard," he continues. "We have had several killings. It has been a terrible time here as well."

"I am sorry to hear that," I say. "We were not aware of this. Perhaps if we had been we would have been more nervous and more careful on our journey through the town."

"Indeed. You have been fortunate," he says, then pauses to take a long sup of wine. "Perhaps I should not tell you, but I am afraid I have been very hurt, disappointed by what I've heard…"

He fades out to silence, leaving us wondering what has annoyed him so much. We wait. He resumes his story.

"Some of the Protestant residents of the town, they'd heard of the massacres near Kilrea and at Ballymoney. They were feeling threatened by some of our local hot-heads, and they guessed that soon Ballycastle would be under attack from the rebels. Well, they tried to take refuge in the castle, the residence of the Dowager, Countess Alice…you know? Lord Antrim's mother. Of course you know. To begin with she took in a few of these fearful people, gave them shelter. But then she must have changed her mind, perhaps afraid of being overwhelmed. When others came begging entrance, well… somehow they got turned away from her gate. Sadly these people were set on and killed right outside the castle walls."

We do not know what to say to this. It is difficult, for Alex in particular. He looks very distressed. We wait for the priest to continue.

"One lady who perished, a Janet Spier, to whom she owed a substantial sum of money….oh, it's a terrible sin if true….the Countess refused sanctuary to this woman, even though the poor woman prostrated herself and held her skirts. In the end, that Miss Spier was dragged out, robbed and butchered, behind the castle stables…apparently by a couple of the castle servants. Our people have become overwhelmed by bloodthirsty and barbarous instincts. And the Countess is implicated in some cases for not providing shelter. I am in despair."

We are both shocked by this and I have to say I find it hard to believe. Countess Alice is an elderly lady, a high-born Irish woman whose father was the great Hugh O'Neill, Lord of Tyrone. How would her son, the Earl of Antrim, feel when he hears this story of her unkindness? But Father McGlaim is not finished.

"I have learned," he continues, "that a William Erwin and his wife were set upon and stripped naked over by the salt-pans. They tried to save themselves by wading out into the sea…but the attackers followed them. They held William down, his wife watching, until the poor man drowned. Then they beat her over the head until she too was dead. Terrible crimes, my friends, but will there ever be justice? More importantly, will there ever be an end to it all?"

We sit silently in contemplation of these horrendous tidings. I feel very sad for Alex having to sit and listen to this catalogue of carnage. Father McGlaim seems to have subsided into a stupor…or perhaps he is praying, I am not certain. After a bit I think I should sympathise with Alex for how he must be feeling.

"I am sorry that you have to hear this news, Alex," I say. "Especially in this place which is supposed to represent the best in our christian tradition."

"It's not your fault," he says softly, "but thanks."

Father McGlaim raises his head and gives us a quizzical look. "And you two have become friends, have you? That is nice," he says.

Alex and I exchange a wry smile.

As we sip I give him a quick account of how our relationship has developed. Alex listens solemnly, on the whole. Perhaps for the first time he is seeing the thing from a perspective other than his own. He doesn't say anything until he obviously feels some need to defend his earlier attitude toward me. He sits forward and asks Father McGlaim a leading question.

"My worries were about my sister getting too close to Darach," he says. "If I am honest I still have those worries. This is no country and no time for Katie and him to be courting. I was concerned that she would get hurt. I still have that feeling; I am concerned for both of them. What do you think about it? As a priest, I mean?"

Father McGlaim sits silent for a long time. One hand is raised towards his low ceiling, the other fingering a rough little cross around his neck. His eyes are firmly closed, as if in meditation yet again. Then he speaks. His tone is soft, thoughtful and captivating.

"I have to be careful about what I say, about how I express these thoughts," he begins. "You see, there is what the church teaches…and I have a duty to be loyal to that as an ordained priest…and then there is what I believe myself, as an ordinary man who tries to follow the teachings of Christ to the best of my ability. Mostly these two perspectives do not differ in one iota. But in recent times I have become increasingly torn between…"

He stops. I think he is reconsidering whether or not to confess his dilemma. We wait. His head goes down on his hand in a gesture of dejection. It is Alex who brings him encouragement.

"Sir, if I could just say, it is nice to see a man of the cloth who has the same doubts as the rest of us."

McGlaim gives him a meek glance. "We are but human too," he says. "It is a question of compassion, isn't it? Compassion that stands against dogma. Myself, I have the deepest regard for my young friend Darach here. And I have no doubt that your sister is a fine young woman. It is clear to me that they love each other and, as love is a gift of God, who am I to stand in their way? On the other hand, I have to ask myself the question. If it were ever to come to marriage…maybe it will, maybe it won't…could I ever marry them?"

"Well, could you?" I ask. "Could you marry us?"

"I don't know Darach. I honestly don't know. I would love to be able to, but I suppose it could only happen if Katie were to become Catholic, you see. That is the teaching of the church."

"I don't think Katie would ever convert," Alex says.

"So we are stuck?"

"No Darach, you are not stuck. God will make a way for you if he wants you to be together. You will see."

"I hope you are right," I tell him. "It must be hard to be a priest, to have the rules of the church to follow but to have your own views on things?"

"Believe me, my son, it is very difficult. My greatest temptation is just to go along with everything, to say nothing, keep my head down and wait for my reward in heaven, please God…which in my case can't be too far ahead."

That weariness again. What canker has entered this good man's soul to so depress him? I want to tease it out of him. He needs to be lifted up again, encouraged as he has encouraged others in the past.

"I cannot see you as someone who surrenders to those temptations," I tell him.

"Can't you? Perhaps you do not know me well enough. I am subject to the same discouragements as everyone else. Do not put me on a pedestal."

"Alright," I say, "but what discouragements do you speak of?"

Again that thoughtful silence. After a while he looks hard at Alex.

"Young Alex, I have to confess a deep shame to you."

Alex looks a bit mystified by this. A priest is wanting to confess to him, a Presbyterian? He says nothing, but his eyes widen and he sits suddenly back in is chair.

"The shame is this," he continues. "Your community is being targeted by the Irish in this rising. There are many who are determined to wipe you out, or at the very least to send you all back to England or Scotland. In a lot of cases the anger that is behind that aim is completely understandable, given all that has been stolen from our people over the years. But what I am so very deeply ashamed of is…"

He coughs hoarsely and takes a long draught of wine from his goblet before continuing.

"I am ashamed of the way my church is acting in this rising."

Alex and I look at each other, unsure of what he is talking about.

"You must understand that, as a priest of the church, I am as annoyed as the next person by the persecution that we Catholics endure. The English have been squeezing us mercilessly. It is so hard to accept. I would love nothing more than for the true religion to be back in its proper place in this holy island. We have always been Catholic Ireland. So I find myself in support of my church in wanting to restore our supremacy in our own land."

I look at Alex. His head is down, his eyes hidden now, his body tense. Father McGlaim notices too.

"Having said that…and you must listen to what I am saying, my young Protestant friend…I do not feel that the blame for this state of affairs is to be laid at the door of ordinary Protestant settlers like yourself. You do not make these discriminatory laws. You are here in Antrim on the invitation of our Earl, and, as far as I am concerned, you are welcome."

"So what are you ashamed of?" Alex asks.

"I am ashamed of the fact that many of our priests, many of our bishops, have not made the distinction between those who have led this plantation, made these laws, and the ordinary Protestant people who are here in innocence because they were promised a place to settle."

"Like my father," Alex says.

"Exactly. The violence has become indiscriminate. The ordinary, decent folk are being targeted. They are the wrong targets."

"And you think the church, the bishops, are to blame for this?" I ask.

"I am afraid their hands are not clean. They have given spiritual succour to the leaders of the movement. For them it is a holy war, a religious crusade to reverse the imposition of the Protestant religion on this nation. It is a continuation of the wars that have been fought between Catholic and Protestant factions in Europe for the last hundred years. So the church, my church, is actually sponsoring this upheaval. These terrible massacres… they lie at the door of bishops and fellow priests of mine who give blessing to the rising. It pains me very deeply. Yet they see nothing wrong in their actions or attitudes. They see it as an inalienable right and duty to try to reclaim Ireland by violent and merciless means. Can such means be reconciled with our Christian gospel? I do not believe so."

This is a very serious subject to have spread its heaviness into our conversation this evening, but it is clearly what has been bothering this good priest.

"I have had these arguments with others, brother priests here at Bonamargy. Opinions differ. The Franciscans, my own order, are fully behind the rising, for example."

"Isn't Randal McDonnell's brother a Franciscan?" I ask. "Do you think he would be on the side of the Irish?"

"Francis, the half-brother?" McGlaim says. "He is highly respected in the order. I am not sure where he would stand on this issue. But, for myself, I cannot be persuaded that the church should ever excuse violence, never mind encourage it. And the thing is…"

We wait quietly as he composes his thoughts.

"The thing is," he continues, "as a person who aims to follow the teachings of Our Lord and the ways of St Francis I cannot be part of such a crusade of cruelty and revenge. I cannot read, 'Love your enemies' on the one hand and be a silent partner in their destruction on the other. Surely if I claim to be Christian I must look for opportunities to bless those who curse me? The inconsistency of it all is tearing me apart."

Tears are tripping the poor man.

Alex and I are speechless to witness this moment of poignant honesty. The priest has bared his soul and is obviously living in a place of pain. After a space of silence Alex finds his voice and makes a faltering reply to his host.

"This is all very confusing for me. I have never had to consider these thoughts before, you understand…Mister McGlaim, you have been very honest, and I thank you. But for me…it is hard to take in that…that you Catholics all seem to think that God is on your side in this row, that he is behind the Irish murderers, that he thinks it was grand for them to turn on us at Portnaw and murder my friends."

"I don't believe that at all," the priest replies, regaining some of his poise. "That sounds like a cowardly piece of treachery."

"Alright, but can God be on both sides of this thing at the same time? We pray to God for deliverance from the Irish; our ministers in Ballintoy preach to us that God is on our side, that he has given us this land and that he will save us in our time of need. But here you are thinking your Catholic God is for the Irish? So, I say there must be two different

Gods."

Father McGlaim is slow to reply. His answer is patient and deliberate. "Alex," he says, "I understand your problem. My own people have the same kinds of thought. In answer I would say that so far as I recall there was only one Jesus. We do share that belief, do we not? It is in both our creeds. 'We believe in one Lord Jesus Christ, the only Son of God.' When I think on him…I think his interest in our fight would not be about who is right, or who is most deserving of his blessing."

"You don't think he would take sides?"

"He would take sides, yes, Alex, he would take sides. I am sure of it. He would be on the side of the oppressed, the weak, the hungry, the sick…surely that much we can agree on. I don't read that he ever supported the Romans in his land…nor, for that matter, the zealots who were trying to fight them. He helped the needy."

Once again we descend into a thoughtful quietness. There seems no more to say. I am wondering how Alex is responding to these ideas in his mind. Then, to his great credit, it is Alex who brings our debate to some measure of resolution. He gets up from his seat and goes to Father McGlaim; he stands awkwardly in front of his frail frame. All he says is, "Blessed are the peacemakers, I suppose."

It is enough. It is a moment of release, of relief. It is like someone has opened a bottle and the scent of summer flowers has filled the tiny room.

Father McGlaim lifts his head slowly, and takes Alex's hand.

"Thank you," he says.

****

We sneak through the back lanes of Ballycastle to the row of low cottages above the seafront. The priest has an idea about who to ask for help with a boat trip to Kintyre, a very able and experienced fisherman who often sails to Scotland. It is late and lights are being doused in some homes but we are in time to catch Marcus Hill before he goes to bed.

If Marcus is surprised to open his door to a priest and two young strangers at this time of night he gets over it quickly. Father McGlaim is known to this fisherman and, after the usual pleasantries, he introduces Alex as a 'good young man of Ballintoy who needs to make a visit to Kintyre'. The boatman shows no hesitation in agreeing to make the journey, saying that there is at present 'a brave dacent stretch o' weather'. A price is agreed and a time set for a morning departure.

"The tide! It's al' aboot the tide. If we dinnae leave at the richt time, at the start o' the flood, we'll be fighting currents and eddies and we'll make little or nae progress. You be here when I say, or I'll naw be taking ye."

After a reasonable night's sleep on Father McGlaim's cold stone floor Alex and I are up well before dawn. We don't bother the priest and take some cold porridge and buttermilk as quietly as we can so as not to waken him. He has agreed to stable Stewart's horse with his own mule at the Friary until Alex can get back from Scotland. Thankfully he did not press us on the reason Alex was making this vital journey to Kintyre. He must have had his suspicions; the journey was significant enough to be 'urgent', yet he had turned away deliberately when I had muttered a scanty version of the explanation Alex and I had agreed on. A wise and sensitive priest.

Back along the lanes to the shore in the dim light of the early morning and we wait beside his front door for the boatman to make his appearance. The sun hasn't actually risen yet and won't do for another hour, so the bay from Ballycastle to Fairhead has a metal hue, the colour of a sword blade. Seagulls are awake and active well before us, and are swooping around the fore-shore area looking for an easy breakfast. Their cries remind me of home; how I miss the village of Dunluce and my lovely life there with John and Eilish. I hope they are safe and well. How long it seems since I have been in my workshop, held a length of oak, planed and carved it into shape? How long since my fingers plucked on the taut strings of a sweet-sounding harp? And when will life return to normal?

Before me the Sea of Moyle stretches out towards the grey shadow of Kintyre's southern headland. There seems to be very little movement on the surface of the water, the breeze from the west being very light. To my inexperienced eye I think that Alex should have a pleasant enough crossing. Marcus, when he finally makes his appearance, agrees with me.

"Aye, it should be grand," he says. "We'll hae ye ashore be late efternoon if it bides like this. But then ye never know wae the sea, dae ye!"

I bid Alex a good voyage and watch as he and Marcus edge slowly out of the shallows by the pier into the bay. The breeze starts to catch their single sail and they begin to pick up some pace.

I wonder if he will be able to make it up through the Mull peninsula to find Archibald Campbell. I wonder how the Argyll will respond and what his response might mean for the people of my home county. I wonder how long before Alex can make it back to his beloved Ballintoy. I wonder what has happened to my own parents, sisters and brother.

I wonder again if I am a faithful servant or a Judas.

These questions torment me as I set out on my return journey towards Coleraine.

Chapter 35

Return to Dunluce

Darach O'Cahan

It strikes me that I will be travelling fairly close to Straid on my way back from Ballycastle; why not make a short detour to see if my family has returned to their house or if anyone has any news of them? So I take the narrow road that leads to Bushmills, across that broad area of bushy bogland where very few people have made their homes. The air is crisp; a deep stillness sits on the landscape as if waiting thoughtfully for something to happen. The great arc of the sky above me has a wintery tinge, mostly cool blue but with high clots of grey cloud curdling on the northern horizon.

I take my time on this ride; *Liath* seems tired and my rear end is sore from all the recent journeys. I just feel the need to be more at rest in myself, more in tune with the softer, slower moods of nature. My experiences with human-kind over the past while have begun to fester in my mind and I resent the dark thoughts that seem to stalk me. I do not want to find myself in the depressive state that has been afflicting Father McGlaim

It is nearing midday when I ride carefully into the town-land of *Sráid*; I need to keep as low a profile as possible, not wanting a reception like I had here on the previous visit. However, I see no-one. Appreciating the solitude, I reach my parent's cottage. It doesn't take long to discover that the house is still deserted. The half-door is closed but unlocked, what furniture there is in the kitchen remains undisturbed. I look around outside and wonder what has become of my father's few animals. I am also curious about the men who had made me feel so unwelcome on my last visit.

There seems little point in waiting around, maybe inviting antagonism from suspicious neighbours, so I allow *Liath* a final drink from the half barrel by the gable and prepare to remount. Turning towards the road I notice a small figure standing by the stone wall along the rodden.

A little old man watches me intensely as I ride towards him and holds up his stick when I come beside him. I interpret it as a threat and am about to spur the horse into a gallop when I sense that, far from being aggressive, the man is trying to be sociable in his own awkward way. I rein *Liath* in and stop beside him.

"Young O'Cahan," he says. His voice is a high-pitched pipe sound, like a boy's voice before it has broken; it matches his physical frame. 'Young O'Cahan' isn't a question, more like a greeting.

"I am," I say.

"Ye'll be luckin' Martin."

"I am; both him and my mother. Do you know where they are?"

He removes his hat and scratches vigorously at the back of his wizened head of thin white hair.

"So you're the wee-fella? The wan they let go tae Dunluce?"

"That is right," I say, "but I am sorry, I don't know you?"

"I'd be a neighbour frae a lang time back. McConaghie is my name, you wouldnae ken me but yer fether woulda helped me the odd time wae the lambin'."

"Ah right," I say, thankful that, with this man at least, my father had a good reputation. "You had a flock of sheep?"

"Damn the flock," he says. "Yin or twa be times."

More scratching at the back of his neck. Nothing a good wash in a bog-hole wouldn't cure, I think.

"Do you know where Martin and the family have gone, Mr McConaghie?"

He considers this, peering up at me, his gnarled hand shading his sunken little eyes from the glare of the sky.

"Aye, likely tae the brither, doon at Dunseverick."

That thought had crossed my mind earlier but I had dismissed it. Gilladubh had never had a lot of time for his poorer kin.

"Are you sure?"

"Naw... but maybes."

"And would you know why?"

"I would. But I wouldnae want tae say o'er much aboot it. Maybe they jist thought they would feel a bit safer in the cassle wae a' the ither Papishes than oot here amang us Prodesins," he says.

"There doesn't seem to be anybody else about," I say.

"Naw a sowl left 'cept mesell. Away tae Ballintoy. Thon boadie Boyd come up an' toul them they wour in danger here, they'd be safer in the kirk doon there. I seen them lea'in', the men wae their guns o'er their shuthers an' the weemen and wains greetin'."

So the men who chased me out of here not that many days ago are now defending my Katie and her family in her church? Strange times, I think.

We who used to live among each other, help neighbours with farming and fishing, share banter and stories and songs, are now securely corralled from each other. The ancient stone walls of castle and church stand between Gael and fellow Gael. How, after this, will we ever laugh together again? Strange times indeed.

I thank this leprechaun of a man and ride on, but not in the direction of Bushmills or Coleraine. I am curious to get a sense of what is happening on the coast around Ballintoy and Dunseverick. I would be foolish to deny that the chance to be in the vicinity of Katie is at the root of my decision, but I do realise that the chances that we might meet are very slim. I tell myself, though, that any intelligence about military activity that I can gather here, even by watching from the heights to the south, will be valuable to Archibald Stewart. I tell myself that this role, being the 'eyes' of the land steward, is completely compatible with my other role, my Irish calling to be a bard. A bard is an observer of events, a keeper of history, a teller of stories. What a rich fount of tales I am gathering for the future, if I should survive to tell them.

****

I pass the Druid's Altar; what poignant memories I have of Katie here, by this time-worn monument. I stop to look down at the view. Beyond the rim of the cliffs, the serene smile of the sea is as broad as ever, and its surface looks every bit as smooth as when Alex set sail this morning. I expect he is close to Kintyre by this stage. I study the church and the castle of Ballintoy on the flatness of the plain below. There is no sign of any soldiers, but I do see one or two figures moving along the lanes or in the fields. I am so tempted to ride down to see if Katie would happen to be one of them, but I resist and turn *Liath* to travel on to Dunseverick Castle.

Arriving before the gatehouse there I am immediately struck by an increased level of defence about the place. Several armed men guard the entrance, their demeanour sullen, suspicious.

"I am an O'Cahan, nephew of Gilladubh," I tell the guard who stands aggressively to bar my entrance. He is a stranger to me.

"Can you prove that?"

"No, not unless some of the family come to vouch for me. Look, I am simply trying to find my father and mother, Martin and Bríd, who have taken refuge here. I have been told so anyhow," I tell him.

"You say you are an O'Cahan? What action have you seen in this conflict so far?" he asks, coldly.

I try to explain that I was part of Tirlough Óge's company. I thought that would be a politic answer, but it only leads me into deeper trouble. The guard sneers at me. He thinks he has caught me out.

"If you were part of that company, where were you when Tirlough Óge and his men were here two days ago?"

This is news to me. The surprise on my face, added to the delay in my response, makes this soldier more mistrustful of me.

"Well, you see, sir," I stammer, "I had a special role with Archibald

Stewart during the…"

"With Archibald Stewart, you say? You were working for the Protestant leader, were you? What exactly was this role?" He is becoming more threatening by the second here. I have fuelled his fire without realising what I am doing. He man-handles me roughly, his forearm pressing on my chest, pinning me against the uneven stones of the gatehouse.

"I simply took messages, sir. Between the various commanders, and here and there throughout the area."

"So you took messages, eh? What were these messages? What did you see in these places you traveled to?"

"I saw a lot of things," I manage to say, "but how would I know what was in the messages? They were all sealed, you see."

A bit of a lie, but a necessary one at this minute. He stares closely at me.

"I think you are a spy for Stewart and the Protestants, what do you say to that? A dirty spy, no other word for it," he hisses. Then he finds another couple of words for it. "And if you are an O'Cahan, then you are also a turncoat. A traitor and a spy. What do you say to that?"

"I was no spy. I was serving Lord Antrim; that was the job Stewart gave me to do. I didn't choose it," I say, my voice starting to sound as nervous as I am feeling. "Gilladubh is my uncle. He knows what my duties were. You can ask him yourself, if he is here."

"He is not here, so you are sunk," he says, delighted with himself.

One of his fellow guards chooses this moment to step forward from the shadows of the gatehouse and speak quietly into the ear of my interrogator. I only hear the odd word of his conversation but, by how he is glancing across at me, I have a feeling he must know me, or at least believe my side of this story. I hear, "…if his family is inside…." The boisterous guard seems to be listening to his advice, thinking things through. He nods dourly and turns back to me.

"You say your family is inside the castle? This soldier will accompany you as you try to find them. If they are here, well and good. Otherwise you are for the cellar," he tells me gruffly.

I follow the helpful guard through the gatehouse. He points to the northerly quarter of the huge castle yard. "They are likely over there among the others," he says.

The others? I soon realise there are several families here. I happen to see my brother in the yard. Henry is a caged animal, roaming restlessly alone beside the sea-wall. I shout to him and we meet.

"I am so relieved to find you," I tell him. "I was at *Sráid* again, but you were all gone. I was worried for you. Where are the others?"

He leads me to a remote corner of the castle yard. My sisters run giggling to greet me. My mother weeps briefly as we embrace.

"None of us feel safe," my father tells me later. "The people in *Sráid* were for burning us out; we felt fortunate to escape with our lives. There is a terrible spate of revenge and then counter-revenge going on. I don't know where it will end. We heard that some of Stewart's soldiers attacked a crowd of women and children at Islandross, near Dervock. Killed sixty of our people. It's unbelievable what is happening, son."

My mother chides him. "But it is not everybody, Martin. There were some who stood up for us, and didn't want to see us leave."

"Aye, until their neighbours turned on them as well. Then they backed down. They had to. They were in danger too."

They are visibly relieved when I tell them that their home still stands undisturbed. I also mention my brief encounter with the McConaghie character.

"Aye, wee Joseph is a sound man; keeps his head down. I just hope your friends at Dunluce are alright," my father says.

"I am sure they will be fine," I say. "Nobody is going to be attacking the castle. It would be pointless for a start, and the Earl has too much respect among both the Scotch and our side for anybody to be…"

I stop as my father raises his hand to interrupt me. He and mother exchange a worrying glance, then she speaks brusquely to Meabh and Rosie.

"Away you two go and play yourselves," she orders. They leave the conversation reluctantly.

"You don't know anything about what has happened here, do you Darach?" my father asks me.

"Know about what?"

"Sorry son, we have bad news for you," he says, lowering his voice, looking around to make sure no-one is overhearing him. I am struck by this sudden change. What can this news be that has to be spoken so discreetly?

"Go on," I tell him.

"Well…a whole company of soldiers arrived here at the castle two days ago, them and a crowd of angry men, no-good hangers-on. I was going to say that they were led by Tirlough Óge and James McDonnell, but to be honest they seemed more out of control than being led by anybody. From what I gather they had killed a lot of folk on their march here."

This doesn't come as a shock to me, having seen what I have seen and heard what I have heard, but my folks are obviously very disturbed by it. My mother takes up the story.

"They were laughing about it," she says, disgusted. "We heard that a whole family by the name of Collier, up near Derrykeighan they were, they must have been fearing an attack. They went for refuge to their land steward. He was their close neighbour…a man called Toole McAllester, one of the Earl's tenants. He took them in at the start. Then his men turned on them; killed the whole family. Shocking."

It is a terrible story, I agree.

"I've seen some tragic things too," I say. "But I have also heard some stories of kindness and neighbours helping each other."

I tell them of two instances I had learned of in my travels. In the first, a Rasharkin farmer called Donnell Gorme O'Donnell came across a Scotch lad by the name of George Thompson. The lad was about to be hung by some ruffians. He rescued the boy, lent him his cloak and a shield, gave him a job on his land. I heard another tale at Clough. An Irish man called Magee had some Protestant friends near there. When he heard of the advance of McColla's soldiers, he took them into his own house and kept them safe.

"That is good to know," my father said. "Some decency still lives."

"What about closer to here?" I ask.

"Some of Gilladubh's tenants have been killed," he tells me. "I would know a few of them; ordinary folk doing nobody any harm. Guy Cochrane's son was one. John Spence's wife was killed…and another boy by the name of McCurdy. In some cases I think it has just been because of bad blood, men settling old scores for things that happened in the past."

"It wasn't that for the McNeill girl, her not even twenty yet," my mother adds. "She hadn't done anything to deserve being murdered; just happened to be in the wrong place at the wrong time."

"Gilladubh was raging," my father says. "These were his tenants. He yelled at Tirlough Óge! 'What good does it do our cause to be killing innocent women and boys', he told him? Even James McDonnell was annoyed at it, but he did say it wasn't Tirlough Óge's fault. It had just got out of control."

"Where are all these soldiers now?" I ask, sick of what I am hearing.

"Well, they slept here at Dunseverick. Then they marched on Dunluce yesterday."

"They surely aren't going to try to capture Dunluce? It's madness!"

"It may be madness," my father says, "but I suppose they must think that if it stays in the Earl's hands it will be a bastion for the Crown and the English forces. This war is nowhere near over yet."

Immediately my mind starts to wonder about the implications for John and Eilish McSparran in the village there. I must find out if they are safe. I must get to Dunluce before nightfall, but I have something else I want to talk to my parents about.

"I have a girl," I say suddenly, softly. My father has not heard me, but my mother turns to me abruptly.

"Say that again," she says. "You have a girl?"

"You have a girl, did you say?" my father repeats.

"I have. We are walking out for a while now so I thought you should know."

"How did you manage to get a girl in the middle of all this trouble?"

"Never mind that. Tell us who she is." Curiosity is leaping from my mother's eyes.

"You remember the young man that Father McGlaim and I rescued up on Altmore, last summer? Alex McKay? It's a sister of his. Her name is Katie."

A stunned silence. I am not surprised. They are unable to hide the moment of processing that this announcement needs. I wait it out for a few seconds. Then I add the obvious comment.

"You'll like her. She's a great girl."

"Is she now?" my mother says. "I remember that boy. But wasn't he a...."

"Katie McKay? A daughter of Daniel?" My father's question is neutral enough, but I feel he may be building up to a tougher question.

"She is," I say. "And I know she is Protestant, but neither of us want to let that come in the way of...."

"Darach, son," my mother says. "You couldn't have picked a worse time to be walking out with a Protestant. Have you lost your senses altogether? And you nearly going to join a holy order at one time! What does your priest friend think of this? Has he not given you some good advice?"

"I have talked to him about it," I say. "He knows it will be difficult, but...he said God would maybe make a way..."

"It's the children is the problem," my father says. "What do you do? She will want to rear them as Protestant, you'll be the opposite. I am sure she's a nice girl and all, but you need to think about the wains."

"I know," I say, "And we already have one!"

That causes a stir!

I have to hasten to tell them the whole story about Nellie and wee Kate. I spin the story out for a good while, for it deflects from the more raw news concerning Katie and myself. I tell them how I had initially brought the child to them at *Sráid*, then, on discovering their absence, to Katie and the McKays in Ballintoy, out of necessity. They listen open mouthed.

"And you say this child is an orphan? And a Protestant?"

"I suppose...but she's got us now," I tell them.

The discussion ranges around in circles for a while. If only they knew Katie, I think. Then they would understand why it has to be her.

"You sound like there will be no talking you out of this," my father says finally. "So let us wish you good luck with it and we will not hold it against you. You'll always be our son, Darach, and I am sure she will be a fine wife for you, but, my God, aren't yous choosing a very difficult path for yourselves!"

****

I leave them. The guard from earlier ignores me this time as I pass through the gatehouse. I take the path west again.

Once more I notice an absence of people and normal activity in the countryside. There is a strange hush, an atmosphere of paralysis about this area that I know and love so well. I am nearing the town of Bushmills when I first become aware of a column of dark smoke rising from beyond the distant headland which hides Dunluce. Dread takes a grip on my heart, an almost physical feeling of terror. I spur *Liath* into a gallop and race across the narrow bridge over the river Bush.

On reaching the summit of the hill just half a mile from Dunluce the worst of my fears are confirmed. The entire village is ablaze!

How could anyone believe that the burning of our lovely homes is necessary for the freeing of Ireland? What has become of all the people who live here? Have they been killed, like the folks around Dunseverick that my father told me of? If so, does that include those two gentle people who have been so good to me for almost half my life? And has Dunluce Castle fallen into the hands of the Irish forces?

My heart is thumping wildly in my chest with trepidation as I gallop down the slope towards the castle, my eyes misted up with furious worry, my nose already invaded by the acrid smell of burning timber and thatch. I must find answers to all these questions.

I become aware of large groups of soldiers and cheering Irish; they stand watching from across the ravine. I pass behind them unnoticed. Somewhere here I must be able to find my cousin Tirlough Óge, or better still Sir James McDonnell. Should I pretend I have a message for them, maybe ask some of the soldiers their whereabouts? Maybe better to ask if they have any communication for me to take to Archibald Stewart?

That is what I do. Soon I am guided through the hundreds of troops and onlookers to the main gate of the outer ward. Looking through the entrance, and down across the long empty funnel towards the Gatehouse, I can see through the billowing smoke that the drawbridge has been pulled up. That is good news. No-one can cross that deep chasm to attack the castle. It has not been taken yet. But Dunluce village is descending into smoking cinders. The home of John and Eilish is no more. The place where John taught me my trade, the shed where we stored years-worth of precious harp materials, is being irredeemably destroyed, burning to ash before me. The roar of the flames and the crackle of splintering timber fill my ears. What a pointless disgrace!

I wonder did John have time to save any of his possessions. What about our precious harps?

Like a knife piercing my ribcage the realisation hits me that I will never see my eagle harp again, never hold its smooth wooden frame, never stroke those handsome curves I carved, or pluck those precious strings. A tear threatens to force its way to my eye as I imagine it, a charred and twisted corpse, pathetically dissembled on the floor. My painstaking labour of many months wiped out in a matter of minutes. Above all I mourn the loss of its plaintive voice. It was my pride and joy; it was who I was. It is of no real comfort to me that the swan harp that I made for the Earl is presumably still safe within the castle. I will hardly have opportunity to play it again.

It feels to me at this moment that what remained of the innocence of my youth has been consumed with this incineration. Yes, I can make another harp, and please God I will….if I survive these troubles. But it will never mean as much to me as my first harp. I half-close my eyes against the emotion of it all, but through blurry eyelids I still sense the gleam of the blaze…and for a brief moment I seem to witness the shadow of a bird rising through the smoke; my eagle harp is chasing the mythical Children of Lir in flight from this troubled place.

I find Sir James McDonnell in the shelter of the wall, presumably taking cover from any firing from the castle ramparts. I observe him for a few minutes before going to address him. His mood does not seem to be good as he swears dismissively at various members of his entourage. Tirlough Óge is nowhere to be seen. Eventually I pluck up the courage to approach Sir James. Before I get my mouth open to speak to him he has me in his sights, both visually and verbally.

"What in God's name do you want? Has Stewart sent you with a message o' surrender?"

"No sir," I say, "but I was wondering if you have a message for him?"

He looks at me as if I am a slimy insect that has just crawled out from a crack in the wall. As he was at Clough, Sir James is clearly on edge now, a much more volatile man, I fear.

"What are ye talking about? Have ye come frae Coleraine or what?" he barks.

"No sir. I haven't been in Coleraine of late."

"So ye won't be aware that Alaster McColla's troops have the place completely surrounded and cut off?"

"No sir."

"So ye couldn't have come frae Stewart!"

"No sir."

"So if ye didnae come frae Coleraine, where have ye come frae?"

"From Ballycastle, sir."

No sooner have I said this than I realise the stupidity of my honesty. I think I must be still in some sort of shock. Now I am going to be quizzed about the reasons for my trip there. I cannot possibly tell this man the truth, that my mission was to dispatch a message to the Argyll, pleading for his help against the McDonnell-led assault on the Protestants of north Antrim. Such a treasonous mission! He must not be able to squeeze that information out of me.

But he tries!

"And what message did Stewart send tae Ballycastle, pray tell me?"

My mind works quickly here.

"Not a message from Mr Stewart, sir," I lie. "It was a personal matter."

He grabs me by the neck, tightly. "Ye're goin' tae hae tae explain that," he growls. "A personal matter in the middle o' a war? The bearer o' messages for the commander o' the Crown forces in this area, but ye hae a message o' yer ain tae deliver? This'd better be a guid message or ye will be spinning o'er the side o' that cliff tae a watery grave."

"It wasn't exactly a message, sir…and it is a bit embarrassing," I tell him, thinking furiously.

He squeezes harder still. Maybe I won't feel a thing when I go hurtling over the cliff-edge.

"Come on," he spits. His face is close against mine, his breath a horrible fishy stench, those eyes wet and gluey. I have an urge to turn my head away, or to hold my nostrils closed, but I resist.

"You see, I had committed a terrible sin, sir…I needed absolution."

"You needed absolution? Frae who?"

"From a priest in Ballycastle. Father McGlaim, sir. He is a friend of mine, used to say Mass here in the castle. You can ask him yourself."

"Ye rode all the way frae Coleraine tae Ballycastle for absolution for some heinous sin ye had committed? At a time like this? Ye're crazy, O'Cahan! What sort o' sin was sae serious that ye needed instant absolution frae a Ballycastle priest?"

Aye, it had better be a serious one alright, I am thinking. Should I confess to an imaginary murder? No, I decide. It needs to be more serious than that. In the present moral climate murder isn't really anything to be worrying about. This man might even consider it a virtue, if the victim was some argumentative Protestant. What a strange time and place to be living in! I clear my throat. If you are going to tell a lie make the performance believable, I think.

"It was about a girl, sir."

"A girl? What girl? What was sae terrible about haein' a girl? Are ye very religious or what?"

"I am, sir…or I was. I was in Bonamargy at a time; I was going to be in an order. That's how I knew this priest. The girl was just a young girl in Coleraine…my conscience was bothering me terribly, and I had to get to confession as quickly as I could. And the poor girl was dying, sir."

He looks at me in disgust.

"I don't understand what ye are tryin' tae tell me, O'Cahan. Your story is as clear as mud."

I feel I need to defend myself here, put my imaginary sin in a clearer light. "It was just something that was weighing heavy on my conscience, sir. I needed absolution and…"

"Get out o' me sight!" he says, turning away.

I stand my ground. I need some information from him, regardless of what he thinks of me and my fictional transgressions.

"Sir, have you any news of my foster parents? They lived here in the village, the McSparrans? They are Irish. I am just worried about them."

"How should I ken what happened tae them?"

"Because you are in command here, sir. I just thought you might have seen what happened to the residents of the place. These are great people I speak of. They have reared me from childhood. It is only right that I should try to look after them now in this time of turmoil. Please, if you know anything about them, or what happened here, it would put my mind at ease."

McDonnell seems to be turning something over in his mind, looking at me strangely for a bit. I wonder what is coming.

"Alright, ye make yer point well," he says. "An' after I tell ye what has occurred here I will want ye tae take a message tae the defenders o' Ballintoy; I have it written already, I was going tae send it in the morning."

"I can do that, sir," I say, hiding the smile of delight at this instruction.

"Alright, so ye want tae know what happened tae your neighbours here. Well, in short, when we arrived here Captain Digby closed the gates again us; he drew up the drawbridge and still refuses tae surrender the castle."

"But the villagers? Where were they?" I ask.

"Most o' them were already inside the castle walls, forewarned o' our approach, it would seem."

"And are they still there?"

"They are, but only the Irish…and them Scottish who refused our offer o' safe passage tae Scotland."

"So the McSparrans are still safe inside?"

"If that is how ye look at it, aye, they are still inside. Unless they went wae the thirty or forty who took our offer and went tae Portballintrae tae wait for the boat tae Kintyre."

"I don't think they would do that," I say. "They are Irish to the core. They wouldn't be interested in leaving their own land at the point of a bayonet."

"Well, those Protestant women and wains were happy enough tae leave," McDonnell says.

"I suppose they would be," I tell him, "if the alternative was to be thrown over a cliff."

He looked hard at me again. "You have a way o' makin' your point that borders on insolence lad, and I cannae make up me mind whether it is intentional or innocent."

I do my best to remain as innocent looking as possible.

"And this letter, sir? Do I take it to Ballintoy now or wait 'til morning?"

"The morning will be fine. Come tae my quarters at first light and then be on yer way. Ye will give the letter to William Fullerton and nae other."

I spend that night in the open, trying to take some heat from the smouldering embers of our Dunluce dwelling. It is all the comfort left to me. How must John and Eilish feel as they look down from the castle embrasures to where they had made their cosy little home? How easily and how quickly a life's work can be erased? In my case, I merely grieve the loss of my harp, and a couple of incomplete frames that I had been crafting in the workshop; in their case the loss must be so much greater. The years of love and creativity invested in home-making must seem like a waste, a pile of glowing ash. How I wish I could be with them inside those dark, impenetrable castle walls tonight. I would hold their weary hands. I would wipe their tears. I would tell them, "Your home was beautiful and full of love. But it was made of decaying timber, and mud and straw, and it was easily wiped out. What will never be wiped out is the love you have shown me. What you have done for me is far more significant and is indestructible."

And I make myself a promise that, if God spares me and I survive this time of terror, I will build them a home in a place of serenity and safety.

Chapter 36

Surrender or Stay?

Ballintoy church had always had a very sombre ambience but it could never have appeared so dismal as that dreich winter morning.

Darach O'Cahan had arrived early at the church door with a letter for the men in charge. He had been directed there by the soldiers manning the gate of the nearby Manor House.

He told the two sturdy lads standing guard by the church door that he needed to speak to William Fullerton and remained outside in the drifting drizzle to wait for him. How he would have loved to be able to slip past the guards into the building and try to get a sight of Katie. He presumed she would still be inside with her family. But there was no chance of him doing that. He was being eyed with suspicion already by the two armed fellows…rightly so, he thought, for who could tell whether or not he was a spy for the rebels.

Reverend Fullerton eventually arrived at the door. He snatched McDonnell's letter from Darach's hand without greeting, not awaiting an explanation either. He began to read immediately.

"Wait here," he told Darach grimly when he had finished. "I need to consider this with the others. There may be a reply, there may not."

Disappearing inside again, he left Darach in the dripping wet of the churchyard. Darach had never felt comfortable in such places. The thought of the decaying bodies down there in the dark soil depressed him and gave him a strange, shivery sensation around his neck. He noticed that there were very few tombstones or wooden crosses here, the Protestant settlers having been present in the area for only a few decades.

Inside the building Fullerton had a quick discussion with his young friend, Thomas Boyd. Word had spread around the tightly packed parishioners of the arrival of McDonnell's message. Now, as they watched their leaders from the shadows, they could not but detect much anger and head-shaking between them.

Eventually the clergyman stood in front of them looking very grave and holding up the fateful letter. He didn't need to ask for quiet as he began his address to the dispirited congregation.

"I have just received a communication here from Sir James McDonnell. I will read it aloud to you and then I will tell you of the decision that Thomas Boyd and I have come to. We are certain that Mr Stewart would agree with our decision, if he were here. This is what the letter says."

Dunluce
19th February 1642

Loving Friends,
I feel it is only right to inform you of the folly you undertake in bringing yourselves to ruin, where you might quietly and without much trouble have safety for yourselves, your wives and your children. Others have taken up our offer of safe passage who were not even in such dire circumstances as yourselves. You will not be able to receive help from any quarter; Coleraine is besieged and the people there are dying for want of food and fire, and of much disease; they have only a few muskets left, having lost so many in the great conflict at Ballymoney. Antrim is also besieged and your people throughout the county have all fled.
Your state is very ill and your only hope is to take the same offer of safe quarter that I made to the people of Dunluce, which they accepted. I vow, by the Grace of God, the same conditions to you. If no-one else then Mr Fullerton, of whom I have heard much good, must take quarter under my protection as others have done.
Therefore gentlemen, to avoid further bloodshed which I have no desire to inflict on you, I beg you to take this fair offer, or else blame your own obstinacy and not us; for be sure we will have our wills of you at last when it will be too late to cry for mercy. I will go to you tomorrow and hear your decision.
I remain your friend,
James McDonnell

The sombre clergyman allowed a period of silence when he had finished. Even the babies and toddlers were hushed. The seriousness of their predicament seeped slowly into the consciousness of the people. Some of the women cried openly, children clinging in sad-eyed bewilderment to their skirts. Most of the men were defenders in the Manor House, but the few who were in the church building looked at each other blankly. What a choice to have to make!

A frail old man spoke first, his voice quivering with age and fear.

"What have yous decided? I couldn't face the sea," he said

"We cannae stay here," said a voice from the back.

"It's surrender or die," came another in a loud whisper.

Boyd heard the whisper.

"I don't agree at all," he rebuked the speaker. "Our choice is to surrender or to stand our ground and defend our rights and our kirk here in Ballintoy."

They looked at each other. A few quiet arguments broke out here and there. Some folk were all for accepting McDonnell's offer, their friends and neighbours who disagreed now quickly becoming temporary adversaries. Others just sat in a stupor of fear. Thinking this through was beyond them. Mrs Smith, whose son Thomas had been slain at Portnaw, began to shake with the trauma of it all. She looked in a very bad way, missing her husband who was stationed over in the Manor House. Her twin losses were weighing heavily on her. Mrs McClure moved to sit with her, just to hold her, try to comfort her as the debate continued.

Jean Kennedy spoke up. "The Dunluce folk have been allowed to escape," she said. "Should we not do the same?"

"Aye! We don't have the protection of a stronghold like their castle. We only have the kirk, if you say we have to stay here and not be in the Manor House. "

Quite a few murmured support for this observation and Thomas Boyd thought the ground was slipping away from him and his co-leader. Fullerton came to his rescue however.

"Friends," he said, "are we not leaving God out of the picture here? Does He not promise to be our shield and defender? Our very present help in time of need? I believe that if we stay calm and patient He will come to our aid. We can see off the attackers."

"There is no guarantee that if we take their offer of safe passage that they won't turn on us as soon as we are out of the building," Mrs McKay added bravely. "I have heard that they did exactly that when William Kennedy believed them at Clough castle. They were massacred. It is too big a risk. We are safer here in the place we know, with the people we can trust."

"Well spoken, Mrs McKay," Fullerton said quietly. "Staying is the safer of the two options. And who knows, help could already be on the way."

"Help from who? Who is going to come? There is nobody to help us."

The despairing voice had a good point but Fullerton would tolerate no such doubt. "The Earl has many friends in high places. He will not abandon us."

"He has abandoned us already," came a disgruntled voice from the back. "I don't see him riding over the hill with an army any time soon."

"If we stay will we have enough food? Will we be able to hold them out if they come at us with cannons? What if they set fire to the place?"

Fullerton held up his hands to quell the rising tide of unrest. "Good friends," he said, "let us not fall into despair so early. We have already stored some food and water. We must ration it of course and we must hope that relief is not too long in arriving, from whatever source. Cannons? I doubt if they have such weapons…maybe in some parts, but here they are more of an angry rabble than a well organised and armed force, I believe. As leaders our decision is to disregard McDonnell's offer. I am not sure we can trust him. We must put our trust in God and in each other. That is all I have to say. I will dismiss this messenger."

Katie McKay's ears pricked up at that word, and she wondered if by any chance this messenger might be her Darach. Little Kate in her arms, she followed Fullerton and Boyd towards the door and had a very brief glance through it to the churchyard beyond before it closed against her. A split second later Darach stepped forward to meet the two leaders, but she failed to see him by the unfortunate closing of the massive church door, just as his glance beyond the two gentlemen was interrupted by the same closing. Unknown to each other, the two lovers were a matter of a few feet apart, but were unable to communicate, even by the briefest of looks.

"You are dismissed," Fullerton told him.

"No message for James McDonnell, sir?"

"No message. I will not dignify his letter with a reply. You may go."

"Shall I tell him this, that you refuse to reply?" Darach asked anxiously.

"You can tell him what you will. If I was you I would stay well away from him. The man is a scoundrel," answered Fullerton.

Darach walked slowly towards his horse, then, on a whim turned to ask a further question.

"Mr Fullerton, can I ask about the people inside. Are you well supplied, if this becomes a long siege?"

William Fullerton was puzzled. He stared Darach up and down.

"What is it to you, young man? Why do you ask?"

"Because…I just wanted to know, that's all."

"You wouldn't be trying to spy for the rebels, would you? Who are you anyway?"

"I am not a spy, sir. I only ask because…because I know some of the people inside."

"Who do you know? I notice you haven't yet confessed your name to me?"

"I am Darach O'Cahan, sir. I know what you likely think when you hear that my name is O'Cahan, and I have to confess that it is my own cousin who is on his way to attack you as we speak, but I do not have any part in his scheme. I only want to help because…"

"An O'Cahan, are you?" Fullerton said, suddenly grabbing Darach by the coat and holding him firmly. He was a big strong man, and no matter how Darach pulled back he could not shake him loose. The two guards leapt to help their leader. Darach was under arrest before he knew it.

"I am no spy! I am telling you the truth," he protested, ceasing his pointless struggling against the two hardy youths.

"You have a nerve," continued Fullerton. "How can you even stand and look me in the eye after the disloyalty of your family? Gilladubh has been a traitor to the Earl, and him meant to be a peace-keeper. His sons should be hung for treason. You have a right neck on you appearing here as a would-be messenger, a spy in disguise."

"I am no spy, sir! If I was a spy do you not think I would have been at pains to hide my identity from you? I volunteered my name truthfully. That is hardly the action of a spy!"

By this stage Darach was being dragged towards the Manor House, a *scian* pushed firmly against his ribs at the back. He realised his only chance to survive this was to somehow convince Fullerton to take him to the church instead, where Katie and the McKays could vouch for his innocence.

"Sir, listen to me. I am a friend of Alex McKay. And I have been working for Mr Stewart."

"A likely story!"

"If you do not believe me take me to the church. Alex's mother will tell you that I am no spy!"

"You know the McKays? How do you know that family?" Fullerton asked skeptically.

"Because…Katie and I…Katie is a good friend of mine. Take me to the church and they will prove it."

Fullerton stopped, thinking.

"Just because you know the McKays does not mean that you are not a spy. That could easily be a very clever cover for your real purpose. My guess is that you have wormed your way into Katie's heart simply to be well placed to carry out your surveillance on our community," he said. Then to the two guards as he turned and strode back towards the church, "Lock him up in the cellar, lads."

The arrest continued. Over his shoulder Darach played one more card, his best hope.

"Sir," he called, "let me tell you of my last mission for Mr Stewart."

But Fullerton wasn't listening. He was a good distance away, about to disappear into the church again. As Darach was dragged towards the sturdy gates of the Manor House bawn he shouted at the top of his voice.

"Argyll is coming! Argyll is coming!"

That did get Fullerton's attention. He trotted awkwardly back to where the guards held Darach.

"What did you say?"

"I said, 'Argyll is coming,' sir,"

"And what makes you think that?"

"Because Mr Stewart sent a message to him. I was involved…"

"Why are you telling me this now? This is very sensitive

information? Don't you understand that?"

"Of course I do, sir, but I would hardly tell you such news if I was a spy, would I?" Darach protested.

"Unless you just made it up on the spot?"

"Sir, I understand that at times like this it is hard to know what to believe, and who to trust, but believe me, I have no interest in giving you false information just to try to save my own skin. What I say is true."

William Fullerton was convinced. Beckoning with his hand as he turned back towards the church he said, "Very well, very well! You made your point. Bring him back and we'll see what Mrs McKay says about him."

They had only taken a few steps when the church bell began to ring furiously. It took a second for its meaning to dawn on Darach, but the panicky reaction of Fullerton and his captors gave him the clue. The guards bolted towards the Manor House. Fullerton took off running towards the church door, leaving him standing behind.

"You'd better get away from here, O'Cahan!" he shouted back.

Darach ran for his horse, untied it quickly and jumped on *Liath's* back. He did not look behind him. He galloped east across the fields, past Katie's farmstead and up the slope towards Knocksoughey Hill. Only at that safe distance did he turn back and watch as Tirlough Óge's troops streamed along the coastline on the flat ground above White Park Bay towards Ballintoy. Before long they were like a dark swarm of bees gathering around the bawn of the Manor House and the church building.

The attack was about to begin.

Chapter 37

Alone

Darach O'Cahan

There is nothing more I can do here.

It is such a dissonant sight below; a frenzy of anger pulsing around the Manor House and its serenely quaint little church; the picturesque patchwork of neat fields now thronged with hordes of dishevelled warmongers.

How has it come to this?

How to proceed?

My duty, I realise, is to ride back to Coleraine. Stewart deserves to know all I have witnessed. He should know that Alex has gone to Kintyre for help. He should know how Dunluce has been attacked, the village there obliterated. Above all, as land steward of Ballintoy, he needs to understand the gravity of the situation here, that his home and his people are under siege.

But it is impossible! I cannot get to see Stewart. I cannot even get a message to him. Coleraine is surrounded, and maybe on its last legs as a settler bastion. It is highly unlikely that I could slip through the cordon of Alaster McColla's soldiers now camped around the place. If I were to be caught trying to do so it would mean certain torture and death...I would rightly be seen as a spy for the enemy and as a traitor to my own tribal cause.

That duty must give way to common sense.

I could ride east to Dunluce again. To what end though? It seems to me that James McDonnell had always intended to march on Ballintoy. Clearly he has not bothered to await a reply to his ultimatum to the people of Ballintoy; his soldiers are here already, them plus a horde of hangers-on.

It is very unlikely that I would be welcome in the castle at Dunluce. There is no-one there that I would consider to be a friend. The carnaptious Captain Digby would have every reason to see me as 'enemy' as well. John and Eilish are most likely as safe there as they would be anywhere.

I could go to Dunseverick and try to gain admittance there to be safe with my family, but I feel no great draw in that direction. To take refuge behind those crumbling stone walls would possibly save my own skin, but it would isolate me from any opportunity to affect what is going on in the conflict. If I ensconce myself in the confines of the castle there, I could be of no possible help to Katie and her family.

I am suddenly shaken by the vagarious uncertainty of my situation. The final dregs of my normal sense of self-assuredness drain away from me. I need to admit to myself just how deeply shaken I am by the new turn of events. Until this moment there has always seemed to be a plan, a duty to perform, a clear way open to me to act on my conscience.

Until now, the responsibilities I have had have suited me. I haven't had to pretend to be a courageous soldier. I have usually known what to do next, sometimes because of instruction, more often instinctively. I have succeeded because I am a solitary person. It has lain easy to me, partly because I have not had to answer to the curiosity of companions.

Now it is different. I am stripped away from myself. It is a new feeling of lostness, of hopelessness.

Am I even the same person who used to spend an entire day happily planing and carving a piece of timber into the shape of a harp?

My role as a messenger for Archibald Stewart has given me the opportunity to be aware of the course of the conflict, but yet sit above the need to identify with one side or the other; a fence-sitter who has been up close to disturbing tragedy and raw human pain. Up until now the most painful experience I have had was the needless death of poor Nellie in Coleraine. Now, with Katie and Kate under siege, I feel more bereft than I have ever been.

Right at this moment I want so much to talk to Katie. I need to be held. Comforted by her physical touch. Restored by her spirit…but that might not happen again for a very long time, if ever.

If ever!

What if this siege is successful? Those poor people would receive no mercy from McDonnell. Nor indeed from my own cousin. There would be a slaughter. Part of me wishes they had taken McDonnell's offer, as some of the Dunluce Protestants had done. At least there would have been a chance of escape to Islay or Kintyre. Now it is do or die.

How can such a feeble church building act as a proper defence against a determined and well-armed force like these Irish troops? They have little chance of warding off attack, especially if the Irish are able to bring in cannons. How long can they hold out? What if their food and water runs out? I have visions of Katie descending into hunger and ending up looking as emaciated as Kate's dying mother had appeared. The thought sends such deep pain searing around my heart area that I hear myself cry out involuntarily.

"Noooo!"

Liath shies below me in surprise at the unusual sound of her master's cry. Unbidden, she begins to move further along the hillside.

"I cannot let this happen," I say aloud. "God help me but I cannot let this happen…but who will aid me? Who can I go to? What can I do?"

I lift my head, aware that my cry has been an unconscious prayer. The sky above me has an unnatural darkness, an ominously thick slate of low cloud that stretches from Knocklayde mountain in the east right across the flattened sky to the Inishowen hills far to the west. An intense blanket of smudged grey and bruise-black gloom blocks out all morning light, apart from some low rays of sunlight that fight it successfully above Fairhead and *An Sruth na Maoile*.

This oppressive sky-scape matches my mood perfectly.

How can such hatred and inhumanity erupt in my lovely country? In this place that the monks tell us is 'the land of saints and scholars'? Where is the christianity now that our Columcilles and Kevins and Brendans had been proudly exporting to far-flung regions? Has it all been a bit of a self-congratulatory myth? Are we just as pagan and blood-thirsty as the heathens that we claim to be bringing light and peace to?

My morose thoughts are interrupted by the awareness that *Liath* is starting to trot, travelling east above the Carrick-a-Rede cliffs, away from Ballintoy, and in the direction of Ballycastle. I let the mare take its head. For some reason I seem to be able to relax into the spontaneous wisdom of my mount. I breathe deeply, deliberately, long and slow, the sea air filling my lungs, settling my churning heartache.

Liath is directing me towards the gleam of light above Ballycastle, towards a source of comfort and inspiration, one that hadn't dawned on me until now. The thought makes me smile inwardly for the first time in a while.

Father McGlaim will know what to do, I imagine

Chapter 38

The Siege of Ballintoy

Katie McKay

It is impossible to properly tell the terrors of those days of siege inside our Ballintoy kirk. The things that I saw and heard I have tried to blank out from my mind, for to remember them is to re-live them. The horrors of those experiences kept me awake during the early nights of our captivity. I was not alone in that; it was the question on everyone's lips in the mornings.

"Were you able to sleep last night?"

We all pretended that we had, but, even in the dull light, the dark shadows around every pair of eyes betrayed our truth. How could you sleep?

The screaming that erupted at some point each night was evidence of the visions and nightmares people were suffering. One person would begin *an caoineadh* with a loud sob, a painful keening, sometimes even a flesh-creeping yell, and that would set off others who joined in waves across the kirk floor. The more sane among us would try to comfort those who were in the tremors with kind words and tight hugs, but even the sane were shaking with dread. The noise always woke wee Kate, and she would add her voice to the din. I held her tightly and tried to sooth her, but it wasn't easy to hear her weak, whimpering cry and know that she would never be comforted by her natural mother; it was enough to melt any heart. How she snuggled into me for solace in those dreary hours. I could hardly wait for the thin strands of morning sunlight to probe their way through narrow slits into our murky prison, relieving the fear in both of us.

We imagined that our clergyman, Reverend Blare, had fled to Coleraine for safety from his residence at Billy. In his absence, our men, under the guidance of Reverend Fullerton and Thomas Boyd, had altered the church building. They had had the foresight to build up the windows of the kirk some days ago, a secure-looking job with sturdy rocks and lime cast over a timber frame which they mounted on the inside. Only thin gaps were left open at the top and the sides so that we could keep a lookout to what was going on beyond the church walls. As it turned out, the slits were to be useful in another way. What happened was this.

Early in the morning, the day after our door was barred against the Irish rebel forces swarming around us, we were woken up by the sound of hammering against the sides of the building. We were under attack. They were trying to break through the blocked-up windows with pick-axes!

I saw Reverend Fullerton signal urgently to us.

"Get the guns! Get the guns!" he said. His command was softly delivered but our men fairly jumped into action. In no time at all, three of them were climbing up on benches beside the south-facing windows, and then there was the ripping explosions of musket-fire as they shot out through the slits. The smoke and odour of gunpowder was in our noses, but worse still was the shouting and screaming in our ears. It was a mad racket of noise out there.

From what we heard, it seemed certain that our men had hit a few of the attackers with their volleys of shots. The angry shouting in Irish made us fairly sure that some of them were injured, maybe worse. Fullerton leapt to one of the windows to peer out and he confirmed that two bodies were being dragged away by their comrades; another man was bleeding from his head. There was no great sense of rejoicing among us at this news, but, at the same time, it was a relief that this first attack had been so easily repelled. The sealed windows had done their job, the little gaps had been a master-stroke of planning, and the naivety of the Irish had been exposed.

I wondered why they had not realised that we would have weapons inside the kirk? Did they imagine we were going to defend ourselves with bibles? It struck me that this was probably the reason they had chosen to concentrate their attack on the kirk rather than the Manor House. To them, we seemed to be weak and vulnerable, whereas the Manor House had its bawn wall and turrets, and was well defended by armed soldiers. We were the easy target…but they had misread the situation.

The following day another letter was delivered to the door of the church. This time it was from Gilladubh O'Cahan; he said he was writing on behalf of all the local men, especially his son, Tirlough Óge, who was one of those in charge of this besieging army. Nobody wanted to hurt the Scotch, he said. We were on our own because Archibald Stewart and nearly all the soldiers from our parish had been slaughtered at a battle outside the town of Ballymoney. There was no point in us fighting on in a war we could never win. Would we not surrender and take the offer of safe passage out of the country through Coleraine or Larne? He would personally guarantee our safety. This was what Mr Fullerton told us in his summary.

What did we think?

Nobody said a word. We all just looked at each other and at our two leaders. Thomas Boyd spoke for us all.

"Not a chance," he said. "For a start, I do not believe this tale of our land steward's death. I think that is a ruse to scare us into surrender. How could we trust the O'Cahans, especially after us shooting a couple of their men? We have begun this and we will see it through to the bitter end."

We agreed, more or less all of us, but we were almost paralysed with fear as this fateful decision was delivered to the fellow with the white flag at the door.

It wasn't long after the huge wooden door was closed in his face that a new attack began. This time it was the kirk door itself that came in for punishment. From what I could make out, someone was chopping at the timber with an axe, maybe more than one person. They were trying to break down the main door. How could we counter this? It was a very sturdy door, but it couldn't withstand this violent attack for ever. And in this case there were no slits to fire through.

But Fullerton was ahead of them again. There was a narrow staircase up to the kirk's bell tower; our leader signalled for a young fellow called Robert Moore to get himself up to the top. I wondered what was happening, waiting and watching the clergyman's face.

After a few more blows against the door there was yet another mighty yelp from outside, very angry swearing and the sound of rushing feet. Mr Fullerton spoke up to Robert at the top of the staircase.

"Good lad! You must have got them!" he called.

It transpired that our leader had foreseen this eventuality and had stored a few heavy rocks up there to push over on top of anyone who tried to destroy the door. We had survived both attacks through good preparation, but it was early days.

As I lay awake at night my thoughts inevitably turned to my lover. What had become of Darach? Was he alive or dead? Where was he sleeping right now? Who was he with? Was he safe? Was he worrying about me? I had not seen him in a few weeks, not since he had arrived unexpectedly that day when he brought Kate to us. We had already heard of that battle near Ballymoney; 'Black Friday' they were calling it. Gilladubh's letter confirmed that it had happened. Now I began to worry again that maybe Alex had been slain there. For some reason I was more confident that Darach could keep himself out of trouble, but I really longed for a sign from him that he was alright. But how on earth could he get such a message to me? It was out of the question. I would just have to say my prayers for him, and for my poor brother who, if he was still alive, must be incarcerated in Coleraine or somewhere and must be worried sick about his family back in Ballintoy.

****

The weeks passed. February faded into March without us really realising it. Days, weeks, months…it didn't matter. Time didn't deserve a name. Everything became a repeat of the day before. That was one of the stresses of it all, that and the apprehension of waiting, not knowing what was happening in our surroundings. We were outdoor people. This was a tight, dull prison. The darkness depressed us all. We did have candles, but as time wore on, so did they. Instead of three or four burning in the evenings we were rationed down to one for each night, its wavering flame providing us with a thin, ghostly light.

When the siege began the women had had enough warning to bring with them a good deal of wool. This had kept them busy until a few days ago. Now all their material had been used, lots of garments knitted which helped in the chilly nights. But it left them with nothing to keep themselves occupied afterwards. All they could do was snuggle together, happed up against the cold under shawls, blankets and sheepskins.

We had Reverend Fullerton trying to bring us comfort and spiritual solace. He would read passages from the Old Testament every morning and some texts from the gospels every night before it became too dark to see. I listened to stories about scriptural characters that I'd never heard of before, men mainly, whose names I will never be able to get my tongue around nor remember. Then there would be singing. Because we were in a kirk it had to be Psalm-singing. If anyone started up a song, or a bit of verse that came from somewhere other than the bible, it was frowned upon and hushed up very quickly. The clergyman was very strict about that. The Psalms! They were alright, but I started to feel that they were all merging into each other…maybe it was just the repetition of all those slow old Scottish tunes. I was itching to lilt a bit of a reel but, if I did, it had to be lilted into myself…and my feet had to shuffle around on the floor from a sitting position on my rock-hard bench. They couldn't be seen to be enjoying themselves. This was kirk after all.

Days passed with no further attacks against us. We had heard what we took to be sorties against the Manor House, but even these had died out. What was happening with the Irish? We could still see and hear them out there. Their mocking threats and laughter could be heard in our stiller moments. It was a tense waiting game, it seemed.

What were they waiting for? Reinforcements? Maybe heavier weapons were on their way, cannon, battering rams or the like? Or perhaps they were content to remain there and watch as we starved to death?

As in everything else, Reverend Fullerton had been planning ahead. He and Boyd had laid in a good supply of food and water, but it wasn't going to last any longer than a couple of weeks at best, especially the water situation. We were told to ration ourselves to a minimum amount of water, and to avoid wasting it…same with the buttermilk, the strips of dried meat and smoked fish, the small amount of oatmeal we had left and the few turnips and carrots. But there were around forty of us in the church. Our leaders felt that, if we were careful, we could hold out for maybe two or three weeks before we ran short, no more than that. But then illness struck us and some of the older folk began to suffer from some sort of fever. It meant that these folk needed extra liquid. It also meant that their use of our latrine buckets became a problem…the smell and the overflowing! This led to our most serious reversal during those first weeks.

The waste buckets badly needed emptying, and our barrels of drinking water were running low.

Robert Moore once again volunteered to take on the task of dumping the slop buckets. Mr Boyd advised the brave lad to do it in the early morning, so, just before first light, the door was carefully opened, and Robert slipped out quietly with a bucket in each hand. He didn't have to walk far to a *sheugh,* no more than twenty paces north of the building. We waited, praying silently for his safety. Relief when he arrived back for the remaining two buckets. He was a cheery lad, Robert, and despite the stench and the weight of our 'doings' hanging from his arms, he had a broad smile on his face. He knew we all valued what he was doing, and he seemed to enjoy the pat on the back from quite a few of us when he returned safely from his second load.

Two mornings later Robert was volunteering again. Our water had dried up. There had been no rain for several days, unusual in March, so not a drop had flowed down the make-shift system that had been rigged up to catch some rainfall from the church roof. One or two of the older folk were complaining, gasping for a drink. Reverend Fullerton and Mr Boyd were scratching their heads to know what to do. Robert went to them with his idea.

"I could go o'er to the spring next Larrybane," he told our leaders.

"It's too far, too big a risk," Fullerton argued.

"You would be sure to be caught," said Boyd. "There'll be a circle of rebels all the way around us. You'll not get through."

Robert was stubborn though. He insisted that, being from a house over in that direction, he knew the lie of the land; he could sneak along the backs of hedges and in the ditches between the fields.

"I can dae it," he said. "I'll be grand. I'll go oot early again. They'll still be asleep. An' if they dae catch me they'll naw dae me a pin o' harm. Sure am'nt I little mair than a wain."

Our leaders eventually consented; Robert left us with two tin buckets in his hands and many good wishes in his ears that morning.

That was the last we ever saw of our friend Robert.

He never returned.

As daylight dawned and we could see each other more clearly, the dread of what might have happened could be seen on every face. His mother grew more and more anxious. Some tried to calm her with hopeful platitudes, even verses of hope and comfort from the bible. It was cold comfort though. By mid-day there was still no sign of him. The waiting was unbearable, the seconds ticking by so slowly. All you could hear was the muffled sound of people praying, some sniffling and crying here and there and Mrs Moore weeping sorely. "Oh my poor Robert," she kept repeating. It was pitiful. Our leaders were strangely silent, hoping against hope as the day wore on. Not many words of reassurance came from them.

James Kerr, a good solid man that I had worked with in the Manor House, sat with his arm around Robert's mother.

"I'll go and look for him, Betsy," he said. "Maybe take a bucket and find some water as well."

Mrs Moore shook her head. "No, James. Dinnae go oot that dour."

"I must. He's the only nephew I hae. Blood is thicker than water."

"Aye, an' you are the only brither I hae," Mrs Moore replied. "If he is kilt you are all I hae left in the world."

But James wouldn't listen to her. He had survived the massacre at Portnaw; he likely thought he was invincible. His sense of family duty was matched only by his courage and he slipped away from us to search for his nephew.

He couldn't have been gone more than two minutes when we heard the gunshot echo against the wall of the building. There was a split second of silence, then a wail of horror rose from almost every throat.

James Kerr had been shot!

Two of our brave men, well…a man and a lad…had given their lives for the rest of us trapped in that dark dungeon of a church. James Kerr now lying dead somewhere out there. Jean and I went to try to console his wife.

I cried all the rest of that day. Nobody had a word of comfort.

Nor was I alone in saving every tear that trickled down my cheeks and making sure it finished up on my tongue. Every drop of liquid was that precious to us then.

When our immediate grief subsided, Mr Fullerton stood before us and made a further speech. He apologised to Mrs Moore and Mrs Kerr, to us all really, for failing us by not being a stronger and wiser leader.

"I should never have permitted these two brave men to leave the safety of our kirk," he said. "Their deaths, if dead they be, lie at my door and I will forever regret that I allowed their courage to out-weigh my own reticence about their ventures. From now on, no-one leaves the confines of this building. We must pray for rain, so that some water can be obtained from what falls on our roof. And, instead of carrying our lavatory buckets outside, we will try to devise a different means of disposing of our slop."

For the life of me I could not imagine how he was going to manage this. The windows were so well blocked that there was no way anything could be thrown out through them. The door was to be secured and guarded against anyone who, perhaps driven to madness by thirst and hunger, might make a rash decision and try to escape the building. So Mr Fullerton's solution, when I watched it unfold, took me completely by surprise.

In one corner of the kirk he had a couple of our stronger folk dig up four of the flat stone-slabs which made up the flooring. This was a difficult job and took some effort, but nothing to the effort required for the next stage. They then began to dig down into the hard-baked soil, and eventually into the chalky rock underneath. At the beginning it wasn't too difficult; the loamy earth that we were used to growing our crops in came up fairly easily and was piled in the corner fornenst the pulpit. The hard chalk was tougher though, and took the men much longer to break and prise out, but gradually we saw that Fullerton's plan was to create some sort of channel under the foundations of the building. It was a huge task; it took the team a few days to complete. The one pointed iron spike which somebody had had the foresight to bring into the church, along with a couple of spades and pick-axes, came in very useful. It was hammered repeatedly into the limestone to try to break it into pieces that could be lifted out and to create holes for the human waste to seep away.

The channel was deep and just about broad enough for one man to crawl along under the church foundations, but he had to be pulled back out by the heels when he had done a few minutes work in that cramped, airless space. Sometimes he dragged a lump of white rock with him, a small victory. When no more could be safely achieved the men moved the slabs back in place, leaving just a small opening through which our waste could reach this escape tunnel.

Such small accomplishments gave us hope in those troubled days. At the same time, what little conversation there was among us was repetitive and very depressing. People who farmed were feeling especially low. Their incarceration in the church was coming right in the season when normally they would be breaking the soil and getting ready to sow corn and plant vegetables. The in-built rhythm of their lives as farmers was being disrupted. They found it so hard to sit around and wait when every muscle was crying out to be active on their land. The paucity of last year's crop would be repeated in the coming months if an end to the siege didn't happen soon. And what about the animals they had had to turn loose before this captivity began? Were they able to fend for themselves on the hills behind the village? Would they still be there when this was all over, or had they become food for our Irish besiegers? It was so difficult not to know answers to these questions.

I watched my mother go downhill as the days dragged by. The last remaining dregs of energy and will to survive seemed to drain from her. The absence of any news about Alex was a huge worry for her. Connie and Alice were in reasonable spirits, but wee Kate was fairly demanding. In the first few weeks after the child arrived in our lives, my mother had been a source of succour and wise support for me, but now even that instinct deserted her and I found myself alone, the child clinging to me more or less all the time, pathetic, too tired to even cry.

We were all so thirsty, desperate for rain, for anything to drink. This was our greatest need; we could all see the desperation grow on the faces of our leaders. What could Fullerton and Boyd do? Not a thing, other than pray for a miracle. And just when it looked as if they would have to surrender to the rebels and trust their humanity to spare at least some of us…just as hope was running out…their prayers were answered.

We got our miracle! And from a completely unexpected source.

Chapter 39

Dilemmas and Discussions

Darach O'Cahan

The cloister pillars are reflecting a brassy glow from the evening sun. I sit opposite Father McGlaim in the still coolness. Bonamargy is the most peaceful place on earth on an evening like this. Apart from the very faint murmur of running water, the occasional cry of a seabird above and the distant quacking of ducks on the river there is complete quietness; *ciúnas agus suaimhneas*. Even the little waves on the beach beyond seem to be respecting the silence.

Hard to imagine that, only a few miles west of where we have been chatting, lives may hang in the balance for want of food and water. While we debate in pure ocean-scented air I try to fix in my mind a mental image of Katie. Her face colourless in the gloomy confines of that darkened building. Other faceless folk crush around her, bodies sharp and boney. Lips are hacked and broken from thirst, eyes red and staring. Children cry, little Kate among them, arms latched around her surrogate mother's neck. This is what I picture, but I realise that the reality may be much worse than anything I might imagine.

Father McGlaim was absent when I arrived here at the Friary. His ministry had taken him somewhere down the Antrim Glens, I was told; I was permitted to take refuge in his abode however, until he returned. When he reappeared he was very surprised to see me but welcomed me and entertained me in his Friary cell. He had listened intently to my story, my deep fears concerning what is happening in Ballintoy. Since then we have argued out several ideas. He has even brought his superior into the discussions, a wise monk whose instincts are reticent when it comes to the question of somehow trying to get involved in helping the victims of this rising.

"While I agree that we must reach out our hands to aid our enemies," the old friar had said thoughtfully, "I would caution. In doing so we should not prejudice the cause of our friends, particularly when that cause is a justifiable one."

McGlaim and I both struggled with this argument. The return of Ireland to our ancestral Catholic faith was an important aspiration for us all, to be sure, but the present situation is a lot more complex than the simple ideal of a just war to achieve the freedoms of the past.

"Are you saying that you would take up arms and join the rebelling soldiers?" Father McGlaim asked him. "If you see the cause as just, and if you believe that God is on our side in this, as you do, why are you not armed and fighting?"

"Because I am a man of God," was the ambivalent response. "I can help the cause in other ways. I am called to serve him by serving God's people. It is for others to take up arms if that is what they believe God wants them to do. That would be the position of the Franciscan order to which we both belong, would it not?"

"We are called to serve people, I agree," argued my friend, "but surely not just the people we see as being 'God's people'? Surely not just our own kind? The Samaritan of the gospel went out of his way to serve someone who was not one of his own, did he not? An outsider? An enemy? That is surely what we are called to do. Otherwise we are no different from the heathen, from the unbeliever who has a mind only for his own group. We must be better than that, don't you think?"

This was a very powerful point and I was proud of Father McGlaim's courage and insight. His superior smiled, a bit smugly I thought, and remembered that he had some duties to attend to in the sacristy.

That conversation had taken place yesterday. Today, while we both feel strengthened in our belief that we are right to try to help the Ballintoy folk, we are not much further forward in having a practical plan.

That is until…

As we sit below the arches, our arguments and ideas exhausted, I am aware of a shadow crossing the grass before us. I look up to see one of the brothers walking slowly towards the kitchens from the direction of the Margy, the river from which this monastery takes its name. The monk's shadow is very long on the lawn, made longer still by the fact that he is carrying on his shoulder one of the tall earthen-ware pitchers from the kitchen. His arm is extended above his head to hold one of the lugs of this well-filled urn, for he has obviously been down to the river to bring a replenishing supply.

"Father McGlaim, look!"

"Look at what?"

"There's our answer," I tell him. "Look at that vessel he is carrying. If you were to arrive at the church in Ballintoy with a container like that, full of water for the women and children inside, surely as a man of the church you would not be turned away? You are only bringing water. You can say you are being a good Samaritan, fulfilling our Lord's command. Gilladubh would have to let you carry out this charity, good Catholic that he is."

The priest does not reply at once. I watch his eyes as he grapples with this notion. The doubt in them seems to be shifting, giving way to a tiny spark of possibility.

"Do you think we could manage this?" he says.

"We?"

"Yes, 'we'! I could never manage that heavy container by myself. You would have to come with me and help."

This scares me a bit. I have a feeling that my presence would contaminate and undermine such a mission. It must be seen to be the churchman and him alone. I have been associated with Archibald Stewart. My cousin, my uncle and indeed James McDonnell will hold me in high suspicion. Already I may be *an fealltóir,* 'the turncoat', in their eyes.

"I can help, but I cannot be seen," I tell him. "I could maybe carry the urn from Ballycastle for you. We could fill it up at a stream closer to Ballintoy. But you must deliver it on your own. If they saw me, those relatives of mine would only laugh at my naivety, that's before they slit my throat."

"Alright, I see that," McGlaim says. "But one container doesn't work. Could I not find two smaller urns, one to hang on either side of my saddle? That way the thing will be balanced."

We are warming to the plan. I notice such a new light in his eyes, eyes that have been depressed by doubt for so long. A further thought strikes him.

"Darach," he says with the excitement of a scheming child, "why don't we try to get some oatmeal to them as well?"

"Oatmeal? How are you going to manage that? They'll never let you provide them with one jar of water and one of food. That's a step too far."

"I agree, but there is another way. We put oatmeal in the bottom half of the pitchers, then fill them up with water. No-one will be any the wiser."

My clever priest is now gleaming with delight at the cunningness of his plan. I haven't the heart to caution him to take one small step at a time. He sees my hesitation all the same.

"If I am going to bless these people then I have to do it with a fulsome heart, with a generosity of spirit, don't you agree?"

"I agree," I tell him, "but are you going to confess that generosity to the besiegers when they question you? To Gilladubh?"

He thinks about this, that mischievous twinkle back in his look. "I won't confess it unless I am asked," he says. "I will talk about water, the water I have put in the urns. I will omit to tell them of my friend Darach who, without informing me, has put some oatmeal in the bottom beforehand!"

"Father," I tell him laughing, "you are my kind of priest. But have you thought of where you are going to find all this oatmeal? I believe it is in short supply across the north coast, but maybe you can command a miracle?"

"Ah, there is always a problem for every solution," he says. "We must pray about this. Yes, perhaps a miracle will happen. In the meantime I am going to suggest we look in the storehouse here at Bonamargy, and talk to the friar who is in charge there. If that fails…let me think now."

I watch as his mind turns the possibilities over. Is he mumbling to himself, or is this a tuneless melody he has started to hum, seeking inspiration? Eventually an idea seems to have occurred to him and he comes back to me, bright-eyed.

"Listen," he says, "I think our supplies come from Hugh MacNeill up at the castle. He has been importing grain from the Scottish mainland for some time. He may be willing to offer some to his friends at Ballintoy. I am sure Archibald Stewart has done plenty of business with him in the past."

"I would be certain of it," I tell him.

I cannot believe how re-invigorated Father McGlaim is by this possibility of trying to help those folk in Ballintoy church. He looks to be a different man, the drabness has fallen off him like an old, threadbare cloak; his very posture has straightened, become more energised. Even if my crazy notion is to meet with no success, even if he fails to convince Gilladubh and the others, to see him come back into himself with such enthusiasm has been worth the dream.

Chapter 40

Water

Darach has hidden *Liath* well back from the summit of the hill beyond Ballintoy's flatlands; now he watches from a distance and from the camouflage of an elevated thicket of trees as Father McGlaim leads his mule towards Ballintoy church. It is a slow procession, deliberately so; there is no threat in an old holy-man ambling so aimlessly beside his beast. Darach would dearly love to be part of the conversation that is about to happen down there, even simply to hear the exchange. He knows, however, that this could be counter-productive. The priest is best on his own.

Two days have passed since that decisive conversation in the Friary. The promise of a generous supply of corn was indeed provided by Hugh MacNeill. The two plotters had visited him in Dunynie Castle that very evening; they found him to be warm to the notion of secretly feeding the Ballintoy Presbyterians.

"I will ask you, gentlemen, to refrain from ever admitting to your source, should you be apprehended in your scheme. My name must never be mentioned. I have to live in this community hereafter, and do business with settler and native alike. I cannot be seen to support one side over the other, you understand?"

Of course they understood, but Darach had thrown in the comment that Father McGlaim, should he be discovered, stood to lose more than business. MacNeill had taken his point well.

"Indeed, and I applaud both his compassion and his bravery," he said. "My contribution is small by comparison, and you must be assured that I will expect no recompense for the corn supplied."

Now, the old priest was nearing the lion's den. Darach blessed himself and said the *"Ár nAthair"* more fervently than he had done for as long as he could remember.

"Ár n-arán laethúil tabhair dúinn inniu" he prayed sincerely. "Give us this day our daily bread!"

Little did he know that Father McGlaim was breathing those exact same words over and over again as he approached Ballintoy church. Out of the corner of his eye he had noticed a group of the Irish soldiers getting up from their resting place behind a hedge. Now they stood like curious statues, watching the progress of this mule and its master across the final field, almost in disbelief at what they were seeing. The little man was clearly dressed in the habit of a religious person, but surely he did not imagine he could just walk up to the door of this church, not in the current circumstances? Was he mad or what? Maybe just a bit simple in the head. Finally, the senior man in the group thought he had better intervene. He shook off the lethargy of his morning stupor and moved forward purposefully to cut off the priest's approach.

"Where do you think you are going, Father?" He spoke in Irish of course, his north coast accent pronounced and lilting.

Father McGlaim looked around at the questioner, feigning an air of surprise that he should be so interrupted; his gait slowed even further and then he pulled *Pádraig* to an unwilling halt.

"What did you ask me, my son?" he said innocently.

"I asked you where you are going...." The lieutenant was unsure of himself when faced with a man of the church who clearly did not recognise the protocols of a military situation, let alone a siege like this one.

"Ah, right. Of course," McGlaim said. "To the church....that is where I am going. If that is alright with you."

"Well Father, now you put it like that, I'm afraid it might not be alright. I need to know why you are going to the church. Do you not understand that it has been under siege for the past while?"

"Indeed, sir...and that is why I am here," the priest said, making moves to continue his journey.

"And why....hold on there...why are you here? What are you intending to do at the church, Father?"

"I am intending to give water to the folk inside."

The soldier almost laughed in his face, but, realising you don't show such disrespect to a man of the cloth, he held himself in check. "I am afraid that you are misguided, Father. You can't be doing that now."

"And why not? Didn't Our Lord give water to the woman at the well when she needed it?"

"That's as maybe, but there's no wells and no women here. If my boss hears what you are up to you'll maybe be seeing your Lord before your time!" The soldier's patience was wearing thin. Time to move to a higher level, McGlaim thought.

"Now, now, my son! Don't be letting me hear any more irreverent talk out of your mouth. Of course there are women in that building. You can't deny that. And I have water..."

"Aye, there's women alright!" the soldier interrupted. "There's that witch, the widow Wilson. You want to give her a drink, do you? They're all Satan's servants, those women. Why would you want to help them?"

McGlaim showed no surprise at how this man was painting these women in the darkest light; he understood the need to demonise those who are your enemies, but he also understood that there was no point in trying to reason with this man, especially in his fraught circumstance.

"I want to do as Our Lord has asked me to," he said calmly. "Maybe you can direct me to your superior, so I can explain the importance of this commission to him in person."

The soldier looked hard and long at McGlaim before responding.

"You'd better come with me," he said, indicating for the priest to follow him. "Gilladubh O'Cahan is in charge here; if we can't find him, his son Tirlough Óge will want to talk to you. They'll be about here somewhere."

The father and son were easily found, taking shelter from any possible musket fire beyond the bawn wall of Ballintoy House. They stared disbelievingly as Father McGlaim and his mule arrived in front of them.

"What in the name o' God....?" began the younger man.

"Indeed, my son," the priest responded quickly, "it is in the name of God I am here."

"He wants to give water to the people in the church," said the soldier, smirking at the ludicrousness of this notion.

"Have you lost your mind altogether, wandering into the middle of a battle?" Tirlough Óge continued angrily. "Water to who?"

McGlaim gave him what he thought was a disarming smile, opened his mouth to say, "What battle? I see no battle!" but no words came. His nerves had briefly got the better of him.

Gilladubh, recognising Father McGlaim from having received Mass from him some time ago, was a little more circumspect in his comments than his hot-headed son.

"Father McGlaim," he said, "I don't know what you think you are doing, but this is not a good time to be trying to interfere. You need to get out of here, and quickly."

"On the contrary, Gilladubh, I need to do what God has sent me here to do. Believe me, sir…I would not be doing this if it was down to me. It is not my idea, not at all. I have come in obedience to God to give water to the unfortunate people who are captive in that church."

Gilladubh reacted badly to this naive proposal.

"Unfortunate people, is it?" he raged. "There is nothing unfortunate about them! Do you know what they did, Father? They damned near killed me! They dropped a rock on my head from the bell tower. If I hadn't had my helmet on I would be as dead as…as dead as the other fellow who was with me at the time."

"He's right," joined Tirlough Óge. "Those bloody Scotch have killed three of our men. Shot two out of the windows… and then Conor died when they threw rocks down on top of him. My father could have been dead too."

Father McGlaim thought about this for a bit. Then he made the sign of the cross towards Gilladubh and said, "But you, Gilladubh….you were spared. God has a special love for you and so he preserved you. You could have been up there talking to your maker today, trying to explain away all your misdeeds, your sins which are many and have not yet been shriven. Instead, Our Father has spared you and given you a longer life; he has afforded you a further chance to atone for those sins. You must take that chance…and I offer it to you now!"

"What do you mean, Father?" Gilladubh was cowed by this speculative little homily.

"I mean what I said to your son earlier. God has given me a commission. His voice was as clear as a bell. The commission is to bring the water of life, the same water as we learn of in the gospels, the same water that Our Lord offered to the woman at the well. I am to bring that water to the sinful people who are behind the walls of that church. You see? And that is where you come into the picture."

"How? I don't see how?" Gilladubh said.

"You are in charge here. God has placed you in charge here. So you are his instrument at this moment in time. You are the only one who can give the permission for this sacrament of mercy, this divine gift of water, holy, blesséd water…for the salvation of those deluded Protestants in that church over there."

The little O'Cahan chieftain now seemed to be becoming more than impressed that, after all his misdemeanours in life, God may have chosen him for this special task. He was certainly coming around to the idea of helping Father McGlaim in his mercy mission, but he had reckoned without taking the views of his more aggressive offspring into consideration. Tirlough Óge was having none of it.

"No disrespect to you, Father, but that is all nonsense. There is a war going on here and…"

McGlaim cut him short. "Hold your tongue, my son. It is not me you are disrespecting. It is your Father in Heaven. He is the one who has given me this commission. It is at his bidding I am here today, not of my own volition. You must understand that, when you speak your objection."

Gilladubh and the listening soldiers nearby looked as if they were tending to agree with the priest but Tirlough Óge took up a stubborn stance, his legs apart and firmly planted before the priest, his chin jutting defiance.

"And you say Our Father in Heaven told you to bring water to the Protestants, Father? Since when did Our Father in Heaven decide to be on the side of the Protestant invaders? Since when are we meant to give any succour to the people who have hounded us off our land and banned our religion?"

Father McGlaim held up his hand for quietness as he pondered this challenge, but words did not come quickly enough to his mind. His mouth opened and remained that way, not a sound coming from it as his mind worked overtime. Tirlough Óge took advantage of his hesitancy.

"This voice that you say you heard, Father? Did it speak to you in the Irish, or was it by any chance in English?"

"*As Gaeilge*," McGlaim said quickly. "That's how I knew it was God the Father talking to me."

"And did he have any message for those who have denied us the right to speak our own language, did he? Did he have any advice about how we should go about getting our land back from the English?"

"He did not," McGlaim said evenly, "but can I ask you a question?"

"Go on," said Tirlough Óge.

McGlaim turned to address the whole gathering of soldiers. "The people you are holding in this church," he said, "can you recall a time when any of them tried to prevent you from speaking Irish? Any of them ever insist that you talk to them in English?"

There was a pause as they looked around blankly at each other. No-one spoke, so the priest continued.

"Of course not, because they are Gaels too, and they have the same tongue, by and large. Is this not true? And have any of these neighbours of yours tried to stop you going to Mass? No? I cannot imagine that. You also speak of losing your land, Tirlough Óge, yet your family remain in your seat in Dunseverick Castle…and many of these soldiers of yours are your own tenants. The others are most likely tenants of Lord Antrim, a Catholic Earl who holds Mass in Dunluce. Am I not correct?"

Nobody raised any objection to his arguments so the priest continued, speaking to the whole group.

"Listen, my friends, these neighbours of yours are innocent people; they are caught up in a war they have no responsibility for. That church is full of thirsty women and children; they could be your own mothers, your own children…and you are trying to deny them a simple drink of cold water?"

Tirlough Óge was aware of the priest's tactic in trying to personalise this matter, to get to the emotions of his soldiers. He had his counter-argument ready long before Father McGlaim had finished his point.

"You may be right in what you say about this special part of the province," he said. "We do have good neighbours, but you have to concede that it is not this way in other parts of our country. Where the planters have been given land in Derry and Fermanagh and the like it is an entirely different story. They have been merciless in their cruelty to our people. When they weren't driving us out by military force they were using their English laws to tell us we don't have official title deeds to say we own the land…land that we have lived on for hundreds of years without any need for these title deeds. They are clever as the devil, merciless thieves and robbers. We have every right to take up arms against them. That is why the church, your own order of Franciscans too, Father…they're backing us."

"That may be true, Tirlough Óge; the church is one thing. Perhaps though…Our Lord is another."

"So do you think he is not for us?"

"Oh, I have no doubt that he is," McGlaim said. "Our Lord, when he was on earth, always took the side of the oppressed against the oppressor."

"Pity he didn't take our side when the English were stealing our land. They have been doing it since the time of Strongbow. All down through the centuries they have oppressed us. Where was Our Lord when O'Neill and O'Donnell and Maguire were so desperate and demoralised that they abandoned us and fled to the continent?"

Father McGlaim's face twisted with displeasure at these allegations, and at the aggressive tone of this young antagonist. He took a couple of deep breaths to calm himself before responding.

"Tirlough Óge," he said, "it pains me as much as it pains you to admit that our chieftains deserted us and left us to face the persecution we have had to endure over the past thirty years. But remember, they were human, these men. They were weak human beings like the rest of us. Yes, they should have stayed and tried to work with the English to protect our homeland, and our faith, and our rights as Irishmen…but they abandoned us. Does that mean, however, that God has abandoned us? No, it does not! Nor has he stopped watching over us. Believe me, my son, he is very grieved at what he sees here in Ireland. He sees war where there should be peace, hate where there should be love."

"How can you talk about peace and love after what we have had to put up with? He is either on our side or he is not," argued Tirlough Óge.

"He is on our side, of course he is, but he asks us to be on his side too. The gospels ask us to free the prisoners, clothe the naked, feed the hungry and, in my case, to give water to the thirsty. That is what he has asked me to do and that is what I am going to do!"

Father McGlaim, his heart pounding in his chest despite his calm exterior, turned away from the soldiers and flicked the reins of his mule.

"*Seo linn a Phadraig!*" he said. "Let's go."

Tirlough Óge took a few aggressive strides after him, but Gilladubh followed him and caught him by the arm.

"Let him be, son," he said quietly. "If he is that determined to give them water then maybe it was God that told him."

"And if the Protestants fire a musket ball through his head," Tirlough Óge said, "it won't be our fault. He'll deserve it, and we'll know he was just dreaming nonsense."

They watched as the priest and his mule stumbled away across the muddied field and cautiously approached the church building.

"They'll shoot him out the window," one soldier said to his mates. "That'll teach him!"

From a distance the soldiers could see the muzzle of a weapon suddenly appearing from one of the window slits.

"Here goes," said Tirlough Óge. "He's a dead man walking."

But no shot rang out. Instead they heard the priest's clear voice carrying across the flat distance between them.

"Friends inside," he called, looking in terror at the weapon which was pointed straight at his chest from a few steps away. "I have water here for you. Can you open the door?"

There was a long silence before McGlaim repeated his request. Then a voice could be heard.

"Who are you?"

"I am a priest from Ballycastle. McGlaim is my name. I have two jars of water here for you."

A further silence, with only the scrieghs of the seagulls circling above the cliffs disturbing the tense stillness.

Father McGlaim could imagine the consternation inside, the doubt and the discussion. So could the watching Gilladubh.

"They'll not trust him," he breathed. "Wait till you see! They'll think it's a clever ruse. They'll never trust him."

Quite a few minutes passed before the voice is heard again. "Why are you doing this? How do we know it is not a trap?"

"I cannot prove it is not a trap. I ask you to believe me. Why am I doing it? Your women and children are thirsty; you need water. I just want to help." He paused to carefully consider his next intended words which he hoped would break the deadlock, then he continued, "Just as when I helped a young man of your church last summer, up by the Druid's Grave on Altmore. His name was Alex McKay."

He could hear the murmur of voices rise in volume as this piece of information was received behind those dark stone walls. He could not distinguish the exact words, but, if he could, he would have heard Katie McKay speak in hoarse but excited tones to those who were surrounding Boyd and Fullerton.

"It is true," she said. "This is the priest who saved Alex's life. Father McGlaim. I know about him. He is a good man."

"Are you sure, Katie? Because this sounds too good to be true."

"I am sure…"

"It sounds like a trap. Never trust one of them," a voice rasped.

Katie's Aunt Biddy came slowly forward, barely able to put one foot past the other, her words grating in the dryness of her parched throat.

"Look," she said, "I know him, this boadie. He talked to me. It's alright. He's a dacent man. He helped our Alex. This must be the miracle yous have prayed for."

Fullerton was convinced; he gave Boyd a weary nod.

"What if it's poisoned?" someone asked from a dark corner. "It could be a trick. We'll likely all die o' it."

"Aye, ask him to prove it is safe to drink," Jean Kennedy suggested.

So Boyd went carefully to the slit in the window opening and stood in a position where he could see the clergyman without himself being in the line of fire. You couldn't be too careful with those trigger-happy heathens out there.

"Let me see you taking a sup of it yourself first," he said.

McGlaim said nothing, simply poured a little liquid into the cup of his hand from one of the urns and put it to his lips. Boyd watched and saw him turn over his empty hand to show he had drunk the water.

"I understand your hesitation. I do not take offence," McGlaim said gently. "Now, if you believe me, can you please open the door."

"We can't open the door to you. Our enemies have been waiting for weeks for us to do that. We cannot risk them seizing this opportunity."

"How can we proceed then? You need this water."

"If you take the jars around to the door of the church we will lower a rope from the tower above you. Could you tie it to the jars, one at a time, and we will pull them up?" Boyd asked.

"I can do that," McGlaim said, moving at once towards the door.

"And thank you," Boyd called after him.

"Not at all. It's a pleasure to do God's work," the priest said. "I will try to be back with more in two days time."

Gilladubh watched solemnly from his distant position and saw the containers being drawn up into the bell tower. He hardly knew what to make of this intervention. In his heart of hearts he had imagined that something would go wrong, that either the people inside would fire a shot at this Papish enemy, or would reject his offer. Even now, as he observed the priest turn away from the church and lead his mule back in the direction of Knocksoughey Hill, he half-expected him to keel over and die from some sort of Divine intervention. Nothing of the like happened. He felt bewildered and a bit betrayed by his God who maybe wasn't as clearly on his side as he had imagined.

It did not help his mood that at that moment the bell of Ballintoy church rang out a two-clang peal of thanks, nor that Father McGlaim raised his eyes and his right hand heavenward in some sort of acknowledgement. *"In aim an athair!"* he breathed in relief. In the name of the Father indeed.

Gilladubh shook his head in sad resignation.

"Well, I never expected to see the like," he said to himself.

"Let them have their wee drink," Tirlough Óge said bitterly. "Just wait till Mortimer arrives with his cannon. We'll see if God protects them from it."

Chapter 41

Hope and Despair

Katie McKay

Should I live to be a hundred, the arrival of that priest was the most incredible thing I will ever experience.

We had been days without water. We were on the point of surrender to the rebels. Some of the weaker ones, the older folk and the sick, were close to death, their speech thin and pathetic through shrivelled throats, their energy levels at rock bottom. The children looked so listless, whatever tears and cries they had left in them so pitiful to witness, wee Kate among them. She was wasting away. In some ways I wondered would she not have been better off staying by her poor mother in Coleraine, and just slipping away from this cruel place in her dead mother's arms. It was very difficult to watch Kate fade. Our Alice had much more resilience in her, but I suppose she had been well nourished over the years, and had a strong bodily constitution after all her work around our farm and her exercise along our beautiful coast. For all that, I did sense her mood going darker and darker as this captivity went on. She seemed to sleep a lot more than usual. Connie, with her deeply-held optimism, never gave up hope, and tried to inspire the same feeling in the rest of us. She was so strong that at times I could sense others getting annoyed at her, Aunt Biddy among them.

"Wud you for wanst go and sit by yoursel' somewhere, Connie McKay" Biddy told her. "Houl yer wheesht, lass. I am in nae mood for your funny oul yarns the day."

Connie just smiled…or tried to smile, for her lips were as dry and cracked as the rest of us. My friend Jean said quietly to me, "You need people like Connie in a siege, but you need them to know when to be quiet as well."

Mr Fullerton led prayers every night. The prayers became shorter but more desperate as time went on, the congregation's "Amens" less enthusiastic, until they near enough faded out altogether. God, it seemed wasn't listening. Was he aware of what we were going through? What about the promises of safety and protection we had had preached at us? How could he ignore our desperate plight?

And then it had happened. The miracle arrived.

Beyond the kirk's thick walls, the voice of a stranger; soft; nervous;

unbelievable!

"I have water here for you."

Slowly heads lifted. Faces that had been turned in on themselves looked at other faces, wondering. Questions in the dull eyes. Tiny glimmers of hope flickered, replacing resignation. Those who had the energy sat up and gave their head a shake or their dry eyes a wipe. Was it a shared delusion, an imagined voice? The forbidden word 'water' had been spoken over us, and lips searched for saliva, tongues divined for moisture behind teeth. Could this truly be happening? A voice from another world, the world of brightness, and wetness, and normality, had called to us…called us friends? Incredible and unthinkable.

But it was true. And when I heard the voice give itself a name my heart leapt in my chest.

"Father McGlaim," the voice said.

Father McGlaim, the priest friend of my Darach?

It was a double blessing. The water, when we would get to taste it, would be twice as sweet. I wanted to shout out to him, ask him if he had any news of my lover but, even if I had had the chance to do that, my voice would have crackled like a burning whin bush and would not have been able to create the sound of the words. As it was, my voice had another role to perform that day; I realised that I would have to somehow convince our leaders, against their better judgement, that this was a good man, one who could be trusted. It helped no end that I then heard him mention our Alex, and the fact that he knew and had helped my brother. Fullerton and Boyd were convinced.

I did think later that day as we took slow, careful sips of this heavenly water, that this man, this priest of the other faith, was becoming some sort of guardian angel to our family. It was all so hard to understand, given the differences between him and us.

"Why would he be doing this?" Connie asked me.

"Just out of goodness, I suppose. Doesn't it taste wonderful," I said.

"It does," she agreed, "but what is it that brings him across our path just when we need him?"

"I don't know, Connie. Keep that question for Reverend Blare…if we ever see him again after all this."

There was a fresh commotion happening near the door. Thomas Boyd was getting excited about something. Our heads all turned in his direction.

"Praise be to God! There is oatmeal at the bottom of the jars," he said, hardly able to contain his joy. "That priest has brought us food."

It was even better news than the water. It turned out that, well below the surface of the water, there was enough oatmeal to make sufficient porridge to give us each a small portion. We were ecstatic. Actual food, under the water!

But how to cook the oatmeal? The children and the very old among us could only eat it if we could cook it into a watery gruel.

We hadn't had fuel to light a fire to warm us in the kirk for several weeks. The cold had been one of our worst enemies and, but for the fact that family groups had been able to cuddle together for heat on the coldest of nights, people would have perished. Connie had joked that some of those poor parishioner women hadn't been so close to a man in years. "It's an ill wind," she had said, her dark humour bringing a smile to the young folk within earshot of her quiet observation.

We had to find a way to cook this oatmeal, and in a manner that would not attract the attention of our captors, either by smoke or smell. We solved the problem of fuel by chopping some of the timber benches into small pieces. It was Reverend Fullerton's idea, so nobody felt that we were doing anything too sacrilegious. The more serious desecration happened when, having failed to get these splinters of wood to light using someone's flints, my friend Jean suggested we should use paper.

"What paper?" Reverend Fullerton asked dubiously.

We all looked at each other. Apart from the letters from McDonnell and Gilladubh O'Cahan, the only paper in the place were the pages of the Prayer Books and Bibles. There were only a few of these in the kirk, given the fact that very few of us could read. It was our Aunt Biddy who pulled a Prayer Book out from below her head and held it up. It had been a handy pillow. Now she thought it had a more important role.

"This!" she said weakly.

"You can't be using these holy books," the clergyman responded, but the tone of his voice was anything but decisive.

Thomas Boyd spoke into the following silence. "William," he said, "we can get more Prayer Books. It's not as easy with people."

To his credit the minister nodded slowly. "Let's try it," he said.

It worked. The dry paper was alight in no time, and a small curl of smoke rose from the timber splinters. We had our fire. Soon we had our porridge...the first food in weeks.

A small handful wasn't much but it felt like a feast. I ate it very slowly, savouring the taste. I watched as some mothers took the tiniest nibble from their hand and fed the rest to their children. I found myself doing the same with Kate, although the poor wain could barely get it swallowed.

"I hope this doesn't make us all sick," my mother said, "after us going for so long without a bite. Maybe our stomachs will throw it all back up again."

Aunt Biddy looked at her as if she was daft.

"If you throw it up again, Isobel, it'll naw go tae waste," she said through a twisted grin. I wondered would she really have done that, eaten my mother's vomit. Knowing Biddy, it wouldn't have surprised me.

Over the next few days that priest brought us more jars of water and oatmeal. He didn't arrive every day; sometimes every other day, sometimes less frequently. It was the same procedure each time, and it got us wondering how he was managing this. Where was he getting the oatmeal from? As far as we knew, such foodstuffs were in very short supply all over the country. It really did feel like a miracle that, after such a period of time without any food or water, now we were getting enough to sustain us. Hope rose in us for a better outcome to this siege than we had feared.

And then disaster struck!

I think we had all become complacent, careless of our safety.

One of the parishioners, a Mrs Ross who was a widow of good age and without any family, made a terrible mistake. For whatever reason and maybe just in a moment of carelessness she went up close to one of the window slots, likely to take a quick keek out. None of us noticed her do this. Maybe she was curious to see how the fields outside looked in the spring sunlight. Maybe she had caught sight of a bird through the gap and went too close in order to follow its flight.

A shot rang out from beyond.

Mrs Ross's body came crashing down to the floor with a terrible thump. I was only a matter of six feet away from where she fell. I saw it all. The image of her destroyed face will stay in my mind for the rest of my days. The musket ball had blown a dark hole where her eye had been. No blood, just a gory mess of a hole. She was dead before she hit the kirk floor. Not a gasp from her, just the strange twitch of her body as her soul departed.

A split second of stunned silence, then a wailing of shock and horror rose from every person in our church. The women screamed, the children cried, the men bustled forward, shouting.

"What happened? Why was she...? Why was nobody watching her? Oh God above, how did this...?"

It was my mother who grabbed a bit of sheep-skin and placed it over that mutilated head so no-one else would have to see that gruesome sight.

"I told everyone not to be going near those openings," Fullerton shouted. "You can never be sure when some divil has his musket drawn on it, just waiting for some poor sinner like Mrs Ross to appear. Let that be a lesson to you all."

His tirade was, of course, completely unnecessary now.

What was necessary later on was to think of how we were going to bury the good woman's body. There was much debate about this over the next couple of days. Nobody was going to volunteer to venture out into the graveyard to dig a grave for her, let alone conduct a burial. It would be far too foolhardy. In the end, and on Thomas Boyd's suggestion, it was decided to ask the priest when he was next with us. Would he negotiate a truce with Gilladubh and Tirlough Óge to give us a safe hour to bury the body before it began to stink?

A couple of days later Father McGlaim listened to the request, straining his ears to hear Boyd's plea from the top of the bell tower because a gale was gusting in from the ocean. Listening inside, we could barely make out what was being said by either man. We waited for an outcome. Eventually Mr Boyd lowered the two jars of water, and climbed down after them.

"He doesn't want to be too presumptuous with our assailants out there," he told us, "just in case they get any suspicion about the contents of his water jars. He thinks it would be a silly risk, so instead he says he will take our spade and dig the grave himself. He thinks they will allow him, as an ordained priest, to bury the body; and he will make them promise to respect the burial, and not rush the door when we open it to pass Mrs Ross's remains out to him. He will give her a christian burial. I think we have to trust him to do that for us. We have little other choice, what do you think?"

There wasn't a single voice against the idea. This man had been risking himself to come to our aid with food and water; why should we doubt him in this matter?

He left us to go to negotiate with Gilladubh and his men. A good while later we heard him back at the kirk door.

"It is agreed," he called above the howl of the storm. "Where will I dig?"

"Dig beside the gate, on your left as you enter," Boyd called. "The soil is light, it should be easy shifted. Don't dig too deep."

We heard nothing more from Father McGlaim for ages, the sound of his work muffled by the storm. Then he banged the door and told us he was ready. We were all that bit nervous as the bolts were drawn and the door edged open. After Reverend Fullerton said an impassioned prayer over her, a couple of the men passed the corpse out to the priest as quickly as the solemnity of the occasion allowed. He was going to have to drag the body to the open grave. The women had wrapped the poor lady in a couple of black vestments…Reverend Blare would just have to get himself some new ones if he ever got to come back here to lead morning worship. We heard nothing more. We had to trust Father McGlaim to do as he promised. We had no idea what prayers he would say over Mrs Ross.

"She is in God's hands now," my mother said. "Whatever the priest says can neither help nor hinder her."

So it was that a Catholic priest found himself in the burial grounds of Ballintoy Episcopalian church, digging a grave in terribly rough weather, and conducting a lonely funeral service for a Presbyterian victim of the conflict at Easter-tide, 1642.

Chapter 42

A Dangerous Weapon

Darach O'Cahan

Alex McKay arrives back with me in Ballycastle at long last. I had been going out to the shore every opportunity, to keep an eye for his return. On one such visit, and completely by chance, I meet him at the pier on a beautifully calm April evening. He has been eagerly and impatiently awaited.

My friend looks very tired, a chastened young man. Dark rings surround his normally bright eyes, very pronounced against the creamy pallor of his skin. The return crossing, he tells me, was a lengthy challenge as the boatman had misjudged the tide. More depressing, though, is his news. The secret assignment in Kintyre has been an exhausting and futile exercise, a bit of an all-round disaster, as far as I can work out.

In many ways I am not sorry for its failure. Am I a hypocrite? I do understand the desire on the part of these north Antrim Presbyterians for urgent help. However, the thought that I as a proud Irishman might have played a small part in bringing over an anti-Catholic army of Scottish gallowglasses has worried me since Alex's departure. I may have been appointed to be Stewart's messenger, but I want no part in the massacres here…those in the past and those that might have been visited upon us if Alex had succeeded. Had the Argyll decided to send an army, I have no doubt that the retribution against my people would have been severe.

He describes in detail his tribulations as he was making his way northwards through unfamiliar countryside on the long peninsula of Kintyre. A horse he had hired for the journey became lame after the first few hours, so he had had to spare it by alternating between riding and leading. A journey that should have taken four or five days had taken double that time.

On his way he had encountered friends and foes. He had no way of knowing who was who in the land of Argyll; some folk he met were Campbell supporters, but many others would have been of the old faith and were antagonistic to the Covenanters and their champion and Laird, Archibald Campbell. Alex said that at times he felt every bit as much in peril as when he had travelled here in troubled Ulster. Where he came across a Presbyterian meeting house he tended to seek out the clergyman and take shelter and succour, just to feel safe for a night.

On his arrival at Inveraray he discovered that Campbell wasn't even present. He had to wait several days for the famous leader. Argyll had been in Edinburgh on political business, and then staying at his main residence, Castle Campbell near Sterling. Alex's presence and the letter from Stewart had seemed more of an annoyance to him than anything else.

"Does your Mr Stewart have any idea about what is happening on this side of the water?" he barked. "The problems of the Presbyterian people of Antrim are hardly a priority for me right now, are they? Anyhow, what would be wrong with Randal McDonnell getting off his lazy arse in Dublin and coming to the rescue of these tenants that his father so rashly enticed to settle in that miserable place?"

Alex had no answer for that question of course. I can imagine him, standing silently before Campbell, wringing his hands behind his back, wishing he had never set out on this pointless quest.

"So he refused to even consider sending help?" I ask gingerly.

"Not completely," Alex says. "He told me to tell Archibald Stewart that he would raise the matter with his Scottish Parliament the next time he is in Edinburgh, which could be weeks away. To be honest, my feeling about him is that he is far more occupied with this new title he has been given by the King, but maybe he'll change his mind."

"What new title? I thought he and the King were at loggerheads?"

"They are, but Charles has made him a Marquess lately. People think it was just an idea to try to buy him off. It seems to have failed though, for Campbell seems to be still determined to join with the English Parliamentarians against the King. Either way, it doesn't look as if he is for coming to the aid of my people, not at the minute anyhow. It's been a waste of time and effort. Stewart's going to be disappointed when I tell him."

"Aye, when you tell him indeed! That could be a long time in the future, for Coleraine is heavily besieged...just like so many other towns."

I had been explaining to him, of course, the desperate situation in his home village, and our attempts to help his people.

"Father McGlaim has made several journeys over there in the past few weeks," I told him. "He has been able to deliver water and oatmeal to them, so your family is at least getting some sustenance."

Alex is incredulous at this news, amazed and hugely grateful. "I must remember to thank him when I see him."

"Yes, when you see him," I say, "but maybe not just now. I have been thinking that it is maybe not a good idea for you to go back to Bonamargy at the minute, Alex. You don't want to be having to answer

Father McGlaim's questions about your fictitious mission, you understand what I mean? It puts both of you in a difficult position, me too. You can't be telling him anything about Argyll, and you don't want to be having to make up more lies to cover your tracks. It just doesn't seem right."

"I understand, but what if he asks you about me? What if he enquires about these imaginary people I told him of?"

"He won't. He is sensitive that way. He won't mention it, and I won't say any more than I need to either."

"Alright," he says, "but where should I go? You say that both Ballintoy and Coleraine are under siege, so there's no point going there. I can't see Stewart to report to him. I can't go back to Bonamargy. Should I just go up into the hills, look for a shepherd's *bothan* on Knocklayde, sleep rough for a while?"

There has to be a better plan than that, I think. Alex looks so worn out that he could fall asleep where he stands. He needs a safe place to hide where he will be fed, and can recover from his ordeal. Alex cannot be caught wandering about the countryside. He could easily end up tortured and dead.

In the end, I take him to Hugh MacNeill at Dunynie Castle. This man has been of great help to us so far, providing oatmeal at no cost so the Ballintoy people can eat. He agrees to give Alex a hiding place in an attic room at the top of his castle. It is an ideal arrangement.

The one request Alex has made troubles me as I lie awake later. How could we possibly get a message to his mother and the family? I have already been wondering how I might communicate with Katie. It has been so long.

I do understand Father McGlaim's point about not wanting to compromise the sanctity of his mission. He needs to keep everything as straight forward as possible, with no superfluous words of any kind passing between him and those in the church. He walks a very narrow path in this whole matter.

I had thought about some sort of letter, a general kind of message to the folk there. Surely somebody in there can read. I wondered if such a thing could be slipped into the bottom of one of the priest's jars, below the oatmeal…but of course the words would probably not withstand the immersion in water. The parchment itself would hardly survive intact.

When I meet with Father McGlaim in the evening quiet of the cloisters, I begin by telling him of Alex's safe return, and that he is resting at the home of his friends. He doesn't ask anything about how the mission went; instead he makes the obvious point that Alex's horse is still in the Friary stables.

"I'm sure he will come and get it, as soon as he has recovered," I tell him. "He was asking about his mother in the church at Ballintoy. He is anxious to somehow let her know that he is safe and well, Father. With all the trouble, she must be wondering if he is alive or dead."

"Indeed; but how are you thinking to get such word into the church?"

So I tell him about my idea of a message contained in his water jar.

"It is likely a useless plan," I say. "The letters would only blur in the liquid. What do you think, Father?"

He gives me a long stare across his small kitchen table.

"Have you ever heard of vellum, Darach?"

I have of course, but I don't see his point. The ink work on the leather skin would still be dissolved in the water surely?

"Not ink," he says. "But if you were to use a red-hot poker, or some similar pointed piece of metal? Could you not create a few words by branding them on to the leather? That way they would survive the water, they would still be there when found in the jar, probably still readable."

"Father," I tell him, "You are as clever as the divil himself!"

We both laugh at this daft comment till the tears are running down our faces. The anxiety we have been living with has been released in a burst of hilarity, and both of us feel much the better for it.

My devious priest goes off to find a spare piece of vellum from the bowels of the library. Bonamargy may be only a shadow of the Friary it was back in its glory days, but it still houses vital gems for all sorts of purposes. He is back with me fairly soon, a roll of calf-skin under his arm. He also carries a thin iron spike, and a narrow branch of a bourtree bush. I don't understand.

"This metal is going to feel very hot in your hand," he says, "so I have found a piece of wood and hollowed out the centre so you can hold the thing." A clever priest.

I get to work, having already thought out a very concise message for the McKay family, one which, should it be discovered, contains no information of use to the besiegers. After a while Father McGlaim reappears and reads aloud over my shoulder. Thankfully I have refrained from any flowery declarations of affection for Katie; I would have been embarrassed for him to read such material.

"'Alex McKay safe and well. Be strong and patient'," he reads. "Good. It is to the point. The letters are quite large and stand out well. That's fine....but why the little black cross?"

"I don't want to put my name on the message," I tell him, "but I am hoping that somehow Katie will see this and recognise it, then realise the message is from me. She can't read, but some time ago I gave her a cross that I had carved out of bog-oak, so it is a sort of secret symbol between us."

"That is a great idea," he says. "She will get the feeling behind the message, I am quite sure. She will understand that you are safe as well, and she will sense your care for her. What more could a girl ask?"

What more indeed. I want to tell her of my love; I want to ask how she is; I would love to ask about Kate…but I know that this will have to be a one-sided communication only. I must simply trust that she is well.

****

I travel with Father McGlaim the following morning. *Liath* and *Padráig*, our two faithful mounts, are becoming familiar with this trek up the hill from Ballycastle, along the coast, past Kenbane, to the backside of Knocksoughey Hill. It is several days after Easter.

What is noticeable on the journey is the stillness of the landscape… not the silence alone, but the absence of any activity in the fields. Even the birds seem to sense crisis in the territory and are showing a reverent hush. In a normal year this season would be marked by a stirring of cultivation, planting and sowing. Men would be active in the small holdings, women too, as every available bit of land at their disposal would be in use, either for their animals or for the crops that would be needed to replenish their larders through the following winter and spring. This year a paralysis seems to have crept over the land. Weeds grow tall in the green of the grassy meadows where no plough has turned a sod since this time last year. Farming is as much on hold as every other aspect of neighbourhood life. The countryside seems to hold its breath. The only comfort to my senses is the strong sweet scent of the yellow whin blossom, an emotive aroma that I always associate with Easter time.

When we reach Knocksoughey we fill the urns from a stream and I seclude myself as usual. I watch the descent of the cleric and the mule towards the church, the two water jars swinging slightly against its flanks. I have watched this procession every day that Father McGlaim has undertaken it…but something is different today, I sense.

From the plain below a different set of sounds is reaching my ears. There are some calls from the soldiers, a hint of laughter and gaiety that I find unusual. From this height and at this distance I cannot quite make out what is going on down there, what the excitement is about. I am so curious that I decide to try to get closer to the source of the commotion. I stay well hidden, gradually working my way around the side of the hill in the direction of the Druid's Altar. Eventually I am overlooking the plain from a more advantageous position, directly above those flat fields that stretch down to the church. I am careful never to be exposed. I keep a roving eye for anyone who might be on look-out duty in these low bushes.

I crawl forward and lift my head carefully to sneak my first look over the tops of the ferns. I get a shock at what I see.

A strange looking weapon is being dragged across the plain, a bulky-looking gun, short and stubby of itself, mounted on a wooden frame, with two great wheels, one on either side. I believe I have heard this gun referred to as a 'sow'…something to do with the pig-like grunt it makes when fired.

So this is the source of all the excitement. Tirlough Óge's company have acquired this weapon from somewhere, and are obviously going to fire cannon balls at the Manor, or more likely at the church. I presume the object is to break through the walls, or perhaps through the wooden door. If they intend the latter they still have a good distance to drag the thing. A single horse strains to pull the contraption, but several men are having to push at the rear, while others spoke the wheels forward. This cannon has a mind of its own about what direction it wants to take. Much of the clamour being generated here is to do with its uncertain course, and the general awkwardness of the transporting arrangement.

It strikes me that Father McGlaim had better hurry himself today. He needs to complete his mercy mission and get away from Ballintoy church as fast as possible. The realisation hits me that, if this cannon is successful, the end of the siege might not be very far off. What on earth will happen to Katie and the others if it is? I start to say an urgent prayer that the cannon balls will miss, or that they will have no effect on the stout walls of the building.

Below me, I hear my cousin giving orders. I am not sure exactly what he has said, but suddenly the attempt to pull the cannon forward has stopped. Instead it is being manoeuvred around and lined up so as to face the church directly. Could it be that they intend to fire from this distance? And why fire at the church rather than the bawn around the Manor House? It doesn't make sense…unless they think that the church is more vulnerable, that perhaps a few cannon balls hitting the walls there will encourage the people inside to surrender. Maybe the intention is to draw soldiers out of the Manor House to try to protect their church, their kin.

I wait and watch…what else can I do? The excited noise level has not diminished. I see Tirlough Óge waving men back out of the way. Someone loads a large round ball. Now someone else is lighting a fuse and placing it…Boom! The gun fires and the sound rises birds all across the plain. The soldiers cheer. Too early though! The celebration dies prematurely as the cannon ball ploughs into the soft earth of a field well short of the church.

It was a first attempt though, and Tirlough Óge is not discouraged. In a few minutes he has managed to have the cannon dragged much closer, lined it up with the church and readied it for firing. Another retort, and the acrid smell of exploding gunpowder wafts up to my nostrils, even at this distance.

This time the shot whistles past the side of the building, narrowly missing the tower. Father McGlaim should have been standing very close to that spot. Has he been hit? I haven't seen him for a while. Where has he gone?

What must those poor people inside be feeling? How is Katie bearing this pressure? I am out here watching, my heart is pounding. And where is Father McGlaim now? Has he managed to convey the two jars with their precious contents to the folk inside? Did he get away from the bell tower in time? I do not see him from where I am secreted. All I can do is pray.

'Holy Mary, Mother of God, hear us sinners now and at the hour of our death…and make this next cannon ball miss as well.'

A bit more resetting of the weapon, lining it up more carefully. The explosion rips through the still atmosphere, and the ball hurtles towards the church. This time it doesn't miss; it thumps against the side wall with a dull thud, but falls harmlessly to the gravel path, no apparent damage done.

They try once more, with the same result. The walls are too thick, too well constructed. I am a good distance away, but even so, no blemish can be discerned at the two points where the balls have hit. Tirlough Óge is deflated. I can tell by the hands to the head, the hunch of his shoulders and the tone of his voice.

"Right," he calls. "These balls are too light to make a breach in the wall from here! But they will make a complete mess of the door. That's where we should be concentrating our fire. We don't have all that much powder and shot left to waste on the walls."

"But it means moving the thing over those two ditches and away round to the east," one of his men complains.

"It does, so get your gang of layabouts organised and start pulling again!"

I watch as a couple of red-headed fellows fumble around, trying to hitch a harness to the big farm-horse. These two look familiar to me. I suddenly realise that I am looking at the Reid brothers, the ones who attacked Alex last year. Here they are now, working with this lethal weapon. The whole process of shifting the cannon starts again. It seems to be working better for them this time. The route is slightly downhill, and the surface of the field a bit more firm and even. The gun picks up speed. It rumbles forward against the horse. The animal is clearly not liking the feel of the thing against its hind legs. It panics a bit. It bucks sideways out of harm's way. The men, having forgotten their steering duty, have not been expecting this. Too late they see the danger. The mighty 'sow' lurches into a deep ditch to the side, one wheel going down with a terrible jerk and a crashing noise which seems to me very like the sound of a splintering axle. Tirlough Óge looks to the sky and swears to the heavens.

"You fools! You fools! The one chance we had to break into the damned church, and you manage to ruin it!"

The besiegers stand around, faces sagging in defeat, arms hanging limp. The jollity of an hour ago has deserted them in that split-second disaster.

It is an outcome I could barely believe. I have to wonder what effect this latest set-back will have on the O'Cahan leaders, and on the morale of their men. They have been besieging this simple little church for almost two months. They have tried pick-axes and hatchets against its walls and door, both with no success. They have tried and failed with this pathetic cannon, and only ended up embarrassing themselves. Before all that, they have tried to starve the people into submission, but they didn't count on the stubborn Presbyterian spirit of these folk. Nor have they counted on the devious way that Father McGlaim and this meek cousin of theirs have been able to affect the situation with a little supportive food and water.

If I should feel any sense of guilt about what we have done I'm afraid I do not. The girl I love most in all the world is inside there. So is little Kate whose mother I promised I would look after. What else can I do but take any chance I have to bring them some hope? As Father McGlaim has repeated to me, "It is not perfidy to do what Our Lord commands us to do, regardless of the risk to ourselves."

If I try to put myself in my cousin's shoes I cannot help but sympathise with his lack of success. He must be asking, "If we cannot take a small church what chance do our forces have against a fortress like Dunluce, or against a properly defended town like Coleraine? Our cause may be just but, if God is on our side, why are we struggling to make gains against these poorly trained and ill-equipped farmers? We have these gallowglasses on our side, with their famous leaders and their great strategies. But such tactics seem to be fairly useless against the ramparts of a town, or when we are having to sit waiting outside the stout stone walls of this church."

These discouragements must surely be damaging Irish morale.

Chapter 43

Message from beyond

Katie McKay

Thomas Boyd had lowered the two empty urns to the kind priest and had drawn up the full ones he had brought. Within seconds we heard an almighty bang from outside. Some huge gun had been fired.

Our bell in the tower above clanged…just once. We thought at first that it had been hit, but Mr Boyd clambered down and explained.

"No, it was only my head," he said, rubbing his skull. "I gave such a jump when that gun went off. I hit my head on the bell!"

"Did you see where it came from or what sort of weapon it is?" Reverend Fullerton asked.

"I did not. All I know is that something went whistling past the tower. I heard it. It wasn't too far away either. The next shot will probably hit us."

And it did. It clattered against the wall beside one of our older men, and I thought he was going to pass out with shock! A screech of panic went up from us all. It was sheer terror to think that one of these missiles would come through and land in amongst us. The crying continued as we waited for the next strike. I saw women shaking like a leaf in a storm. I smelt pee as some of us lost control of ourselves. Not a single person looked at the water jars, thirsty and all as we were.

Mr Fullerton did his best to calm us down.

"Look folks," he called above the hullabaloo, "the cannon ball hasn't come through the wall. It must have just bounced off. These walls are good and thick. We will be alright, but just get on your knees and beseech the Lord above to protect our wee kirk and all of his people in it."

We needed no second instruction. We were on our knees on the floor in a second, and we were still there when the next cannon ball hit the side wall of the kirk. Every eye blinked open and heads turned to the wall. We needn't have worried. It had held. We waited and waited in trepidation, but no more shots came. We had no idea why but we thought God must have heard us and answered our prayers.

Eventually we got off the floor and formed a queue as usual to get our mouthful of water. Being one of the younger fitter ones I was almost at the back of the line, along with Connie and Jean. I looked at their solemn faces. The smiles that used to play around Jean's mouth and the devilment in Connie's eyes were becoming a memory. They both looked strained, pale, gaunt. Actually, when I looked at my own arms and legs I saw that, like these two, I had lost weight. How could it have been any other way? The wee bite of porridge I got each day was great, but in a sense it only left me hungrier than I was before. I was more worried about Aunt Biddy and my mother though. Biddy was so weak she spent most of the day just lying on a bench half-asleep. I suppose that way she was saving energy.

Mummy tried not to let me see it, but I know she was crying a lot of the time, her arm around Alice for comfort. Those were tough days.

'Please God,' I thought so often, 'Let this be over soon before someone else dies in here.'

Up in front of me, at the head of the queue, there seemed to be a commotion. Thomas Boyd was getting excited about something. Everybody had started to gather around him. I couldn't see what was going on, so I moved forward to listen from behind the swarm of bodies.

"It is some sort of parchment," he said. "I wondered what was obstructing the flow of the water. This roll must have been concealed down in the bottom with the oatmeal."

He held it up for us to see, water and oatmeal dripping off it, some of the children near him trying to gather the drips in their hands.

"Let's have a look at that," Reverend Fullerton said, coming forward and taking the rolled-up parchment. He unrolled it before our eyes and we hushed as he examined it.

"There's some sort of message branded on it," he said, wiping the surface carefully with his sleeve, "if I can make out what it says. Let's see."

We watched as he read it quietly to himself first, his eyes widening in surprise.

"Goodness," he said, looking around us, and trying to locate someone in the tightly jammed sea of faces before him. "It is a message about Alex. Mrs McKay? Where are you? It is a message about your Alex."

If my heart leapt in shock when that cannon ball hit the church wall, it did another serious contortion right then. Alex! What had happened to our Alex? My first instinct, God forgive me, was fear. I could only imagine bad news. My mother, I saw, was exactly the same, her hand at her mouth.

"No, no!" the clergyman said, looking at us. "It's not bad news at all. Listen! 'Alex McKay safe and well. Be strong and patient,'" he read.

He repeated it. There was a growing murmur of relief among us that grew into a chorus of joy. Alex is safe! What amazing news! Wonderful news!

I was hugging my mother, Alice squished in between us, Connie joining in with a sudden burst of energy and elation. Poor wee Kate stood wondering what was going on, so I had to grab her; she deserved to be included in this. Poor Biddy, though, hadn't the strength to join us in the celebration, but she did burst into tears of relief on her bench. Everybody was delighted for us, slapping us on our backs, shaking hands as if we had had a miracle...which we had! It lifted the whole mood, though I am sure that several others in the congregation were thinking about their own sons who were also away with Archibald Stewart. Our good news just made things tougher for them, Thomas Smith's mother and Mrs Moore especially.

It was only after several minutes of thankfulness that I started to wonder how this message had come to us. Who was behind it? Who knew Alex? This priest...had he had any recent contact with Alex? Surely not? Had someone heard something and persuaded the priest to write the good news down and pass it on to us? It was a mystery to me.

I went to Reverend Fullerton.

"Who sent this, sir?" I asked. It was all I could say. I was suddenly feeling exhausted after that burst of delight.

"I have no idea, Katie," he said, "but isn't it the best news you've ever heard?"

"It is," I agreed, "but who wrote it?"

"How would we know? There is no signature," he said.

"No signature?"

"No...perhaps this priest heard the news and wrote it down for us. I don't know. I am only surmising," he said.

"Alright," I said, turning away. Then, on a whim, I came back to him and asked if I could see the parchment.

"Of course," he said, "but sure you can't read, lass? There's no name on it anyhow so I don't know what sort of clue you are going to try to...."

"I know!" I interrupted him. "I know who it is!"

I had opened the document and, below the writing, the first thing I saw was a wee black cross, its outline burned into the leather, and its centre dark and charred...it was exactly the same as the black cross Darach had carved for me from the bog oak all those months ago.

Darach had written the message, I was sure of it! He had found out about Alex. Maybe he was with Alex. Somehow he had also discovered that this priest, this friend of his, was being the good samaritan and bringing water and food to us in the Kirk.

Unconsciously I was fingering the little bog-oak cross which had hung around my neck every day since Darach had given it to me back last summer. I brought it to my mouth and kissed it, tears starting to appear in my eyes. I couldn't help it. Darach was alive and well. And he was able to communicate with me. That was amazing news in itself, not to mention the actual message about our Alex. It felt like the best day of my life.

The minister noticed my joy. He saw my tears; he saw me kiss the wooden cross; he couldn't help but notice this emotion.

"Tell me who, Katie…and how are you so sure?"

So I told him. I confessed everything, my love affair with Darach, the story of the bog-oak cross, his connection to our family and his relationship with this priest, Father McGlaim, when together they had saved Alex on the mountain. I also explained how I came to have the child, Kate. The poor clergyman just sat and listened, finding it hard to take in this torrent of elation as my heart burst with pure bliss that Darach, my Darach, had been our hero again in these, the direst of circumstances. I don't know what Reverend Fullerton made of it all. It was probably the longest flow of words anyone had spoken to him since this whole incarceration began. He heard me out with great patience, I'll say that for him.

"I have met this lad," he told me then. "He is the one who brought McDonnell's letter to us just before the siege began. We were about to arrest him as a spy, but he told me he knew the McKays. He was concerned for you."

I wish I had known this earlier, but I could not blame the minister. He had plenty on his mind at that time. It was enough to know that Darach was still alive and still thinking of how to help us.

Afterwards I collapsed in a heap on the floor with sheer exhaustion. The minister got me a cup of water; he lifted me to a bench where he laid me down gently.

"You have tired yourself out, lass," he said. "Rest now…but we will have to talk a lot more about these matters when we get time, after all this is over, you understand?"

I nodded as I surrendered to the sleep that overcame me.

Chapter 44

The Earl Returns

At the beginning of the rebellion, the Earl of Antrim and his wife were over one hundred miles and several days travel from Dunluce. They were safely ensconced in Slane Castle with Randal's sister, Anne. Anne's husband, William Fleming, was the 9th Baron of Slane, an important man in Leinster politics. But when Fleming decided to lend his support to the Irish party and support the rising, Randal saw trouble ahead. He had tried to steer a middle course and, although he had a certain sympathy with the goals of the Catholic Irish, he felt he needed to distance himself from their aggressive campaign. He was a Gael in his blood and his bones, but first and foremost he was a pragmatist…a pragmatist and a survivor. He also thought of himself as a friend and a close confident of King Charles. The sovereign, under huge pressure from the Puritan element in the English Parliament and from his Covenanter enemies in Scotland, needed the loyal support of old friends. And, at the end of the day, he thought, Charles' rule in Ireland would be infinitely preferable to the extreme anti-Catholicism of those English Parliamentarians. So Randal made the decision that, to avoid any tainting of his reputation and to maintain his ability to be a peace-maker in his Ulster homeland, he and Katherine should leave the opulence of Fleming's Slane Castle.

Having a good colleague in the Earl of Castlehaven at Maddenstown, near Kildare, he took up residence there. During the several months he spent in Kildare it was reported that he and his Protestant wife gave practical and moral support to groups of Protestant refugees and, in particular, to Crown soldiers, men who were wounded and destitute after a bloody battle at Kilrush. Many of these people he was able to get to the safety of Dublin. Such charity was purposed to silence those who speculated that this powerful Gaelic Earl from the north was secretly a supporter and sponsor of the rebellion.

While in the south, Randal had heard the stories of atrocities being committed by the Irish in Ulster. He was disgusted by what he heard, and very concerned for his tenants. In early April of that year, he heard that a Scottish Army under General Munro had come to Ulster. By the end of the month he had reached the decision that he needed to travel back to Dunluce to try to ameliorate the situation in his lands in the Route. His main intention was to negotiate a settlement between the Irish rebel leaders and the Crown, especially with General Munro. He sent his countess to England for safety and eventually began his journey home, protected by a small company of soldiers. It took six days. For some reason he kept a diary of where he stayed each night and who he talked to…perhaps worried that his loyalties to either cause might be called into question later.

The diary recorded that, beginning in Offaly, he travelled to Westmeath, then to a relative in Louth, then to Armagh where he lodged with the Franciscans rather than another of his sisters, Eilish, who had rebel connections. He made a strong public statement there, denouncing the Irish party and the merciless violence of their rebellion. From *Ard Mhacha,* he traveled up the western side of Lough Neagh in O'Neill country until he reached Moneymore, where he met the Irish rebel leader, Sir Phelim…apparently to plead for restraint in the campaign, and to urge for a truce and a settlement. He then moved north through Magherafelt, eventually crossing the Bann into Coleraine.

The siege of that over-crowded town was continuing. He heard that as many as one hundred were being buried each day. Disgusted by the lack of humanity being shown by his cousin, Alaster McColla McDonnell, leader of the besieging Irish troops there, he insisted on an urgent meeting with McColla.

****

Alaster McColla McDonnell was not impressed by the Earl's interference. Their argument, in McColla's pavilion, continued for several hours, during which McColla's temper reached boiling point. The Earl had to be at his most clever and controlled to survive the verbal onslaught from the furious Highlander. For a long time the disagreement sat on an impasse, a tipping point between Randal's desire for moderation and McColla's insistence that these Protestants in Coleraine should be starved into a humiliating surrender.

"How is the future of this part of Ireland to be served by the continuing deaths of so many good people in this town, Alaster?" Randal asked. "I have spoken to our friend, Phelim O'Neill, not longer than three days ago. Can I tell you that he is as disgusted as I am by the wanton and indiscriminate violence of many of your troops. Even more so by that of the native Irish folk. This is not what he intended."

"It may naw be what he intended, but it is what he unleashed," McColla argued. "Maybe it passed your notice in your big castle at Dunluce, but the native people o' Ulster are very angry, aye an' wae every right."

"They may be angry, but that does not excuse your attacks on my innocent tenants, these people that you are holding hostage. If you could explain what these women and children have done to merit your cruelty, I might consider listening to your argument."

"They are Protestant! They are sympathisers wae Campbell an' the Covenanter cause. And they are trespassing on the lands they stole frae the Irish!" McColla shouted.

"They are women and children, man! They stole nothing. No Irish were dispossessed by my father in settling these Scots in the Route. Nor by myself! These good women could be your own mother. They cannot help the faith into which they were born. Not one of them was responsible for stealing land, not one!"

"That maybe so, but they hae been misled by people like yoursel'. You hae them thinkin' that it is acceptable tae live in this lan' that is naw their's, that they are entitled tae this... inheritance."

"So it is the fault of people like myself?" Randal scorned. "I have misled them by offering them a decent tenancy here in Ulster, and at very low rates? Not at all. My late father gave them a chance to better themselves here in this fertile land, whereas before they were scraping a living amongst the rocks and bogs of some distant Scottish island. I have been committed to continuing his great work of settlement."

"Ye make it sound like a fine act o' charity on your part, on your fether's part...providin' for poor Scots," McColla said. "Ye ken that is naw the case. It was al' done tae advance your position wae the English King. Your family could as easy hae settled Catholic Scots in these lands. But naw! It had tae be lowland Protestants, just so the Crown couldnae complain that ye were building a bulwark o' Catholic-controlled territory against the Protestant King."

"That is nonsense. The people we settled here are good, sound, hard-working Scots..."

"Rubbish!" McColla interrupted. "They are naethin' but pawns in your power game, Randal! Pawns!"

The Earl paused and waited for his warlike cousin to settle. Then in a much softer voice he told him, "Better to be pawns than to be dead, Alaster! These people you are starving to death are my tenants, and I will defend them. More than that, I will feed them."

McColla laughed scornfully. "And how, pray, will ye dae that? I hae them completely surrounded. I hae them demoralised. I hae them at the point o' surrender. How dae ye think ye're going tae feed them?"

Again Lord Antrim spoke with quiet confidence. He would not be ruffled by this man's sneering belligerence. "Tomorrow a cargo of corn will arrive at the western gate, by the riverside. You will instruct your men to let it pass through. Over the next few days sixty tons of corn and other foodstuffs will be permitted to enter the town to feed the residents, my tenants."

McColla laughed derisively at this. "Where will ye get that amount of corn? The countryside haes nae food. Ye are talkin' nonsense."

"I am not. It has been ordered and paid for, and it is on its way already. What is more, as many cattle as I can rustle up from my lands all over Antrim will be driven here to Coleraine. You, Alaster, are going to concede pasture to these animals…and furthermore you are to concede grazing lands to the many animals which my tenants have harboured within the ramparts of Coleraine. These animals are starving also. It is a pitiful sight. So you will move your troops back to a distance of three miles from the ramparts, and there they can stay and continue their siege; but they will not harm these animals, nor the youths who come out of the town to herd and tend them. The cruelty you have perpetrated upon these loyal tenants of mine is at an end, you hear me, cousin? You will attend to these matters forthwith."

The Earl rose from his seat and moved serenely towards the opening. Behind him he heard the undertone of sarcastic laughter from Alaster. McColla's stool got roughly kicked over as the huge soldier jumped to his feet. He towered above his cousin, but Randal stood his ground, refusing to be cowed by the Highlander.

"Those are my orders, Alaster. You have heard me," he said.

"I hear ye, but just how dae ye think ye are goin' tae enforce these ridiculous orders?" McColla responded in a quieter tone, though still full of obduracy. "Ye may be the Earl of Antrim, but while you hae been skulking aroun' in the safety o' the south, I hae been the one making the decisions here. What makes ye think ye can arrive back here and countermand me?"

"Because, sir, I am the Earl of Antrim! Because, sir, you are my guest. You have been hosted in Ballintoy by a good Scot, your friend, Archibald Stewart. The same man who now holds Coleraine against you. This is the man who has shown you kindness and hospitality. And this is how you repay him? Have you no sense of decency about you? You are trying to starve your host to death, the man who has generously fed you from his own table! What say you to that, eh? Where are your principles? Disgraceful, I say! Shame on you, sir!"

Alaster McColla winced visibly at this verbal attack. He could think of no further reply, so he turned his back on the Earl and stood contemplating something in the far distance, hoping that Lord Antrim would slip away and leave him alone. But Randal was not quite finished.

"Has it occurred to you," he said, "that this rebellion is likely to lead to even worse outcomes for the Irish people than resulted from the departure of the Earls in 1607? Do you imagine for one minute that the English King is going to let you and your gallowglasses get away with this? The Crown will be delighted that yet again the Irish Lords have rebelled. More opportunity to beat the natives into the ground and seize more of their land. You are aware that General Munro is already here, with three regiments at his command?"

"We dinnae ken if that is true; it's just a rumour," McColla said sullenly, feeling that this argument was getting away from him.

"And that is not all. I cannot tell you how I know of this, you understand….but King Charles has been casting around in Scotland, trying to have the Covenanters there raise an even greater army to come across to Ulster to save their co-religionists and avenge the massacres that you and your like have been perpetrating."

McColla stared at him disbelievingly. "That must be a false report," he said. "The Covenanters are the King's enemies. Everybody kens that. They would never agree tae such a campaign."

"They might…if the incentives were right. The King might tell them, 'Beat the Irish rebels and you can join the Presbyterians in Ulster, and take as much land as you want.' He has already promised them Rathlin Island as a base. Think of that, Alaster. Campbell in Rathlin! Charles is clever, you know."

"Aye, and he's a freen o' yours," McColla grunted.

"He is, and he knows a good trick when he sees one. He has enemies in Ireland? So why not persuade his enemies in Scotland to go fight them…it would be a masterful plan, don't you think? Pit his two enemies against each other! That way he would be keeping the bulk of his own troops in England where he needs them to protect the Crown against the Parliamentarians. As I say, Charles is extremely clever, far too clever for the rather stupid leaders of the Irish rebels."

McColla smarted inside himself at this insult. He was starting to realise that he may be out of his depth in these troubled political waters. "And hae ye heard that this is definitely happenin', that the Argyll is involved in the scheme?"

"He could well be; if not him, then some of his generals."

McColla swore. "Those bloody English!" he said. "They can never be trusted."

"Well Alaster," Randal said reflectively, "I wouldn't say that. You can trust that they will always have a disparaging opinion of anyone who is not English. I lived among them; I listened to them at the highest courts in the land. I know how the English mind works. Fundamentally they see themselves as superior; the Irish are savages…less than human, and, even if we are human, we are not quite the same kind of human as they are. That makes their conquest of our land easy. They see conquest as a positive value, almost as their God-given duty; like their duty to civilise these poor natives, get them speaking English, give them English law and order, give them the true religion, introduce them into the polite ways of English society."

"Aye, and that's why the Irish hae tae fight it at every opportunity," McColla insisted vehemently.

"Ah yes, but it is about how you fight it, don't you see?" argued the earl. "When the Irish get violent, it confirms the English perceptions of us as barbarians. Our disorder plays well to an English audience. It gives legitimacy to their crusades to subdue us, to destroy our Gaelic way of life, to take our lands."

"So the Irishmen should just sit back and let them get on wae it? That sounds cowardly tae me, Randal."

"It may sound that way, but when you realise that you can't beat them at their own game, militarily I mean, you have to devise more clever schemes to work with them, and work around them. There has to be a better way than fighting them, you understand?"

"Let me know when ye think of it," McColla said. "In the meantime, if you are right, if a Covenanter army is going tae be marching in our direction soon, we should be getting ready for it."

"That is my point, Alaster. How will the continuing sieges of Coleraine and Dunluce help you in your preparations to face a Scottish army? Don't you see that, on the contrary, it is now beholden to you to begin to treat these besieged Scottish Presbyterians with some care and respect? You wouldn't want to incur the wrath of either Munro or Archibald Campbell, would you? Their revenge would be savage."

McColla was silent, defeated by the Earl's canny words, well chastened by this final, veiled threat. His confused mind was full of new questions which had not been on his horizon until now. His patience at the doggedness of the Protestant garrison was wearing very thin. He had to admit that he had underestimated the tenacity of Archibald Stewart and his fellow leaders. Despite the huge numbers of deaths, and the desperately hungry plight of those still remaining alive, the garrison had shown no sign of surrendering. Might now be the time to try a different tactic, the time to show some mercy?

The Earl gave him time to ponder. Then he changed his tone and put the question, "So, Alaster, you will follow my orders and withdraw your troops to the three mile radius. And you will permit the passage of food convoys tomorrow."

McColla inclined his hoary head. "Aye, I will dae it."

"Good," Lord Antrim said. "Now I will be on my way to Dunluce. I am sure Captain Digby could use a bit of moral support. And I will be investigating what the O'Cahans have been doing in Ballintoy."

He turned on his heel and left McColla to ponder the difference between power and authority.

****

Captain Digby accompanied Lord Antrim as he wandered around his castle. They stopped to talk to each of the villagers who had taken refuge inside its walls when the Irish had attacked. The Earl sympathised with them on the loss of their homes in the village next door. He promised to do all he could to put the little settlement on its feet again.

John McSparran took courage to ask the question that was in everyone's mind. "When do you think that will be, m'Lord?"

"I don't know the answer to that, John," he replied. "As soon as we possibly can we will get the houses rebuilt. I met James McDonnell out there. He stood aside and let me into my castle alright, but I need to spend some time with him, and persuade him to pull his troops back from this foolish siege. Once he does that we can make a start. I will be relying on you, John, to organise teams to clear what remains of the old homes and start getting timber to rebuild."

"I will undertake that task with pleasure, sir," John said. "So many of our young men have perished in this affair…and others of our village have fled back to Scotland."

"I understand that and I sympathise, John. It's a bad business. But we must get the place back into shape, eh?"

"Indeed, sir, but can we stay in the grounds of the castle until our homes are up and ready?"

"Certainly," the Earl assured him. "Stay as you have been. Captain Digby will continue to make sure you are fed and sheltered…after he gets back from Ballintoy."

Captain Digby turned in surprise. "I am to go to Ballintoy, my lord?" he asked apprehensively.

"You are, Digby. I need someone of your authority to take a message to Gilladubh O'Cahan. He and that foolish son of his need to withdraw, and allow those good people to go about their normal business. How are they to pay their tenancy dues to Archibald Stewart if they are not able to work their land? It is high time they have a chance to get their crops in, and tend to whatever stock they have been left with."

Captain Digby looked less than enthusiastic. "With respect, my lord," he said quietly, "do you think the Irish will desist simply because I bring them such a message? They have besieged Ballintoy for many weeks. I hear that, in their determination, they have even used a cannon against the church. They may not listen, sir. They may even arrest…."

The Earl interrupted his objection. "You will take my order, Captain. Once I have persuaded James McDonnell to withdraw from Dunluce, I will get him to counter-sign this instruction to O'Cahan. The Irish will do as they are told if both James and I tell them to. They cannot afford to mess around any longer, not with Munro's army now in the country."

Captain Digby's smile evaporated. "Aye sir," he said quietly.

"Good. Now, I think a large goblet of Spanish wine is called for. Will you partake with me, Captain?"

"I will, my lord, thank you," said the Captain, turning to follow the Earl into the Manor House.

Chapter 45

Uncovered

Darach O'Cahan

Another journey from Ballycastle to the Ballintoy church.

The priest and myself. Two disciples bearing the bread of life… secretly.

In my sleep before these missions I am always haunted by the fear that things will go wrong, that, when we get there, the Irish will have broken through the church door; or, worst of all, that Father McGlaim will be discovered. Obviously I lock these thoughts up in my head. He does not need any doubt, any discouragement. His poor heart must be already sick and tired of the nervous strain of these repeated visits. But the kindness of the man is matched only by his courage, his resilience.

I had been with Alex before we left. Poor Alex, restless and bored in his attic hide-out at Dunynie Castle. He is desperate to help, but so far he has listened to our wisdom.

"Alex, it would be madness for you to leave here, suicidal," I told him. "Just be patient."

"But this wait is even more maddening," he argued. "I cannot sit a minute longer in this gloom."

He begged me to ask some of the leaders inside the kirk to put a message in one of the empty containers, just something to let us know how his people are.

This is a repeated request. It is one that I cannot answer, except to say that by sending such a message out they would be endangering Father McGlaim. He does take that point, but it does not do much for his patience.

Today's journey to Ballintoy has been uneventful. The animals are well accustomed to the route now. They know the humps and hollows on the path, the rough surfaces to avoid. There is little conversation between the priest and myself. He seems preoccupied, his emotional energy running low. I watch him from the corner of my eye, and I sense that he is in some deep contemplation. I want to ask him how he is feeling. I want to encourage him. But I cannot find the words to begin the conversation. He ignores me, unusually so. Today's anguish, whatever it is, remains unspoken, locked up in his private mental dungeon.

I tie *Liath* to the same tree as always, and watch the priest's slow descent from Knocksoughey Hill. I can see the two water jars bouncing against *Padraig's* flanks. No vellum inside this time, no good news from beyond. No message other than that contained in the actual water and oatmeal, a very distinct message in itself. 'Someone cares about you. Cares enough to put their own life at risk. You are not abandoned.'

I watch the activities on the plain stretched out below me. It dawns on me gradually that there is something different in the atmosphere today.

The Irish troops are somehow disturbed. From this distance it looks like a wasps' nest that has been interfered with. Small figures are buzzing around. There is a sense of confusion, of anger even, about their movements. I wish I had travelled further around the hillside to where I had observed the cannon episode some days ago. That way I could hear the conversations, perhaps discern what is causing this unsettled atmosphere. Up here, I have no way of knowing. I can only wait and surmise. And surmise I do.

I cannot make out the figures of Gilladubh or Tirlough Óge from this distance. I sense a lack of order in what I am observing. It is not so much a panic, as would be the case if they were being attacked from somewhere, just a feeling of disarray and confusion…a few men running one way, and then the other, while others appear to be gathered in a tight huddle, as if in conference. It certainly doesn't feel like the patient waiting game of the last few days. After the failure of the cannon attack, there had been an atmosphere of resignation, stalemate. Something has happened; I cannot begin to guess what.

My eyes have been fixed on this behaviour, as I have tried to understand it. Now I look north to see how Father McGlaim is progressing. He should be at the church by now…or very close to it but…where is he? I scan the fields around the church.

I cannot see my friend, the priest.

He is not where I expected him to be at this stage. What could have distracted him, delayed him in his…

To my horror I suddenly see him! Father McGlaim is in difficulty!

His slight, dark-robed figure is surrounded by several soldiers. He is being held by them, physically held, pushed and pulled in a brutal manner. I see him stumble and fall to the earth, his frailty and weakness suddenly exposed. He struggles back to his feet with difficulty.

It all looks very aggressive, even from this distance. I hear shouted oaths, faint at this distance but ugly, abusive language. No-one should be shouting such things at a clergyman.

Padráig is being towed away roughly by one soldier.

Another man has one of the jars in his hands.

'Oh no!' I think, as I watch this man turn it upside down. The water floods out around Father McGlaim's feet, followed by the wet splurge of oatmeal. It hits his legs, and slowly curdles to the earth.

Someone has him by the throat; another screws his arm up his back. This is my worst nightmare!

Everything inside me screams out to run to his aid, this man who has been the epitome of goodness, now in the danger of his life. Inside myself I send an urgent screaming prayer to Saint Michael and Our Lady. 'Let him survive this. Please let him survive!'

In all the tragic things I have seen since this unrest began, in all the shocking things I have heard, in all the sadness I have been involved with, this is the worst experience of all. It is even more painful than finding the girl, Nellie, lying in her death. My heart is aching as I watch this pummelling of my friend. Tears of sheer grief are coursing down my cheeks. I am so helpless. I can do nothing. Am I shirking my duty here? Is it simply that I am afraid for my own life if I get involved? Yes, I am a pathetic, self-protecting coward who does not even deserve to have known this man.

Yet I cannot move. I tell myself that to do anything at this stage risks everything, and for no good outcome. Is there no-one else who can stop this? No-one to speak for this holy man? Where is Tirlough Óge and my Uncle Gilladubh? They would surely not suffer any harm to come to a man of the church, a priest who has often served Mass to them. But I cannot see them.

Where, oh where is God when he is needed? Why does he not act to save this good servant of his?

Why doesn't someone from the church look out and see what is happening, someone with a musket who could fire a warning shot and save their saviour's life? But no-one is doing anything. It all seems so inexorable.

Father McGlaim is being dragged away in the direction of Larrybane, that area of starkly beautiful white cliffs just a half-mile from the church. His body is already limp, up-turned, surrendered to their cruelty. He is sliped roughly over the field, like you would with a dead calf. His head hangs back, swinging low to the grass. The procession is slow and painful. The gang of his attackers disappear from my view behind a rise in the land.

It is to be my last ever view of the saint who is Father Patrick McGlaim.

****

Back in Alex's hiding place I lie howling on a couch. I am inconsolable.

The words to explain to Alex and Hugh MacNeill what had happened have struggled to climb out of me; they have congealed in sourness in the drought of my mouth. Every word a sob. Never have I felt such waves of grief.

I feel so alone in the depth of this agony. My friends here try to comfort me, but I long for Katie. I long to tell her of this man. He is the reason she is alive. He has now saved both her and her brother, and she may not even know. As well as that, he is the one man I know who might have been able to marry the two of us. Now I fear he is gone. I know it in my bones.

But Hugh MacNeill tries to give me hope.

"Maybe he will survive this, Darach," he says. "You saw him being taken towards Larrybane, but that does not mean they have killed him, does it? You may be jumping to false conclusions."

"He is right," Alex tells me gently. "You are imagining the worst. Maybe they will just give him a beating. Maybe they'll stop after they have tortured…"

Tortured him? The thought strikes me forcefully. If Father McGlaim has been tortured, might he have confessed the secret of where he got the oatmeal? Might he have had to tell of his accomplices? Could we be in serious and immanent danger ourselves?

I blurt out my worries to MacNeill and Alex. Fear has taken over my senses, unbalanced me, turned me inside out.

"Do you seriously think the good priest is the kind of man to implicate you in his scheme, Darach?" MacNeill asks.

I am rebuked.

"I can't see that happening either," Alex agrees. "You are safe; we are all safe. I think you are just distressed by what you witnessed over there and so you fear the worst."

"No, Alex," I tell him. "I don't fear the worst. The worst has already happened."

Chapter 46

Release

Katie McKay

No-one actually told us that the siege was over. We had to work it out on our own. We grew into the realisation of it ourselves, rather than hearing from someone in the outside world.

It was hard to believe, almost impossible to take in.

We had heard, with great sorrow, the commotion around the unmasking and arrest of Father McGlaim. It happened not thirty paces from the door of the church. While it would not have been wise at that stage to have made an attempt to help him, or even to try to see from our window-slits what was happening, we were all hushed in dread as we heard what was going on. The voices of his attackers, raised in screaming rage, could be heard echoing off the sides of the kirk. Every word that they said came in to us. Between the oaths and curses of them, we heard the brave priest condemned to hellfire for ever out of their filthy mouths…though I am quite sure God will take a different view of it. God will likely have him sitting in a very special place in heaven, along with all the other martyrs to kindness.

One of the things that I heard repeated several times by his interrogators was a query which worried me. It was the question of who had been his accomplices.

"We know you couldn't have carried out this deceit on your own," yelled one voice. "So come on, Father. Tell us who helped you!"

They kept going over this. It was like a repeated prayer, a senseless rant. I never heard a single word from the priest though, not a sound did he make at that time.

"Who supplied the corn to you?"

"Where have you come from? Ballycastle, was it?"

"Are you a Bonamargy priest, are you?"

"Where did you get the oatmeal?"

"Who helped you? It surely couldn't have been one of your brother Friars! So who was it?"

Then, this question. "What possessed you to turn your back on your own kind and help your enemies, you oul reprobate?"

Then, unbelievably, I heard the faint voice of the priest above the clamour as he answered that question…and that one only. His voice quivered with fear, God love him, but he made it bravely through to the end of his statement.

"*Chuala sibh go ndeirtí, 'Tabhair grá do do chomharsa, agus fuath do do namhaid.' Ach is é a deirim libh, 'Bíodh grá agaibh do bhur naimhde agus bígí ag guí ar son lucht bhur ngéarleanúna.*"

I understood enough of his Gaelic to know that he was quoting the words of Jesus. "You have heard that it was said, 'Love your neighbour and hate your enemy.' But I say to you, Love your enemies and pray for those who persecute you."

Their voices faded after that. Father McGlaim had been taken away somewhere, and we feared for him. Reverend Fullerton had us all on our knees praying for him…aye, and giving thanks to God for the man's kindness and sacrifice.

There were many tears shed that night in our dismal kirk.

Mine were mixed with pride that my Darach had been associated with this priest. I thought of him all night, prayed for his safety, and held him tightly in the arms of my longing imagination.

It was the next day, a very thirsty day, for we hadn't had water since the Tuesday. At one point, Mr Boyd told us he was sure the Irish had gone away. There hadn't been any noise from outside, apart from the fact that the birds were singing with what sounded like a new joyfulness. He and one or two other brave folk peered carefully out through the window-slits, and Boyd climbed to the bell tower to spy out across the fields. Nobody saw any sign of our besiegers. Could it be that they had upped and left us in peace, after so many weeks of capture? There was a sense of anticipation and relief among us, but above any other feeling there was thirst and hunger. Could we not slip out to the air and see what food we could find? We would even scrape the remains of the priest's oatmeal off the gravel, just to make some porridge. Our leaders counselled us to have patience, to take care that the Irish weren't trying some trick. Perhaps if we left the building we would encounter a band of them hiding somewhere nearby, waiting to ambush us and use us as hostages. It was a point well made, after what we had heard happen to Father McGlaim.

It wasn't long, however, until we heard the sound of galloping hooves coming down the lane from the village. Horsemen were arriving in a mad hurry, that was for certain, but were they friend or foe?

A severe banging on the door, and then a voice we all recognised.

"Open up, Reverend Fullerton. It's me! Archibald Stewart! It's all over!"

Mr Stewart was visibly failed when he appeared inside the kirk. He had lost a lot of weight, his usually full, round face hanging loosely, deep, dark bags surrounding those huge staring eyes of his. Even though he was smiling, he looked completely worn out…and we watched his smile fade as he saw the same symptoms in all of us that day. The three months of near starvation had left us just about hanging on to life. What would we not have been like without the smuggled water and oatmeal?

But now, according to him, it seemed to be all over. The Manor House had not fallen. Our men who had been guarding it had fended off the attackers and were waiting to be reunited with their families. The realisation was dawning on us that we had somehow survived.

There would have been dancing in the place, kirk or no kirk, if we had had the energy. Instead we all just hugged each other, laughed and cried, and jigged up and down, and giggled some more. What pure joy to flock to the door and step out into the brightness of the world. We couldn't contain our excitement, tasting the clear air of freedom for the first time in so long. I say 'we', but in truth there were a few folks whose relief was tinged with a great sadness. Not far from the church door Mrs Kerr and Thomas Smith's mother stood at the grave of Mrs Ross, holding each other in deep sorrow. Neither of them knew where their loved ones lie buried, of course, or even if they had had a decent burial. I noticed Robert Moore's mother turn from this sight and hurry away towards the village in a bent-over stumble. The poor woman could handle no more public grief, it seemed. But following her, trying to catch up, was Jean Kennedy. How kind of Jean, I thought, to be the person going to give the grieving woman some support and consolation.

Wee Kate's eyes screwed up against the light, and she cried at the shock of it. The breeze was blowing in from the west with the fragrance of the flowers of White Park Bay on it. The silvery-blue of the ocean was like salve to the eyes. The yellow sun, high and bright in the May sky, was glinting off the wings of the seagulls. Our fields looked rich with deep, green grass, crying out for the scythe…and not a soldier of any kind in sight!

The young ones among us ran and cavorted in the lanes and fields. It only took a few moments, however, for them to discover that they did not have the energy they would have had before. They gave up quickly, and stretched out on their backs on the grass, staring up at the patterns of the clouds in the sky as if they had never seen such a display. I saw several go down the track towards the harbour, Connie and Alice among them. I almost did the same myself. The thought of washing in that cool seawater was a powerful attraction. I started to follow them, but turned back. I had Kate in my arms; I felt I should stay with the older folk. Apart from anything else, I wanted to hear the news from Mr Stewart… and I wanted to make sure he knew about Father McGlaim. Did he have any word of Alex, or of Darach? I joined the other parents, including the McClures and the Taggarts, who were asking about their boys. Bruce and Matthew, I heard, had survived and would be home soon from Coleraine. Their folks were weeping with relief. Standing on the edge of the circle of the listeners, I waited my chance to ask my questions more privately.

I heard all about the siege of Coleraine, but then I had known most of that information. The news about the arrival there of Lord Antrim was very welcome. It was great to hear that he was back in Dunluce, and organising food for his tenants. Stewart was hopeful that a load of grain would be arriving here with us in Ballintoy soon, but we would have to be patient.

"What persuaded the Irish to give up and leave us," Fullerton wanted to know.

Stewart's answer was that the Earl had talked some sense into Alaster McColla and James McDonnell, and they had pulled back their soldiers from Coleraine and Dunluce.

"He also sent word to the O'Cahans here, telling them of his displeasure at their actions, and ordering them to desist," Stewart said. "I think once he informed them of Munro arriving in Ulster they were convinced."

"Munro arriving?" Fullerton said. "We haven't heard anything about that. Is it true?"

"Aye William, it is true," Stewart replied. "The great Scottish General landed in Carrickfergus a while ago, sent by the King after some clever deal between him and the Covenanters. From what I hear, he has a good sized army, some say over two thousand soldiers. He has already secured Belfast, and then he marched on to deal with Newry. After that we expect him to come to the Route to quell the rebellion here. It is great news for the Protestants of this place."

"Aye, but not such good news for the Irish, I'll warrant," Fullerton said quietly. "He will be ruthless with them."

"Indeed, and I believe he has been already. There are stories…but, enough about that; they had it coming to them, the Irish," Stewart said. Then, turning to the crowd, he continued, "Now, good friends, I am going to dismiss you and send you to your homes. I hope you find them in good order, not damaged by the rebels. You will need some time to come to terms with your freedom, so take it easy. Remember, you are weak, and you will not be able to do all you feel you need to do at once. The priority, I suppose, is to see what you can find to eat. Leave the cleaning up of the kirk for a few days until you have the energy for it. We will meet again here on the Sabbath."

Slowly our people began to disperse. It was a very strange feeling, watching these folk who had been so intimately involved with each other's lives peel off uncertainly from the assembly with slow steps and many backward looks. Soon they would be starting to scavenge around for any sort of food they could find. There seemed to be no cattle left on our flat plain around the Manor House; some animals might have made it up to the safe grazing of the hills behind the village, but probably a lot had been killed for food for the Irish. The same fate had probably befallen the hens and pigs as well. It was going to take a while to get things back towards normality. In the meantime there would be fish to be caught, plenty of limpets on the rocks below and lots of black mussels and crabs to be easily found.

I gave Kate to my mother and watched as she and Aunt Biddy wandered away from me on the short walk along the path to our house; they had the child between them, each holding a hand and sort of half carrying, half-swinging her. They seemed to be stumbling uncertainly at times. Both seemed to have aged ten years.

I stayed where I was, however, needing some answers to my questions. When had Stewart last seen his messenger, Darach? What did he know about Alex?

I slipped closer and listened from around the corner of the kirk to the conversation between himself and Reverend Fullerton.

"It was a priest," the clergyman was saying. "A Father McGlaim. We would never have survived without what he did. We would need to try to find out what happened to him. I hope the rebels let him go, but I fear the worst. We all heard the interrogation he was being put through out there."

"And you think he did this on his own, of his own volition?"

"As far as we can make out," Fullerton said. "But there was one strange incident that puzzled us. There was a message inside the water jar on one occasion."

At this point, Fullerton drew the roll of vellum from somewhere in his cloak and showed it to Stewart.

"You see this message, Archibald," he said. "'Alex McKay safe and well. Be strong and patient'."

Stewart took the vellum and studied it, initially with a puzzled look. "And when was this received?" he asked, a great excitement in his voice.

"Not long ago. Young Katie McKay seems to know who sent it," Fullerton said. "A friend of her, a young man called O'…"

"If this is genuine, it is the best news I have heard in a long time," Stewart interrupted. "You say it came from the priest? I wonder how he knows anything about Alex?"

"I have no idea," replied Fullerton. "Why should he want to tell us about Alex McKay in particular?"

"There is a very good reason. Alex had been on an important and dangerous mission for me, you see. I had no idea if he had survived it."

At this point I knew I had to join the conversation, so I came forward. They looked at me, a bit taken aback that I had been eavesdropping around the corner.

"I am sorry. I shouldn't have been listening, sirs," I said, "but I did want to ask Mr Stewart about our Alex."

Reverend Fullerton frowned and tutted in slight annoyance, but Mr

Stewart nodded in that wise and caring manner which, for all the chaos he had been through, had not deserted him.

"That's alright, Katie," Stewart said kindly. "Mr Fullerton tells me you have some knowledge concerning this document? It has no signature but apparently you know of its sender, is that the case?"

"It is, sir. I was able to work it out from this wee black cross. You see, I believe it was written by the same person who gave me this cross," I told him, pulling my bog-oak cross from my bosom.

"And that was...who?"

"It was Darach O'Cahan, sir," I said. "Darach and I are...we are good friends. Have been for nearly a year now."

"Ah, Darach, my messenger. So that is the way the wind is blowing, is it? I think I have some memory of your connection to him from a long time back," Mr Stewart said. "So you are convinced he sent this message into the kirk with this Father McGlaim?"

"I am sure, sir. There can't be any other explanation," I said.

"Well, if so," he replied, "it is very good news. It means that both of them are alive, or at least they were when this was sent. And that was just a few days ago, you say?"

"Six days ago," I told him.

He smiled. "You have clearly been counting, Katie. And you must be very thrilled that, not only did young O'Cahan think so kindly as to send a message to your mother about Alex...he also was telling you that he was alright?"

"I am," I said, "but even more thrilled that he was helping his friend, Father McGlaim."

"You know that they are friends?"

"I do. Darach told me about him months ago. He said I should meet him sometime. He said that Father McGlaim might be the one to..." I stopped short, realising that I was about to spill out one of our most private secrets.

Stewart and Fullerton both seemed to intensify their look at me at that moment, and I caught a flicker of a glance go between them. I knew they were correctly guessing what I had been about to say. Neither of them, however, were about to discuss the issue just then. I jumped quickly back into my inquiries.

"Mr Stewart, do you know anything of their whereabouts?" I asked.

"I do, Katie, but..." He paused, briefly weighing up what or how much to tell me. "Look, my girl, this is a very delicate subject. What I tell you now must never be repeated. Reverend Fullerton, you too must never breathe this. You understand? It would be dangerous for the two lads if their part in this were ever to be uncovered."

We both nodded, in my case very bewildered.

"Some weeks ago," Stewart continued, "when things were looking so bleak in Coleraine after Black Friday and the terrible slaughter at Laney, I came to the decision that we needed aid from outside…to save us from the rebels. So I gave Darach and Alex a commission. I sent them to Kintyre, to Archibald Campbell, the Argyll. I was begging for him to come and bring an army to help us defeat the Irish. I have heard nothing back. Obviously I was holed up in Coleraine, so no message could get through to me, if there was a reply. I was very worried about the two lads. Anything could have happened to them. They could have been apprehended by rebel troops before they left Ballycastle. They could have been arrested as spies in Kintyre or slain by bandits. You have no idea how relieved I am to see this message."

"Not half as relieved as I was, sir," I said. "So you have no idea where they are now?"

"I had no idea whatsoever, Katie," he said, "until now. If Darach wrote this message, as he most likely did, then he must be local to us. He must have been in contact with the priest, somewhere around here, and he must have either heard from or met Alex. So they are in north Antrim somewhere. My guess would be Ballycastle, or maybe in the Glens. We can only hope and pray they are lying low and safe somewhere. It may be a while before they even hear that the rebels have backed off."

"Indeed," the Reverend said. "I can see why you insist that their part in your scheme with Argyll must remain secret. They would both be prime targets for the Irish, and especially for McColla McDonnell, if word of this ever got out."

I left the two men shortly after these words, and my heart was in a new turmoil. On the one hand we were all free. Here I was walking our lane again, birds hopping in the hedgerows beside me. I was able to look over the cliff and see the waves break around Sheep Island; I was free to breathe deeply in the sea-fresh air once more. I saw a hare rise in the field beside me and bound off towards the hills; another survivor, I thought. I was sure many's another one of its family circle got trapped and eaten by hungry people all over our countryside in the past while. May it enjoy its freedom, I thought. And, on top of my own freedom, I believed that both Darach and Alex were safe… at the moment, at least.

But now there was a big part of me that was bowed down by the thought that nothing here could ever be the same again…in particular, that these two lads, the two most treasured men in my little world, were going to be having to watch their backs for a very long time to come. What would be the future for us all in this special place? Was this idyllic life of ours on our beautiful Antrim coast going to be tainted for ever by the tragedy of what had happened here in the past year?

Chapter 47

Home-coming

Katie McKay

We were in our beds. The softness and warmth of our own beds. Heavenly, after clinging together against the chill of the nights on the board-hard floor of our draughty kirk for the past months.

We were in our own beds, but we felt a taint of contamination. The sanctity of our home had been violated by those men who had used our house during the siege. They had slept in our beds, fouled the place, and made use of our kitchen ware. To be fair to them, everything was still intact; we found no breakages, but the cleaning of everything took us hours on that first day of freedom. There was nothing left in the house that we could have eaten, so our hunger continued. Not one of our stock had survived the occupation of our farmstead. Even our donkey was gone, and Alice's lamb. Our kitchen felt so empty without the animals. It was easy to imagine that, our farm being closest to the scene of the siege, our stock had been slaughtered over time to feed the attackers. This was a huge blow to us of course, but as my mother said, "Look, we have survived. We will be able to get more animals eventually." Connie had gone rummaging in vain around the fields and the shore for food. Anyhow, our stomachs were not ready for substantial food. The taste of the few limpets she found among the rocks seemed tainted by a bitter remembrance.

Aye, we were in our beds, but not yet asleep, worried for our men, afraid perhaps that when we awoke again we would still be captive, that this freedom had all been an illusion. We were almost too tired to sleep. So many strange thoughts crowded through our minds. The present was being distorted through the eyes of the past, as if we were seeing this new life through a rain shower.

Our conversations had, in a similar way, been very stilted. Thoughts were slow, words were even slower. How did you begin to understand what we had been through? There was a lingering grief about those we had lost, but a grief also for ourselves at the loss of our innocence, our trust in other people. This was a silent emotion in us all, I think.

So, after that first day of anti-climactic freedom, we were trying to get to sleep.

At first I thought that what I heard was a door rattling, or maybe some timber falling over in the yard. The wind had got up. I paid little attention.

Then it happened again, a little bit louder. I heard mammy stir in the bed next door. I looked to my left and, even in the gloom of the room, I could see that Connie's eyes were open.

"What is that noise?" she whispered.

"Nothing," I said.

But the third time it definitely was not nothing. The rattle was distinct. Somebody was trying our door, trying to break in. My heart seemed to jump into my mouth. 'Not again,' I thought. 'Haven't we suffered enough?'

I heard mammy get out of bed. I did too, just in support of her. We went together to the door.

"Is there somebody there?" she said, her voice a quiver of apprehension.

"It's me mammy!"

We looked at each other. Disbelief, shock and delight in that glance, and then a fumbling to open the barred door.

Our Alex stood there. It was either him or his ghost, I wasn't sure which. But in a second he was in my mother's arms, and reaching out past her for me. His arms were strong. He was no ghost. He was alive and well…and he was home.

Mammy started babbling, talking and crying at the same time, not making a lot of sense. Connie and Alice came tripping from the corner and joined in the hug. And then Aunt Biddy, laughing and bawling her head off at the same time.

"You are a sight for sore eyes!" she cried. "I thought you were deed. I dreamed you were deed; I never toul a sowl you were deed, though, but I really dreamed it. But now you're back to life. It's a miracle!"

Alex still hadn't said anything. He pulled himself away from Biddy's clutches after a bit. Alice was jigging up and down as if she'd been given a lovely red apple all to herself. I don't think I'd ever seen her so happy.

"Where have you been, son? Where have you come from?" my mother asked, taking his hand. Lord above but he looked like a different fellow, now that I got time to stare at him properly. Far less burly of himself, his freckles seeming more spaced out on the paleness of his face. I had never seen his hair so long and straggly. He looked like he had been through a lot of hardship.

He still hadn't said a word. It was almost as if he'd been struck dumb by some illness. There was a brokenness in him that almost scared me. That look of resignation in his eyes, a melancholy that bordered on despair. Then he spoke.

"I am glad to be home," he said, quite formally, quite detached. "You have no idea how glad. I have seen too much…" There he stopped.

My heart was heavy for him, and instinctively I went forward to hug him again. Half-way through the embrace he sort of pushed me out from him, but still held me by the shoulders, looking intensely at me.

"Katie," he said slowly, thoughtfully, "I am sorry. It has been so good to be home and see you all that I forgot to tell you…."

'Oh no, no, no!' was my first reaction. Something had happened to Darach. Dread rose in me like a wave surging through a gap in the shore-rocks. Alex saw my reaction.

"No, no, it's not bad news," he said. "I was to tell you to step outside."

"Step outside?" I said, completely confused. Had my brother gone crazy?

"Go on," he said. "Step outside. It's alright."

Everyone was silent, as baffled as me. I took one step towards the door, then seemed to freeze in doubt.

"Come on, sister," Alex said, taking me by the arm and gentling me towards the door. I stopped again.

He pushed me on out into the summer night air. A tall, dark shape stepped forward to me from the shadows of our barn.

I heard, "It's just me, Katie," and I found myself instantly wrapped up in the strong, hungry arms of my lover.

"Darach! Darach! Darach!" I cried.

"My Katie," he said. "How I have looked forward to this moment."

He wasn't alone in that.

What a feeling, just to be held again, kissed again, loved again!

We stood outside under the night stars for ages. The only sounds were the faint murmur of conversation from inside our kitchen, and a sleepy-sounding owl hooting from the direction of the hills.

We said little to each other; this was a re-melding of two separated souls, an intense physical reuniting, the passion between us just about being kept decent. The words would come later…and they did.

"Let me look at your eyes," he said, stepping back briefly, studying me closely.

"What are you doing," I asked, impatient for the firm strength of his body on mine.

"I had this fear," he said.

"What fear?"

"Your eyes have always had a great humour in them," he said. "Ever since the first time I saw you…your eyes had this green glint of laughter in them. I suppose I was worried that everything that has happened would have dampened it."

"Well, what do you see?" I said, knowing full well that my eyes have never been more full of joy than at that particular moment. He stared down into them.

"I see the stars reflected in them for a start," he laughed, pulling me tightly against him again. His hands were everywhere on me then... as hungry as I was.

"Am I too thin and boney for you now?" I gasped, breathless.

"Too thin?" he laughed. "You're just so perfect, Katie. I have no words."

After a while my mother, God bless her, came out to us. We disentangled quickly, though he did still hold on to my hand.

"What are you keeping this poor lad standing out in the cold for, Katie? Bring him in to the kitchen," she said.

It was a lovely moment, one of acceptance and generosity from my mother. Shyly, he followed me in.

Aunt Biddy was embarrassingly delighted to see Darach again, fawning over him like a long-lost cat.

"Just let the fellow be, Aunt Biddy," Connie said laughing. "You'll scare him off and Katie will never forgive you."

My mother came from the bedroom, a bottle in her hand, full to the neck of an amber liquid. I had never seen my mother holding a bottle of whiskey, not once in my entire life. She saw the astonishment on our faces.

"No better time to open this," she said. "It's the bottle your uncle Donald brought us from Islay. I've kept it hidden all these years. Would anybody like a wee dram? You two deserve it after all you've been through; maybe we all do. Biddy, reach me a cup or two."

Biddy obliged, and a few cups got passed around between us all, all except Alice.

"You walked from Ballycastle tonight?" I asked Darach and Alex. "What happened to *Liath*?"

"*Liath* is still in Hugh MacNeill's stables," he said. "Alex's horse is at Bonamargy. We can let Mr Stewart know where they are later. It is far too dangerous for us to be caught on those horses at the minute."

"Why dangerous?" I asked, a bit naively.

"Well, it's just that...if certain people found me on Stewart's horse that would be the end of me."

"How could that be?" I asked. This sounded far-fetched.

"It's true," Darach said. "I am associated with that horse. I can't afford to be seen on it again, not now. I can't afford to get caught by my own side, not after being a messenger for the Protestant captains. There are still angry Irish prowling around. It is a very dangerous time."

Alex joined in. "You have no idea how dangerous it is for him," he said. "If they ever found out that Darach was helping Father McGlaim to feed you all in the kirk he would be killed, make no mistake about that."

"You were helping Father McGlaim?" My mother's voice choked with emotion as she spoke.

"Not really...I just..."

Alex interrupted him at once. "Let me tell you, for Darach will play it down, as usual. The priest told me it was Darach's plan, or his idea."

Darach protested and shook his head.

"The priest wouldn't have been lying to me, would he? And you helped him bring the water every time he came. Father McGlaim did the handover, but Darach was as much a part of it as him."

"That is not the case," Darach insisted. "He took the real risk. I hid in the hills while he put his life on the line. I watched from behind a tree as they arrested him and dragged him away. I am no hero, I am a coward. I should have tried to save him."

"You couldn't have saved him," I told him, taking his hand again. It wasn't hard to sense his despair at what he had witnessed. "Inside the kirk we heard it all happen. You would have been in the same trouble as him. Maybe more, for at least he was a religious man."

"He was a saint," Darach said. "Now he may be dead."

"Nobody knows that for sure," Alex told him. "They may have spared him, maybe locked him up in Kenbane Castle or somewhere."

"Maybe," Darach said.

My mother joined in. "What he did for us will never be forgotten, and what you did as well, Darach. If he is dead, at least he died trying to help us. It was very brave and very kind."

"Alex did a very brave thing as well," Darach said. "He took on a very difficult job and he did it..."

Alex interrupted again. "I only did my duty. I took a message. We aren't allowed to say where. If that got out my life would be in danger too. So," he said with a half-smile, "you are looking at a pair of on-the-run renegades here. Him especially. He will be seen as a traitor to his own side, and at the same time he is an O'Cahan. So he won't be safe from our Protestant neighbours either."

The seriousness of Darach's dilemma was just starting to dawn on me. My Darach a renegade! And under suspicion from both sides. I suppose that was why they had come tonight, under cover of darkness. Where was he going to go now, I began to wonder. If it was going to be so important to hide, where could he hide? There were no obvious safe places in our area.

We talked on into the wee small hours of the morning. The conversation was flowing, the stories, and the tales of the tragedies of the past months. The whiskey flowed as well and, as it did, I sat in my own home kitchen with the arm of my lover around my waist. It felt like he couldn't let me stray from his side, and it was wonderful. But at one point he did ask me about Kate, and I took him to her crib at the foot of mammy's bed. He stood and looked down at her for a good while, and I wondered what was going through his head.

"Katie," he said eventually, "what do you feel about all this?"

"All what?" I asked...but I knew.

"About this child? About me landing her in on you and your mother without even a warning? Without asking?"

I was silent for a bit. Could I open up my heart to him completely, tell him my doubts, my secret fears? This was not a good time. He had just materialised back in my life. But maybe there would never be a better time. I had to know, to know everything.

"Come on, tell me what you are thinking," he said. "I need to know. It will be alright. Tell me."

His arm was around me. My head was against his chest. I took courage and opened my mouth.

"Nellie," I said. "Who was this Nellie?"

"She was a complete stranger. She just walked up to us, in the square in Coleraine."

"You didn't know her.... before?"

"I didn't."

"You never saw her before?"

"Never saw her in my life."

"What was she like?"

"She was the skinniest girl I ever saw. Pathetic. Big round eyes. She'd have been nice at some stage, but she was like a corpse walking."

"What did she want?"

"She wanted food. Food for her and her baby, she said."

"Is that all?" I asked.

"No, it's not exactly all. She offered herself...to all three of us. Alex, Bruce and me. If only we could get food for her."

Oh Lord. This was what I feared.

"What did Alex and Bruce do?"

"Well...they listened to her. They were as shocked as I was."

"But you were the only one who went and got food for her?" My voice was cracking with some emotion I hadn't felt before.

"I was," he said. "I just felt somebody had to do something for her. Nobody else seemed to be wanting to help. So, I went and found some eggs and a hen..."

"And took it to her...somewhere? How did you find her in a big place like that, with all those people?"

"She had told us where her hovel was. Out by the river. I had to ask as well. It was very dark."

"So you found her and..."

"I found her. I got the eggs cooked and she ate one. I left the hen for her to cook the next day."

"And before you left...?"

"Before I left... what?" he asked.

294

My heart was quaking.

"Before you left… did you….did you do anything…?"

Darach tried to draw me into his arms.

"Aye, I touched her, Katie. She fell asleep as soon as she had eaten and I touched her. I stroked her hair."

"You stroked her hair? Darach…please no, don't tell me…"

"Listen to me, Katie. I stroked her hair as a father would… as her mother should have been stroking her hair. The girl had been abandoned by everybody who was supposed to love her. By her Presbyterian hypocrite of a father, by her mother who should have been standing up for her, by the filthy Catholic married man who had made her pregnant. The least I could do, as a complete stranger, but as a fellow human being, was to stroke her hair."

I could say nothing. I was fighting with the mixed emotions of possessive jealousy and of admiration for my man. I wanted one to go away and leave the other one in peace.

"I love you, Darach; it's just that I don't want to share you with anyone," I told him.

"And you don't have to share me with anyone, not as your lover, not as your husband," he said. "But together we have to share ourselves with whoever needs us. Surely we've learned from Father McGlaim?"

"I understand that," I said. "But I need to ask you one more thing."

"Go on."

"What happened between you that you felt you had to promise to look after her child?"

He thought about this. "What happened was that she died," he said simply. "Just picture this, Katie. The girl is lying cold and dead on her rickle of a bed. Starved to death in christian Coleraine. The child is crying. It's alone in the world. You know…alone. There is nobody who knows her. Nobody to love her. To walk away would have been the same as picking her up and throwing her into the river. So what else could I do? I thought of taking her to John and Eilish, but then I thought my folks, especially the girls, would love to rear her. But they'd been hunted from their home. So I brought her to you."

"There's only one thing wrong with what you did," I told him.

"What's that?"

"You should have thought of bringing her to me first."

This pleased him, and we stood in intimate closeness for a bit. Then a further shock to me. Darach had been thinking up some other ideas.

"Aye, we have to look after her, Katie, and we have to look after each other. The trouble is …I don't think we can do it here in Antrim."

I let this sink in. "What are you telling me?"

"I think we have to leave, do you not think so?"

This was a lightening bolt. A massive thing to take in. This was going to take a lot of thinking through. I couldn't reply, not straight off like that. I just squeezed his arm, really hard…to let him know this was a big issue.

I didn't say another word about it.

When we came back in my mother had a little speech to make.

"Darach," she said, "you have nowhere to go where you'll be totally safe. Ballycastle won't be safe, not now with the priest gone and no-one to give you protection. Your folks have had to leave Straid. Dunseverick Castle is going to be over-run sooner or later by our side. Dunluce will never be the same safe haven again for you, not now that the village is burned to the ground. Where can you go?"

"I'm not sure, Mrs McKay," he said with a rueful look. "I need to think of a place to hide for a while till things settle down. Somewhere safe, away from both sides. The only idea I have is to find a cave somewhere along the coast. Over beyond Dunluce we have a few deep caves, at the White Rocks. I think you have some here as well, down near the harbour below. Do you think I'd be safe there?"

Alex shook his head. "Everybody knows about those caves," he said. "Around here, anybody who is trying to hide away for a while heads into those caves. That's the worst place to go. Once you are in there you are trapped."

Darach went silent for a bit and we waited. "I just don't know where to be going," he said.

"Well, until you have a better idea you can stay here," my mother said.

My heart leapt with delight. Darach hiding in our house? How I loved my good mother. Connie was grinning, her eyes twinkling playfully at me like candles in a distant window.

Darach was speechless. Alex helped him out.

"We've just talked about this," he said. "We can hide you. You probably need to stay inside during the day, just go out at night."

"You are very kind," Darach said eventually, "but are you sure you have room? What about sleeping? Do you have a barn I can use?"

"We will think of something," my mother said.

"I'll try and think of something too," Aunt Biddy joined in and, whether it was the whiskey or just the innocent look on poor Biddy's leathery old face, in seconds we were all falling about the kitchen in one of those laughing fits that releases the tension and just refuses to be quenched. That night none of us went to our beds. Every single one of us slept where we were, on a few sheepskins and well-dried rushes, cuddled in against each other in a slightly drunken bond of family love.

It was a night that neither Darach or I will ever forget. Our first night together, in each other's arms, on the floor of my mother's kitchen, surrounded by my family.

Chapter 48

Future Plans

Darach O'Cahan

Hiding away in the McKay home, and sleeping in their outhouse, is not what I want to be doing. I would far rather be catching fish out in the bay with Alex. He seems to have turned a corner since he got home. There is a fresh lease of life about him. He's full of delight at the amount of herring and mackerel he has been bringing up from the harbour everyday. The family is being well fed now. This nourishment is just what they have needed. How I would love to be part of that. Instead I am a trapped fugitive, watching dust dancing in shafts of sunlight, thinking back over the events of the past year.

The one creative thing I have been able to do is carve a play-doll for Kate from an old log that I found in a dark corner of the barn. Biddy finished it off with a piece of material fashioned into a simple garment. Kate is delighted, her wee eyes sparkling at what might be her first ever plaything.

Katie and Kate are much improved. Their strength is gradually returning. It is so good to be with them, but most of my time is spent indoors, being very careful not to be seen by anyone in the community. You never know who is about, or what might happen. Only late at night do Katie and I get to walk outside. I love these times of courtship in the moonlight. But underneath it all I am discontent. I wonder how long this seclusion must go on for. When will it be alright for me to wander about the area again? How will I know when it is safe to go back to Dunluce? What might life be like there now, with the village in ruins and John and Eilish no longer having their own place? Will I ever be able to go back to harp-making as before?

This idyllic strip of coastline is where I was born and reared; I know its legends, its secret stories and moods; it is in my blood and my bones. From the White Rocks and Portrush in the west to Fairhead and Ballycastle in the east is my landscape; I know every bay and harbour, every cliff and strand, every bog and grove. How intensely I resent this feeling of this my place being unsafe, of being not 'at home' in my own homeland.

But I also know how dangerous it will be to remain here with Katie, to try to make a safe life together in this caldron of distrust, hate and revenge. Our conversations about the future have become quite intense. I have sometimes involved Alex as well, just for his perspective and wisdom as a friend, as Katie's protector. I sense that he is now accepting that Katie and I will be together. This, regardless of his strongly held religious convictions and his loyalty to the normal expectations of his 'clan', for want of a better word. I appreciate that this is a big step for him, as it will be for his mother when we have a clearer plan for our future.

My growing conviction is that it can't be a future here in Ulster.

It is after midnight, certainly well after the hour when Katie and I might be expected to be in our separate beds, but it is the safest time to be together. Nobody else with any sense of propriety will be out at this hour. The moon hangs above Knocksoughey Hill to the southeast. Tonight it is at its fullest, casting deep shadows where the white cliffs fall to meet a narrow bed of near-horizontal rocks by the sea. We walk down the winding lane towards the harbour, the sweet fragrance of honeysuckle wafting to us from the hedgerows. I pick some strands and twine them around Katie's neck. These have to be sniffed, of course… over and over again, and from very close range. She knows what I am doing and teasingly pushes me away.

"Just wait," she tells me.

We sit together on a grassy bank beyond the harbour, listening to the shushing sound of low waves breaking against the shore. The light of the sea is incredible, a luminous, silvery flatness stretching away to an invisible horizon. Silence grows between us. Our conversation has reached an inconclusive impasse, it seems. Katie is a home bird, pure and simple.

"I am already in hiding," I tell her again. "I fear that it will always be like this, that either you or I will always be having to shield ourselves from the opposite side. That is no way to be living, constantly in suspicion and worry. There has to be another way, another place."

"Don't you think it will pass, Darach? When all this dies down?"

"But that's the point. When will it ever die down? This could go on for years. Now that this General Munro has arrived from Scotland with his Protestant army he will beat my people into submission. He already is; his soldiers are brutal beyond belief, and that's according to Alex. How long is our submission going to last? All Munro will do is create a new generation of bitterness and before too many years have passed a new rising takes place. It is like a child swinging on a rope. Push it one way and it will always swing back to the other. The thing will just keep repeating itself."

"But surely it doesn't have to, Darach? You have shown the way, you and Father McGlaim…by just being decent. Those kind things you did are far more important than all the killing and burning, do you not think?"

I consider this. I don't see any comparison; the import of what we did is a thousand times outweighed by the vileness of the conflict.

"I doubt it," I tell her.

"Time will pass. The river flows on. People will forgive and forget."

I wish I could believe her.

"Katie, this river," I say. "We will live our lives down-stream from all these violent events. The poison of what has happened in this rising will pollute the river for many generations to come. The waters will be stirred by the re-telling of myths, and the eddies will continue. Victories and defeats will become part of our tribal memories. The battles will be fought over and over again, until someone works out a way for the two sides to live together without celebration of victory, or without the memory of defeat."

She is silent after this pessimistic homily, maybe feeling defeated herself by my wordiness. But I plough on.

"For you and me, and for our children, the only solution is to leave them to it. We need to find our own source of water at some spring or stream that hasn't been tainted. Put down our roots beside it."

She is quiet again for a bit. I stand up to skip a few flat pebbles, creating patterns of expanding ripple-circles on the glassy surface of the sea. Katie comes behind me. She slips her arm around my waist.

"Where are we going to find this spring?" she says.

"I have no idea. There must be somewhere…"

We say no more about it, as I sense Katie's despair. I turn to her, hold her tightly, stroke her hair. She turns a solemn face into my shoulder.

"We will be alright," she tells me. "Long as we have each other."

"We will," I say, "and for as long as we possibly can make it last."

We walk back to her home very slowly and drag ourselves apart towards our separate beds. This is getting harder and taking longer every time, the passion between us growing nightly, fighting more and more urgently against our half-hearted attempts to suppress it.

"Soon, Katie," I say. "Very soon."

"I hope so," she says. "Otherwise I might die of this."

Strangely, the next day her brother wants to talk to me about our dilemma. He makes the same point as myself, but from a slightly different perspective. He brings some fried *glashan* out to me in my barn hide-out. We spend a while just recounting some of the barbarity we had witnessed at Portnaw and such places over the past six months. We tell each other of some of the acts of mercy and bravery, as neighbours helped and protected each other in places. These stories give us some comfort and hope, but we both realise that the terrible sights we experienced are so ingrained in our minds that we are reliving them, even as we talk about them.

"The thing is, you cannot sweep all these lost lives under the mat. History doesn't forget. The smell of their rotting bones will rise to our nostrils in every coming generation. We'll always be reminded of the savagery."

"What you say is true, Alex," I reply, "and it is the same in my community. What we have endured as Irish people, as the dispossessed in our own land…those feelings will not go away, no matter how many battles we fight, and how many victories we win."

"So…you and Katie?" he says. "What can you do? I don't see any future for you together in this place."

"My point as well," I tell him.

Then we sit in a depressed silence together.

As it happens, it is Mrs McKay who, whether inadvertently or consciously, provides us with a glimmer of light. I suspect that Alex has had a conversation with his mother about our plight. She brings Katie out by the hand to the barn not long before nightfall. I look at Katie as she arrives; she seems a bit nervous, not to say mystified, by her mother's behaviour.

"Sit there beside him," Mrs McKay commands with a sweet authority.

'Oh dear! This doesn't sound good,' I think as Katie comes to me, almost reluctantly. It all feels really awkward between us.

"I have been giving this a lot of thought," her mother says. "This predicament you two are in. It's not an easy path to be walking, all this uncertainty. I hate to see you both unhappy like this. Your father would say the same, Katie. When he and I started walking out together we had similar problems. It wasn't religion, it was family. Who was getting what and all that kind of thing. We had to make up our minds. Were we going to be brave and face it, or were we going to go our separate ways? Well, as you know, Katie, we took the brave road…otherwise you wouldn't be here. It wasn't easy. We had to say 'Farewell' to our family and friends in Islay and move over here. There was nothing for us in Port Ellen. Here we had a chance."

She pauses, as if to reflect, or gather strength for what she wants to say next.

"I know all this, mammy," Katie says. "But it's no use for Darach and me, is it? It's not the same. There's no Archibald Stewart this time, nobody sending for tenants in some happy land."

"Katie, it's maybe not the same, but the principle is the same. Look, there's a hundred and one things against you and Darach marrying. Religion is only one of them. As you know, I was against it at the start. Reverend Blare will be dead set against it. You would have been marrying Darach over my dead body right up until I learned what a good man you have got here. So I am going to say something to you now…

and I am very sure your father would be saying the same thing if he was here, and if he knew all that Darach has done for us in this family…"

She pauses again, stifling something like a dry cough in her throat. She takes Katie's hand tenderly.

"You know, Katie, how much you mean to me. I love you as much as any mother loves her first-born. If we were in a wedding ceremony in our kirk the vicar would be asking, 'Who giveth this woman to be wed?' Well, I am saying, 'I do.' I am giving you to Darach, for your father isn't here to do it. Alex agrees with me too. You two are meant to be together, it is as plain as the nose on your face."

I am really moved by this. I start to make a sort-of thank-you speech but Mrs McKay hushes me.

"I am not finished yet, son," she says.

'Son?' I think. Lovely.

"You have been wondering where you can go to escape the problems of this place. I think I have the answer…or at least one answer."

Katie and I look at each other.

"Go on," Katie says, her eyes widening by the second.

"I think you and Darach would feel a lot safer if you moved to Islay."

"Islay? Why Islay?" Katie looks bewildered.

"Because it is my home place," Mrs McKay says. "Islay is a lovely place. When we left there, the farm that your father should have inherited was left to your uncle, Donald. You met him at Ballycastle, and he came here after your daddy died, remember?"

"I do, but what has he got to do with this?" Katie says.

"Well, he and his wife never had any children. He has a farm there, a business as well. Darach might be able to get a job with him…if you were able to explain everything to him. He would remember you."

Katie looks at me, wondering what I am thinking. I am thinking a score of thoughts all at one time; chiefly I am thinking that Katie's mother is some lady, even wanting to help us and come up with such ideas for us; I am also thinking that the last thing I want to be doing for the rest of my life is farming on the backside of some mountain in Islay.

"What is this business he has?" Katie asks.

"As far as I know he is an undertaker," Mrs McKay says.

This is not getting any better, I am thinking. Burying people sounds even less appealing than farming. Cows and corpses! Not my calling at all. I cannot see myself doing either of these things. What about this huge drive I have to be working with wood, especially to be making harps? Would that be possible in Islay? Do they even have the trees, the right type of wood for me to use? Would there be many people interested enough to buy a harp from me? I know nothing about the place, nor about the people and their traditions.

But Mrs McKay isn't finished yet. This brother-in-law of hers must have built up a small empire. "And," she adds with a tantalising incline of her head, "he has a carpentry business. Maybe Darach could work for him; maybe even take it over from him in the future."

Carpentry? Great! So you would think there must be timber about the place. Katie and I just stare at each other. It is hard to know what to say. I don't want to appear immediately enthusiastic in case the whole thing is not to Katie's liking. I am trying to judge her reaction, and I sense that she is doing exactly the same. I see the question in her eyes. I turn back to Mrs McKay.

"Thank you very much for this," I say. I don't have to pretend appreciation. "Will you let us think about it? It sounds a very interesting solution."

"What about us getting married, mammy?" Katie asks. "We want to be wed. Do you think that is possible over there?"

"I have no idea, Katie, but it may be a lot easier there than if you were to stay here. They haven't had the same kind of troubles that we have had in Ulster. Aye, there's the two religions, but at least yous wouldn't have to be looking over your shoulders for the rest of your lives, for the folk won't know you or what your background is. We could ask Donald to try and help with that problem as well. As an undertaker, he is bound to know the clergy, which ones might be willing to marry the two of you."

Goodness, I am thinking, she has put a lot of thought into all this. She is very convincing. It sounds like the most hopeful plan we have had to think about so far.

"Would you not mind me going away, mammy? Would you not prefer us to be still around Ballintoy?" Katie asks.

"Of course I would mind," she replies, "but I would mind even more if you lost each other and had to live with a broken heart, a broken dream."

"We could come and see you every year at the Lammas Fair," Katie says.

I am beginning to see her mind coming around to this notion. We talk about the idea most of that evening on our moonlit dander. The sea has got up a bit tonight; the crash of the breaking waves mingles with the echoing swish of rattling pebbles. It is a mild night and the draw of the privacy of the sand-hills is hard to resist, but we keep walking, talking. There is so much to talk about.

"We would need some sort of letter, some recommendation from an adult," Katie says. "Someone who knows us both. Just so my uncle doesn't think we have eloped together."

"Now there's an idea. Why didn't you mention that to me before?"

"What, the letter or eloping?" Katie says. "I would have, but I thought you were far too honourable."

"You could talk me into it fairly easily," I respond. "But this letter? Who is there who knows both of us, someone who can write?"

"Maybe Mr Stewart? We have both worked for him, haven't we?"

"Great idea," I say. "He is the man. I think he likes me; certainly he trusted me enough to send me on some dangerous errands. Do you think you and your mum could go and beg him to give us a reference….and an explanation of our plight?"

"Darach! Mammy would do anything for you. She's near as smitten as me!"

"Sure why wouldn't she be?" I tease.

Her next question is one I have been pondering.

"What will we do for money?"

"I have been wondering that as well. We will need enough to pay a boatman. And enough to see us through until I can earn."

"I don't think we can ask my mother for any," Katie says, "not after the year we have had. I have no idea how she is going to scrape enough together for our rent to Archibald Stewart. Maybe he will waive our dues for a year."

"I wasn't thinking of asking your mother," I tell her. "I don't really have any money myself. I did have, but it will be lost now after the fire in Dunluce. Unless John rescued it for me. It was only a few shilling anyhow. I must go to them as soon as I possibly can, just to see how they are."

"Where are they staying now?"

"I am not entirely sure. Hopefully still in the grounds of the castle until this trouble dies down a bit, if the Earl has been generous."

"Would the Earl not be generous to you? Could you not tell him your situation and ask him for some money? After all, you worked for him. I'm sure you didn't get much by way of wages from him," Katie says.

Ask the Earl for money? A strange notion. I have been waiting for the Earl to… Suddenly I know exactly how I am going to get some money.

"Katie," I say, "you are a genius. I am going to talk to the Earl and he is going to give me…maybe five pounds."

She turns to me where I have stopped short on the sand. Little flickers of pale moonlight in the green of her wide eyes; a light gust of sea-breeze sweeps her long hair back from her face, pushes her clothing against the tantalising shape of her nubile figure. She is unbelievably attractive tonight, this girl, and she is mine, all mine…as much as I am hers. I cannot believe how much I am enthralled by her

"He is going to give you five pounds? How can you be so sure?"

"Because he never paid me for the harp I made for him and the countess. He still owes me. I never liked to go back and pester him for the money because I was working there and I didn't want to get myself into his bad books by being too brash. But he does owe me, and he knows it."

Katie is laughing at me now. "You know how to put a smile on a girl's face. All this time you have been owed five pounds and you had forgotten about it? I will have to start looking after your finances, Mr O'Cahan. Are there many other creditors out there with money owing to you?"

"Not that I can recall," I tell her. "But at least now I know where we can get the cash to pay our boatman. I just have to pick up the courage to travel to Dunluce and ask the Earl."

"Right," she says, far too jovially, "and I have to persuade my mother to go and get a letter from Archibald Stewart, then we can be on our way."

"Are you sure you want to do this, Katie? It won't be easy leaving your folks. We can wait for a while to see what way things turn out here, if you like. I don't want to force you to do something that you will regret later."

"And keep you in hiding for God knows how long? No Darach. I want to be with you in the open, I want to be able to walk down the road holding your hand with pride, not wondering if the person coming towards us is a rebel coming to take revenge on you for being Stewart's man, or for helping Father McGlaim to feed us. I don't want some embittered Presbyterian woman spitting on my child because it is of a Catholic father. I want us to live as man and wife, without all those kinds of worries. I want to bring up Kate and rear our own wains in a normal sort of place. Maybe someday we will be able to come back here…if this place can just get over its anger. It would be nice to do that, wouldn't it? But for now, I want to be with you, soon married… and always together.

"Katie," I tell her, "you have never spoken more sense."

Chapter 49

Farewell Dunluce

Darach O'Cahan

I am nervous about this journey from Ballintoy to Dunluce. That may seem strange, given the perilous nature of the journeys I have undertaken over the past six months. The difference is, I suppose, that now I am out on my own little venture. I do not have the legitimacy of being on a mission for either Colonel Archibald Stewart or Sir James McDonnell. Those messages gave me cover, where now I am feeling exposed, vulnerable.

I have no idea who is abroad in the neighbourhood. I would not want to encounter any of my cousins' soldiers. Neither would I wish to run into some vengeful Scotch settlers, newly freed at Ballintoy. My name alone could get my throat slit before I had time to explain anything.

I have no horse now, so it could take me a long time to walk to Dunluce. I leave early, well before sunrise, so as to cover as much of the distance as possible before people are up and about. Even then, I am very careful and avoid any settlements. I give a very wide berth to Dunseverick Castle. It is possible that my parents are still taking refuge there, but I dare not risk showing my face. I will try to find them later.

The morning sun is just peeking over the mound of Kintyre behind me as I reach the eastern end of the Causeway cliff path. I trudge along the pebble-strewn strand at Runkerry towards the river Bush, its peaty, brown water gurgling to the ocean over a deep bed of rounded stones. Crossing the rickety wooden bridge there I climb up the slope and pass two remarkable circular earthworks at Lissandubh, mysterious remnants of a long-forgotten age. Thankfully the tiny fishing village of Portballintrae seems still and asleep; I have only another two miles to walk to Dunluce.

It is still early when I reach the Castle, not long after what would be normal breakfast time. How relieved I am to see that the surrounding area is so much more peaceful than during the earlier attack. The Irish troops and Scottish gallowglasses seem to have fled. I have encountered no strangers on my journey, and no soldiers of any kind. My first instinct is to look to my former home. The charred remains of Dunluce village are a sad reminder of the debacle that I witnessed on my last visit here.

As I arrive at the gate before the Castle, however, I am surprised to see a good deal of activity. Servants, male and female, are scurrying around, clearly engaged in some busyness. I am well known here so I am waved through by the guards.

It does not take me many minutes to find John and Eilish McSparran in the outer ward. Our reunion is full of emotion; I have not seen them since leaving Dunluce with those three regiments, almost six months ago, although to be honest it does seem a far longer time. After the hugs and, in Eilish's case, the tears, the questions begin. They want to know about what has been happening in the places I have seen. I have questions concerning the reason for this activity in the castle today. I can tell, however, that John is under pressure to start working again at whatever task he has been doing, Eilish as well.

"Look," he says, "we are very busy here, but if you could see your way to join in and help we could talk as we work."

"Good plan," I say. "I can do anything you want."

"Great," he replies. "We are making trestle tables, would you believe. Eilish is having to help me, for the last apprentice I had deserted us and may have forgotten everything I ever taught him."

I catch the twinkle in John's ageing eyes. "Not at all," I tell them, "and he can't wait to get his hands on a nice length of oak again."

In a matter of minutes, I am comfortably back into the old routine of carpentry with John, measuring, sawing, planing, hammering, and all the time answering questions from him and Eilish. I am especially pleased that they ask about Katie, and I explain to them the dilemma of our future. I mention the possibility of Islay; John surprises me by being very positive about the idea of emigrating….actually, of emigrating to a place even further away.

"Have you heard of the American Colonies? A place called Virginia…away on the other side of the world?"

"I have," I tell him, "but if Katie is finding it difficult enough to think of moving to an island that is within sight of Antrim I don't think she will be too interested in crossing an ocean. I think we can only consider doing it because we can be back once every year to see her mother. Anyhow, we have no money, so where could we ever hope to get the fare for a place like America? I am hoping to ask the Earl today if he could pay me the money he was supposed to give me for the harp. It's the only way I have to pay a boatman to take us to Islay. Is he available, do you think?"

Eilish and John look at each other. "This might not be the best time to be bothering him with that sort of thing," Eilish says. "It's a very busy sort of day here."

"Aye, I can see that," I say. "What is all the bustle about? What are we making trestle tables for?"

"Well, if all goes to the Earl's plan, this could be a very historic day in Dunluce. What we were told is that the Earl has invited a very important Scotsman, a General Munro, to come to the Castle. It's all about some peace plan that Lord Antrim wants to negotiate with the Crown. He doesn't want any more fighting; that's why he got rid of McColla, and your uncle Gilladubh, and Tirlough Óge and the rest of them."

"He got rid of Alaster McColla?" I cannot imagine how he did that.

"Aye, and Sir James as well."

"The two McDonnells are gone? How did he get rid of them?"

"Don't ask me that, son, for I wouldn't know the answer," John confesses. "But whatever he did the pair of them aren't to be seen or heard around here any more. They have fled."

I am a bit amazed by this news. The great warrior Alaster McColla, the bane of my life a few months ago with his sneering and bullying.... now fled like a coward?

"Have you any idea where they have gone? Are you sure they are not still prowling around this neighbourhood?" I ask selfishly. I would rather they had disappeared to Donegal or somewhere...I would feel safer. At the same time I have a small thrill of satisfaction somewhere in me that I have survived in this conflict longer than the big persecuting Scotsman.

"From what I gather," John says, "some of them have gone to take refuge in the Dowager's Castle in Ballycastle, but others have fled into O'Cahan country, across the Bann, trying to get as far away from Munro as possible."

"So, this Munro is coming here tonight?"

"He is, as far as we know. Hence the rush for these tables. Remember he sent his best tables away to England. Munro will have a big entourage of men with him. The Earl wants a massive feast. He's had men out fishing all day for the last while, both in the Bann and the Bush...some even out in the bay. And he wants singing and dancing, and the best of entertainment. It is to be a big night to impress this General. Where he is going to get the players and singers and dancers now I don't know. So many have left and gone away to Scotland."

How fortunate I am, I think, to be right in the middle of yet another pivotal episode of history. Imagine! A possible peace settlement being agreed in the castle tonight and here I am making tables for the feast. More than that....

"John," I say, as a fresh idea begins to take shape in my mind, "do you think I should go in to the Earl and volunteer to play the harp for this General?"

Eilish grins with enthusiasm. She puts both her hands on my shoulders. John laughs happily at my audacity.

"A great idea," Eilish says. "He will be delighted, I am sure...and then you can ask him for the money. He won't be able to refuse you."

Exactly what I was thinking too. I work hard until Eilish brings us some vittles from the cook-house. As I finish the oaten bread and mackerel, I suggest to John that now might be a good time to go in to the Manor House, to try to see Lord Antrim.

"He'll be in good humour after his lunch," I tell them. "Anyhow, he can only refuse, and no harm is done."

"Go on with you then," John agrees. "He'll not be fit to say 'No' to that silver tongue of yours."

Soon after I am face to face with the most senior Gaelic Over-Lord in all Ulster, and I find myself very gratified that he remembers me by name…well, surname at least. We have only ever met on those occasions when discussing the harp he had requested, and then only briefly. What a mind he must have that, after all the places he has travelled and the important people he has encountered, he should remember a mere peasant like me. He stands tall and impressive in a new wig, long and curly, his hand resting on the intricately carved post at the bottom of his grand staircase, one foot on the first step, the other on the floor. It is like he is posing for another painting.

"O'Cahan, if my memory serves me right? The maker of harps of unique quality; where have you been hiding?"

"Not hiding, my Lord," I stammer. "I have been active as a courier for Mr Stewart of Ballintoy, sir, since the very first engagements of this…"

I stopped, unsure of what name to put on our recent upheavals.

He is about to turn away, disinterested, busy. I have to speak.

"My Lord," I say, "I was wondering if you would like me to play some music for your guests tonight."

The Earl stops short, pauses in mid-step, then spins around. As he does, one of his equerries, Captain Digby, approaches from the main door, a message in his hand for the Earl. He pauses and listens as Lord Antrim addresses me.

"You are a God-send, young man," he beams. "How did you know exactly what was required, and at exactly the most propitious time? Thank you for offering…of course you can. And you shall be handsomely rewarded."

He turns to engage with a slightly impatient Digby. I must continue to strike while the iron is hot.

"Begging your pardon, my Lord," I say, "but just when you mention payment…"

"Yes, speak quickly. I am very occupied just now, as you might expect. What is it?"

"Sir, I am to marry very soon and travel to make a new life in another place. I was wondering if you could see your way to honouring me by paying me the monies owed for the harp that I made for you. I am in fairly immediate need, sir."

"Oh dear, my lad. You choose the most inopportune time to make such a request. Pray patience. Play for me tonight and tomorrow I shall reward you handsomely on both scores, alright? Captain Digby, will you see to that for me? Good-day to you, sir."

He takes the message from his Captain and I no longer exist.

"Thank you, my Lord," I say. "I would need to go and tune the harp now, if that is alright?"

Digby turns and looks at me, agitated and disdainful. He says nothing, just waves me upstairs towards the Great Hall. I climb silently away from them. Behind me I am aware that the Earl is becoming quite excited, whatever his message is. I make my way upstairs to find the swan harp.

It is a deeply satisfying feeling to be with it again. I haven't seen, let alone played, a harp in several months. I run my hand along the frame, stroking its smooth curves, caressing the swan's head. 'Dear God!' I think, 'in another life I made this beautiful carving!' I am conscious of not being able to control a half-smile of pleasure around my lips.

First I wipe some dust off it. I hear myself talking to it, soothingly reassuring, as if it was a favourite spaniel that I had just been reunited with. I am apologising for my long absence.

It will take a while to have it back in tune, I imagine. The tuning key is there, tied loosely to the frame as always. I undo the knot and begin the tuning process. The strings are very far from pitch, the instrument having been silently waiting, impatiently so, I imagine, for many months for someone to play it. As I tune I am reminded of my strange dreams involving this instrument. Eventually I am satisfied that it sounds reasonable. I begin to play an old slow air, twanging the strings with my fingernails. They have become very soft through lack of usage. It is going to be difficult to play later for this General with any gusto or proper feel, I am realising.

As I approach the end of the old Irish melody I hear a very unusual sound.

A trumpet is being played somewhere. Played, or perhaps more accurately, tooted with enthusiasm.

It crosses my mind briefly that the Earl has managed to recruit another musician from somewhere for tonight's festivities....but the longer I listen to this blast of what seems to be quite a military sound I begin to doubt that this is a musician for a concert. Frankly, the sound he is making is more intimidating than anything else. My hands stay on the harp strings, but are silent while I try to understand this trumpeter. As I listen, the racket from outside increases. Feet running, people shouting, horses neighing...a complete change of atmosphere though, from the creative busyness of earlier.

Ah, I think. Maybe this General Munro has arrived early. I go to the bay-window, but I cannot see much from there….just a view of the Earl's back as he hurries with Digby and a few others of his staff from the upper ward towards the gatehouse.

I rush down the staircase and outside to follow. I do not want to miss any of this historic encounter when our great Earl greets his Scottish adversary. As I pass through the gatehouse and start to cross the drawbridge I happen to look up over the heads of the crowd of folk now following Lord Antrim towards the outer gate. What I see gives me a severe shock.

Beyond the castle's outer wall, and ranged along the rise of hills on the other side of the charred and jagged corpse of our village, there seems to be a vast army of kilted soldiers. General Munro has serious intent here. There must be hundreds, maybe thousands of soldiers…and, at first glance they do not look like they are here for a feast, nor for some sweet Irish airs on the harp! Did the Earl know that so many were going to be coming? Had he invited Munro and all his regiments? Why are they here so early in the day when the feast is tonight? I am puzzled.

Ahead of me I sense that the Earl has slowed in his hurry to greet Munro. His head is raised…he is now seeing what I have just seen. I notice a slight hesitation in his step, a momentary pause, but then he strides on again, full of welcoming bluster.

Lord above, I think, as my eye catches sight of two massive cannons, their barrels trained on the outer ward where we are gathered. I hope those are only for show and to impress the Earl.

He has just reached the outer gate.

"You are most welcome, General Munro and gentlemen, to my residence, to the famous Castle of Dunluce."

I move a bit to get a better view of the General. I am tall enough to actually see his face over the other onlookers.

His face!

I have seen softer blocks of Causeway stone…and more handsome ones. This man is not friendly. He is staring at our great Lord Antrim as if he is some low vagabond caught stealing sheep. There is a taunting cruelty in those eyes, in that dry, sarcastic cackle of a laugh.

The Earl looks discomforted but continues. "I hope your journey from Carrick has been a pleasant one, good sir. It will most certainly have whetted your appetites…" Here he falters a little, looking at the huge number of men that he may be promising food to. "We have a great feast laid on for you and…and for some members of your most senior entourage…I am not sure we have enough for all these…"

Munro interrupts.

"Enough sir!" he spits. "Stop your foolish rambling and be silent. We ha'e-nae got all nicht here. I am tae inform you…"

This time, and not to be outdone, Randal does the interrupting.

"I beg your pardon, sir, but your hostile mood and unkind words do you no credit. I have generously invited you to my abode, to dine with me here in Dunluce, all for the purpose of conducting negotiations with you concerning a peace settlement for both Irish and Protestant people in my estate, indeed for all of Ulster. Do not commence, sir, by displaying such absence of courtesy and manners. Now, would you like to follow me to the…"

As he speaks he turns to retrace his steps into the outer ward. I see Munro nod to the two large guards who stand on either side of him. I have never seen such large men move so quickly. The Earl has barely taken two steps when he is grabbed on either side by these soldiers and spun around to face Munro. My Lord splutters and whines, but no more intelligible words make it to my ears for several seconds. Munro fills the air with accusations and arrest warrant pronouncements.

"Randal McDonnell, Earl of Antrim, I hereby place you under arrest. You ha'e been charged wae treason, treason against His Royal Highness, King Charles. You will be taken frae this place tae Carrickfergus where a cell awaits you in the castle dungeon. Your crimes will be investigated and you will be given a proper trial."

"This is an outrageous mistake, General Munro! There must be an error somewhere." Lord Antrim's voice rises and falls, alternating between a pleading tone and an angry one. It squeaks and booms like a poor musician fighting with an unwilling set of pipes. I feel so sorry for him in his ignominy. "King Charles is my very dear friend," he continues. "How could he suspect me of anything other than the greatest devotion and loyalty to his royal person? Treason, you say? In what way have I been treasonous?"

"Do you deny, sir, that you hae consorted wae the leaders o' this dastardly rebellion? Do you deny that just last week you fraternised with Phelim O'Neill, the chief protagonist on the Irish side? You are a known sympathiser with the Catholic cause. That point, sir, it is impossible for you to deny. Your actions have given succour tae the rebels at every turn. You were clever enough tae station yoursel' well away frae the rebellion in Ulster, but it is weel kenned all o'er the country that you have financed and sponsored this rising frae its inception right tae the present. Noo you will hae tae answer for your treachery. Your brother's castle at Glenarm has already been burned tae the ground. If you don't want the same tae happen to your precious Dunluce you must surrender your person tae me withoot further delay."

I am getting very angry inside, boiling up with the injustice of these accusations. Why is nobody speaking up for the Earl here? I have worked for this man. He is many things, many things that I do not like or admire. He may be as slippery as an eel, but he is not a traitor, nor is he a sympathiser with the rebels. Isn't he just after freeing the besieged people of Ballintoy and Coleraine, chasing McColla McDonnell and his Highlanders, organising food for his tenants? I am hopping from one foot to the other in exasperation.

"What hae you tae say for yoursel', sir?" Munro finishes.

Antrim has run out of words, or at least seems to be trying and failing to wet his dried-up mouth.

I have to speak here!

I am a mere ten paces from where the Earl is pinned between these two guards.

My mouth is open before I can stop myself.

"Listen, Lord Antrim is no traitor. He is…" I begin, but choke to a sudden stop as a very powerful hand grips my mouth from behind. I splutter to continue but it is no good. I can't get a word past those fingers. I am being stared at by the whole crowd. The two guards look at me astonished. Lord Antrim's eyes meet mine for the briefest of seconds, wide with surprise. Munro peers through the folk in front of me to try to discover what the commotion is. I am still being firmly held; actually I am being pulled down and backwards, away from the situation. My heels slipe across the cobbles.

Until my captor has dragged me well away to the edge of the crowd I have no idea who is behind that powerful grip. He is still holding me tightly. Then I hear a gentle Bushmills whisper that I know so well.

"Darach, son! That was brave, but it wasn't the wisest thing you've ever done."

John McSparran takes his hand away from my mouth and I breathe again.

"John," I say, "I didn't know you were so strong."

"Were you trying to get yourself locked up along with the Earl, were you? Do you not think that lassie of yours deserves a fellow who is a bit more sensible? One who wants to stay alive long enough to be married to her?"

I hang my head.

"Aye, maybe I was daft," I say, "but nobody else was speaking up for him."

We listen from a safer distance as the noise rises and the arrest continues. I get the impression that there is no point in the Earl arguing any more. This Munro has his army here for a reason. Not only is Lord Antrim going to a dungeon in Carrickfergus Castle, but this, his seat of power, is going to be his no more. Dunluce is going to be forfeit to the Crown, or at least to General Munro and his Scottish Protestant army.

The two guards are now leading Lord Antrim back towards the Manor House. He is trying to maintain his dignity, but I see that he looks entirely deflated, his sad eyes trying to make contact with as many of his people as possible as he is marched unceremoniously through us. Captain Digby and his man, MacArthur, are trailing along behind him, no doubt to help him get organised for the journey. I wonder who will be accompanying him to serve him in captivity. I wonder how the Duchess will take this news, wherever she is now. I wonder what fate awaits him. Might he be imprisoned for the rest of his life? Might he, as an accused traitor, find himself on the gallows, or have his head chopped off? It strikes me that I can think of a few others of his clan who better deserve such a fate.

As he comes in my direction I stare intently at his diminished figure. Approaching John and me, the Earl turns his head slightly and I stare into his defeated eyes. He meets my gaze and seems to attempt to give a rueful smile, then moves away, disappearing from our view into the shadows of the gatehouse.

I find myself thinking of Katie. The sense of our decision to leave this place and go to Islay has just been confirmed. Any peaceful settlement which might have been reached between the Irish and the Crown has been well and truly scuppered by this arrest. Randal McDonnell was, for all his faults, probably the best chance of peace. Now, with Munro in this vengeful mood and his Protestant army itching to even up the score, this country is not going to be a pleasant place to live. The agitators have shot themselves in the foot yet again, and the ordinary people will bear the brunt of their ill-conceived campaign.

****

John, Eilish and I leave Dunluce Castle the morning after Lord Antrim's arrest.

Yesterday we had watched him emerge across the drawbridge. Surrounded by Munro soldiers, he walked slowly up the slope of the funnel and through the outer ward. His gait was as dignified as he could command, his head unbowed, but his eyes holding a clear and desperate sadness. Mounting his favourite stallion, he steadied himself in the saddle. Then he turned around and gave a sorrowful wave to those of us who had stayed to watch his humiliation.

Finally, the Second Earl of Antrim, the enigmatic Randal McDonnell, made a slow and sombre salute to his precious Dunluce. For all he knows, it may be his final sight of the castle he calls home. It was an emotional moment.

MacArthur followed his lordship out through the gate; the two horses were then surrounded and hidden from our view by Munro's mounted guards as they headed away on the narrow track south.

There was nothing for us in Dunluce any more. From the safety of John's workshop beside the brewhouse we watched and listened as the

Scottish soldiers plundered their way around the place. We heard their laughter as they devoured Randal's festive dinner. The noise increased as beer and wine flowed. Soon we were hearing the screams of the small group of female servants who had been in the kitchens to prepare and serve the feast, and had been unable to escape. Then more pandemonium as they ransacked the Manor House. Windows were being broken as an intoxicated madness took hold; we heard dull thuds as items were thrown from upstairs.

Then, to my horror, the unmistakeable sound of splintering wood and crashing strings. I realised at once that the lovely swan harp had joined other furnishings on the stone cobbles of the upper ward. This was the ultimate sacrilege for me. I pictured its twisted frame, the tangled strings, the fractured sound-box. The swan's head on the neck could not survive this impact.

Heart-breaking to hear its dying cry.

The final song of my precious swan harp.

If only I could have seen ahead I could have saved it. This was the second of my harps that had been ruined in these attacks on Dunluce. I was on my feet, agitating to enter the upper ward to try to salvage what was left of this one.

"Maybe I could get the neck itself. Maybe some part of it will have survived," I begged John, but he forbade me.

"It is not worth the risk, son," he said, probably rightly. "You could finish up with a *scian* in your ribs from those ruffians. It is likely beyond redemption anyhow, but you have many more harps inside you. So think of them and think of your future. Not the past, not even the present."

Eventually we heard some shouted rebukes as Munro's sergeants got their drunken troops under control and restored some order. A sombre twilight settled slowly and brooded over Dunluce.

We slept ill, huddled in the cold shelter of John's workshop.

This morning, as we gather up a few of John's tools and what possessions Eilish had salvaged from the day of the fire, we talk about where they should go now for refuge. They are next thing to destitute and I want to help them as much as I can. I suggest that they come with me to Ballintoy. Archibald Stewart is surely the best-placed person to give them some help. Perhaps they could stay in a home made vacant as a result of the rising. They think not, however.

"Mr Stewart will have his hands full with his own people," Eilish says. "We couldn't expect help from him."

I suggest that they come with me to Straid, to my parent's home, but again they see too many risks in that.

"Sure you don't even know yet if your family has been able to return to live safely in their old house yet. We would only be an additional burden," they say.

They are determined to go to John's cousin, Doole, in nearby Bushmills. I cannot argue with that idea. Doole may be able to keep them until things settle down and they find or build another house. I do feel guilty that I am abandoning them, unable to offer them anything to help, but they will hear no such chat from me. The best of people. I owe them so much and will never be able to repay.

****

We have decided to leave Dunluce as early as we can. The Scottish soldiers are mostly still asleep or dealing with their hangovers, but we certainly do not want to be in the vicinity of the castle when they wake up.

We are making our way out through the main gates as surreptitiously as possible when I hear a rush of feet on the gravel behind us. Then a call to wait. I turn to see Captain Digby striding quickly up the incline. I am surprised that he is still in the castle. After last night's shenanigans I would have imagined he would have put as much distance between himself and Dunluce as possible. Perhaps loyalty to this place that he has been constable of has been stronger than his instinct for self-preservation.

"O'Cahan," he says, "I did not know you were still here until I happened to look out from one of the turrets of the gatehouse and saw you emerge from the shed. So you hid there last night?"

"We did, sir," John says, defensively. "We had nowhere else to go, just my old workshop. I hope that was alright?"

"Of course it was alright," the Captain says. "I hid in the turret myself! It is just that I was looking for the harper; I thought you had gone, but no harm done; I am glad I caught you."

"Why is that, sir?" I ask.

"Before he left yesterday the Earl asked me to speak to you."

I wait.

"Two things," Digby says. "The Earl heard your words….right here, when that Scottish buffoon was arresting him. He thought it very brave, what you did, what you said, or attempted to say. So that was one thing. The other thing was to give you this."

Digby reaches me a small leather bag. I take it. Its weight surprises me.

"Thank you, sir," I say.

"It is payment for the harp; also a gratuity for the music you were supposed to play last night until that peculiar set of circumstances prevented your performance."

I repeat my thanks. This does give me a warm feeling inside. And the bag is heavy. I suspect it is well in excess of what I was owed. I will wait to count it later.

Digby makes some small talk with John and Eilish. I judge that any other kind of conversation is just too painful for him right now. He keeps looking over his shoulder to the castle. I am sure he is wondering what the rest of the day holds for him and where his duties lie, now that his Earl has gone. Suddenly I have an idea.

"Captain," I say, "when all that commotion was happening in there yesterday… I think I heard the sound of the harp being…." I struggle to finish the sentence, but Digby nods in understanding.

"Aye, I'm afraid you are right," he says. "I think some drunken soldier pushed it through the window. I'm sorry."

"Could I ask a favour of you, sir? I'm sure it must be badly broken, but if there is even a piece of it still intact would you be able to bring it out for me? I would like to have it, maybe use it for another harp. Especially if the neck with the swan's head has survived in one piece."

"I cannot do that, son," he says sorrowfully.

"Please Captain. I am begging you."

"That's enough, Darach," John says. "The Captain says he can't."

Digby looks me in the eyes for a few seconds, a pained look in his.

"I can't do what you ask, because your harp is no longer there."

"Where is it, sir?"

"One of Munro's men threw it over the curtain wall. I didn't want to tell you, but… I saw it happening. I am sorry. There was nothing I could do about it. The place was in turmoil; I was trying to stay alive, high up in the Gatehouse. The last I saw of your harp it was bouncing off the rocks on its way down the cliff to the sea."

There is no more to be said.

The knife in my ribcage has been twisted even further. My favoured swan harp, smashed to pieces. Splinters of alder and oak bobbing on the tide; the soundbox floating away on the Atlantic waves. The brass strings silent, entwined with strands of swirling seaweed.

Instantly a tune forces its way into my head. It takes a second for me to recognise it, then I realise it is one of my own compositions…the one in which I tried to capture the sound of breaking waves on the strand by the White Rocks and the swell of the wide ocean. Involuntarily my arms stretch out for the briefest of seconds and my fingers flex, as if to reimagine the harp in my grasp.

But there are no harps remaining here.

One is burned, one drowned!

We take our leave of Captain Digby; he wanders away much more slowly towards the drawbridge.

Through misted eyes I investigate the contents of the bag he has given me. I am astounded by the Earl's generosity. I don't take time to count the coins, but I know what I must do with them, with some of them at least. I take a handful of coins and grab Eilish's hand.

"Here," I say. "Take these, Eilish. I haven't been able to give you any help in getting a new home. The Earl has been more than generous…so take…"

John interrupts, stepping between me and his wife and taking a firm hold of my arm. "No, Darach, no! It is not us who needs it. We will be fine, we have enough to get by for a while. We are near the end of our time. You and your girl are just at the start. You don't know what lies ahead of you, but this money is your money and you'll have far more need of it than we will."

They will hear no more of it. I have to relent. The three of us climb the hill to the east on our walk to Bushmills. Up on the summit we stop briefly for a final look back at Dunluce, its dark battlements catching the low morning rays of a watery sun. The village of our home is no more; the hearth of my fostering lies in its ashes; the castle of our carpentry has been carved from us. It is a deep and painful cleaving.

I know John feels it even more than I do.

My foster mother and father hold hands on the hill top. I have never seen them so loving before, not in all the years of living in their home and working with them.

John turns away first. A regretful sucking sound through his teeth, then, "*Níl maith sa seanchas nuair a bhíos anachain déanta.* Come on now. No use crying over spilt milk."

We wander down the hill towards Bushmills.

Chapter 50

Reunion

Darach O'Cahan

The long walk back from Bushmills to Ballintoy. I am preoccupied, my spirits at their lowest. Saying farewell to John and Eilish was less a parting, more a tearing. Painful and emotional for all three of us.

The leaving of Dunluce is equally grievous for me. The place has been my life for so long. And what a privileged life it has been. To learn my trade there with a master craftsman like John. To work in the grandeur of the castle. To walk its magnificent gardens and its wider surroundings. To be a part of the rich Gaelic traditions of music and song, of poetry and story-telling, of dance and games. To have been trusted with a first-ever commission to make a harp for Lord Antrim's great hall. To witness, from close quarters, the character and life of such a legendary man as the Earl, not to mention his enchanting Countess. To have had a hand in creating and repairing the opulent fabric of that ancient fortress over the past few years…these have been experiences I will never forget. Now I have a deep and foreboding sense that I have just witnessed the end of an era, a final death knell that signals the burial of such a precious set of our native Irish traditions. Gaelic Ireland is hanging by a thread.

What Munro's men are doing to Dunluce at the moment is a desecration, an outrage of revenge and sectarian hatred. How I despise them for it. The sneer of superiority on the Scottish General's face as he humiliated the Earl has produced a fury in me that I find hard to contain. I do not like being this disturbed in my thinking. It creates an imbalance of spirit and distorts everything around me. Even the ocean seems to be agreeing, riotous waves rolling in from the north with powerful urgency over Runkerry strand.

I drag myself up the long slope of the land towards the Causeway. It may be a sub-conscious thing but I am being drawn to the path where I first met Katie. That chance encounter, if chance it was, changed my life. Now it is about to be changed again. In a few days time she and I will sail away from these tortured shores to begin a new life in a new place, one without the support of those who have nurtured and loved us since birth. We two will become one, and the one will be stronger than any two…I do believe that, but what will I do if Katie misses the closeness of her family too much? What if I am unable to meet that kind of need in her?

We are going to be completely dependent on each other, and for almost everything...certainly at the beginning. I wonder how we will be as parents to Kate, and then to our own child. That is probably the circumstance which will leave Katie feeling most vulnerable. Her mother and sisters, and indeed Aunt Biddy, have been very good at sharing the load of looking after the wee one.

I hope we will be able to make friends easily on Islay. I have no idea of the nature of Port Ellen, in terms of its mix of traditions and churches. At least Katie has some knowledge of her uncle and aunt there. It is possible that she will have other kin as well. I will be feeling my way for a while. A lot will depend on the references we get from Archibald Stewart, if he is willing to provide these. We must make a point of seeing him soon, I think. I have no idea how he will react to the nature of our plan, but surely he will see that at least we are trying to do things in the proper way, rather than by some sort of indecent elopement. If all else fails, though, such a course of action is still an option.

It has become very windy up here as I trudge along on the edge of the cliff. A summer storm has been blowing in from the south-west, sweeping rain-showers across the flat bleakness of the bogland beside me. It is something we are well used to in north Antrim; the Sperrins seem to send us these squalls far too regularly, even in the height of what should be summer. I pull my coat tighter around me. I wonder if I wouldn't have been safer today to take the inland route through Lisnagunogue. It is dangerous to be too near the cliff-edge here, but I suppose that intuitively I had made the decision to stay clear of any area where I might run into strangers.

Beside the path ahead of me a flame of colour; a cock pheasant shelters in the lea of a tangle of whin bushes. It struts away resentfully as I approach, then clears its throat hoarsely and takes off across the flat of the rushy bogland, its wings whirring furiously into the breeze.

Far below me the darkening ocean beats relentlessly against black Causeway rocks. The swell really has risen in the last couple of hours since I left Dunluce and this off-shore wind is whipping the tops off the breaking waves as far out as I can see; sea-spray streams wildly behind each one, reminding me of *Liath's* white mane. Islay is just about visible in the north under a brooding sky, gravel-grey clouds scudding in its direction.

This is it! This is the exact spot where she first appeared.

Almost exactly a year ago, if my memory is correct.

I stop, stand back from the cliff edge, close my eyes to recall that sacred moment. That image of feminine beauty is etched so clearly on my mind. And now she and I are one. It is barely believable, especially given all the trauma we have both had to endure over the past year.

The wind howls in my ears, but above its noise I think I hear something else, something like a call. A seagull's cry? No, this is more like a shout. A human shout. I open my eyes, look around. This is such a lonely place. I had not expected anyone…who could be calling in such a place?

I see two figures. They're approaching from the east. Climbing up the slope of the path with great vigour. Two men, well muffled up, their bodies bent determinedly into the buffeting wind. I watch as they get closer, wondering, nervous, hoping against hope that they are not young Protestants with an axe to grind. This is no place to be encountering trouble. The storm is giving me enough to contend with.

I only realise who they are when I hear the shout.

"O'Cahan!"

Bruce McClure!

Bruce and his friend! Matt somebody, if I remember correctly. Not a pair of men I want to be running into.

I try the smile tactic as they close on me, but my face is cold and the lips don't seem to want to co-operate. I raise a hand in greeting, an empty hand. I have no axe, nor any other weapon. I cannot say the same for these two. Both are carrying sticks. It is not a good start. It puts me on the back foot straight away. But maybe my initial judgement is all wrong. Maybe they are going to be friendly. I should not jump to conclusions. The conflict around here is over after all, isn't it? They are back home in their own place. They survived, unlike their friend at Portnaw, unlike so many locals whose deaths I have been told about. Oh Mary, mother of God…what to do!

It is amazing how many thoughts go through your head in that split second. I have an instinct to run.

I could turn and flee as they are still a few paces from me. I am quick enough, I think. But then I don't know how quick they are. And anyhow, where would I run to? Going back the way I have just come leads me to nowhere safe. Bushmills? Hardly the best place for an out-of-breath Irishman. I cannot run towards Ballintoy where I might expect help from Alex…these two block the path in that direction. Running isn't an option.

I can stand my ground. I'll try to charm my way out of this. I can talk to them. They will listen to my wise, peaceful words, won't they? Maybe I am being fearful for no reason. I should give them the benefit of the doubt. Maybe they will just pass me by on their way to wherever they are heading. Maybe we can exchange the time of day and they will wander on peacefully into the rest of their lives. Or maybe not….I cannot judge their mood, but their stance as they stop a few feet away from me is sort of cat-like. Cat stalking mouse, ready to pounce.

I have the Earl's bag of money hidden in a pocket inside my coat. I could offer them cash to let me go if they get aggressive. I reject that idea immediately. It wouldn't dissuade them if they intend to do me harm, might only encourage them. Anyhow, Katie and I need it, don't we? Why would I even think of trying to save my skin by doing such a spineless thing?

Time for conversation, I think.

"Hello lads," I begin.

Matt opens his mouth, turns to glance at Bruce, shuts his mouth again and steels his face, his eyes squinting, his hands both gripping his cudgel, holding it firmly in front of him. Bruce, on the other hand, grins maliciously.

"Hello is it? Listen to him, Matt. 'Hello lads,'" he sneers sarcastically. "I have been looking for you for weeks, O'Cahan. Where have you been hiding? I thought you had maybe scarpered over the Bann with the rest of your gutless clan."

"No, I'm still here…as you see. How are you Bruce?" I ask, doing my best to stay calm, be sociable.

Bruce isn't deflected from his sarcasm, I notice. His features twist, his lips seem to snarl like an angry dog. God but he looks a fierce size.

"Not great, to be honest," he says. His words appear friendly, his face belies it. "Haven't been in the best of form lately."

"Oh right? How's that?" I ask, ignoring the undertone of fake civility, still trying to be as normal as possible, but eyeing this stick of his which he is switching from hand to hand.

"Well, you see," he continues, "a lot of reasons. I saw a lot of corpses over the past while. Thing about them was, they were all bodies of Protestant people. Some of them were women. Some were children, wee girls and boys. Some that I heard of were people I knew, you see… friends o' mine."

"I know, Bruce, I know…and I am really sorry for your loss." I am sincere, of course I am, but my words sound so hollow in this circumstance.

"And the other thing is….my mother and father. They are older folk, older and not in the best of health. But they were doing alright, you know; keeping fairly well…until a crowd of dirty, low-down scoundrels who used to be neighbours, friends even…until these bastards came to our village and my mother and father had to take refuge in the kirk, them and a lot of other decent people. And the bastards outside kept them in there, for months they held them prisoners, and them starving to death."

His voice rises and falls, crescendo to whisper…all to good effect. The impassioned way he speaks these words is sending shivers down my spine. The fellow is a bit deranged.

I can tell where this is going. What can I say to calm him? There doesn't seem any point in trying to explain to him what Father McGlaim had tried to do, nor to give him a hint of my own part in the mercy mission. I think it would only be counter-productive. I'll just keep him talking, play for time.

"I know all about this," I say. "It should never have happened. I hope your father and mother can get over it…" He raises his stick to stop me. I listen.

"Never you mind about my father and mother," he shouts. "They'll be alright, but there's ones that went into that kirk who will never be alright again, never…for they are dead. Robert Moore, a sound young fella, killed by your cousin when he went out to get water for the others. He'll never get to come home again. I knew him well, a good lad."

"I know, I'm sorry," I say.

"And a woman that got shot through the window-slit and her only looking out to see what was going on!"

"I am so sorry about her too. I heard about that."

"And old James Kerr that never did nobody a pin o' harm, a good man. Shot by you bastards. Our village will never get over it. We will never forget. These were decent, God-fearing people. Your people, your family, O'Cahan…they killed them!"

What could I say? I could feel his pain, his anger. It was all completely understandable. He and his friend had my full sympathy.

"Bruce," I say, "and you too, Matt. I am so sorry all this happened. Those people did not deserve to…"

"Just shut up!" he shouts at me, looking more and more jumpy as he works himself up into a frenzy. "Nothing you can say can make it any better, so just shut your mouth."

I stand silent for a bit, wondering all the time how I am going to be able to survive this anger and what violence it may lead to. Maybe I can get through to Matt. He has said nothing as yet. Maybe he will be more reasonable, maybe help to calm his friend down before he does something crazy. Should I try some appeal to him? I don't have much to lose.

"What about your folk, Matt," I say, "were any of them caught up in the siege in…"

I don't get any further.

"I told you to shut up," screams Bruce. "Why are you still talking?"

He drops his stick. Why is he….he is fumbling under his coat for some reason. I watch in dread.

He brings out a pistol.

Points it at me, his hand shaking.

Oh my God! I could die here. I could die in the very spot where I met Katie, I am thinking. I could die here and never see her again, never make it to Islay with her, never hold our baby, never….never anything. Talk! Talk quickly! Talk or run? Take my chance? Run like hell? I don't....I am frozen to the spot. My feet won't run. The ball in my back...that would hurt so bad. I'd rather face him, face the ball.

My arms go out automatically, as in a gesture of pleading. Of begging. Of saying, 'Have a bit of sense, Bruce. You don't want to be doing that now. Let's talk a bit more.'

His hand is shaking. The pistol weaves about. His face contorts with pain and determination.

Oh Katie, Katie...pray for me now. Pray for this sinner now at the hour of his death...which might be closer than I had hoped.

"You stole my girl!"

"What?"

"You stole my girl," he repeats.

"I don't understand."

"No you don't, do you? You stole my girl!"

"Who?" I say. What daft questions you ask in times of stress, I think.

"Who? You know right well who."

Matt joins in at this point. He is looking at Bruce, his eyes widened even further, this time it is surprise, adding to the horror that appeared when the pistol came out.

"Where'd you get the gun, Bruce?" Matt asks.

"Never mind that. I want him to say her name!" Bruce says.

"Soon as he says her name he's going to hear a bang, and he's going to feel a terrible pain in his chest, and he's going to go falling backwards over the edge of that cliff."

"You kept your pistol instead of handing it in to Stewart, didn't you?" Matt persists.

Bruce swears furiously at him, tells him to shut up now. If Matt goes on like this Bruce is as likely to shoot him as me. Matt raises his hands in submission. Bruce turns his attention back to me. Glaring through narrowed, hate-filled eyes.

"You are a dirty rat, O'Cahan."

"I don't know what you are talking about, Bruce...but look. Put that pistol away and we can talk about it," I say.

"Talk about it? Aye, you're good at the talkin'. You sweet-talked Archibald Stewart into giving you a job as a message boy...just so you could spy on the Protestants. You were all sweet-talk to thon hoor in Coleraine. And long before that you sweet-talked my girl away from me. Everything was fine until then. She and I were getting on great. Now she won't even look at me. And, from what I hear in the village, she has a child now! Your wee bastard of a wain! What do you say to that, eh?"

I smile... I can't help it. It is so laughable. So now wee Kate is our child! How false rumours can begin and spread.

"I say it is not true. Not a word of what you just said is true."

"Aye you would say that, wouldn't you? Does she have a wain or not?"

"No, she doesn't have a wain. The child has nothing to do with her. You mentioned that girl we met in Coleraine, the girl that was begging? The one you called a hoor? Well, she died…and she left her wee girl an orphan. There was nobody to look after her. You saw what Coleraine was like then. So I brought the wain to the McKays to look after."

He thinks about this for a second. Matt joins in again.

"That's what I heard too, Bruce. That's what Alex was saying."

"That's as maybe, but this villain is still a Papish bastard and he is going to pay for what his Irish rebels have done to us, so you stay out of this, Matt. This is between him and me. He stole my girl, so he did…and nobody does that and gets away with it.

"I stole nobody's girl. Katie came to me of her own free will. We met here at this very spot and I loved her from the very first minute I saw her. So you'll just have to get used to that. It's not for changing."

"You think?" Bruce yells. "Well, think again. If I can't have Katie McKay then I am damned sure no rebel Papish dog is going to have her either."

He steps forward, raises the pistol, cocks the hammer, points the long barrel straight at my chest.

My arms rise again, all by themselves, surrendering.

"Don't do this, Bruce." My voice is a whimpering meow.

"You have five seconds to save yourself. Promise me now, on your mother's death, that you will disappear out of this country and never see Katie again. I'll count to five. Make up your mind."

He starts.

Before he gets to three I have my answer, just in case he forgets a number.

"Bruce, listen to me. Katie and I are going away. We will be getting married."

He is still counting.

"There is nothing you can do or say can change that."

"You think?"

The wind rips his words away. But I see his lips. Read them.

"Five!"

I watch his finger tighten. There is a faint click. No bang, no explosion. No pain. He cocks the hammer back and tries again.

Click!

Nothing. My mind is racing, almost as fast as my heart is. Has he even loaded the thing, I wonder. If the powder is wet it could still fire.

He stares down the barrel of the pistol. Very foolish!

"Damn the bloody thing," he shouts and throws the misfiring weapon with all his enraged power straight at my face. My reactions are slow. I try to duck sideways but it catches me full on the temple, painfully so. I stagger a little to my left. Maybe it is just as well that I do because Bruce has launched himself at me in a manner that a Deerpark stag would be proud of. A head-down charge. Dangerously so. We are on the edge of a sheer cliff. It is many feet to the bottom, to certain death.

His madness has so blinded him that he almost misses me. Instead of catching me full in the stomach with his head he glances off my hip, one arm wrapping itself around my middle, dragging me with him. Instinctively I grab on to his coat. We both clatter to the ground, him about to be on top. But my body is doing things that I haven't the time to be telling it to do. It twists on impact, throwing Bruce off, using his own momentum to propel him over and to the side of me.

He screams!

His head and shoulders hang over the abyss! His face is staring down at death, at a three hundred foot drop. Most of his torso is over the edge, but from the waist down he remains on the safe side of the precipice. His legs scramble for some purchase on the grassy bank, with no success. He tries to turn so as to pull me with him. He is wailing the foulest of oaths at me.

"If I can't have her, neither will you!"

God, what a thing to be saying in the face of your death, I think. Not once has he begged for help. What madness this is.

I am fairly well connected to the earth on which I lie, fairly secure. And I am still gripping his coat. It is a flimsy garment. But my grip is nowhere near secure enough to be able to haul him back over the edge. These seconds of impasse seem to stretch into minutes. It is a dead-lock, in so many senses. He could still easily squirm enough to take me with him.

"Do something, Matt," I call.

Matt is petrified, his face a mask of horror, hands clasped behind his head. "What'll I do?"

"Pull him back up by the legs, you idiot," I say.

"Aye," he says. "I'll do that."

He jumps forward, grabs Bruce's brogues. A few good tugs and Bruce is sliped back to safety beside the path. He doesn't get to his feet at once, instead lying face down in the soft summer grass, his features buried away from us. Initially he is prone and motionless, but he is soon overtaken by violent shuddering sobs. No words, just soul-deep painful moans.

"Come on, Bruce," I say, reaching down to put my hand across his shoulders. "Let's get you up and back to your home."

"Take your bloody hands off me."

He rises in a sudden burst of vehemence, leaping to his feet. "You can go to hell. You too, Matt. You could've pushed him over."

With that he takes off running. Heading west along the cliff edge, a dangerous place to be running so madly, so out of control.

"I hope he's alright," Matt says.

"Me too. Will you follow him, Matt?"

"Aye, maybe I should."

"What were you two doing out here in weather like this anyway?" I ask him.

He grimaces. "Looking for you," he says. "He was out to get you. He's been searching for you for days on end."

My good Lord! I suddenly realise how fortunate I am to have survived, how thankful I should be that Matt wasn't as keen on my demise as his mate.

"Will you shake my hand? You did a good job there. We could've both been over the edge," I say reaching out my arm towards him.

He waits a bit, looking at my open hand, then gives me his.

"Aye surely," he says. "And you look after Katie, won't you? She's one of ours, one of our Ballintoy lasses."

"I will, Matt. I promise."

He follows Bruce. I watch him jog away. Then, feeling a cold sweat break on my brow and a sudden churning of my stomach, I retch and empty myself beside the path. A euphoric sense of relief sweeps over me as I rise from that release. I have survived my closest brush with death.

And Katie McKay awaits me at Ballintoy.

Chapter 51

Leaving

Katie McKay

We sailed out of Ballintoy's little harbour. My tears flowed freely, salty on my tongue. Darach sat by my side, holding me lightly, his arm around my waist, wee Kate on his knee and her trying to make sense of what was happening as our boat rocked on a very gentle swell.

The late July morning was quite calm. Before us the sea stretched flat, the colour of milk in a churn, the sky being blanketed with high hazy-white cloud. Islay was just a misty suggestion of a shape on what would have been a horizon, if you could have distinguished one. It was all as hazy as our future.

A good crowd of people had gathered on the pier to wave us away. My family had been joined by a few of my friends and neighbours, Jean Kennedy among them. The farewells had been solemn, the good wishes and hugs warm and supportive. At the same time, nobody could have failed to sense the misgivings that these good people shared concerning what I was doing. The community of my kirk, nowhere near recovered as yet from the ordeal they had been through in the past while, could not give me their full blessing in this course of action. Even as Marcus Hill's sturdy boat had pulled away from its mooring I could see doubt, maybe even a hint of something closer to rebuke, in one or two of those watching eyes.

Alex had gone to Ballycastle and negotiated a price for us with Mr Hill to transport us. The village of Port Ellen lay on the southern coast of the island. It wasn't a port that he had sailed to before, so he was a bit uncertain, telling Darach that he would only undertake it if we had a spell of settled weather, with a light south-westerly breeze and leaving during a slack tide. He had sailed to Ballintoy from Ballycastle the previous day, moored in our harbour and climbed the hill to find our house.

"Tomorrow is the day, the only day, and in the mornin'," he had announced. We had to ready ourselves and our baggage that evening, while Darach went to his family at Straid, to tell them why he was leaving and to say his goodbyes.

It was just as well that, only a few days before, Darach and I had gone to see Archibald Stewart in his Manor House. The conversation with him and his wife had gone well. Mr Stewart was very understanding of our predicament and he had had no hesitation in writing a letter of recommendation to my uncle Donald regarding employing Darach and helping us find accommodation.

"I will explain to him that you were a very reliable courier for me. I'll tell him that you are on your way to being a master carpenter. I'll mention that you have made a number of harps. That should impress him, I think."

"It might," Darach said laughing, "unless he is tone-deaf, or maybe thinks the harp is the devil's instrument."

"That will likely be the least of your worries," answered Stewart.

Mrs Stewart gave us one of her gracious smiles. "I hope you can put all this trouble behind you," she said. "Move on with your lives."

"We will try," Darach said, "but it will be hard. One of the things that has happened to me during it all is that I have almost forgotten who I am."

"I don't follow you. You'd better explain."

I was puzzled. I wanted to hear his explanation too.

"Well, when I was working in Dunluce with John McSparron I understood my place in things, I knew who I was there. I thought of myself as a person who could play music, make songs and tell stories, a sort of young bard, if there is such a thing. Better still, I could make harps for other people to enjoy. I have almost forgotten how good that feeling was…and that was me. That was who I was. That was me at my best."

"I see. Go on," Mrs Stewart said, kindly encouraging Darach to get this burden off his chest.

"I watched the Earl taken away the other day, and I watched the castle being stripped. I even heard the harp I had made for him and his Countess being destroyed, as if it was a piece of worthless driftwood. I took it very personally and it made me wonder. Will I ever again get that sense of pride in what I did, in the harps I made? Pride in who I was back then? If we stay here I doubt very much if I will get that chance. Who is left of our chieftains to ever want me to make a harp for them?"

Mrs Stewart seemed to be turning this over in her mind. "You shouldn't despair of that," she said. "The chieftains may all be gone, but I am sure there will be other people who would buy from you in these parts."

"I doubt that," Darach said, "but at least I know there are still Gaelic lairds in the islands and highlands of Scotland. I think that is my best chance of getting back to harp making."

"You are right," she agreed. "You know, Ireland isn't the only place where the harp is played. In Scotland, on the islands especially, the harp is every bit as important as our pipes. You'll find manys a person to buy your instruments."

Then a more difficult question arose.

"And what do you want me to say about marriage?" Mr Stewart asked.

We looked at each other, unsure of how much to say.

"Well, we want to get married, sir," Darach said.

"Of course, of course," Mr Stewart said, "but shall I tell him the background? Shall I raise the issue of your differing church affiliations?"

"He will likely be able to work that out for himself," I said.

"You see, it is possible... likely even, that you run into the same kinds of objections to your marriage on Islay as you do here," he said. "The people there have similar attitudes. These divisions regarding religion run deep in all parts of the kingdom, I am afraid. People are people wherever you go."

"That may be true, sir," Darach said, "but at least in Islay they won't have the legacy of this rebellion to be drawing on. Here in Antrim, well, everything is so raw. The pain runs deep on both sides. We can never escape that, if we stay here. Over there we have a better chance, do you not think?"

"I do agree," Stewart said thoughtfully. "You may be right." Then, after a pause, he continued. "But...look, my young friends, I should tell you that Reverend Blare has been to see me about this matter."

My heart sank a bit at this.

"Aye, and he is not happy about it at all," Stewart continued. "He told me of your conversation with him, Katie. I think he regards you as a very headstrong young woman. There was no talking to you, he told me."

"Mr Stewart," I said. "With respect to him, the way I looked at it was...there was no talking to him. He was intense about it, sort of dangling me over the pit of hell because I have fallen in love with Darach and want to marry him. I hope when we get to Islay that we don't have a man like him to deal with."

"You well might meet such a man, Katie," he said. "But maybe if you find a clergyman who is prepared to listen to your story, maybe if he sees that you two are determined to bring up this wee lassie, Kate...is it? If he hears your determination to bring her up as a Protestant maybe he will see his way to blessing your marriage. You can but try. In the meantime, it is my intention to write a letter to him now, explaining the honourable part that you played in the alleviation of suffering in Ballintoy kirk during the siege, Darach. If he cannot see the christianity in that he is not worth the title of minister."

We were so grateful for this.

Mr Stewart's letters were now securely hidden in our baggage, perhaps our most important possessions.

I will never forget those final goodbyes on the pier. Alex seemed to have taken it upon himself to make sure that I was protected from an overwhelm of feelings, trying to manage everything in such a measured way so as to shield me from the rawness of this leaving.

He needn't have bothered!

A leaving it was…and there was no disguising the wrenching that we were all feeling. Even Alex himself was shuddering with suppressed emotion as we engaged in that last hug. My mother was the most controlled of all. I suppose she had been through this all those years ago when she and my father had left Islay. For her there may even have been a sense of a circle being completed in her daughter's return to her home area. Certainly she had Connie and Alice bound close to her as we all stood in near wordless desolation on that pier.

Connie tried, as always, to be funny. Her wit, ever irrepressible, brought smiles and laughs which soured into sobs almost as soon as the quip had left her lips.

"I want to be there for the birth of your first baby," she said as she hugged Darach and I at the same time, "just in case he throws a lot of holy water round it and claims it's a Catholic!"

I think Alice found saying goodbye to Kate even more difficult than parting with me. The two of them had grown inseparable over the months since Darach had brought her into my family. Kate had become Alice's real-life play-doll; it was going to be very hard for her to readjust to imaginary playmates. I had never witnessed wee Kate show so much attachment and feeling as when she and Alice were cuddling for the last time. The child's normal demeanour, right from when she first arrived with us, had been a wide-eyed look of apprehension…understandable, considering her poverty in Coleraine, the loss of her mother and, I suppose, being deposited in this family of strangers… and then the thirsty, hungry weeks she had had to spend with a crowd of people she had never seen before, under siege in our dark kirk. To watch her love for Alice, the last person she hugged before Darach gentled her away to the boat, spoke of a huge and welcome change in the child. I hoped that she and I could bond in a similar way in the days ahead.

As Darach stepped down into the boat beside Kate and me there was another moment I will treasure.

Alex had been talking a fair bit to Marcus Hill, having become well acquainted with him on the earlier voyage to Kintyre. He was aware of the boatman's impatience with the slow pace of our farewells and the need to be getting this journey underway, so he had been almost rushing us to get aboard, arms outstretched like he was ushering a flock of ewes down the pier for the short crossing to Sheep Island. Now that his work was done, and as Mr Hill was casting off, Alex made a sudden leap on to the deck of our craft.

The boatman's eyes widened in surprise.

For a second I actually thought, 'Goodness! Alex is for coming with us!'

But I needn't have worried.

He hadn't said his farewell to Darach!

They shook hands quite formally, but with a great warmth of respect and affection between them.

I was so proud of my brother at that moment and, of course, even more proud of the man who would be my husband… and the father of my first child when our own baby is born in the new year.

Poor Alex had to jump out of the stern and swim ashore as Marcus began to pull on the oars.

Looking back at the pier I noticed hands to mouths in fretful concern. Now those fears quickly turned into cheers.

We watched as he staggered up on to the shingle and into the outstretched arms of my mother and Jean Kennedy. The water was raining off him. Jean didn't seem bothered by it. Aye, that was interesting, Jean holding my sodden brother steady, holding him close, like a lover would, as he tried to get his balance on the loose pebbles.

Our boatman shipped his oars as a sudden flurry of breeze caught the sails and our craft picked up speed, tacking out to the north-west. The figures back there on the pier grew smaller and smaller, their waving arms more fitful until they seemed to stop altogether.

Darach turned to look at me, sideways on. We stared at each other without any language passing between us. There did not seem to be any need for words. Behind us the white cliffs of Ballintoy faded into the distance until they were barely visible.

We shifted our positions to face north, looking over the bow, waiting for the first sight of Islay.

Farewell to the Antrim Shore

Farewell to the grey cliffs of Antrim
And the white rocks of Ballintoy
Farewell to Dunluce Castle
Where I worked in the Earl's employ
And although I love my homeland
I love my lady more
And please God when things are settled down
We'll return to the Antrim shore

On a summer's day when I saw her first
As we walked near the Causeway stones
I knew that I would marry her
I could feel in within my bones
Her eyes they did enchant me
Her smile I did adore
And her hair blew long in the summer breeze
That day on the Antrim shore

Courting has always been a pleasure
Just so long as we hid away
From the spying eyes of the neighbourhood
For you know what the people say
'You must not marry the other sort
What is wrong with the girl next door?'
But I'll marry none if I cannot have
My girl from the Antrim shore

So farewell to friends and to family
It's to Islay that we must go
To seek for a life of contentment
Far away from the place we know
My harp I'll play in a sacred key
And we'll sing from a common score
And in harmony I will always be
With the girl from the Antrim shore

Author's Note and Acknowledgements

This story has been fermenting in my sub-consciousness for far too long. It began life as a stage musical in Limavady High School where I worked for many years. The 1999 production of "The Fairy Thorn" is a treasured memory. The development of the narrative into novel form has been both challenging and rewarding.

I have always felt a strong connection to the events of the 1641/2 Rising. Having learned in school history class of the destruction of my home town of Ballymoney and after spending forty years living very close to the site of the Battle of Laney, (11th Feb 1642), such interest was inevitable. In the course of research for this book it has been an added fascination to discover two members of my ancestral family who were intimately involved in the events described, one a leader in the besieged church in Ballintoy, the other resident in Dunynie Castle. Both feature somewhat in the storyline.

Readers of my previous novels will recognise a recurring musical theme in this story. Having initially imagined my lead character as a harper and harp-maker in Dunluce Castle, it was a wonderfully confirming sensation to discover that the 2nd Earl, Randal McDonnell, had played harp himself; even better was to read of a harp tuning key from the period being found in the uncovered streets of Dunluce village during Colin Breen's recent excavations there.

I wish to extend my thanks to the following who assisted my inquiries; Barbara Harding of Coleraine Historical Society; Maurice McHenry and Robert Corbett of Ballintoy Historical Society; Donnell O'Loan of Glens of Antrim Historical Society for his advice on McDonnell genealogy for the 2nd edition; Maire Nic Cathmhaoil; Dónal Mac Ruairi; Lucy Kerr; Nodlaig Ni Bhrollaigh; Rev Stanley Johnston.

The late Bertie McKay of Ballintoy was also a mine of information back in the 1990ies when I first developed an interest in writing about this subject. I named my heroine Katie McKay in honour of this lovely gentleman.

I really appreciate Jim Allen's engagement with this project, in particular his creativity and expertise in producing the harp design for the front cover.

Thanks also to Mark Strong for his wonderful sketch of Dunluce Castle.

Finally, my deepest gratitude to my wife, Mary, whose forbearance, rigour and painstaking dedication in her editorial role have been invaluable as ever.

2022 and here we are again! As I complete this story from 380 years ago, war rages again in Europe. Sieges are happening in so many beleaguered Ukrainian cities. Refugees flee in their millions. Atrocities are happening on a scale that people in 1641 could never have imagined. 'How long, oh Lord, how long', before humankind can learn to live in peace with each other? In the midst of it all, however, there are the intensely moving stories of grace and goodness. In the worst of times we also witness the best of humanity; therein lies a hope we must cherish and hold tightly to.

Appendix 1

Fictional and Historical Characters in 'The Last Harp of Dunluce'

Fictional	Historical
Darach O'Cahan	Father Patrick McGlaim
John McSparran	Randal McDonnell, 2nd Earl of Antrim, Dunluce
Eilish McSparran	Countess, Lady Catherine (Manners)
Martin & Bríd O'Cahan	Archibald Stewart (Land Steward, Ballintoy)
Henry, Rosie & Meahb O'Cahan	Alaster McColla McDonnell
Maeldearg, Sean & Michaél Reid	Raghnall McDonnell
Mrs Mary Stewart	Gilladubh O'Cahan (Provost, Dunseverick)
Katie McKay	Tirlough Óge O'Cahan
Mrs Isobel McKay	Manus O'Cahan
Biddy McKay	Captain Digby (Dunluce)
Alex McKay	Captain McPheadress (Dunluce)
Connie McKay	Thomas Boyd (Ballintoy)
Alice McKay	Rev William Fullerton (Vicar in Derrykeighan)
Thomas Smith & his mother	Rev James Blare (Vicar in Billy & Ballintoy; also spelled Blair)
Bruce McClure	The Dowager Countess, Alice McDonnell (nee O'Neill, Ballycastle)
Jean Kennedy	Alexander McDonnell of Glenarm Castle
Matt Taggart	Sir James McDonnell of the Vow

Fictional	Historical
Nellie & Kate	Hugh MacNeill (Dunynie Castle, Ballycastle)
Murdo McDonnell	Doole McSparran
Marcus Hill	Archibald Campbell, Laird of Argyll
McConaghie	Coll McAllester (Derrykeighan farmer)
Jimmy & Thomas Stewart	Robert Moore (killed at Ballintoy)
Reverend Patterson	James Kerr (killed at Ballintoy)
Mrs Betsy Moore	Wm & Mrs Erwin (killed at Ballycastle)
Mrs Ross (the lady killed in Ballintoy church was un-named)	Janet Spier (killed at Ballycastle)
Donald & Mary Gilchrist	Thomas Robinson (killed at Ballycastle)
Tadhg McAleer	General Robert Munro
	Toole McAllester & the Collier family
	A McNeill girl, Guy Cochrane's son, John Spence's wife & a McCurdy boy- all killed near Dunseverick
	George Thompson & Donnell Gorme O'Donnell
	Archie Boyd of Dunluce
	The widow Wilson

Appendix 2 - Notes on Historical Characters

While the following are indeed historical characters it should be noted that I have used creative license in attributing to them certain characteristics and personalities.

Randal McDonnell, Second Earl of Antrim (1609-1683)
The Second Earl of Antrim was a shrewd political operator. At a time when most of his peers in the upper echelons of power ended up on the gallows, Randal was an incredibly resilient survivor.
After his arrest at Dunluce by General Munro (in 1642) he was imprisoned for several months in a dungeon in Carrickfergus Castle. Eventually he escaped, made his way to York and continued his campaign as a negotiator between the King and the Irish earls. Returning to Ireland in 1643 he was re-arrested and incarcerated once more, accused of plotting a rising in Scotland with Montrose, only to escape a second time from Carrickfergus.
He had a unique capacity to read the political situation and place himself in the most advantageous position. He switched sides several times during the period subsequent to the 1641 rebellion, at one stage being a key leader in the Irish Catholic Confederation during the Irish Confederate Wars between 1641 and 1653. At one stage he was involved in a plot to have the Irish Catholic Earls and their armies support the English King Charles in his war against the Parliamentarians in England and the Covenanters in Scotland. In 1647, however, he rejected the King in a fit of jealousy over the Lord Lieutenancy of Ireland and began to support Cromwell instead.
After the Restoration of the Monarchy, the Earl spent 11 months in the Tower of London, accused of treason. The Queen Mother secured his pardon and release, and he received his lands in Ulster back in 1665.
His first wife, the Duchess, Katherine Manners, died in 1649. He then married Rose O'Neill of Shane's Castle in 1652. He did not have any children. He died in 1683 and was buried in the family vault at Bonamargy Friary, Ballycastle.
His brother, Alexander of Glenarm, became the new Earl of Antrim. The McDonnell castle at Glenarm was eventually rebuilt in 1756 and is still lived in by Alexander's descendant, the present Earl of Antrim, Randal Alexander McDonnell.

Acquaintances of Earl McDonnell who were executed while he survived
Strafford (Sir Thomas Wentworth, Lord Lieutenant of Ireland)   1641
William Laud (Archbishop of Canterbury) his patron   1645
Charles 1 (his king and friend)   1649
James Hamilton, 1st Duke of Hamilton (his friend)   1649
Sir James Graham, 1st Marquess of Montrose (his ally)   1650
Archibald Campbell, 1st Marquess of Argyll (his rival)   1661

Archibald Stewart continued his faithful service to the Earl for many years, administering his estate in the Route as land steward. He worked to protect the interests of the Antrim tenants, despite the presence of 1,200 Scots soldiers who had quartered on the Earl's lands and who had threatened Antrim's tenants, levying intolerable taxes on them. Among Stewart's notable tenants were the Shaws, Stewarts, Dunlops, Boyds and Kennedys.

Alaster McColla McDonnell
After the Siege of Coleraine was lifted McColla went with the Irish forces across the Bann. He was injured at the Battle of Glenmaquin. Later that same year he appears to have deserted the Irish Confederates and tried to switch sides, seeking terms with the Scottish General Alexander Leslie. He returned to the Scottish Islands to fight alongside Montrose against the Scottish government forces. His troops committed many atrocities against Campbell and his Argyll forces. McColla returned to Ireland where he commanded a regiment in a battle against the Parliamentary forces in Co Cork, in 1647. Surrounded and defeated in the battle, McColla surrendered, only to be shot dead. He was buried in Clonmeen, Co Cork.

General Robert Munro
Munro's ruthless campaign against the Catholic Irish began in April 1642 and continued until the Battle of Benburb in 1646 where he was heavily defeated by Irish forces led by Owen Roe O'Neill. In the meantime he had laid waste to large swathes of Counties Antrim and Down in a 'scorched earth' policy. Carrickfergus Castle, where he based his campaign, was besieged in 1648 and Munro, betrayed by some of his own men, was arrested by General George Monck. He was imprisoned in the Tower of London for five years. In 1654 he was allowed by Cromwell to live in Ireland, where his wife, the widow of Hugh Montgomery, 2nd Viscount of Ards, had estates. He lived near Comber for many years.

Father Patrick McGlaim
In oral tradition Father McGlaim is said to have been a local priest, possibly a Ballycastle Franciscan. All that is known of him is his act of mercy in providing water and food for the besieged Protestants in the church in Ballintoy in 1642. He may have been arrested and martyred for his act of generosity; that story has been passed down through the generations as oral history but is difficult to authenticate with actual evidence from source material. The late Bertie McKay, formerly verger of Ballintoy Church, told me of the story in 1998; he recited one piece of evidence to support its authenticity, that in the oldest records of the church finances there is record of a stipend which was paid annually from church funds to a family in Ballycastle by the name of McGlaim, an on-going mark of gratitude for the priest's sacrificial actions. (I have been unable to confirm this information.)

Additional Characters
The names of the following people appear in the 1641 Depositions, recorded variously between 1643 and 1653. These Depositions are held in the Library of Trinity College Dublin. They are available online as referenced in Appendix 5. It should be remembered that, while the existence of the records of the 1641 Depositions provides a detailed first hand account of some of the happenings in the area in which this novel is set, the information is contested for the following reasons;
- the accounts were heard at various times and places during that period up until 1653, 11 years after the events, so memories of the original events may have been distorted by further happenings and/or rumours in the intervening period;
- stories may have been altered to fit with a prevailing narrative, particularly the need in England for propaganda to legitimise and finance further suppression of the Irish;
- participants may have been selective in their accounts; while some examinees may have wanted to avoid accountability most were in the business of trying to claim reparations for losses incurred during the rebellion.

Actual victims mentioned in the Depositions and in this novel
Robert Moore and James Kerr (killed at Ballintoy)
William Erwin & Mrs Erwin (killed at Ballycastle)
Janet Spier (or Jennett Speer- killed at Ballycastle)
Thomas Robinson. (killed at Ballycastle)
The Collier family
A McNeill girl, Guy Cochrane's son, John Spence's wife and a McCurdy boy- all killed near Dunseverick
A woman inside Ballintoy church, killed through a window opening. (I have given her the name Mrs Ross)

Others who are mentioned in the Depositions
The Dowager Countess, Alice McDonnell (Ballycastle)
Captain Digby (Dunluce Castle)
Captain McPheadress. (Dunluce Castle)
Gilladubh O'Cahan, Manus O'Cahan and Tirlough Óge O'Cahan
Hugh MacNeill (first Constable of Dunynie Castle in Ballycastle)
Toole McAllester (tenant farmer of the Earl of Antrim)
Coll McAllester (Derrykeighan farmer)
Doole McSparran (or McSporran)

Appendix 3 - Notes on Historical Places and Events

The settlements at Dunluce and Enagh Cross were thriving villages in 1641, but were both entirely destroyed by fire during the rebellion. Neither village was ever rebuilt, although a fair continued to be held at Dunluce well into the 18th Century. An archeological excavation was undertaken at the site of Dunluce village by Dr Colin Breen, (Ulster University). In his 2012 account he mentions the find of a harp-tuning key, apparently left lying on a village street. No sign remains of Dunluce village. However, at Enagh Cross the remains of earthworks, including a small rath, are visible between the Glenstall Road and the River Bann. ('Enagh' comes from the Irish word for 'Fair', '*Aonach*'. Presumably this crossing point on the Bann was the scene of regular markets/fairs.)

The ruins of Bonamargy Friary (Ballycastle), Dunseverick Castle, Dunluce Castle and the old church in Ballymoney remain, and can be visited. The current church building in Ballintoy was built in the early 19th Century, replacing the original church which was attacked in the 1642 conflict. Nothing remains of Ballintoy Manor House (Castle). It was disassembled in 1795, but its staircase, beams and oak panelling were taken to be used in Downing College, University of Cambridge. The Druid's Altar (or Grave) sits high above the plain of Ballintoy.

The following events which appear in the novel are historical; the arrival of Alaster McColla and Raghnall McDonnell at Ballintoy in 1641, the removal of the Earl's possessions from Dunluce to Chester, (a detailed inventory still exists), the outbreak of rebellion in Oct 1641, the attack on Stewart's troops by the Irish and Scottish at Portnaw, the Battle of Laney and the burning of Ballymoney, the sieges of Ballintoy House and Church, Dunluce Castle, Clough Castle and Coleraine, the killing of escaping settlers at Ravel River and of various members of the Ballycastle and Ballintoy communities, the letter appealing to Argyll for help, the capture of Lord Antrim at Dunluce and the castle's seizure by General Munro.

The author has exercised some artistic licence where there appear to be contradictions and disputed details in the testimonies of participants, as presented in the Depositions. The order of events during that period, muddled as they are in the accounts, have been simplified for the sake of this narrative.

The dates given in the text are according to the Old (Julian) Calendar which was used in Britain, though not in Europe.

The actual letters sent from Clough by James McDonnell to Archibald Stewart, and later from Dunluce to Wm Fullerton at Ballintoy are still in existence. (See for example, The 1641 Depositions; TCD; M838 folios 239r and 240r. Also in George Hill's 'The Stewarts of Ballintoy). The versions of these texts in this novel are ones simplified by the author, hopefully presented in more understandable English.

Appendix 4 - Ulster-Scots Glossary

aboot/oot	about/out
aff	off
ain	own
awa'	away
baith	both
blether	someone who talks too much (Also used as a verb)
bleutered	drunk/tired
boadie	person
brither	brother
clabber (*clábar* in Irish)	mud, muck
cleggs	horse-flies
dinnae	don't
doon	down
dreich	dismal
efter	after
eejits	idiots
fether	Ulster Scots prononciation of father
footerin'	fumbling
frae	from
freen	friend
hae	have
hallion	rascal
hame	home
houl	hold
hoor	whore

gae	give
gan	going
gern	complain
glar	mud, muck
greetin'	crying
guid	good
gulpin	uncouth person
ken	know
langer	longer
loanin	yard, lane
a lock of	a lot of
luk	look
mair	more
maist	most
midden	a pile of farm-yard manure
mooth	mouth
naethin'	nothing
naw	no, not
noo	now
oul & toul	old and told
quare	very, a term of emphasis
richt	right
rodden	narrow lane
santerin'	talking aimlessly
screigh	screech
scunnered	annoyed, disappointed

sheugh	ditch
shuthers	shoulders
sowl	soul
teemin'	raining heavily
thon	that (yon)
twa	two
wae	with
wanst	once
wain	child
weel	well
wheen	a few
wheest (houl yer wheest)	quiet (be quiet)
wrang	wrong
wud	would

Appendix 5 - References

Antrim, A. (1977) *The Antrim McDonnells*. Belfast
Boyd, H.A. (1994) *Olden Days in Cushendall and the Glens*. In 'The Glynns; Journal of The Glens of Antrim Historical Society Volume 23 1995'
Breen, C. (2012) *Dunluce Castle; History and Archeology*. Dublin
Day, A. & McWilliams, P. (1830-38) *Ordnance Survey Memoirs of Ireland; Parishes of County Antrim V; 1830-5, 18-8. Giant's Causeway and Ballymoney*
Forde, C. (1927) *Sketches of Olden Days in Northern Ireland*. Belfast
Gribben, C. (2021) *The Rise and Fall of Christian Ireland*. Oxford
Hamilton, J.B. (1957) *Ballymoney and District in the County of Antrim Prior to the 20th Century*. Ballycastle
Hill, G. (1865) *The Stewarts of Ballintoy*. Ballycastle
Hill, G. (1873) *Historical Account of The MacDonnells of Antrim*. Belfast
Mac Coitir, Niall. (2003) *Irish Trees; Myths, Legends and Folklore*. Cork
McDonnell, H. (2004) *A History of Dunluce*. Belfast
Ohlmeyer, J.H. (1993) *Civil War and Restoration in the Three Stuart Kingdoms; The Career of Randal McDonnell, Marquis of Antrim* Dublin
Smyth, Wm. J. (2006) *Map-making, Landscapes and Memory; A Geography of Colonial and Early Modern Ireland c.1530-1750*. Cork

The 1641 Depositions, Trinity College Dublin. https://1641.tcd.ie from the following 22 witnesses; Gilladuffe O'Cahan, Henry McHenry, Donnell Gorme O'Donnell, Alice Countesse Dowager of Antrim, Edmund O'Haggan, Brian O'Haggan, Coll McAllester, Donnell O'Cahan, Shane McVickar, Donnell Magee, Fferdoragh Magee, Tirlagh McRichard O'Cahan, Thomas Boyd, Fergus Fullerton, Robert Hamil, John Kidd, Robert Ffuthy, Rorie Ó Deaghan, Shane O'Coll, William McPheadress, John Duffe McGillchatton and Isabell Kerr.

For detailed information on the work of Prof Jane Ohlmeyer and her team at Trinity College Dublin on the Depositions and the process of making them available online see - https://youtu.be/LbeW8sAFY0o

http://www.ballintoy.connor.anglican.org/ballintoychurch.html
Wars and Conflict; The Plantation of Ulster, BBC
The Wars of the Three Kingdoms-Part 2: The Irish Rising
https://youtu.be/kz6mBN3KbFk
Devlin, A. (2021) *Showcasing The Downhill Harp*. https://youtu.be/QqFoTJw1KBg
Billinge, M. (2010) *Building a Reproduction of the Downhill Harp (the Harp of Denis Hempson) for the Irish Television Documentary Banríon an cheoil*. Bulletin of the Historical Harp Society, March 2010; and online at https://www.wirestrungharp.com/harps/historic/downhill/downhill_print.pdf

Other books by David A Dunlop

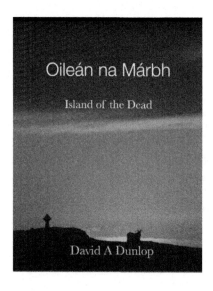

Oilean Na Marbh (2014)
When Sean-Bán Sweeney finds a body of a stranger washed up on a Donegal beach he can never imagine the hidden backstory that intertwines his simple life with that of the unknown youth, nor the connection to Annie, his mute, childhood sweetheart.
Set in 1898 when a new railway was being planned to link the impoverished regions of west Donegal to the centres of commerce and trade in the east, this is a story of tragic misunderstanding, but ultimately of the triumph of love.

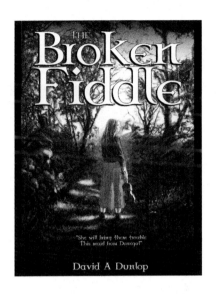

The Broken Fiddle (2016)
As partition carves Ireland in two in 1922, Matthew Henderson, a young Protestant farmer in Tyrone's border country, goes to the hiring fair and finds himself a maid. Sally-Anne Sweeney is a feisty, Irish-speaking Catholic from west Donegal. As Matthew falls for her charms, his maid proves equally attractive to Joe Kearney, Matthew's friend and neighbour across the new border. Inadvertently this pretty, fiddle-playing maid causes a feud between the two friends, lads whose fathers had fought beside each other at the Somme, six years previously. No-one is immune to the political violence of the period and, in the end, a tragic set of circumstances leads to the maid leaving for home. As she goes, a distraught Sally Anne takes out her anger on a gift which Matthew had given her, his late father's precious fiddle. The broken fiddle haunts her over the years until she writes a letter of forgiveness to Matthew. Can there be any reconciliation of the fractured relationship?

A Maid Again (2020)
The concluding part of the trilogy.
The letter is dated 25th July 1945. The handwriting looks familiar, even after twenty three years. The signature confirms his guess. Sally-Anne Sweeney, his former maid, almost his lover, from all those lonely years ago. The warm tone of the letter stuns Matthew Henderson. It is a letter that reaches out across time, that transcends hurt and offers forgiveness, that tempts him with the possibility of reconciliation. But it is also a letter of farewell. She is leaving Donegal for a new life in America, and very soon. Matthew drives from his borderland farm in Co Tyrone to try to find her home in The Rosses before she sails away for ever.

We, The Fallen (2018)
"Without really meaning to I somehow found myself part of an All-Ireland study trip to the war cemeteries of the Somme, 100 years on from the infamous battle. This changed my life, for the simple reason that I met Magdalena. Lena, as she prefers to be called, is from Germany, though she is not exactly German. She has fascinated and frustrated me ever since. Most of my songs are now about her, about us. So is this book, but not only about us. With all that's going on in Europe, Brexit and all that, how could it be?"
Patrick McAleese 2017

These novels can be purchased online through the usual websites, from selected outlets in Ireland and N Ireland or by direct contact.

email- dadunlop50@gmail.com   Twitter- @dadunlop50

Printed in Great Britain
by Amazon